Two very different men with a single, shared destiny

Kherin of Khassan

It was said in Khassan the Chosen could read a man's soul, sift truth and falsehood, and strike down the wrong-doer if that was the Will of the Goddess. The Goddess' Chosen was Priest, Warrior and Mage; Kherin had been trained from childhood to be all three.

Rythian of the Shi'R'Laen

He was a skilled hunter, as talented a wood-worker as his father had been, and in Syth's judicial opinion, probably the most handsome man among the clans. He also had the rare gift of mind to mind contact; he could bring his horses from the common herd without leaving the hearth if he so wished, but rarely practised such laziness. He could entice the birds from the trees and gentle the most savage hound. But he undeniably lacked the height, strength and weight of every other warrior in the Shi'R'Laen tribe. Not that it had hampered him, being little taller than she was herself. Rythian could more than hold his own in combat; what he lacked in strength he made up for in speed and agility. There was no war-scout as skilled as he. The fact that he had no other status in the tribe meant nothing to her.

Tribute Trail

Terri Beckett and Chris Power

Speculation

Press

TRIBUTE TRAIL

A Speculation Press Original.

Speculation Press
P.O. Box 543
DeKalb, IL 60015

ISBN: 0-967-19790-2

Cover art by Arlin Robbins

Cover design by Terry Tindill

First Printing June 1999

Dedicated, with love, to Terence, for unstinting support:
and to Phill and Kathy.

Chapter One

He was a prince, the son of a Royal House that had ruled for time out of mind a great kingdom, bounded by the sea to the north and tall mountain ranges to the south and west. Horizon to horizon stretched Khassan, the land of the Goddess, peopled by Her children.

The Prince's name was on their lips now, a chanting paean, as his horse paced the street lined four and five deep with cheering people.

"Kher - in!" A two-syllabled praise-song, "Kherin— Kherin — Kherin!" Flowers were tossed from balconies, petals red and white and dawn pink, soft on the breeze, tangling in his unbound hair, their scent as heady as his victory.

At his stirrup paced T'Shayra, the great hunting cat, coat sand-colored as the desert itself. To his right and half a length behind, rode Tarvik, Captain of the Khori, the Five Hundred. There was no rider to his left, and the emptiness of that space was a deep pain, hidden behind the visible joy. It must stay hidden; the Chosen could not show grief, especially not in the midst of rejoicing. Later there would be time, and privacy, to mourn his friend. But not yet.

The people cheered Kherin to the gates of the High Palace, where the Khori were dwarfed by the massive Black Guards on their greathorses. Kherin dismounted, walking past the saluting swords to enter the Hall of Audience with T'Shayra at his heel.

Amidst all the splendor of white and veined marble, chiseled stonework, inlay of precious woods and metals, he walked clad in his dust-grimed, unadorned, white campaign tunic. His titles went before him, proclaimed by the heralds.

"Kherin the Chosen, Prince of Khassan, Beloved of the Lady, Protector of the people, Son of the Wind, Whose Name is Sung Among the Warriors — Kherin the Hawk!"

Teiron, the High King, used none of these names as he rose from his chair of state, smiling, and holding out both hands in greeting. "Kyri!"

The affectionate name of Kherin's childhood was used now by few. The last time he had heard it had been from the blood-flecked lips of his dying friend. *Later*, he told himself sharply, *later*.

"Sister's son, you are well come in our sight. Truly the Goddess smiles on Khassan this day!"

Kherin gave the Royal Salute before returning both smile and embrace. Kherin had no acknowledged father, but this man filled a father's role, and gave him a father's love. Teiron's First Son, Alzon, heir to the Empire, stood at Teiron's right hand; Kherin walked at his left — the heart-side, and all knew it.

"My lord," Kherin began, "I and my Khori salute you. We bring Khassan victory." The words were pure formality, since a warrior of Khassan would die before bringing news of defeat.

"We - and all Khassan - rejoice with you." Teiron's smile and the pressure of his hands said there would be time later for private talk. Kherin turned with the High King to face the small knot of people at the foot of the three steps leading up to the throne. "Sister's son, let me make known to you the merchant embassy from Tylos."

"May your visit prosper both our lands," Kherin said politely, dismissing them from his mind as he turned again to Teiron. "Lord, I would go to offer thanks at the Sanctuary."

"Then let our eyes be gladdened by the sight of you soon."

There would be time for public thanksgiving and festivals soon enough, but now Kherin needed solitude. In the temple he wouldn't be harassed by crowds or courtiers.

The great hunting cat found a shaded spot to lie, and in the quiet of the fountain court, Kherin stripped to bathe in the deep plunge-pool. He was taller than most, lean-muscled, with battle scars showing silver on skin that was tanned to copper by the hot sun. His hair was long and black, the waterlogged weight of it clinging to his shoulders until he shook it back. On his brow was the sign of the Goddess, a winged spiral etched in blue that indelibly marked him Hers. There was an impression of contained power about him, and for a moment he seemed as alien as the hunting cat to the walls and colonnades. As if he belonged more to the wide plains and deserts rather than the city. A warrior in the midst of a gentler civilisation.

Kherin replaced his dusty war tunic with a garment brought for him; a belted blue silk robe oversewn with silver. A silver circlet that was the symbol of his rank replaced the Khori headband, gleaming metal shaped to echo the tattoo on his forehead. Kherin the warrior leader became the Prince again, the Goddess' Chosen Consort.

Cleansed and fresh-clad, Kherin approached the Holy Place of the Lady, a natural cleft in the rock, faced now in white marble and rose-quartz, embellished with carvings in graceful fluid lines that almost belied their stone, the work and love-gift of the finest artisans in the land.

It was dim after the sun's brightness, and cool. *"Yth'n t'yr-aith, k'al-nir'at'yn Yth..."* Kherin whispered the salutation in the ancient tongue of Khassan, heard it drift in sibilant echoes throughout the silent chamber. In his soul, he had other words for Her. *Beloved, Lady, Mother and Queen...* Kherin opened his heart to Her and let Her peace flood through him, transmuting raw grief to gentle memory, washing away the stresses and pains and filling him with new serenity.

Beloved, Son — thou art come home.

The setting sun painted the white stones a pale ochre as Kherin came out of the Inner Sanctuary. He saw T'Shayra fed and tended; he paused to smooth the blunt head. Her fur was dense, soft under the coarser outer coat, and she purred at his caressing, wiping a harsh tongue across his wrist. He had cared for her since he had found her a year ago, a blind mewling kit half-starved beside her dead dam. She had repaid his care with unstinting love and trust, and the fierce loyalty of her kind. He stroked her for a while as she ate, then left her to the attentions of the Precinct servants.

In the Outer Court Kherin discovered Undabi, a captain of the Black Guard, sitting patiently, his bay greathorse beside him. Kherin paused as the man rose to his feet and gave the Royal Salute.

"Undabi. Do you wait here for me?"

"Yes, Prince. And no, for I had a request to ask of the Lady, and this I have done."

"May She grant it," Kherin said, smiling.

"With your aid, my Prince, She may do so indeed." The dark face broke into an answering grin. "My first-born son is of the age to serve in arms. I ask that you look upon him for your Khori — to become one of your warriors."

Kherin knew the boy. "He has fifteen years already?"

"This Fallowtime, lord. And I have trained him myself."

"There is no better teacher, as I know."

Undabi's answering smile was both pleased and proud. "But I grow old, my Prince ..." and it was true: the cropped black cap of hair was threaded with grey, like the frosted muzzle of his mare. Man and beast, they had served Khassan for twenty years. "I would have a son of mine serve after me."

"But not in the Guard?"

"By the Lady's grace, and your will, Lord, he is for your Khori. This has been his wish since first he carried a spear."

"Then when the time comes, my friend, I will remember his name." Kherin gave the man his hand in the hard clasp of warrior to warrior. "The Khori are no longer Five Hundred. I shall need good men." That was another truth. Drawn from the elite of Khassan and her allies, the Khori were the Chosen's Honor Guard and the vanguard of the Royal army.

Undabi bowed low, touching his brow to the narrow, tanned hand he held. "I thank you, my Prince. May the Goddess prosper you in all things. I am at your service and Hers."

Kherin glanced at the horizon and the sinking sun, and laughed. "Then take me up on S'uldira as you were used when I was small. It is past the time when I should have been at the High Palace!"

"That would no longer be fitting, my Prince. Besides, S'uldira would carry you to the world's end, if you wished it." He put the reins into Kherin's hand.

"The High Palace will be far enough. And you?"

"I stay to offer thanks to the Great Goddess. Go in peace, Prince Kherin."

"Stay in peace, Undabi."

Kherin swung up into the saddle and gave the massive black-maned neck a caress. The greathorses, bred from a single stallion and two mares so far back in time it was now a matter of legend, held a special place in his affections. Gentle in peace and savage in war, they were as famous in Khassan as the Khori.

In keeping with her size, the mare had a pace as smooth as silk and Kherin's thoughts were free to wander. It was good to be back in the city of his birth after the long summer campaign. Even though his spirit had no yearning for the closing-in of walls and roofs, this place was full of familiar, and much-loved, things. The simple beauty of dressed stone, of water falling in the frequent fountains — the smile of a woman, the laughter of children — and after hard living, the luxuries of good wine and meat and bread, and a soft sleeping-place without the need to lie hand on swordhilt, were a balm to his soul.

Such little things, to be so pleasing. There were the greater things, too. The Festival of Gathering which he would lead for the people, remaking his own dedication at the same time — and the unfailingly wise counsel of the High King. Yes, it was worth enduring the diplomatic fencing of the feast tonight, to be able to talk afterwards with the man his soul called father.

Kherin gave the horse into the keeping of a groom and went up the wide stairway into the Palace. In the Great Courtyard, with its open pool and fountains under the clear sky, a feast was laid out on long tables. The guests were already gathered. As Kherin passed, they made deep obeisance, most smiling with their greetings. He offered smiles and quiet words in return.

Tarvik, in the full panoply of a Tsithkin Captain of the Khori, saluted him gravely, then grinned and fell in at his heel. The Tsithkin were Khassan's oldest allies, a desert people of fiercely independent ways and unswerving loyalty. Tarvik was also called the Hound, and like the trusted packleader a huntsman relies upon, he was as true as steel. He was Kherin's right-hand in battle, confidante and companion in peace. As Jeztin had also been. The sorrow of that loss was still there, but the edge was off the sharpness of it now, by the Lady's blessing.

"Cousin, I salute you." Alzon, First Son of the High King, Heir to the Land, made the obeisance due to the Chosen, then took Kherin by the shoulders and gave him the kiss of kindred. Two tall men, as alike as if born at one birth, from the blue of their eyes to the curl of the black hair and the wryly humorous smile. "The merchant-embassy has a desire to meet you."

"Those I saw earlier?"

"From Tylos, beyond the Middle Sea. They wish a stronger tie between Khassan and the North."

"What do they offer, that Khassan has not already got?"

"Little, indeed!" Alzon chuckled. "Grain and woods, mostly. I have counseled my father to require breeding pairs of some of their beasts — like the Northern long-haired goats —·"

"Or a few stallions of the greathorse breed, if any can be found. I would mount my Khori on such horses."

Tarvik converted his snort into a cough. "By your leave, Princes — fine though their greathorses are, let me keep my Khassani stallion!"

"There speaks my Hound," Kherin chuckled. "Nor do I blame you, when your war-steed is one such as Benith."

"Nor I," Alzon smiled, then became more formal. "Kherin, Chosen of the Goddess, I would ask you to Read these people for my father's sake."

"Of course."

The First Son beckoned and a group of men approached. There were five of the Tylosians present, the chief among them being Hasoe. He was a tall, heavy-featured man, with sallow skin and russet hair. He was much hung about with jewelry, as were the rest of his party. Khassani nobility might wear one or two favorite pieces, or none at all, as it pleased them. Hasoe's display gave him an alien, barbaric appearance.

However, Hasoe's grasp of the Khassani language was excellent, with scarcely an accent. He was spokesman for the delegation, smooth-tongued and impeccable in his courtesies. Perhaps too smooth-tongued. Kherin found himself disliking the man, which disconcerted him, there being no reason for it that he could see. He looked at the Tylosians a little deeper, using a deeper Sight than eyes could provide.

It was said in Khassan the Chosen could read a man's soul, sift truth and falsehood, and strike down the wrong-doer if that was the Will of the Goddess. The Goddess' Chosen was Priest, Warrior and Mage; Kherin had been trained from childhood to be all three.

He saw nothing within Hasoe but myriad webs of woven plans, all of them tangled about with 'trade' and 'profit' with no care for anyone else's well-being. Three of the others were no different. The fifth, a plump, smiling man with thinning blond hair, and rattling with crystal charms, made obeisance. He was introduced as Lord Prenin, Astrologer-Mage to the Lord Hasoe. He called Kherin mage-brother. Kherin felt more webs and tangles in him, along with the energy-sparks of small spells as irritating as gadflies. But he felt no danger, no menace. As soon as he could, Kherin excused himself with the polite phrases that told Alzon all was well, and left them to the First Son.

Seated in his place with Tarvik beside him, neither man ate much of the multitude of rich food. But still they ate well and the entertainment was lavish. The dancers in their light bright silks were as graceful as birds in flight. The singers and musicians gave joy a voice and stirred the heart to tears. Kherin gave the chief singer a silver armring in token of the pleasure their art had given him — and besides, he had seen some of the foreigners looking sidelong down their noses, and did not want the artists to feel slighted by the ignorance of the guests.

"No doubt they have other entertainments in Tylos," Kherin murmured to Tarvik.

"Aye, my Prince." Tarvik selected a candied fruit from the dish offered. "Slaves to sing and dance and pleasure them."

"Counterfeits. These sing as the birds sing, for joy in living; the dancers tread the measure to honor the Goddess, freely. Can a slave do these things?" He frowned, gesturing a sweet dish away. "My Hound, I like these traders less and less; it is in my mind that we should have nothing to—·"

Tarvik's hand brushed against his wrist in a seemingly accidental touch. The code was an instant warning, and shocked Kherin into silence. He had seen nothing in the foreign envoys to threaten Khassan. But the light contact warned him to be on his guard.

"I will try that fruit-ice," Tarvik said easily. "Is it not a masterly confection, my Prince?"

It was jade-green, sculpted into the form of growing plants, leaf and stem delicately fashioned. Kherin murmured agreement to the praise, but he did not taste it.

"Where lies the shadow?" Kherin asked in the dialect of Tarvik's tribal lodge. "I see none here but the small deceits of the marketplace."

"I don't know, my lord," Tarvik said in the same language, lounging back with a deceptive smile, "but the chill in my spine tells me it is here. Somewhere. How mighty is this Trader-Mage?"

Kherin gave a quiet snort. "Should I test him now and risk breaking every window in the Palace? Not to mention any treaty that might be made for the good of Khassan. I have looked in him and there is no threat to Khassan nor Teiron in his heart. No one else here would think on such a betrayal."

Tarvik nodded. "Then my spine is mistaken." Even so, his eye was never far from the Tylosian delegation from that time until the feast was finished and the High King retired.

Kherin took his leave at the same time, making his way to the Royal apartments in the high towers. There, in the cool of the airy rooms lit by fretted metal lamps, Teiron dismissed his servants. They were at last alone. Formality dropped from them like discarded cloaks.

"Come, Kyri," Teiron beckoned. "Sit with me on my balcony, where we can watch the Lady of Night on Her journeying amid Her stars. It is long since we talked."

"The summer has been long." Kherin leaned on the balustrade, looking out over the sleeping darkness of the city. "I told you before I left that I sensed a grief to come."

"And Jeztin, your captain, is dead."

"He was my friend before he joined my Khori. The Goddess called his name, and I opened the path for him to go to Her." He fell silent, remembering each detail. Sweet-rich scent of blood on the dusty air and the gasping rattle for breath. The feel of life ebbing beneath his hands in spite of all he could do, so that in the end there was but one course to be taken...

"I do not know what to do with this grief. I thought I could beat it into a blade to avenge him, but the pain did not ease. I offered his death to the Mother and She has taken him to Her, but my spirit is still heavy. I do not understand—-"

"You are young, Kyri." Teiron laid gentle hands upon his shoulders. "By Her mercy, grief has passed you by until now. It is as it is. Accept it, and learn from it."

"I know. But I think — I think that if I had been able to mourn as Tarvik did, as the Khori could, it would have been easier. To keep always the face of the Chosen, to show nothing — it was a flood pent up, a wound that festered. Until She healed me, in the Sanctuary. I know that nothing of Her creation dies save by Her will. Still I grieve. Counsel me, my lord. Is She testing my worth?"

"If anything, She is teaching you. May it be the hardest lesson you need to learn, Kyri."

Kherin bowed his head. "I am justly rebuked. Forgive me."

Teiron smiled at him. "Enough. Now give me your counsel — tell me your view of the Tylosians."

Kherin hesitated. "I do not like them," he said slowly. "Even though I know the Goddess has many children, and shows Herself in different fashions, yet I cannot greet them as brothers. I am glad that Alzon is the one who must be pleasant to them, and not I."

"I would not ask it of you, Kyri. Do they come in peace, do you think?"

"There is no thought of war in them," Kherin said slowly, remembering what his trained senses had shown him of their minds, "but they are thick with deceits. They think always 'How shall this profit us? What shall we gain?'"

"Well, they are traders," Teiron pointed out. "That is their way. Be easy. After the Moon of Gathering, they will leave Khassan. They asked that they might stay to witness the Festival, having heard how we celebrate the Goddess' bounty. I have given them leave to do so. Be not swift to judge the nation by the few."

Kherin smiled. "I deserve that censure. The Lady of Harvest turns away none who come before Her in praise, be they from Khassan or Tsithkian or Tylos. I can do no less than bid them welcome in Her name. So they worship the Goddess in Tylos?"

"In their fashion, but their ways are not ours. They have not been gifted by Her knowledge — they think we select Her Chosen as a matter of rank. There is no word in their tongue for what you are, Kyri."

"May the Mother of All Wisdom grant them knowledge in Her time, then."

"Her will be done in all ways and all things." Teiron spoke the ritual response. He poured wine into cups of black jade and gave one to Kherin. "In three days you will lead the people in Festival and make your yearly dedication. It has been fifteen years since Her mark was put on your brow, Kyri. For ten years and more you have served Her in all Her ways. Are you happy, my son?"

Kherin blinked. "Father?" They used these words of kinship rarely. "Can I be other than I am?"

"It was no fair question. Alzon is five years your senior. Of all my acknowledged sons, he is the best fitted to take up the rule of Khassan after me. Yet it was at your birth the prophetess spoke, and I thought... well, no matter. I do not grudge the Goddess Her Chosen, but truly is it said She chooses only the finest."

Kherin reached for Teiron's hand, touched it to his brow. "My lord, father, I ask for nothing, I desire nothing that is not mine. And surely She blesses us both as we do Her bidding."

"I know it, and all Khassan knows it. We are blessed in Her Chosen — and Alzon will hold the Empire after me, by Her will, since She will not have it otherwise."

"May She call my name before that day comes, my father," Kherin said softly. It was no polite wish, rather a prophecy — Teiron, barring accidents, was good for another thirty years' rule, whereas the Consort of the Goddess always went back to Her while still in his prime. So is he called the Ageless — for he never grows old. In all probability, Kherin had another fifteen years before She called him home, and the sadness of that foreknowledge was in Teiron's eyes.

"May She choose another as fit to guide our people, then."

Garlanded and crowned with flowers and ears of corn, the children sang the Goddess' anthem. Kherin's embroidered robe was lifted from his naked shoulders. His hair was loosened from the silver circlet and he knelt, bending his head in homage to the invisible presence of the Goddess.

"Great Mother, Giver of all good things — I am Thy Chosen, Son and Beloved, Thy servant and Thy sacrifice. My life is in Thy hands. Accept the offering."

The chief priestess took up the sacred shears and dedicated them to the Lady of Harvests. There were sharp snipping sounds, then the acolytes gathered up Kherin's shorn silken curls, laying them on the spread cloth on the altar. They lay black against the white of the fabric. His hair no more than a few inches long, Kherin rose to his feet and stepped down the slope into the still, jet darkness of the Lady's pool. It was fed by an underground spring and cold enough to make his bones ache. The smooth rock floor under his bare feet dipped sharply — he felt the tug of the unseen current and gave himself to the water's embrace, sliding down into its darkness.

Accept the offering...

The chill water cradled and supported Kherin's unresisting body; he felt the touch of air as his head broke water, and heard the cry of the watching priestess echoed by the waiting people outside.

"The Goddess is good! She returns her Chosen to us, the Risen Lord, the Beloved, given back to us out of the Waters of Life...!"

The chants rang in his ears as he waded out of the pool. The servants of the Sanctuary brought fresh robes, and combed his hair into a neat cap, setting the silver circlet on his brow once more. As always after the cutting of his hair, his head felt strange — cool and light without the weight of his dark mane. He walked out into the sunlight, feeling the touch of the sun on the tattooed Mark of the Goddess on his brow. He lifted his voice in the Hymn of the Gathering, his song ringing clear and and strong in the morning. The children joined the refrain, then the young men and maidens came into the melody and all the Precinct was filled with it.

This was the sunlit side of the Festival — the smiling face of the Goddess turned to Her children. There were other aspects to the Goddess as well — Maiden and Bride as well as Mother, and at the last, the Veiled One who calls all men home.

The people rejoiced, and Kherin led their celebration. Tonight would come the Moon Dance, the ritual in which the Beloved is joined to his Bride. The time when the Chosen is one with the God whose mortal part he is — the Horned One, the Seedgiver, Lightbringer and Lord of the Dance. It was the most solemn of the duties of the Chosen, never taken lightly or without due reverence. Tonight when the moon rose silver-full he would no longer be Kherin, but instead be the Ageless God Incarnate, Consort of the Great Goddess Herself. But for the day time he was Kherin still, yet no less honored by the love of the people who brought their First Fruit offerings to his feet and stretched out their hands for his touch, his blessing. He was the Luck of the Land, their Hope and their Salvation.

As twilight came he led the dancing on the great threshing-floors, circling in the sacred measure, bare feet dusty with the chaff of this season's grain. He partnered this girl and that, their faces laughing and flushed, tossing dark ringlets on modestly covered shoulders. Though the slender bodies were ripe and clad in their Festival best, none of them was touched by the Goddess' choice. Their waists were supple in the curve of his arm, but their hands met his and parted, met and parted, until his head spun with the spinning dance, the dust swirling up under the beating feet, the music lifting, soaring, carrying him with it —-

Until She came to him, and loved him, and they were One.

The Moon of Gathering and Thanksgiving waned, and Khassan put off the air of Festival. For Kherin, the richness of the autumn days always woke a restlessness in his blood. This city was his home; but he was also the Hawk, never to be caged, flying free beyond any man's call, answering only as he willed.

Kherin began to yearn again for the silences and timelessness of the deep desert instead of the crowded busy thoroughfares; for the hardy companionship of warriors instead of the precise formalities that entwined life in the palace. Such things were part of his duties, but he did not always find it easy to keep the smiling mask in place.

He found a measure of peace, at least, with Tarvik and his captains as they choose from the scores of men who competed for the honor of riding in the Khori. They had to replenish the ranks of the Five Hundred, replacing the men who had died that summer.

Kherin's standard was high and he selected only the best. Men came from every quarter of the land, from every country that owed Khassan allegiance, and from every walk of life. There were the sons of noble blood, and the nomads of the deep desert; dark skinned or copper, clad in silks or skins. Nine of every ten returned disappointed to their homes, or stayed to take a lesser post. The one-in-ten received the cherished scarlet silk of the Khori headband and thanked the Goddess on his knees for his good fortune.

As he walked from the parade-court at the end of the choosing, a man fell at Kherin's feet in the dust. Kherin thought him a latecome petitioner for the Khori, until he saw the lines of age and the grizzled hair.

"What is it, venerable?" he asked gently. The man kissed his sandaled foot, not lifting his eyes.

"Lord, most high Prince, I come to beg your aid."

The man's looks identified him as being from the northern hills. He wore rough sheepskins and loose wool trousers; his hill-tribe origins were clear in his speech.

Gaze downcast, he related his tale. "Our village is small, we eke a living on the mountainside with our herds. Now a terror stalks our lives. A great bear kills our livestock and only last month it took a child. The men of the village have tried to drive the beast away or kill it, but without success. Our wisewoman says the bear is sent by the Goddess."

Kherin listened patiently while the man spoke, ignoring the whispers of his companions. He laid a hand on the bowed shoulder. "You did right to come to me. If indeed this beast is a

Sending, be sure I shall discover it, and by the Lady's grace, free you of it."

"Cousin, this is madness!" Alzon was at his side, pushing through the group that had gathered. "You cannot go to tackle this beast alone. No, let me take the Guard and deal with this matter—-"

"Alone?" Kherin caught the one word out of his objection. "I had not intended to go alone, but — yes, I see that I must. If it is a beast of the Goddess, who else should be asked to hazard his life?"

"Lord, let me go!" This was Tarvik.

"No, my Hound. Your charge is the Khori when I am absent from them. And who else can I trust with my great cat?"

"Then I shall accompany you," Alzon said, "and you shall not deny me. The hunt shall be yours, and the kill if you wish it. But I ride with you, cousin."

Tarvik cut in on them, irrespective of propriety. "Lords, I say this is folly! Two of Khassan's princes..."

"Aye, and how shall any beast stand against us?" Alzon laughed and struck his cousin lightly on the shoulder. "When shall we ride, Kherin?"

After the heat of the city, the mountain air was cool and fresh. The hunters camped on the lower slopes, where streams cut the wooded flanks of the hills and there was grazing for the horses. Kherin and Alzon scouted for sign of their quarry. The villagers had given the last-known direction, but so far no sign of the animal had been found. They pressed on up to the ridge that passed through the mountains to the distant sea, and there halted in the dusk.

"We shall be well enough here," Kherin said, swinging down from his mountain pony near a small freshet gushing through a narrow channel between rocks. "In the morning we'll try higher."

"As well we thought to bring food. And wine." Alzon led his pony beneath the dark conifers, and dropped the bundle of provisions onto a mat of needles. "I'll find wood for the fire."

The shadows crept long and violet over the mountain, but the small fire Kherin built was brisk and bright with resinous wood, flames crackling. Alzon broke the hard journeybread in two, crumbled a little salt onto it and passed half across to Kherin with a wedge of goat's cheese. Kherin spoke the Blessing on the food, and they ate.

They were thirsty afterwards, and Alzon scorned the spring water, bringing out his leather flask. He drank first, then passed the flagon to Kherin. The tart draught was cool in his throat, and welcome.

It was only when Alzon spat the mouthful of wine into the fire that Kherin saw the bright triumph leap in the other's eyes. Kherin stared, uncomprehending as Alzon's expression changed, a soft, sinister smile touching his lips. Kherin felt a numbness begin in his fingers and knew.

Poison. But no poison could kill the Chosen and Alzon knew that. Unless it was his time. But Kherin had had no warning, had Seen nothing of this — something or someone had blinded his Goddess-given Sight. He tried to gather his power and failed.

"Too late, far too late, cousin," Alzon whispered. His eyes were shining in the firelight like a feral cat's. "Yes, you are drugged, and it cost me much to secure so swift a potion. But it will be worth the price. They offered me a binding spell but I refused," he went on. "You would have sensed the weaving and broken it, and once on guard against arcane attack, it would be impossible to snare you. Best to stay with simple poisons."

The wine hissed in the flames as Alzon poured it out. "Their mage is very skilled — you have never met such a one in combat, have you? He wove a net of many small spells, to mislead, to turn aside, to dazzle a little. You did not suspect a thing. Perhaps you are not so skilled a mage as we had thought. Besides, if you do not look to find an enemy, you cannot see one." Alzon laughed softly. "You are very trusting."

"—-why?" Kherin's lips and tongue felt thick, slurring his speech.

"Why? You ask that? Are you blind and deaf as well? Do you not hear the palace rumors that swarm like maggots in carrion flesh? Have you never looked in a mirror since you grew to manhood, my noble kinsman? We are like enough to be brothers of one womb, yet you do not know your father's name?"

"I am a Child of the Goddess..."

"Fine words and superstition. Well, I have eyes and ears, if you do not. I know my father's heart, Kherin. He need not name me his successor, unless he wishes. And he wishes you to hold Khassan after him."

That was impossible. Kherin tried to say so. "The Law..." His mind was working at half-speed, as in a nightmare. He tried again to summon his will, to gather power, but there was nothing there. None of his limbs would answer him and his sight was shivering out of focus.

"Oh, yes, the Law. The Chosen of the Lady may not rule. Kings made that law, Kherin mine, and a king could change it. There was prophecy at your birth: *He will make the mountains to dance and bring change to a great nation.* Well, it will not be Khassan. I would kill you if I could, but it is forbidden to shed your blood and I will not risk Her wrath. As it is — you chose this hunt, you drank of your own will — my hands are clean."

He pushed the drugged and unresisting Kherin bellydown and pulled his arms back, tying the wrists tightly. "I take no brother's blood upon my head. I will take you to those who will take you far from here. I shall return to the palace saying that you chose to track the bear alone, in spite of my protests. And you did not return."

Alzon's voice blurred into a humming drone. Kherin's last conscious thought was still of disbelief, of utter denial. Then thick darkness clogged eyes and ears and mouth, ran turgid through his veins and drowned his mind...

Alzon finished tying the rawhide thongs, lifted the senseless body and slung it over the pony's broad back. Kicking earth over the fire, he led the laden beast through the trees, down over the pass towards the border. The glimmer of torches below was all the guide he needed and it was not long before the circled caravan could be seen in the moonlight.

The Tylosian sentries spotted him and raised a shout. There was a sudden flurry of activity in the camp and one man came forward to meet him.

"Prince Alzon..." Hasoe made obeisance. "Be welcome to what poor travellers' hospitality we may offer you. We feared you would not arrive before we were forced to leave."

"I keep my word," Alzon said shortly. "See that you keep yours. Here is the merchandise, as we agreed." He tumbled the slack body from the pony's back.

Hasoe gazed down at the unconscious Kherin, sprawled at his feet. "Oh, we bring a prize out of Khassan indeed," he murmured. "Such a one as this, princely and proud, to be tamed and trained to serve the great lord of the Horse People. Surely he will count us as his allies for such a gift."

"Kherin must not return," Alzon said forcefully. "Not one word must come to Khassan."

"Ah, be assured, Prince. Where he is destined to go, the people have no knowledge of Khassan. They live on the edge of the world. He will never set foot to his native soil again, this I swear."

"So. Give me his outer robe." One of the guards stripped the heavy silk from the captive and handed it over. Under Hasoe's questioning eye, Alzon gave a grim smile and drew his dagger. "It will be found, rent and fouled with blood, at the edge of the mountain trail where the rock falls sheer to the river," he said. "As if the bear he hunted this night had taken him in truth."

"Truly Khassan has a judicious prince in you, my lord," Hasoe bowed. "But we have little time and must take our leave. You two — see our prisoner secured and place him in the first wagon. Before he wakes, we must be on shipboard and away."

Alzon turned his pony back onto the high trail as Hasoe called for his roan mare, urging the caravan into ponderous motion, a smile of extreme satisfaction on the sallow features. "You spoke more truly than you know, my princeling, when you claim your cousin-brother is taken by a bear. So do the D'Shael call their great lord, their Sun Stallion — Caier the Red Bear. And it is to the D'Shael on the rim of the world that Kherin of Khassan goes — a rich tribute from Tylos, to their friends, and protectors, the Horse People."

Chapter Two

As the wagons crested the last rise, Rythian stood on the wagon box and shaded his eyes against the glare of the sun on the snow. Ahead and below, still some hours' journey distant, the buildings of the Summer Hold were dark huddled masses among the snowdrifts. Beyond the settlement, the lake was a vast expanse of dull silver, patterned by waterfowl swimming on it and flying above it. The land about the shoreline was for the most part white, but here and there stretches of turf showed brown, swept clear by the wind. There would be grazing for the herds, though they might have to scrape for it. By the look of the clouds and the smell of the wind, there was still more snow to fall.

In earlier years the clans would have waited until the plains were clear, but since the treaty with Tylos five springs back, the warriors had to be at the distant GodStone by the Equinox. And this year winter was slow in retreating. Rythian wondered if the treaty to protect the Tylosian caravans was worth the trouble, and dangers, of such an early return.

Syth glanced over her shoulder at the long line of herds and wagons winding like a sluggish serpent over the snowscape ahead and behind, but her major focus was checking on her own household. Alais, her hearthsister, handled her team with casual competence. Ronan, Alais' son by her short marriage to Syth's brother, drove another wagon. Between Alais and Ronan were the two milk mares, the small Tylosian mare in foal and the house cow, all kept close by half a dozen dogs. Emre, hearthsister and birthsister to Alais, rode on the box beside Syth, her heavy skirts wrapped around her feet and legs. Her pregnancy was too far advanced to allow her the more practical garb of thick breeches that the other women wore. Everyone had on several layers of quilted shirts beneath furred cloaks. Spring it may be, but the cold was intense.

Rythian was driving the family's lead wagon and the sight of him warmed the chill from Syth a little. The wind pushed back the hood of his cloak and his long pale braid gleamed against the black fur. He glanced back as her eyes rested on him and she felt the gentle caress in her mind, tangible as his mouth on hers. Husband, father of her children and always her lover, he had been a choice that had surprised her family. Certainly, it went without saying that he was a warrior. He was a skilled hunter, as talented a wood-worker as his father had been, and in Syth's judicial opinion, probably the handsomest man among the clans. He also had the rare gift of mind to mind contact; he could bring his horses from the common herd without leaving the hearth if he so wished, but rarely practised such laziness. He could entice the birds from the trees and gentle the most savage hound. But he undeniably lacked the height, strength and weight of every other warrior in the Shi'R'Laen tribe. Not that it had hampered him, being little taller than she was herself. Rythian could more than hold his own in combat; what he lacked in strength he made up for in speed and agility. There was no war-scout as skilled as he. The fact that he had no other status in the tribe meant nothing to her.

Sounds of a different kind of combat rose from her wagon. Beneath the curved roof were the three younger children of the hearth, and after the four-day trek confined in their cramped quarters, their tempers were frayed to rags. She could hear their squabbling voices, shrill as jays. She pulled an expressive face. "Emre, take the reins. I'm going to have to separate those brats again. 'Thian!" she called, "will you take Dreyen up by you? He won't stop tormenting Fyra and upsetting Lirren."

Rythian held back his team to allow the second wagon to glide alongside. Syth scrambled back over the baggage roped to the arch of the roof, swung inside, and sounds of dispute became squalls of distress as the crack of palm on flesh sounded clear.

Flushed and sullen, Dreyen scrambled onto the tailboard and jumped from one wagon to the other. His expression lightened into a grin as he settled himself beside his father.

"Can I drive?"

"No. Wipe your nose."

"We weren't really fighting," Dreyen offered thoughtfully.

"Then it was a good imitation."

As the other wagon dropped back, four-year-old Fyra was being carried forward to sit between the two women. She waved cheerfully at her brother, and Dreyen chuckled.

"We guessed that if we made enough noise, Mam would fetch us out."

"Brat." But Rythian was smiling, and the boy leaned against his side.

"And I was feeling sick. But I'm better now." For a while the only sounds were the grunts of the oxen, the creak of harness, and the hiss of the wagon-runners over the snow. Then: "Da, Shenchan said the warband will be leaving tomorrow."

"That's right."

"Do you have to go? You went last year."

"Only on the early ridings. For late summer and leaf-fall I was at the Hold."

"I know, but why can't you stay home now and just go out on the ridings you missed last time?"

"Because I have already said I will ride south to the GodStone."

Dreyen accepted that and lapsed into silence again, for which Rythian was grateful. The child had all the persistence and curiosity of his years, and could be trying. Rythian did not wish to lie to his son, but neither could he tell him the whole truth.

Caier was not a popular leader with many of the tribe. This, the sixth of the yearly treaties with the Tylosians, would be a time of severe strain on the self-control and temper of many of the warriors. The temptation to Challenge would be strong. In the past all those who Challenged Caier died. Caier, Sun Stallion of the Shi'R'Laen tribe of the D'Shael nation, was both immensely powerful physically — and immensely cunning. Now in his forties, Caier made up in sheer brute strength what he might lack in speed. And for ten years he had led the tribe.

Once down on the plain, the caravan began to divide. The herds peeled away from the line, urged by riders and dogs, and spread over the wide expanse of snow-covered grass. The wagons continued on into the settlement, threading through the wide haphazard streets to respective longhouses.

"Ronan," Rythian called, "Take your wagon to the back." The boy nodded, raising his whip in salute, and turned the team down the side of the barn. The runners lurched and bucked over the hard-mounded snow, but the six beasts leaned well into their collars and kept it stable. Alais steered her team in his wake, while Rythian brought his six to a halt beside the longhouse doors. The snow was drifted deep, almost to the top steps.

Syth pulled her team alongside. Rythian lifted Emre down. The two women looked at the snow-laden roof, the hidden steps, and the threatening sky. "I think," Syth said, not for the first time, "that the Elders were foolish not to wait another week."

"Caier," Rythian said shortly, "has plans that will not wait on late thaws, or poor weather. Emre, stay where you are until I've cleared the steps. Another fall won't help matters."

"My ankle is strong now," she objected, but stood still, skirts bunched up out of the snow. She was finding it increasingly irksome to be limited by a difficult pregnancy, a rare thing among the D'Shael.

"It isn't your ankle we're concerned for." Syth pulled off her heavy gloves, thrust them through her belt, and started untying the lashings of the wagon. Rythian unstrapped a shovel and began scraping the snow from the steps. Dreyen tumbled down from the wagon and promptly disappeared into a drift with a squawk of surprise.

Rythian swept the last step clear, then, using the blade of his belt knife as latchkey, he opened the first door into a mass of cobwebs festooning the porch. Brushing them aside, he used his knife again to open the inner door. The air smelled cold and stale, but not damp, which was good. Raised some four feet off the ground, the boarding of the floor was dust covered, but dry. The closed louvers of the roof would need to be cleared, but the hearth could be lit. It was a stone-built trough some twelve feet in length. Most of its depth was filled with flints used to bed the layers of coals, logs, and peat which would burn continuously until the tribe moved out again with the first snows of autumn. The hearth provided heat for cooking and comfort; it was the central focus for each family unit.

At last year's end, wood had been left ready. Rythian fired it with flint and steel, the strengthening flames highlighting the Sun Symbol carved and painted on the end wall beyond the hearth. The Symbol glowed red and gold as if freshly made, as welcome as the fire.

With the day so far advanced, there was little time to spare. Emre tended the hearth while Syth investigated the state of the rooms that opened off the main chamber. Rythian went through the door to the right of the Sun Sign and down into the stable block as Alais swung open its doors. In the swathe of light he could see that the earth floor was dry and he gave a nod of satisfaction, not unmixed with relief.

"I checked the other barns," Alais said. "The fodder and straw are still sweet, the seals on the storage pits are safe and the roofs are sound. If the house is the same we'll have come through the winter well."

"Well enough," he smiled and she laughed quietly.

"Better than some, I'll wager," she said. "I'm sending Ronan to the herds for our horses. He'll bring Goldstar and Chyren for us. Who do you want for your war-string?"

"Zaan, Frost, Llynivar and Stormrunner, but tell him to bring Amber in first. We should get her bedded down and watered before the rest."

Alais nodded and disappeared.

With the swiftness of long practice the wagons were unloaded, their contents stowed in the longhouse and the barns. The three mares, the cow, and two of the oxen were stabled, fed and watered, and stalls were made ready for the stallions from the herds. By nightfall it was all done and they were sitting around the glowing hearth, eating the rich stew Emre had prepared. Lirren, the youngest, was more than half-asleep, but Dreyen and Fyra still had plenty of energy left. Their exuberance was in marked contrast to the subdued quiet of the women, and Rythian was uneasily aware of it. He did not have to guess at its cause.

Unobtrusively he watched the faces of the women he loved; Syth, Spear Woman and Lioness; she was the center of his life and the core of his heart. She possessed the enduring strength and dignity of the mountains — and a temper that no one sought to rouse. She was only a few fingers width shorter than he, and it was not only the directness of her blue gaze and the straightness of her carriage that earned her the name of Spear Woman. Before their marriage and the birth of their children, she had ridden the wartrails at his side.

Alais, She-Wolf and Firechild, swift to anger and often restless. Yet she was warm and loving and fiercely protective, and almost as dear to him as Syth. She matched him for height and could use sword and spear with equal skill, if not strength. In the past she, too, had ridden the wartrail with him, hearthsister and spearsister. She was the Huntress of the hearth, sharing with him the teaching of the children the skills they would need.

Emre, Summer Woman and Flowerchild; not for her the wartrail or the hunt. Small by D'Shael reckoning, she seemed almost placid beside her birthsister's fire. There was a gentle strength about her that was as rich and generous as the earth itself, and she had a special place in the hearts of all who knew her. Though Syth was wife and First at this hearth, in many ways Emre was the heart of the hearth, beloved by all. If he should lose all this —

Frowning, Rythian stared into the hearth and refused to acknowledge the chill that slid down his spine.

Syth, her concentration split between her husband's face and making sure Emre did not peck at her food, was the first to break the ominous reserve. "You should not be going," she said abruptly. "There is too much to be done here."

Rythian glanced up. Syth met his gaze, and there was a shadow of fear in her blue eyes which startled him.

"I have to go," he said, voice quiet. "You know that. It takes both Arun and myself to ride herd on Voran's temper, and it gets no easier as the seasons pass."

"I know. They should stay at Hold as well."

"We fear for you," Emre whispered.

"The danger is no more than on any other trail," he said, touching light fingers to her cheek, but he would not hold her gaze. He took another piece of bread.

"Perhaps," Alais said with something of a snap. "But Emre has dreamed a darkness about you. Death hangs close. Too close."

"Hearthsister," he said levelly, "is that good enough reason for a man of the Shi'R'Laen to stay with the herds?"

"But what of your word?" she cut back and as if on cue, Syth took up the attack.

"You promised us after Alais bore Lirren that you would extend the porch along the housefront. Lirren is now a year old and there is no more porch than there was then. The thatch will need repair in the old barn, and you said that this year you were going to replace the axles and wheels on the wagons."

"All that is beyond Ronan as yet," Alais continued. "Indeed, he needs to learn more of the woodcraft from you, and he cannot do that if his hearthsire is with the warband. As for Lia and Shelais — how many years have they waited for a second barn and an extension of their house? Voran has no skill with wood or thatch and Arun will need help there."

"We do not want you to ride south this year," Emre said, laying a hand on his arm. "You are needed here."

"Besides," Syth went on as he drew breath to speak, "though a man has duty to spear and sword and the wartrails, so also does he have duty to herd and furrow and hearth, to his wife, his sisters and children. You have given enough dues to warring, Rythian Lyre'son. Now it is time to give dues to Hold. Furthermore, that is as true for Arun and Voran as it is for you and you know it."

"I was in Hold last summer," Rythian pointed out. No matter what the future held, he had the memories of last summer to hold dear. "There are new rooms, new roofing —"

"You were here because the SwordBrothers brought you home with a Surni blade in your thigh," Syth interrupted. "You stayed because Arun came down with the marsh-fever and there was no need to ride herd on Voran since he wouldn't leave Arun."

"If you talked to Arun," Alais carried on quickly, "he would listen and not go on the riding. And if he did not, his Brother would not, so there would be no need — "

"Unfortunately for all this logic," Rythian cut in, "Caier has already given us our orders. After the Tribute we are to scout into Surni lands."

"So?" Syth demanded, head high.

"So," he went on, "am I to stay in Hold and let another face the dangers my hearth won't have me face? Will those dangers be less for another man? More to the point, am I to go to the Sun Stallion and ask him to give me leave not to ride south?" Syth's jaw set stubbornly but color rose under her fair skin. He did not have to say more.

"We would not shame you — or this hearth," Alais spoke for them all. "Just take care."

"And forewarning is another weapon to your hand." Syth leaned forward and hugged him. "See that you use it, husband."

"I will," and he dropped a kiss onto her hair where the part was warm cream under the gold. "You could always come with me, Spear Woman." Laughing, Syth threatened to box his ears, but Alais was wistful.

"If Emre was not so close to her time and Lirren was weaned, I would ride with you."

"Alais, you'll do no such thing!" Emre snapped with uncharacteristic sharpness. "And neither will you, Syth!"

"I'm away," Rythian laughed and stood up. "It's a brave man that intervenes between women, and I have not that kind of courage."

As the porch door swung closed behind him, Rythian let out a sigh of relief, his breath billowing white in the cold air. Two tall figures lounged out of the gloom at the foot of the steps.

"Thian, there is a hunted look about you," Arun drawled, his voice warm with affection.

"Nor he alone," Voran muttered. "Gnawing at me like beavers at a stump — nag nag nag — and not just Lia and Shelais. They've even got the brats at it. Fire take it, my own son —!"

"A conspiracy," Arun agreed. "Our wives don't want us to go south."

"Of course it is," Voran grunted, kicking at a clump of hard-packed snow, "and I'm the one they blame. You'd think I'll deliberately go out of my way to risk your lives. As if I would! My SwordBrother and my spearbrother — would I risk your lives? Would I?"

"Hush," Arun said as the angry voice grew louder. "We know you would not. But we also know your temper. And our Sun Stallion's way with those who irk him. If you flare up, Voran, I swear I'll duck you in the lake if I have to break the ice to do it."

Voran glared at him, but remained silent. Arun was taller, heavier, and did not make idle threats. Moreover, Voran knew that any aid his SwordBrother might need would be given by Rythian.

While that one didn't have the height or weight of either of them, he possessed a whiplash speed that few could match and a deceptive strength. Voran knew from past experience that it was difficult to win against either in combat; against them together he stood no chance at all.

"I'll be glad when we're riding south," he growled. "I'm sick of walls and people hemming me in."

Rythian was wholeheartedly in accord with that. The close confines of the rock-cut Winter Hold were only made bearable by hunting trips on skis or snowshoes, and herd mustering. Summer Hold was better, but... "We won't have long to wait," he said. "Come the dawn we'll be on our way."

"Aye," Arun said grimly, "but I'd sooner fight the Tylosians than treat with them."

"They always were our enemy before the treaty," Voran said with a nod.

"True," Rythian said. "But that wasn't a good enough reason why they must remain so."

"Seems good enough to me," Voran snorted.

"Peace, man," his Brother grinned, tugging the thick braid. "Your temper is redder than your hair. So, Rythian Elder, do you have a better reason?"

Rythian gave no outward reaction to the gentle gibe. "Land," he answered succinctly. "Every year the Tylosians settle closer to the GodStone. The old songs say the hills were their boundary. Somehow, somewhen, it became the river, which has since changed its course northwards. Now our Stone is in a no-man's-land."

"It's empty," Arun shrugged. "The God left it generations ago, when the river shifted."

"He's not likely to return when Tylosians build their cow-byres against it," Voran snapped, anger growing again.

"Gods don't return," Rythian said impatiently. "If they were ever there in the first place. Still, Tylos has no right to push out her borders. That is the bone under contention as I see it, and neither is Tylos alone guilty of it. The Surni are encroaching on D'Shael lands."

"You don't mean that," Voran said, "do you?"

"Of course I do. We're losing valuable grazing every year and it's common knowledge to those who pay attention to — "

"No. About the Gods." Voran made the Warding sign with his left hand. "'Thian, the Lord and the Lady — "

"Leave the Lady to the women," Rythian said coolly. "As for

the Sun Lord, I think Caier is proof enough that He cares nothing for the Shi'R'Laen D'Shael." He pitched his voice low so it would not carry beyond the three of them. "We rule our own destiny. Caier will die one day and when he does it will be by a man's choice, and by a man's hand — not any God's intervention. It seems to me," Rythian went on over Voran's inarticulate protest, "that the Lady is the only one close to our lives, but She has too many faces — and Hoods — for my stomach. Besides, what has She done to prevent Caier's damage, or to repair it? Perhaps She is as disinterested as Her Lord. No, Caier is a problem for men to resolve."

"He's wrong, isn't he?" Voran said to his SwordBrother. "Tell him he's wrong. He makes me nervous when he talks like that."

"I don't know," Arun muttered. "My head says he's right, my heart says he's wrong. Which do I believe?"

"While you decide," Rythian said briskly, "I have four horses to prepare for tomorrow."

"And willing hands to help you do it," Voran said, leaping at the distraction.

It was warm in the barn. Double walls, heavy thatch, lantern flames and body heat from six large horses defeated the cold outside. Rythian and Arun worked shirtless while Voran took his ease and watched them with lazy affection. There were times when Rythian talked rubbish - unsettling rubbish at that, but only Arun, his SwordBrother, was closer in his heart.

The stallion's winter coats were thick and shaggy, and thanks to the slow thaw, they were well-plastered with mud from the river-crossings. It was a long task, combing the tangles from manes, tails and leg-feathers. Chestnut Zaan with his mane and tail as pale as Rythian's own braid; grey Llynivar dappled in shadow-black; white Frost; and Stormrunner so dark a bay as to be almost black. Good blood and bone, Voran mused drowsily. Even lightbuilt Llynivar had proved his speed and stamina, though it was as well that 'Thian was not amongst the tallest of the Shi'R'Laen. A picture formed in his mind of Kardan Elder astride the grey horse, and he chuckled.

"What's so amusing?" Arun demanded, leaning on the bay's rump.

"Was just imagining Llynivar's disgust if he had to carry Kardan," Voran smiled. "All that weight. It would buckle his knees, poor colt."

"He's no colt," Rythian said drily, "and he has more sense in his head than you have in yours."

"Not difficult," Arun grunted, but the lanterns' light caught on the slender bracelet of Voran's copper-red hair bound with gold wire. Voran's wrist bore the the bracelet's mate, Arun's ripe-wheat blond caught within narrow bands of metal. It was a physical affirmation of the bond between them.

"SwordBrother," Voran whispered and Arun glanced up. He met Voran's gaze and his grey eyes widened.

"No," Rythian laughed. "Not here. If you want to roll in the hay with him, Voran, wait until later. Fill the water-troughs for me, that should cool you."

The three Priestesses, representing the three aspects of the Goddess: Maiden, Mother, and Hooded One, gathered in the house of the eldest.

Velra Etha'sdaughter represented the Maiden. Tall and lean, her once-handsome face marked by battle-scars and a cold bitterness, she was First of the Huntresses. Each year, in late spring, another Maid would be chosen in ritual to join with the Sun Stallion, but all times Velra carried the Arrow carved from bone and bladed with flint. There was no one, man or woman, to match her in the hunt.

The Middle Priestess was Myra, as tall as Velra but wide of hip and full-breasted. Her jaw had a stubborn line, but the warmth and generosity of her smile tended to disguise it. She could be ruthless when there was need for it, and it was a fool who forgot that Mothers punish as well as nurture. She had Healing in her hands, a Gift that could release life as well as strengthen it. Those hands were clenched in her lap now, and she was not smiling.

The Hooded One was named Chiera. Taller than both women, no one knew her age, save that it was great. Barren with years, she was deep with ancient secrets, cloaked and hooded in the darkness of death and of the womb before birth. Power hung about her, as tangible as the black cloak she wore; power born of Gifts, of ancient knowledge and Weavings. If the Shi'R'Laen tribe had a mage, it was Chiera.

They knelt around the circular hearth in Chiera's house, tension quivering in the air.

"The Red Bear," Velra said, cold anger in her voice, "has survived another winter. Is he to live through another summer?"

"Good men have died," Myra said quietly. "Remember them, Daughter." It was an honorary title as the Huntress was a scant four years younger.

"Clearly they were not good enough!" Velra snapped. "Why do you still not strike at him directly?" she demanded, her eyes on the Third Priestess.

"Because to do so will turn the Elders and most of the men against us," Chiera said. "He must fall by right of Challenge."

"Why not accident or illness? They are weapons he uses himself — and all know it."

"All the more reason why we should not. Better we use the traditional ways."

"And more good men will die before it's done," Myra sighed.

"Yes. For the greater good. Sacrifices must always be made, yes? Besides, I have been working on one that will give us success."

"Who?" Velra leaned forward, face avid in the firelight.

"Voran Yena'son."

"That fool?" Velra sat back with a snort of disgust. "My horse has more brains!"

"Do not underestimate him," Myra said sharply. "Even so, I don't think he —"

"He is not one man, but two, remember," Chiera spoke over her. "He is hot-headed and hates Caier. I have been feeding that flame. Soon he will Challenge. He will fail, but there is Arun. The Sword Vow will not let him do other than Challenge Caier when Voran falls. Where the one fails, the other will succeed before he follows his Brother to the Eye of the Sun."

"And then what? We will have two dead men and no Sun Stallion," Myra demanded, meeting the Hooded One eye to eye.

"There will be others ready to Challenge each other," she said cynically. "Men are ever ready to kill for gain. That, or the Elders will decide; there is precedence for that."

"Still to lose both Voran and Arun ..."

"Yes, the price is high," Chiera agreed fiercely, "but the cost of failure is far more. I have Seen this, and it is no less than the destruction of the Shi'R'Laen tribe. Not only is Caier destroying us from within, but a darkness comes from without to threaten us. I have Seen this Hold empty and decaying, the grasses of the plain growing tall between crumbling longhouses. With Caier gone, we can turn back to the old ways and regain our ancient strength to confront that which comes."

"We are not so weak," Myra countered.

"No? Who among the Elders who can match one of us? Even Velra, who has no Gift but has learnt the Weavings well? No Elder can match us." Nor would she ever countenance such a threat to her supremacy, but she did not say that. Besides, she had taken certain measures to ensure that any spark of curiosity towards magical experiments was deflected. Again, that was something no one else knew. "Other than the smiths who have their own special Earth-Gifts, there is no man in the tribe who has the slightest knowledge — indeed, they scorn it as much as they fear it."

"The potential is still there," Myra said over Velra's snort of agreement. "No few of the men have the Long Sight, and there are those who can communicate with animals —"

"And do they give the Lady due honor when they use their gifts? No. It's done as casually as braiding their hair! Moreover, there are some who speak blasphemy, are there not, Myra? Your sister's son for instance. He is a greater fool than Voran —"

"No," Myra disagreed sharply. "Rythian has a cool, wise head on his shoulders. He'll be an Elder one day."

"He will not." Chiera stated with cold finality. "Fortunately, Rythian is just a blasphemous nobody who takes his Gifts for granted. But if he lives through this war-season, then in the Lady's Name I will deal with him. It'll be a salutary lesson for the others."

"How will this avert the destruction you have Seen?" Myra demanded, "and what of this threat? Mother, tell us more."

"You show scant respect!" Velra barked.

"Hush, Daughter. Things will still happen, although the reasons why will change. More I do not know; it has not yet been shown to me. Myra, you are riding with the War Band. If Arun also fails to kill Caier, then stop his heart when you tend his injuries. I want him dead before this cursed Treaty can be sworn. By the Lady's Will."

"By Her Will," Myra whispered, mouth set to a grim, determined line.

In the grey chill of a frozen dawn, the Warband assembled in the wide forum between Sun Hall and Elder Hall. Despite the cold most of the warriors wore only breeches, boots and cloaks. With their hair tied up and the black hawk-shadow painted across their eyes and temples, they awaited their Chieftain's word. The Warband was comprised of half of the tribe's men of age and fitness to ride to battle, and the women without child-ties who chose to ride with them as warriors, herb-wives and priestess-healers. Of the tribe's twelve elders, six would ride with the war band to the place of treaty making.

In all, two hundred and thirty warriors would be riding south, among them boys and girls in their last year of childhood brought to care for the remount herd, provisions, and to train in war. Additional warriors remained behind at the Hold for defense and care of the land and herds. These remaining warriors, along with the rest of the Hold, hemmed around the Warband, sitting on their fidgeting horses. They all waited for their Sun Stallion.

The six Elders who would be Trail Council sat on their horses in a half-circle in front of the Sun Hall. Kardan Elder, on his massive roan, towering by more than head and shoulders above all others, held the great Standard.

Only the Sun Stallion himself was not dwarfed by the bulk of the Elder and his horse — Caier, Son of Storms, the Red Bear, Sun Stallion of the Shi'R'Laen, Ninth Tribe among the D'Shael. He came out of the Sun Hall and mounted his horse, heeled it forward into the square. The hubbub stilled. What little light came from the rising sun collected in him and was transformed into redness. The man's close-fitting breeches and boots were of red leather; his mane of bright copper hair flowed over shoulders in a wind-tossed tangle. A ruddy pelt of body hair covered his chest and a belly ridged-hard with muscle. Even his restless stallion was a red chestnut. From mane to boot heels, Caier was vibrant with angry, aggressive life. He crackled with it like the static of a dry summer storm, and the force of his personality was a battering ram to the senses.

Rythian hated and despised him, but did not underestimate him. Not yet could any man hope to stand against Caier and win.

Against all that redness, the gold of the massive Sun Disc that hung around Caier's neck seemed pallid. The pectoral moved on the deep chest with the man's breathing, the ancient patterning catching the meager light and throwing out a glint or two, as if there was a spark of knowing in the Eye of the Sun.

The Eye of the Sun, the symbol that nothing was hidden; nothing lay in shadow. The symbol of all that was bright and clean and honorable and true.

Zaan shifted restlessly, jerking at the rein. Rythian stilled him with mind and touch.

The SwordBrethren rode out of the press of warriors and formed a crescent behind Caier. Eleven pairings vowed through life and into death, oaths taken that linked each man to his Brother in an unbreakable bond. Like the Sun Stallion, the Brothers' hair was loose, swords drawn and resting across their horses' withers. As usual, Voran was at the far end of the line, as far from Caier as possible. His hair, lifting in the wind, was the same fiery color as the Sun Stallion's.

It's a wise Festival Child that knows its sire. And a wiser one still that accepts it. Voran had yet to find that greater wisdom.

Caier's deep voice rolled out in the ritual speech, calling on the Lord to shine His light on their paths, grant them victories so that they might bring honor to the Sun and to their hearths. Then he drew his sword, held it aloft, and the Brethren led the paean. Along with the other warriors, Rythian unfastened the thong that held his hair up on the crown of his head, shook it free. The D'Shael were riding to war. Later their hair would be braided and clubbed for ease in travelling; for now they would ride from the Hold as they would ride into battle, with the living banners of red and gold and white loose on the wind, worthy trophies for any who was hero enough to take life and head from a D'Shael.

Caier took the Sun Standard from Kardan Elder, holding it as if the mass of shaped gold that topped the bone-white staff weighed little. Hanging from it, the flowing crests of past victories blew in long stranded clusters, all bleached uniformly white by many summers, many campaigns. History and song knew the name, lineage and battle-death of each one.

Rythian let the Standard fill his sight: a stallion rearing in a fountain of nine shafts of lightning, one for each of the D'shael tribes, and on each tip the Sun Disc in a circle of curling flames. The Eye was within it and above it the Hawk balancing on wide wings, talons in the flames. The Hawk that carried the souls of the dead into the Sun...

Intricate gold, its making lost in legend. Rythian would follow that, not the man who carried it.

In a warband of two hundred warriors and nearly eight hundred horses, most of the time it is easy enough for three men to avoid one, even if the one was their leader. There were many who would not grieve if Caier fell, but the Sun Stallion had enough adherents to make plain-speaking a risky enterprise, so discontent was rarely given voice. It was not fear exactly that held tongues back, more a wariness of convenient accidents. Death in battle was one thing, but to fall from your horse because a girth broke, or to be taken sick and die in your bed, was another thing entirely. And above and beyond that was another, far weightier consideration: the Sun Stallion was, after all, sacred in the Eye of the Sun.

It was not a quandary that Rythian shared; he had his own plans. The little time he spent in Caier's company receiving his orders taxed his endurance to the limit.

For years Rythian had effectively effaced himself, using his Gift to best advantage. Summoning of Beasts, the D'Shael called it, but the subtle touch of mind on mind could also turn a man's or woman's attention away from him. To everyone he was no more than one skilled hunter-tracker among others. He only came to Caier's notice when his talents were needed. He had done his best to extend a certain amount of anonymity to Arun — and especially Voran. Sooner or later, though, their good fortune would run out.

Camp, this night, was set up in the shelter of Wolf Tor, eight days riding from the Summer Hold and another three from the GodStone and the Tribute Gather. The tents were laid out in the same pattern as the Hold, with SunFire burning in the center space between the Stallion's tent and the six tents of the Elders. As with most evenings, the warriors drifted to the center fire after they had eaten at their own.

Rythian, arriving late at the fire he shared with Arun and Voran, was in no hurry to join that company. "We go early to the Surni border," he said, helping himself to the inevitable stew.

"Good," Arun muttered. "Apart from anything else, the weather's going to break soon, and we may not be able to get into the hills."

"That's what Mettan Elder said," Rythian smiled. "So Caier's sending us the day after tomorrow. We've made good time up to now and we should be at Stonehand's Ridge by then. We'll take the forest trail —"

"The men of Tylos are weak fools!" Caier's great voice bellowed over the camp, echoing back from the rocks behind and above the tents.

"Oh, no," Arun groaned and the other two exchanged rueful grins. "Not that speech again. Doesn't he know another?"

"Not by what we've heard every night so far on this riding." Rythian smiled, and glanced over his shoulder.

The Stallion was on his feet by the SunFire, the leaping flames and night-shadows transforming him into a massive red-gold monolith hewn into man-shape and crested with streaming fire. "I hold them in my hand," he roared, and Voran mouthed the words as he said them. "I, Caier, Son of Storms and Sun Stallion, can crush them when I choose, and they know it!"

"Aye," Arun snorted. "He'd bore them to death."

"They tremble and abase themselves before me like whipped curs!" Caier was well into his stride and so was Voran's mimicry.

"They are not men but pale reflections — so why should they not be treated as such?"

"Uh?" Voran's head snapped round. That was a new thing. The warband was gathering more densely around the SunFire, many on their feet, drawn by the force of the Stallion's personality. In mutual, unspoken agreement the three men left their fire and joined them.

"This year the Tribute will be richer than ever before, and I'll ensure the next will be richer still. Already Hasoe Trader knows what I want, wines and silks and gold for my warriors, and virgins for my pleasure!" Caier laughed, head thrown back, while a few dutifully echoed his amusement.

"More children for your bed?" Voran yelled before Arun could clap a hand over his mouth.

"Caier," Kardan Elder stood up quickly, cutting in on the echo of Voran's fury. "Our laws are clear and our customs are not those of Tylos. No one may take an unwilling —"

"I am Sun Stallion!" Caier roared. He turned on the Elder like an enraged bear. "It is for me to say what is law and what is not! I stand in the Eye of the Sun, I speak the words of the Sky Lord to the tribe!"

On the fringe of the crowd, Arun and Rythian had wrestled Voran to the ground, Arun's hand clamped firmly over his SwordBrother's mouth. In front of them the warriors stood shoulder to shoulder, a living screen, ignoring the struggle at their backs.

"I lead you by His will! Does He deny me my right to order things as I choose? Great Lord of all the D'Shael, if I have transgressed, then strike me down!" He flung his arms wide, massive chest exposed for the lightning bolt.

It did not come, of course. The night sky was clear. But as a dramatic gesture it was well performed. Rythian, bruised and winded by Voran's fury, gave his chieftain that.

"So be it! For ten years now I have led you, and led you well! Any who Challenged me died before my wrath and the will of the Sun! Do any Challenge me now?"

Voran heaved under the combined weight of the two sitting on him, but he could not shift them, nor make much sound through the hard palm gagging him. Several men in the crowd coughed to cover what noise he did make.

Caier's triumphant laughter boomed back from the boulders of Wolf Tor as Arun freed one hand long enough to put pressure on Voran's throat, choking him into semi-consciousness. When they were sure he was at least temporarily subdued, they bundled him in their cloaks and half-carried him out of sight among the tents. Another confrontation averted. Voran's life saved for him to risk another day.

"By the Sun," Arun whispered as they carefully laid the limp body on the floor of the tent, "Caier shames us all, 'Thian. For years I've prayed there might be some truth in the old songs and legends — even if they were only half-truths, surely he would have been struck down the moment he treated with Tylos?"

"It's for a man to remove him," Rythian muttered, "not a God. It's a pity Kardan isn't thirty years younger — he'd do it. Can you manage Voran now?"

"Yes," Arun smiled ruefully. "When he's cooled a little, all I have to do is point out that if he dies, I die; and die he will if he Challenges. He has as much chance against Caier as a babe in arms, and we all know it. They may be bloodkin, but look at him. All Arun has of Caier is the head-mark, none of his bulk and cunning." Arun wrapped a cloth around his bitten palm, and rested his good hand on Voran's brow. "Are you sane again, Brother?"

Voran's eyes blinked open; they were still glittering with anger, but controlled now. "Get that oaf off my belly," he coughed and Rythian obligingly shifted to kneel at his other side. "You shouldn't have stopped me! He has to be put down!"

"Aye, but not in the heat of anger," Rythian said quietly. "That gives him the advantage. Besides," he went on, "it would take five men, not one."

"Five?" Voran asked blankly.

"One for each limb and one to close his throat."

Voran swore, chuckled, swore again. "Perhaps. But something has to be done."

"He's right," Arun agreed reluctantly. "Thian, what was Caier leading up to out there this evening? It stinks, what ever it is, worse than any midden."

"I know," Rythian said. "Perhaps someone should ride to the Heartland, put the matter of Caier before the Sun Council and the Stallion Gather. Let them decide."

"Yes!" Arun's expression lightened. "Who? Not one alone."

"I'm thinking along the lines of the three of us," Rythian said. "Four if we can persuade Kardan, or Mettan, to come as well. An Elder's voice carries more weight than ours."

"We can talk to him now!" Voran started to struggle to his feet, but Arun caught hold of him.

"Not now, fool! If Caier gets wind of it, accidents will start happening to us. And if I am to die in battle I'd sooner it was from an enemy's blade than one of the Sun Stallion's shadows."

"All right," Voran said, subsiding. "But soon."

"Soon," Rythian promised and left the tent, wrapping his cloak around him.

Against his will he was drawn back to the SunFire. Caier was still holding forth, arguing with Mettan now.

"It is easily done!" the Chieftain was bellowing.

Rythian could not remember Caier ever speaking in a quiet voice. Everything about him was thunder and crackling energy. The man was more than impressive, a true leader of men and a fearless warrior, but flawed.

"We will take hostages." The word was Tylosian since the D'Shael tongue did not have that term.

"And I'll not release them until there are more pleasure-slaves," again using Tylosian for the alien concept, "for the beds of my greatest warriors! I ask you, has there ever been a Sun Stallion like Caier, Son of Storms?"

A roar went up. To that, at least, all men could honestly agree.

Rythian stood in silence, fighting to control the fury that was boiling up in him like molten metal.

"That is not the D'Shael way," Mettan Elder said grimly.

"Do you speak against your Sun Stallion?" Caier returned sharply, and after a pause Mettan bowed his head and took his seat once more. Rythian did not wait to hear more. He turned on his heel and walked blindly away, knowing that if he stayed he would speak the words of Challenge. With anger ruling him, he would have no more chance of victory than Voran. He needed to control his own heat.

"Rythian." Kardan spoke out of the shadows. "Join me." Obediently Rythian ducked into the Elder's tent. "Voran has gone too far this time," Kardan said as soon as the tent flap closed. "Caier will not overlook him any longer, he'll swat him like a gadfly."

"I know. 'Ran's stings are too public."

"Exactly. You've been given the Surni border to scout. I think the three of you should be changed to the southern passes and leave at dawn. I'll put it to Caier later on when he's cooled his temper somewhat. But if I fail, stitch Voran's mouth shut and guard him day and night."

"Kardan," Rythian said quietly through the anger that filled him, "have you thought of the Stallion Gather?"

"Aye, frequently. But what can they do? What if the Stallion Gather decides Caier is in the wrong and unworthy? How would they enforce their ruling? He isn't likely to obey any direction from the Heartland if he does not listen to his own Elders. The Gather would either tell us he is a Shi'R'Laen problem, or send warriors to depose him. Or to Challenge him. And if they did that, then the clans would be at each other's throats. Peace between the tribes is uneasy as it is. Can you truly say that if D'Shael came from the Heartland tribes to Challenge or slay Caier, that you would stand by and let them attack your Sun Stallion, even knowing what he is and what he has done?"

"No," Rythian muttered after a pause. "I could not."

"And thus D'Shael would once again turn on D'Shael, and there would be no victory for any save the enemies beyond our borders."

"You are saying, then, that Caier is indeed above the Law?" Rythian demanded incredulously.

"Yes, I suppose I am. In one sense, at least. In older times such a one would have been driven to his own destruction by the madness sent by the Sun Lord."

"This is now," Rythian snapped, "and I cannot believe he is outside the Law, any more than the Council is. It makes a mockery of — "

"Rythian, he is Sun Stallion. His victories are guided by the God."

"No!" Rythian flared. "They are permitted by men who fear his anger and retribution!"

"And who can say they are wrong to do so? Guard Voran well, boy. We cannot afford to lose such as he and Arun."

Rythian did not trust himself to answer. He left the tent, his rage bitten back behind clenched jaws. But he did not return to his own tent. He needed to get as far away as possible from camp and Chieftain alike.

Chapter Three

There was a place up on the Tor among the outcrops that offered solitude, a place for a man to think. Rythian pulled the hood of the black fur cloak over his head to hide the pallor of his hair and merged with the night beyond the firelight.

The bowl was too small to be called a valley. Almost circular, its sloping floor was perhaps ten paces across, but the sheer rock walls were twice that in height. Rythian had first discovered the place when he was a boy riding with the warband for the first time. By the signs, or rather the lack of them, only an occasional wolf or cat had come here. The single entrance had been easy for a child, but it was a tight squeeze for a grown man through the leaning rocks and the tangle of undergrowth. Inside the bowl was the freshness of new grass, the trickle of water from the small spring and a feeling of warmth and welcome as if he had returned to his hearth. Moonlight filled the bowl like water, and in the shelter of the circling rock the air wasn't as cold. There was no snow in here, though it lingered in great drifts out on the plains. In this one place, it seemed that spring had already come. The rawness of Rythian's anger was cut through and soothed. With an unconscious sigh of relief, he settled crosslegged on the turf and relaxed at last, seeking the still center deep within himself.

Finally he could think objectively and without emotion.

Years ago, after the first Tylosian treaty, Rythian realised Caier was no longer fit to be Sun Stallion. There were, of course, others who thought the same, but those who Challenged Caier always failed. And those who were openly critical, or gave advance warning that they would one day contest his leadership, met with unfortunate and fatal accidents. Or were taken suddenly — and equally fatally — ill. Many saw this as the Sun Lord's will. Rythian saw it as Caier's cunning and execution. The man did not intend to be ousted from his position and slain.   But Caier's methods of preventative defense were without honor. His flouting of the ancient laws and customs was a deep shame on the man, his kin and the tribe. It wasn't long after that first Tylosian treaty that Rythian had decided that, when the time was right, he himself would Challenge. And he would win.

Under normal circumstances it would never have occurred to him to make such a Challenge. The price of being Sun Stallion was too high. The Sun Stallion lives apart in his own Hall without the day-to-day intimacies of family life. Rythian was more than content with his wife, his children, hearthsisters, friends, and his place in the tribe; he didn't want to lose his wife and hearthplace to become Sun Stallion. However, Caier was beginning to taint the Shi'R'Laen — something would have to be done to stop the rot.

During the four years since he had made his decision, he had honed his speed and stamina while time took its toll of the Red Bear's wind and muscle. And now?

Little had changed, save that the rot was spreading further. Caier was still as strong as his namesake. Rythian was into his adult height and weight and was little more than a stripling beside the older man's bulk. But he was fast. Very fast.

It would take more than simply speed to win against Caier. It would take a certain skill in combat that Rythian had perfected over the last few years.

Begun out of sheer self-preservation, the inventiveness of a boy who was neither as tall, nor as heavy, as his peers, Rythian had agility of mind as well as body. He had developed flashing speed and a darting attack that had him away before someone with longer reach and greater strength could defeat him. But on his first adult wartrail Rythian learned the hard way that he needed something more than speed and weapon-skill. Faced with a Surni warrior who had the bulk and girth of a boulder, and with only a broken sword in his hand, Rythian would have died but for the timely arrival of Arun and Voran. As it was, Rythian had collected wounds that not only had him sent back to the Summer Hold, but kept him from the wartrail for the rest of that year. He'd had plenty of time to think then.

The result of those thoughts was a different way of fighting, a grim dance learned from the animals he'd watched since early childhood; the horses and hounds, and later the rock-lion and the wolf. Knowledge of how best to kill an opponent was combined with his speed. He'd tested and honed his skills further when scouting in enemy territory where a swift and silent kill was essential. Over the years, he'd come to realise he could use his speed and knowledge against Caier, so long as no other of the tribe saw how effective he could be and warned the Sun Stallion.

Only Voran and Arun had seen those quick and skillful kills in enemy territory, and with small, mental nudges Rythian had 'suggested' they forget what they had seen. He'd had the uneasy feeling that was not the way such Gifts should be used, but he judged it necessary.

Now he was twentyfive. He would grow no taller, no stronger; his speed and stamina were at their peak. There should be no more waiting. Even if Rythian failed, he could inflict such damage on the Sun Stallion that it would invite a second Challenger to come forward and finish what he had begun. There was precedence for that in the old songs. And if he won...

Syth.

A Sun Stallion has no wife.

Emre and Alais.

Yet did not the code of his people say that a D'Shael should die with honor rather than live with dishonor? Victory — or defeat — would cost him dear, but surely the sacrifice, whatever its price, would bring protection to those he loved?

Then doubt took him by the throat and choked the breath from him. Who was he to presume so? Greater warriors by far had Challenged Caier and died in the combat. It would be better, perhaps, if he did nothing, said nothing, stayed anonymous and overlooked.

While the honor of the Shi'R'Laen rotted like a corpse in the sun.

No. He would not let that happen — not if he could prevent it.

His decision made, Rythian wrapped his cloak more closely around him and stretched out on the grass. He saw no point in returning to his tent. This place had been a safe haven in his childhood; it seemed fitting that he should spend what could be his last night of life within its rocky embrace.

A high, thin cry woke Rythian and he sat up with a jerk. The bowl of rock was bisected with shadow and pale yellow light. To the east the sky was lemon streaked, and the silhouette of a hawk spiraled slowly across it. If he was given to follow omens, he could read that as blessing — or a curse. However it might be, in the dawn of the new day, his resolve was unshaken. He broke his thirst at the spring and left, heading not for the camp but the horse herd. Standing among the boulders and snow-covered bushes he sent out a silent call to Zaan, then stripped off cloak and shirt, breeches and boots. He took handfuls of snow and scrubbed at his body and limbs until his skin glowed and life sparkled through his blood, fierce and exhilarating.

Finally Rythian loosened his hair and combed out the night-tangles, shaking it back over his naked shoulders. He stretched long muscles and lifted his face to the spring-warmth of the sun.

There was an impulse to laugh aloud with the sheer joy of living, and he reached up with both hands as if he could touch the bright fire in the sky. Then Zaan was there and he swung up onto the horse's back. There was no anger in Rythian now, nor was there doubt or uncertainty. Caier would die. Or he would.

It was time.

The chestnut stallion caught his mood. Heavy neck arched, cream-blond mane rippling in the wind, Zaan swept into the camp. Warriors, sensing what was coming, followed silent in his wake.

Clear and sharp, as if he saw them focused through crystal, Rythian saw Arun emerge from his tent with Voran at his side. He saw their faces mirror shock, grief and hope; saw them reach up as one to unfasten their hair. Rythian knew what that meant: if you fall today, then so will Caier — or both of us. Rythian smiled at them so they'd know all would be well; youth and vitality ran smooth and potent through his body. It was a good day for dying. Better still for living.

Warriors ran ahead of him; Rythian heard the bellow of fury that rose from Caier's tent. Apart from that wrath there was no sound in the camp. Warriors made a silent wall behind him, following close on Zaan's heels. Ahead of him they formed a great circle where the Fire had burned the previous night before the Standard. The last cinders were being raked clear even as Rythian halted on the edge.

Caier burst out of his tent, already stripped for the coming fight, hair hanging loose. The Elders Ellar and Gorryn came behind him, and Ellar hung the Sun Disc from the Standard for the victor to claim.

Rythian dropped from Zaan's back and sent him away. "I am Rythian Lyre'son of the D'Sheolyn clan," he shouted, "and I am called Lion of the Mountains. I would lead the Shi'R'Laen, by the God's will."

"Whelp, are you drunk?" Caier bellowed. "I've a half-grown daughter with more bone on her than you!"

"Caier." Kardan stood forward a pace, his carved staff planted firmly on the ground. "The Challenge has been given. Answer it."

The red man laughed. "Peace, old Uncle. I was being generous to the lad, but if he is so eager to die, I'll not keep him waiting long." Feet spread apart, fists on hips, Caier stared long and hard at Rythian, then nodded. Only the framing of the actual Challenge was set by ancient custom — but the answer had to fit a certain form. "I stand in the Eye of the Sun," he said, voice booming, "and I've no mind to step from it." Neither did he seem to be in a hurry to come forward and meet the upstart.

"It's long since you stood in the Sun's Eye, Caier Kistre'son," Rythian answered. "Now shadows lie about you. It is your time to die. Look up and see the Hawk above your head, waiting for your soul."

"Or yours, boy."

"Oh, no. Not mine," Rythian said softly, laughter threading through his voice. "Am I not also called the Son Of The Sun?"

"Aye, so is any brat born at the Long Day's noon."

"Caier Red Bear, you are dead," Rythian said flatly. "And in your heart you know it. Why else do you talk so much, if not to delay? The Challenge has been given. Come into the Eye of the Sun and at the least die with honor. The Lord knows you have not lived so." He had lost awareness of his surroundings, all his concentration was on the giant opposite him — so when Caier suddenly charged Rythian was already moving.

Naked a man is born, and if he would gain the God's honor and favor, then naked he fights the Challenge. The stallions who dispute the leadership of the herds have neither clothing nor weapons; when one man contests with another for the leadership of the clans, he is not greater nor lesser than the horses who are already beloved in the God's Eye.

So it was, custom as ancient as the Sun Standard and Disc. Only the strong and the swift could lead, and a blade could make a weak man an unworthy victor. Caier would fight with the size and strength he was born with and had honed over years. Rythian's swiftness, stamina, and cunning were the only things that would keep him alive long enough to find an opening. If Caier managed to get in one single, powerful blow, or pull him within arm's reach, then Rythian would certainly die.

Rythian evaded the first charge easily, but for all his vast bulk Caier was fast and light on his feet. The Stallion spun and lunged again. This time Rythian kicked out as he leapt away from the clutching hands, a swift strike to the side of the man's knee. Caier did not even wince, let alone stagger. Rythian had not expected him to. It would take more than a few such blows to knees, elbows, kidneys, before any effect showed, but each one would slowly weaken and hamper the bigger man.

"You'll need to do better than that," Caier jeered, turning on his heel to keep the fast-circling Rythian in sight. "Or do you seek to make me giddy with your dancing?"

"And make more of a fool of you that you are already? Too easily done." Rythian knew that as long as he avoided those boulderlike fists he could keep this up until the sun set. "If you were not such a dishonor to the clans, you'd be a laughing-stock, Caier. A misshapen mockery of a man."

A howl of rage drowned the words, and Rythian needed a leaping salmon-twist to escape Caier's sudden lunge. Yet despite the blood-engorged face and snarling mouth, Caier's eyes were cold and watchful.

Rythian was not there to be taken by the next rushing attack, either, but his heel drove hard to the tendons at the back of Caier's right leg.

It was a pattern to be repeated twice more; the smaller, younger man moving too fast to be trapped or blocked, his kicks landing with the speed and accuracy of a serpent's strike. A new grimness settled about Caier's mouth and he changed his tactics, no longer seeking to close with Rythian. Instead he remained in the center of the circle, pivoting to keep his opponent always in view. Almost imperceptibly he was favoring his right leg.

"You're nothing but a gadfly, boy," he jeered. "Speed is no substitute for courage. Come, I'll give you a swift end."

"Have you forgotten the old story, Bear?" Rythian's lips were drawn back from his teeth. "About the little stinging insect that sent the bull to his death?"

"Aye, but it takes more than an insect to lead the Shi'R'Laen," Caier barked.

"Indeed." Suddenly Rythian's voice was chill and deadly. "It takes more than the strength and appetites of a rutting hog. You have forgotten how to be Sun Stallion. If ever you knew."

"I know enough to trample you in the dust, brat," he hissed. "And you'll die slow, I'll make sure of that. Will they grieve for you, your wife and hearthsisters? Don't fear for them. I'll comfort them and warm their lonely beds."

Rythian let the lascivious voice wash over him, marginally aware of the warriors' response. They did not like that, but for him to react with rage and disgust would be to play into Caier's hands.

"They have the pick of the Shi'R'Laen, why should they choose a hog above a man? Try another weapon, Kistre'son. That one is as dull as your wit."

"I'll break you, boy!" Caier's roar had little human in it bar the words. "By the Sun's Golden Blood I swear I'll master you as you've never been mastered before! Think to be Sun Stallion, do you? You'll be the Stallion's mare before I let you die!"

A yell of scorn went up from the crowd and brought a darker scowl to the man's face.

"I'm no Tylosian slave to be broken for your pleasure," Rythian said scornfully. "But it's a fair measure of how much you've grown towards the ways of Tylos. Your death is long overdue. You'll shame the clans no longer."

Caier howled with frustrated fury and sprang forward. Again Rythian was too fast, and again a hard heel landed on Caier's right knee. But the Stallion was already turning, lashing out, not to strike but to snatch at the flying mane of pale hair. His fingers clutched and twisted in the heavy tangle and at once he threw his weight back. Rythian went with it, foot scything up to impact with unerring accuracy on Caier's elbow.

The hand in his hair spasmed and he was free. As Caier staggered off-balance, Rythian sent a double kick crashing into the man's lower back.

The only sound the giant made was a peculiar grunting sigh, as he lurched a few steps before regaining his balance. He spun to face Rythian fast enough but his breathing was ragged, and his mouth was a twisted scar across his face.

"Nothing to say now?" Rythian taunted, his own breathing deep, but steady and unhurried. "No Stallion are you, Kistre'son. An ox, more like, castrated by Tylosian vices —"

With a wordless yell Caier charged, his eyes reddened pinpoints of blind rage. Foam flecked his chin and he moved with the speed of a goaded bull.

Yet Rythian was faster, spinning around him in a terrible graceful dance that finally battered Caier to a halt, his massive body bruised and welted by the flying kicks.

Sanity was back in Caier's eyes now, and a cold determination. His breath rasped unevenly in shallow gasps; he was limping and his right arm hung useless. Sweat and wet red hair netted across his face, clinging to his skin and interfering with his vision. For a brief moment Caier blinked, gaze wavering, and Rythian saw the end of it. Snake-swift he struck, not with fist but heel, as he had so many times in their contest. All his weight was behind it, the target chosen with precision, and he felt the man's breastbone break under the blow. Caier went down like an oak riven by lightning. He did not move.

Slowly Rythian straightened from his crouch. The great chest was still, open eyes glared up at the sky and baffled fury was glazing in their depths. Caier was dead.

Rythian drew in a deep breath, a fierce exultancy rising in him that was almost like the touch of battle-fire.

Then Voran punched the air with a howl of wild joy, and the paean rose spontaneously from many throats. Rythian threw back his hair and stalked towards the Sun Standard where the six Elders stood. Faces nearly as white as their hair, Kardan and Mettan had the beginnings of a smile pulling at their hard-set mouths.

Rythian reached up for the pectoral, took it from the Standard and held it aloft so that the new sun struck yellow fire from it.

"I am the Stallion of the Shi'R'Laen!" Rythian shouted above the paean, and Wolf Tor was alive with echoes. "Will you follow where I lead?" The roar of assent was doubled and redoubled by the rocks, and in the midst of the noise Rythian put on the Sun Disc. The metal was chill and very heavy.

"Now I know it will be a good year," Kardan said. "I rejoice that the Sun Lord favors all His children with this victory."

Rythian gave him a smile then turned to face the warriors again, one hand on the Standard's shaft. Instinctively his eyes sought his friends; Voran was pounding his Sword Brother on the back, laughing and yelling with the rest, but Arun seemed frozen, a dawning grief and consternation whitening his face.

"Go into the tent," Mettan said softly. "The wind is cold and it will chill you. Go in and find stillness."

Stillness, with such a wild surge of elation in his blood? But commonsense told Rythian the Elder was right. There were orders to be given, decisions made and enforced. He would need a clear, cool head.

"Send a rider to the Summer Hold," he said. "And choose four warriors to follow with Caier's body."

"It will be done."

"His weapons are in the tent," Rythian went on. "Gallan, you're his eldest son; do you claim them?" The man moved out of the jubilant crowd, a kind of relief showing behind the stubborn pride that marked his heavy features.

"No, Sun Stallion. Do with them as you see fit and I speak for my brothers here also. I have made the swords I'll give to my sons."

Rythian nodded and started for the tent, but a grim voice stopped him.

"Sun Stallion, I claim Caier's weapons if his blood kin refuse them." Marikyr stood alone in the circle. There was a subtle challenge in his stance. It sparked a controlled anger in Rythian.

"Do you so?" he said, locking the gray-green stare with his own. "On what ground?"

"Friendship's sake. I have no cause to speak ill of him. He has brought us much wealth and profit."

"True, but little honor, Marikyr. It is refused. Caier has other sons at Hold, too young for these trails. They shall make their choice, and if they both reject them, then ask again."

"They are children," the man began scornfully but his eyes shifted away from Rythian's.

"They have the right to inherit their sire's weapons if they so wish," he interrupted. "In the Eye of the Sun, I have said it!"

"So be it!" Kardan, Mettan and Ellar said as one and their staffs thudded on the ground.

"And I would have words with he who challenges my brothers' blood-right," Gallan said, deep voice deceptively mild.

"I challenge no one," Marikyr said quickly. "I spoke in haste," and he backed into the crowd and disappeared.

It was a timely reminder that Caier had not been without supporters. Rythian would face resentment and opposition, if not outright Challenge, from some. So be it, he thought. He'd cross that river when he reached it, but he would not let slip the reins he had taken up.

"Go inside," Kardan ordered, "before the sweat freezes on you." Rythian obeyed with a wry smile.

It was by no means the first time he'd entered this tent, but always before it had been filled with the bulk and personality of the Red Bear. Now it was empty and surprisingly spacious. The man's belongings were tidily in their places, clothes folded, swords and spears in their rack. Only the disarray of the bedfurs pointed to his sudden departure.

Rythian took off the pectoral and hung it on the center pole. The brazier was glowing steadily and he knelt beside it, tried to find the required inner stillness.

What had been so easy to consider the previous evening was now all but impossible. Restlessness attacked muscles and nerves. The leather walls of the tent became oppressive; an interruption would be welcome.

As if summoned by the wish, familiar voices were raised in dispute at the threshold and Voran came in fast, ducking under the swing of Kardan's staff. He was carrying Rythian's discarded clothing and on his heels came Arun with Rythian's weapons.

Voran dropped the bundle and pounced on him, lifting him to his feet and into a fierce embrace. "There's never been a contest like it!" he whooped, bruising Rythian's ribs in his enthusiasm. "'Thian, you'll go down in legend for this victory, Sun and Moon, there isn't a mark on you! It looked so — easy! You made a fool of him!"

But it was Arun's silence that Rythian was more aware of. The SwordBrother was carefully removing Caier's weapons, setting Rythian's in their place. Little could be seen of his face past the sweep of his hair.

"It may have looked easy, but I'll wager it wasn't," Arun said quietly. Then, "Fire take it, 'Thian, why?" and the words were torn from him, harsh with pain.

"Because it was time," Rythian said. "Because I knew I could kill him."

"'Run, Caier is defeated." Voran went to his Brother, concerned and surprised. "'Thian is Sun Stallion and without a scratch on his hide. The clans are free of Caier and Tylos both, you should rejoice, not grieve."

Arun leaned briefly on his shoulder. "I do rejoice," he muttered, "but —"

"What did you See?" Rythian asked softly. The grey eyes slid away.

"Nothing." It was a lie and they all knew it.

"'Run, put it aside," Voran pleaded. "'Thian is the God's choice, he stands in the Eye of the Sun. What greater glory is there than that?"

"What, indeed." Arun's smile came with an obvious effort, but he hooked a free arm around Rythian's neck and hugged him close before releasing both men and becoming brisk and practical. "Voran, heat some ale and spice it. Get him something to eat. Kneel down, 'Thian, I'll braid your hair. The Elders will want to be in here soon, they'll have to pack Caier's belongings before we can move south."

"Tylos has quite a shock waiting for it," Voran said gleefully. "I would give blood to see Hasoe's face when we attack them."

"We won't attack them," Rythian said quietly.

"What?" Voran gasped incredulously. "Why not? Burn it, they're our enemies! Let's sweep them into their sea, clean them out of our land!"

"No. Not yet."

"Why not? They —"

"No."

"Give me a good reason!"

"I'll give you nothing until you calm down and think," Rythian snapped. "Between men like Marikyr who'll want Caier's way unchanged and men like you who'll want blood-feud on all things Tylosian, there is a middle way. We will make treaty with Tylos again this year and perhaps the next," he went on over Voran's spluttering denials, "because there are some things we need from them."

"No! Nothing save their deaths! Rythian, you cannot treat with them! Have they not tainted the D'Shael enough?"

"Brother," Arun said quietly, "listen to him."

"But —" It came out as a bleat of protest.

"Swords," Rythian said, taking Caier's blade from where Arun had put it. He drew it from the scabbard and laid it on the bedfurs. The hilt and alien cross-piece were ornate, chased with gold, and the long straight blade was the shimmering grey of water under a clouded sky. Beside it he laid his own sword, the mellow golden-brown long leafshape, its patterning catching the light in fluid lines.

"Iron that is not iron," he said. "A metal that holds a cutting edge better than bronze. It does not bend so readily, yet is not so brittle in weapon-shape as the iron of our own smelting. We need more of such blades. We need the secret of their fashioning. For both, we need Tylos."

"He's right," Arun murmured, and Voran scowled.

"I prefer my bronze blade to any other."

"And I mine," Rythian agreed. "But think if we marry the two — our shaping in their substance. Besides," he added, as Voran thought about it, "I prefer that Tylos does not see us as enemies until I am ready for them to do so."

"I don't disagree with any of that," Arun said. "But what of the people they give as Tribute?" He would not use the Tylosian word 'slave'.

"Send them back." Voran was adamant.

"No. It sticks in my craw, too," Rythian added before Voran could say anything more, "but that would make the traders suspicious. I want them to think that nothing other than the leadership has changed. The people we get in Tribute will be treated according to law and custom. If they wish to return to Tylos, or any other land, they'll be free to do so."

"'Thian," said Arun fondly, "I can recite you a list of names who will Challenge you for these decisions."

"Not yet they won't." Rythian's grin was boyish. "It'll be a while before they forget how Caier died — and how I won without a scratch on me."

"Oh, aye, witchcraft for sure!" Voran's teeth flashed white. "I've never seen you fight so before. And so fast! Ae-shae, it must have taken practice!"

"You planned this!" Arun hissed suddenly, fingers biting into Rythian's shoulders. "Damn you, Lyre'son! How long?"

"Four years," Rythian admitted.

"Four — Mother of Mares! You devious, conniving —" his voice broke on a sob of indrawn breath.

"Why didn't you tell us?" Voran demanded. "All that time, you said nothing!"

"We'd talked," Rythian defended himself.

"Many times, about what we would do if —"

"Exactly. If. Leaf-dreams." Voran was not pacified. "Wishful thinking, with never a hint that you meant it to be reality. Didn't you trust us?"

Rythian winced. "It wasn't a matter of trust. No wall shuts in all sound, and men have keen ears. It only needed one to overhear and all three of us would have been dead."

"There were times enough when we were on the open plains with no other ears about," Voran insisted.

"True, but can you say that once spoken of, it would never be mentioned between us again? I know I couldn't. It was hard enough to keep it to myself — three times more difficult if I had shared it. Besides, I only decided I would Challenge today after you had gone to your rest."

"Excuses?" But Voran was smiling again. "Well, when do we put those leaf-dream plans to work?"

"Changes don't happen overnight," Rythian said cautiously. "For good or ill. If I push for too much too soon, the people will balk."

"So what if they do? We stand with you!"

"So will the rest of the Sword Brethren," Arun confirmed. "We have been ousted from our true place too often under Caier's rule."

"Sun Stallion!" Voran laughed, and embraced Rythian again. "The Sun Lord chose well!"

"Ran, it was my choice," Rythian said, a little irritably. "No God pushed me to Challenge, or gave me the victory."

"Yes, 'Thian, as you say. You won't mind if I give thanks to the Lord and the Lady anyway, will you?"

"Fool," said his SwordBrother, lovingly.

"Sometimes," Voran told them both, "it is possible to think too much, which is as bad as not thinking at all." They stared at him, and his face flushed an unbecoming crimson. "Well, isn't it? You've both yelled at me often enough for not thinking. 'Thian can doubt all he wishes, but I know what I believe, and his victory confirms it."

"I am glad to hear that," Kardan said, pushing back the tent-flap and entering. "There is altogether too much questioning of our ancient beliefs. Anyone who doubts the power of the Lord is a fool, regardless of victories."

"I do not question, or doubt, His power." Rythian stood up and Arun rose with him, tying off the finished braid. "It's His concern and involvement in our lives that I would argue. Ten years we endured Caier. If the stories were true, he should have been struck down long since by the Sun's wrath. Aye, and the Lady's."

"I'll not debate with you," Kardan said, "not when you use logic like a sword-blade. Sun Stallion, the Warband awaits your instruction. Do we ride south in blood, or make treaty?"

"For now we follow Caier's pattern; we meet the Tylosians at the GodStone."

"The treaty stands?"

"For now. I've thought long on this, Uncle."

"That I do not doubt."

"Four years," Voran muttered. "Four years he's been planning this."

Kardan did not appear surprised. "I would rather have seen you with a Elder's staff, Rythian, than with the Eye of the Sun on your breast."

"I doubt I would have lived long enough to bear a staff, Uncle. The tribe needed to be rid of Caier. Of all people, you know that. Too many of our young warriors were making the Challenge in hot anger, and losing. And the longer he ruled, the easier it was to condone what he was doing."

Voran snorted. "Well, I say the Sun set His Eye on you, Lyre'son, four years ago if you will, but He chose the time and place and the victor."

"If the Sun were concerned enough to want Caier dead," Rythian reasoned, "then he'd have fallen to the first Challenge."

"Enough of this!" The Elder thumped his staff on the ground. "Save arguments for the evening fires. Sun Stallion, we have work."

"My apologies, Uncle." Rythian dressed quickly, put on the pectoral, and swung the cloak about his shoulders. "We've lost time with the Challenge. We'll need to move fast to make the next camp by nightfall." For a few heartbeats the enormity of his new responsibilities rose up to swamp him. Plans and strategies aside, he had not looked beyond removing Caier and the danger he represented. Now, as Sun Stallion, he had the future and well-being of every man, woman, and child of the Shi'R'Laen tribe in his keeping. His own beliefs aside, in many eyes he now represented the Sun Lord, as the Three Priestesses represented the Lady; and as such he was suddenly far more than war-leader and chieftain.

Kardan's hand rested firmly on his shoulder. "Stand steady," he murmured. "Did Mettan not tell you to find stillness? You are in the Eye of the Sun, and that would not be unless you had the strength to carry it. Do not scorn the ancient songs and stories. They have counsel for you. Now, go out and speak to your people."

Chapter Four

It had been a long and arduous journey across the ocean. Now, back in his own palace, Hasoe was less enamoured of the bargain he had made with Alzon, Prince of Khassan.

As soon as the captive came out of the drugged stupor, he became very difficult to control. Because Hasoe had not wanted him damaged, care had to be taken, so Prenin Mage had been summoned. Even he had not found it easy to subdue the captive. The maintenance dose of drugs that kept the Priest-Prince docile had stolen much of the high-bred beauty that had first caught Hasoe's eye. Kherin's skin tone was sallow, the dark curls were tangled into elf-locks, the blue eyes dull and unseeing. Not even the talents of Merse, Hasoe's current favorite, could do much to repair the damage, and the situation wasn't likely to show any dramatic improvement. Only luck would have Kherin presentable when the Tribute time came.

Hasoe had more than negotiating skills at his disposal . He also had a network of spies and informers without equal in Tylos. He prided himself on having eyes and ears in every city-state and tribe that had trade dealings with Tylos, including the Surni nation, which shared a border — and an ancient hatred — with the Shi'R'Laen tribe.

One such pair of eyes and ears, a Surni warrior, had watched the duel between Caier and Rythian. He had witnessed Caier's rise, and now he watched him fall. Then he rode south to give this information to a man who paid well.

Merse was intrigued by news that a barbarian warrior had arrived at the palace. The man was said to be of the Horse-People, and might have news of the coming Tribute. That Tribute was assuming a great deal of importance in Merse's life — it meant that he would at last be rid of the Khassani Prince: Hasoe's interest was becoming more and more obvious. Merse had been Hasoe's favorite for some eight months now and he did not intend to be usurped by anyone. It would be well if this Kherin was gone from under the Lord Hasoe's eye, and quickly. Or Merse might well be tempted to dose him with something more deadly than the sedative drugs he was currently fed.

Merse had also never seen one of the legendary Horse-People; this would be his first opportunity to remedy that. He made his way to the private chamber where Hasoe entertained important guests and slipped silently into the listening-alcove behind the fretted screen and silk draperies. His view was far from perfect, but when his master and his guest entered, their speech was clear enough; Hasoe's voice smooth and mellifluous, the other accented oddly.

"You are welcome here, Seran," Hasoe was saying as the servants put chilled wine and goblets on the low table. "We did not look to see you until Year's End."

The visitor waited until the last of the servants had withdrawn before he spoke again.

"Indeed, Lord. But there is word from the North that I think may be worth gold to you."

"As to that, we shall see. Sit, my friend. Take your ease and let us be comfortable together."

Their conversation was followed by the liquid gurgle of poured wine. Secure in his hiding-place, Merse eased a fingertip through the fretwork and made a small gap between the drapes. Hasoe reclined on cushions of azure silk, his back to Merse. The other man was clad in leather and furs that emphasised his height and width. His grey-blond hair was drawn up into a braid that swung forward over his shoulder as he leaned over to pick up his cup. The clean-shaven face was hard-featured, wide across the cheekbones, marred by a hacked scar that sliced down almost to the jawline. The mouth was thin-drawn, and looked cruel. He was a stark contrast to the cool lapis and ivory mosaiced elegance of the chamber.

"To business, Hasoe." The guest came to the point of his visit with what seemed to the hidden watcher to be a boorish lack of common politeness. "The D'Shael who guard your caravans have a new Sun Stallion."

"Have they, so!" Merse heard the hiss of drawn breath. "That is a word worth reward indeed, my friend. So the Red Bear is no more?"

"Caier is dead, and Rythian of the D'Sheolyn clan stands in his place." Seran took a deep draught.

"Rythian? That is a name I have not heard. But he must be a warrior in ten thousand, to have defeated Caier."

"He is young, half the Bear's bulk," Seran said. "I've seen little of him, and know less, but the Surni will be testing him soon, I promise you," the warrior added with an unpleasant smile.

"I wish you fine victories." From the tone of Hasoe's voice, Merse could guess at his smile. "Seran, I thank you."

Now the usual formalities followed with more tangible thanks in the form of gold. A clap from Hasoe summoned servants to escort the barbarian to quarters for the night, and Hasoe did not stay long in the room once the man had gone. As soon as the door had shut behind his master, Merse slid from his vantage point and returned to his own rooms, his mind working busily.

"Your spies are efficient, Hasoe," the Year-President of Tylos' ruling council, Lord Behmath, stroked the fur of his pet monkey idly. "And the Khassani prince? Still for the Tribute, with circumstances changed? Or will you reconsider my offer?"

"Your pardon, Lord Behmath." Hasoe bowed, smiling. "Tylos cannot risk war with Khassan at this juncture. He will have more difficulty in escaping from the edge of the world than from your pleasure gardens. For the good of us all, my decision must stand." This was not at all what the President wanted to hear. Hasoe knew it and they both smiled engagingly at each other.

"There are other changes in the Tribute this year?"

"NaLira and the Prince are as we decided. But since we know little of the new Sun Stallion, I will add two who may be of more use to us. Added at great expense to myself, I might say. LyDia, a courtesan of the Flower Isle and the eunuch Merse, of my own household. These will keep us apprised of events among the D'Shael. Now, if there are no further matters...?"

There were none and the council dispersed. Hasoe bade each a courteous farewell precisely calculated to their status, and returned home, deep in thought.

Hasoe was glad that winter was almost over. Soon the Tribute could depart and he would be rid of the liability of the Khassani prince. He would also be without Merse, which was an irritating prospect. He frowned and sent a slave with a summons for the eunuch.

Swiftly, but without unbecoming haste, Merse followed the servant to the fountain-court. He knelt in an artful flutter of silk to kiss the ground at his master's feet. "My lord has sent for me."

"Prettily done," Hasoe complimented him absently. "Stand, my jewel. Turn around... and again. Bring me wine. Yes..."

"Lord?" Merse murmured, wondering what was afoot.

"With the spring, Jade-eyes, I am to lose the delights of your company."

Merse's heart gave a great panicked bound in his breast. He was to be sold on? Why? "Lord, how have I offended...?"

Hasoe's hand tousled the young man's hair. "Child, child, do not think that. I am not displeased with you. The Tribute must be changed, since there is a new Sun Stallion. We know nothing of this man, and we need an ally in his tents. I am sending you, my jewel, with the Tribute slaves, so that we may learn what manner of man leads the Shi'R'Laen now, and how we may treat with him."

Merse hardly heard the rest of Hasoe's speech. His mind was in turmoil. Why had he been chosen for this task? His master said he had not offended, but that must not be true, or why was he being sent away? And why on this mission? Everyone knew the Tribute slaves did not survive long. Hasoe was sending him to his death! Why?

He could think of only one reason. He had been supplanted.

"Lord...?"

"Yes?" Slightly irritated.

"Prince Kherin — he is still for the Tribute?" *If he is not,* Merse vowed, *then I will kill him before I go!*

"Of course. Much though it pains me to part with such a one."

So, it was with regret that Kherin was sent, but there was no such reluctance over Merse? Hatred simmered in him, and unable by long training to direct it at his master, he selected the next best target — one unlikely to strike back. The Khassani Prince.

* * *

The organised chaos of setting up camp went on around Hasoe without encroaching on him. He stood in the doorway of his pavilion, his hands behind his back under the heavy silk and fur of his over-robe, gazing out to the north. The view was, as always, impressive.

The GodStone was a massive pillar of black rock rearing over two hundred feet into the leaden sky. At the base, its diameter was that of a large house, and it narrowed only marginally towards the summit. The sides were sheer, but there were signs that once a narrow path had wound up to the top. Now bushes and slender trees grew about its jagged feet and the grass surrounded it like a frozen tide.

Beyond the GodStone was the river, wide and fast-flowing, the colour of dull iron save where the water broke whitely over submerged boulders. Beyond that, on a shallow ridge where the land rose a little, were the painted tents of the D'Shael, as they had been in past years.

Hasoe nodded to himself. Thus far all was at it should be. The change of leadership had not changed policy, it would seem.

The ceremony would begin at noon. The D'Shael had insisted on that right from the first treaty, superstitious savages that they were. Which reminded him of the Giftings. The girl-child and the prince did not matter. The courtesan was as poised and unruffled as ever; she knew her role and it held no terrors for her. But Merse was less wise and every glimpse of him showed he was becoming paler with every passing minute. It would not do for him to succumb to an attack of nervous fright. A gesture and a word sent a slave running to do his bidding, and within minutes Merse was there, making obeisance.

"There is no need to fear," Hasoe said quietly. "I know all this is strange to you, and it is only natural to be afraid of the unknown. Therefore ask what you will about them and I will answer you. Speak freely, boy," and he smiled, holding open his robe. Merse crept into its shelter, shivering. "I'm not angry, my jewel, and I don't look to send you to your doom. You'll have a task to do for me among these barbarians, remember? Now, ask those questions that are turning you green."

"They are giants," Merse whispered, "tattooed and hideous."

"Well, taller than most, certainly," the trader-prince agreed cheerfully, "but not tattooed. They wear warpaint to the meetings, to remind us they are as ready for battle as for peace, but that's not as fearsome as it sounds. Each man wears the same, a black bird-shape across his eyes and temples. Look beneath it and you'll see they are not an ugly race for all their barbarity."

"None of the Tribute has lived long…"

"Ah, yes. The northern weather is fierce. Why do you think I'm sending packs of warm clothing to go with you? You'll stay warm. More important, Caier, who was indeed a giant and intemperate to boot, is dead. A man of savage appetites, that one. Perhaps I did too good a job of introducing him to our ways, eh, my jewel?" smiling down at the pale face by his shoulder.

"Everyone says he was great and terrible, my lord," Merse muttered. "What then is the man who ousted him?"

"A younger man. Now, listen to me. I know about them. I have some knowledge of their language, which is simple and unwritten. They have a hundred words for 'grass', and none at all for money! And yes, they are barbarians, and can be brutal. But they are also unsophisticated and easy to manipulate. That is your task. You are going to deliver a nation into my hand."

"Yes, lord," Merse said obediently, but he was still shivering. Hasoe laughed and gave him a swift hug, then released him.

"All will be well, you'll see," he promised. "Go and ready yourself, and see that our prince is also suitably prepared. I'll send for you when it's time and you can ride at my side to the treaty place."

The Shi'R'Laen were waiting, men and women sitting tall on their huge, restless stallions, spears glinting gold in the sunlight. The long hair of the warriors and horses rippled like woven silk on the wind; they were poised, as ready for battle as for treaty. There was no order to their line, no discipline, and neither armor nor shields.

Still, Hasoe knew their fighting skill. In his youth he had faced a D'Shael warband. Their attack had been as remorseless and unstoppable as an avalanche. Sheer luck was the only reason Hasoe lived through it. These warriors did not know defeat. That was one rumor about them that was frighteningly true. And it was the main reason for the Treaty and the Tribute.

Five years of these Tribute Meets had lessened Hasoe's awe of the people. The D'Shael were, for all their height and ferocity, like many others in the world. All people had their price. Hasoe had found Caier's quickly enough. Whoever now led would be much the same.

Hasoe's ornately canopied litter, carried by eight large slaves, paced sedately over the turf. Merse was curled close to his side among the cushions. Hasoe's retinue fanned out behind him, bright with gold and jewels and brocades, displaying all the pomp and authority of a trader-prince. His features impassive, Hasoe scanned the mounted ranks of the Shi'R'Laen as he approached.

The barbaric splendor of their Standard glowed in the sunlight, and Hasoe recognised the white-maned giant who bore it. Beside Kardan was a much smaller, younger man on a chestnut stallion; both horse and rider were dwarfed by the Elder on his massive roan. The younger man's pale blond hair blew in the wind, and on the naked chest beneath the cloak of black fur, gleamed the great Sun Disc of the Stallion.

Hasoe guessed that the new Sun Stallion could not be more than twenty-five or twenty-six years old. Beneath the warpaint the young man's face was handsome in the D'Shael fashion of planes and angles rather than Tylosian-rounded softness. His body, though hard-muscled, was slight compared to the bulk that had been the Red Bear's. *How in the Goddess's Name had he?* But of course — it was obvious. A man drunk — or drugged — does not fight well. What could be simpler than to slip a potion in the Bear's ale and then the Challenge? A clever man, then, this new Stallion. Or rather cunning, which was not necessarily the same thing.

"To the right of the white-haired giant," Hasoe whispered without moving his lips. "The fine-looking young man in the black cloak. That is the Sun Stallion." Merse's tension did not lessen, despite Hasoe's carefully chosen words.

"Him?" It was close to a squeak. "My lord — witchcraft!"

"Poison, more like," Hasoe drawled, and finally felt Merse relax a little. Poison and palace intrigues were the eunuch's life-blood and delight. He would feel on familiar ground.

"Now pay attention. The old men, and that giant with the Standard, are six of the twelve Elders of the tribe; the warriors immediately about them are the SwordBrethren. They are the most savage of their fighting men. The Sun Stallion leads all of them, Elder and SwordBrethren alike. Control him and you control the tribe." Hasoe didn't think it politic to mention that the courtesan had received the same instructions. "And see, he is young, my jewel."

The litter came to a smooth halt scant yards away from the mounted barbarians. The slaves had been chosen for their height, the litter itself specially designed. Consequently when Hasoe carefully rose to his feet his gaze was level with the Elder's and he could actually look down on the smaller man. A subtle test of superiority.

Hasoe's satisfaction didn't last long. Chill blue eyes stared up at him, patient, judgmental and entirely unimpressed by the weight of majesty and authority that Hasoe represented.

"Great Lord of the D'Shael," Hasoe began, his rich voice pitched to carry. "We of Tylos welcome you across the river." He spoke slowly and clearly, knowing that few of the D'Shael had bothered to learn more than a few words of Tylosian. Only a couple of the Elders spoke it with any degree of fluency, and then with atrocious accents. "In earnest of this, and of other things, we bring you many fine gifts — rare and exotic treasures for your pleasure." There was a restlessness among the SwordBrethren, but the Sun Stallion on his chestnut horse might have been carved from stone. Hasoe waited for Kardan Elder to translate his words, but the old giant did not speak.

"Of these other things," the Sun Stallion replied in a clear tenor, his Tylosian fluent despite the inevitable lilting accent, "we will talk later. In the Eye of the Sun, I greet you, Hasoe Trader. I am Rythian, Son of the Sun, and I stand before the God for my people."

"So we have heard, my Lord." Hasoe made obeisance, hands on breast. "And to honor you we have brought great riches." The Goddess was indeed generous. With a language in common, Merse's task was made yet more simple. Hasoe clapped his hands, and the

Tribute litany began. "Gold I bring you, mighty lord; silver, pearls, and jewels from many lands. Carpets of perfect weave and design, silks and brocades from far islands, spices and exotic fruits. Rare wines from the finest of our vineyards."

Slaves brought out the Tribute as he named the gifts; glittering caskets and bales of silky brilliance, barrels and tubs and amphorae all laid out in display on the turf.

"Six pairs of coursing hounds, finely bred and trained to hunt the hare. Six gyrfalcons from the ice-bound fjords of Seaholme, majestic birds fit for the wrist of a king. They can kill a deer, take a heron from the sky." He was very proud of those falcons. They had cost a small fortune. They sat on their jeweled blocks, hoods like miniature crowns glittering in the sunlight. There was a stir among the Shi'R'Laen; yes, he'd known the falcons would be appreciated by a people who lived by the hunt. "Six mares from the desert tribes far to the east, swift as the wind, gentle as royal maidens, chosen for their excellence and colouring."

They were delicate beauties, with limbs like gazelles, dark courtesan-eyes unafraid and trusting. Their coats gleamed burnished gold; their manes and tails were blonde silk, pale as the hair of the Sun Stallion himself. For that fortuitous happenstance Hasoe promised the Goddess a suitable gift.

"And finally, great lord," he went on, "slaves hand-picked to serve your every whim. Two trained in pleasure, two whose untouched virginity are jewels of delight for you alone."

The chestnut horse threw up his head, ears flattened, then became still again. His rider had not moved a muscle. Nor had his face changed expression throughout the Gifting. In fact he had not glanced at all at the riches spread out before him. All the time those cold eyes had remained on Hasoe's face. It was not a comfortable stare.

Was the fool being deliberately insulting, or was he so new to his position that he must seek to impress Elders and SwordBrethren alike? The Gifting was rich — there were, no doubt, many he would need to bribe, young as he was.

"LyDia, the Butterfly of the Flower Isle, the most famed courtesan in all Tylos," Hasoe announced and she glided forward, Unveiled mahogany hair, her fine robes fluttered about her as bright as the wings of her namesake.

For the first time Hasoe saw a reaction from the Sun Stallion; his steady gaze left the trader-prince and lingered on the courtesan's loveliness. She smiled, and the hard young face warmed a little in an answering smile. So, the boy was not immune to beauty. Hasoe gestured to Merse and the eunuch slipped gracefully to the ground and made obeisance.

"The Jewel of the Court," Hasoe announced, "Merse, also trained from childhood in the arts of pleasure. A eunuch whose beauty shall not coarsen nor age, but will remain ever-young, ever-pleasing."

The Sun Stallion acknowledged Merse as he had the courtesan, with a slight smile, and even though the eyes that returned to his face remained cool, Hasoe was by no means discouraged.

"And now a virgin for your bed, great lord," he went on. "The fairest daughter of an ancient, noble line, picked for her gentleness and beauty and knowing nothing of men. She is ripe to learn the ways of pleasing her new Lord. She is NaLira, Flower of Gossamer."

She had been coached over many weeks, and was, indeed, of noble lineage. She managed to walk with proud grace to the courtesan's side, but there her courage failed her and she half-knelt, half-collapsed on the grass.

The chestnut stallion bugled suddenly in fury, surging up on his haunches, forehooves lashing out. NaLira screamed and the great beast was still, trembling and sweating. Now the man's eyes were no longer cold. They burned like blue fire in a rage that struck into Hasoe's guts and turned them to knotted rope. A rumble of anger went through the ranks of the D'Shael and swords were raised, underlining the extent of his misjudgment. This gift was more than unwelcome.

Rythian had schooled his face to show as little as possible. He had not been as successful in schooling his mind, and Zaan was sensitive to his mood.

"Father of Fires!" Voran blazed in their own language. "What are they in that land? Animals? Rythian, we cannot deal with such people!"

"Be still," Kardan said still in the same language. "The child will fare better with us than with Tylos."

"It's as well Rythian is Sun Stallion," Arun snapped, "and not Caier."

"Peace," Rythian cut in, and they fell silent. Across the expanse of turf Hasoe's eyes were narrowed and watchful, and Rythian held that suspicious gaze with his own until the pale eyes shifted aside.

The trader raised his arm again, and three men came forward, two of them obviously attendants. But the third, between them, wore gilded chains on wrist and ankle, like a prisoner.

"A prince, Horselord, from far Khassan," Hasoe went on quickly, "that distant land where chimerae dwell in the sands. A great prince, and warrior, taken in battle, brought here to be part of this tribute we lay at your feet."

"A prince?" Rythian repeated non-commitally. He sensed the seething fury behind him, stilling to a cold contempt as the translation was passed among the warriors. Most of them had no idea what a prince was, save that it was a Tylosian title of high-standing, but all knew the warrior's honor code. Rythian took his eyes away from the trader and stared at this 'prince'.

Like the boy Merse he wore long tunic and loose trousers, of an iridescent blue silk with the shimmer of a bird's spring plumage. His hair was short, curling on the collar of his tunic, a heavy mane of raven-black curls. The shirt was open to his waist, and in the fashion of Tylos, his honey-brown skin had been oiled. If he was freezing in the chill wind, he did not show it.

There was something about him that hovered on the edge of recognition; that and the contradiction of the hard-bodied man beneath the perfumed oil and silk held Rythian's attention. This particular gift did not walk forward with any aspect of submissiveness. This one had the grace of the hunter, rather than the dancer. Enhanced by arrogance, contempt and a fierce hatred, he had walked between his attendant guards as a conqueror enters a captured Hold, proud head high, eyes and mouth expressive of his scorn. By Hasoe's hastily hidden consternation, this was unexpected and unwelcome.

"Indeed, Lord," Hasoe said quickly. "Kherin is called the Hawk of Khassan."

"Again they insult us and the God!" Mettan hissed. "And they call us savages?" The hawk was sacred to the D'Shael, carrying the souls of the dead up to the Sun.

"Hawk?" said Arun loudly in Tylosian, "Peacock of Tylos more like." That was translated as well and a snicker went through the warriors. Hasoe paled a little, and the slaves holding the litter shifted restlessly; if they were horses they would have bolted.

Not so the prisoner. Manacled hands clenched into fists, and dark blue eyes, icy with frost, swept the SwordBrethren, as a leader might mark out an insubordinate troublemaker.

"This peacock has spurs," Rythian said quietly in D'Shael. "Are you Shi'R'Laen, or cattle herders?" he demanded of his own people and there was a shuffling of hooves behind him, as some of the tension ebbed. "So," he went on in Tylosian. "A prince and a warrior, you say?"

The trader snapped his fingers and the guards pulled the man's shirt off his shoulders and tugged it to his elbows. The stance did not alter, but suddenly every muscle was taut. "As you see, Lord, there are battle scars."

And undoubtedly there were, pale on the tan, the marks of edged weapons. But not one of them was a fresh wound, not one less than a year old by the look of them.

"When was he taken prisoner?" Rythian asked Hasoe coolly.

"Three moons since, great chieftain."

Rythian nodded. Taken in battle and unmarked? A direct contradiction, that, particularly considering the pride the man displayed. If he had been captured in battle then surely that pride would have given him the Inner Path to honorable freedom. But all Tylosians lied. Rythian met the chained prince's freezing gaze and held it with his own critical stare. "Indeed," he said, as much to the prisoner as to the trader, "Khassan is a land of wonders."

His sarcasm struck home with both. Hasoe bit his lip. And the man Kherin grabbed towards his hip for a sword that was not there, and the chains went taut for a moment. Then the captive stood unmoving again, his face a mask, only his eyes betraying the rage and shame within.

There was a story here; Rythian realised that he should not be so swift to leap to a conclusion. Truly how the man had been captured was unknown. Rythian gave the man a brief nod of the head, acknowledging his error, then flicked his gaze back to the Tylosian.

"Hasoe Trader," he went on, "the gifts you bring are in truth a reflection of all that is Tylos. We will have much to discuss when you come to the Sun Fire."

"But, Lord, we have a great feast prepared for you and your warriors, as is the custom."

"No," Rythian said. "It is not *my* custom, Hasoe Trader. You and your Council will be before my tent an hour from now." He looked down at the courtesan and the weeping child wrapped in her embrace.

"Nor harm or threat will come to you from any of my people," he told the two quietly. He made a sign and the D'Shael were abruptly in motion, the massive horses pacing with ponderous grace to form a barrier between the Tribute and the men of Tylos.

"Kardan, tend to these four; the child and the prince look to be frozen. If they have none, give warm clothing to them. Mettan, get that stuff onto the wagons and across the river without delay. There will be a full Council meet in my tent as soon as possible." The cold bite of command in his voice was given immediate and unquestioning obedience, but he did not wait to see the orders carried out. He headed Zaan towards the river at a swift canter, the SwordBrethren following in his wake.

* * *

The effects of the drugs that had kept Kherin docile during the uncounted weeks of his captivity were waning. He could think coherently for the first time since Alzon's betrayal. He had felt trapped in a nightmare; now he discovered it was reality. The sunlight, weak as it was, was painful to Kherin's eyes; the wind cut through the flimsy silk like a knife. It took a concentrated effort merely to stand upright and straight, and not join the crumpled child on the grass. It came to him that he should do something for her distress. The child had crept into the courtesan's arms, but plainly the woman knew nothing to calm her. Kherin took a step towards them, reaching inside himself for the power, the healing touch that would soothe the child's frightened mind.

He found nothing. His hand, already extended, dropped uselessly to his side and he stood shocked, mute and blind.

Surely it was an after-effect of the drug, clouding his mind so that he couldn't find his way within. Calming his mind to stillness, Kherin went inside himself, seeking the shining path of Knowledge and Power given him by the Goddess Herself when he became Her Chosen. He had walked that path every day of his life, secure and proficient. Now where the path should have been, there was nothing but confusion. The wellspring of his power was dry.

Kherin opened his eyes, stunned beyond belief. A keen of grief rose in him, to be bitten back because a Prince of Khassan does not show weakness to an enemy.

Incomprehension swamped him, leaving only the question — *why? Why had She forsaken him?* Or was this yet another thing that Tylos had stolen from him with their drugs, spells and humiliations? Kherin's confusion only increased. *You should have died before you let this happen*, a small voice inside whispered — but that too was forbidden him. He could only go to Her at Her Call.

* * *

Rythian's coldness was surface only. Behind the icy mask his fury was hot, threatening to break the bounds of his self-control. He had been prepared, he'd thought, for anything Tylos would do, including the offering of slaves. But he had not expected the blasphemous travesty of the hawks, hooded and hobbled against all custom and belief. Above all he had not expected NaLira, so frail and tiny. Six years old, if that! Not as old as his own son! And chosen to serve Caier's pleasure. Part of him wanted to echo Voran; 'We cannot deal with such people!' But he would. For the time being. Because Tylos had what they needed.

Rythian dismounted in front of his tent, and Kardan's grandson came running to take Zaan to the horselines. Rythian tossed the reins to the boy with a brief smile. There was a thing to be done, more urgent than all else.

He went to where certain of the Tribute had been put for safety's sake. The hawks were hunched on the padded crests of their golden, jeweled tree-stumps. Their feathers were ruffled in the ceaseless wind; he could feel their illtemper and uncertainty, and their need to have that wind under balanced wings. One by one the blind jewel-crowned heads turned towards him. How long had they been hooded? Did they remember freedom? The eyrie on the rocky height?

Slowly he approached the nearest hawk and knelt in the grass to remove the hood.

Hot eyes stared at him, alien yet familiar. He unfastened and took off the straps that tethered its legs. The bird did not move. They ride on a wrist, the trader had said. Rythian didn't relish the idea of those talons closing on his skin. He saw a much-decorated gauntlet among the rest of the paraphernalia, and pulled it on, holding out his arm in silent invitation. With a lift of its wings the hawk stepped onto it. Talons flexed, then locked into the tough hide.

Rythian stood up slowly, turning so that they both faced into the wind. Then he lifted his arm and the gyrhawk was suddenly in flight, climbing swiftly. He watched it soar in a tight circle then arrow eastwards into the clouded distances.

Go free, brother. And good hunting.

He did the same with each of the birds, and when they were all gone Rythian felt his anger lessening. He dropped the gauntlet and turned away, striding past the stacked fuel made ready for the Sun Fire and into his tent. Most of the Elders were already there.

"We'll wait for Kardan and Myra," he said over their rush of questions. The five Elders settled to the floor talking quietly among themselves.

Rythian didn't join them. He paced the width of the tent, his anger rising again. Suddenly the words were there and had to be spoken.

"While we wait," he said, "think on this: as Elders of the Shi'R'Laen, you are the spokesmen of the Law. Given that at least one of the lives given to Caier every Tribute has become progressively younger; given that none of them survived the winter — and some not even the summer; given that no formal charge was ever made against Caier, even though it was common knowledge that he preferred the young in his bed, and got his pleasure from rape — what if he had defeated me at Wolf Tor, how would this Trail Council deal with the young NaLira?"

Ellar Elder came to his feet. "Rythian, that is unfair!"

Rythian took a step forward, head up, eyes blazing. "Is it? I am Sun Stallion, and I stand before the God for my people! So do I stand before my people for the God! Did you fear the wrath of Caier more than the wrath of the Sun? The Law is the Law, and no one is above it, neither Sun Stallion nor Elder! He was one man — you are six — twelve when all are gathered at Hold! In the past the Elders bound those Stallions who brought shadows to the D'Shael, took them to a high place and threw them to their deaths as expiation and sacrifice. Any of our children can name half a dozen who met that end! Why was not Caier so dealt with?"

Ellar sank back to his place, white hair sweeping over his shoulder as he bowed his head. No one spoke a word.

"So," Rythian said quietly. "I have some matters for this Council to debate — the status of these four shall be as any guiltless outlanders who seek asylum within D'Shael. They are of the Shi'R'Laen, subject to our laws and customs. They are now my hearthkin, as Domen Stonehand claimed Suri Mai's daughter and her children."

Mettan got to his feet, using his staff to help himself up. "I think we are all in agreement," he said. "If there is a dissenter, let him speak his reasons." Silence stretched until Mettan struck the heel of his staff on the ground. "In the Eye of the Sun, so be it."

"So be it indeed," Kardan grunted from the entrance, the Priestess at his side, "and the Lady will also agree with that, eh, Myra?"

"In truth, though it's taken the Sun long enough to put His house in order," the Priestess said crisply. "I'll say to Trail Council what I'll say to Hold — that if Caier had not fallen at Wolf Tor, the Lady would have moved against him, Sun Stallion or not. For what use is the heat of the Sun's wrath when the Earth is cold and barren?" she went on over the snorts of indignation. "It's a very foolish child who risks the Mother's punishment as well as the Father's."

"Fine words," Rythian said, an edge of impatience in his voice, "when the deed is already done." Myra smiled at him, indulgent as a mare with a yearling set on trying his new strength. Rythian bit back the angry words that rose to his mouth. "How is the child?" he asked instead.

"I gave her an infusion and she sleeps. LyDia, and one of the priestesses will stay with her, waking or sleeping. She is nine years old, poor kitten, though she is so small we all thought her younger.

She never left her mother's hearth until they took her for Tribute. I told LyDia the little one would be kept safe and cherished, but I don't know if she believed me, even though I speak for the Lady and she is supposed to be from Her Shrine in Tylos. However," she went on, "she had something to tell me of the one named Kherin. She knows something of the customs of Khassan where he is from. It seems the Lady is given the highest honor there, and Kherin is Her Chosen. LyDia says his power is greater than Khassan's ruler."

"What does that mean?" Milgan Elder said blankly.

"I don't know," Myra said over the growing consternation of some of the men. "I haven't spoken to him, but," and she hesitated, remembering what she had felt when she had gone to help the little girl — something like a faltering power, "there is something chancy about him."

"Chancy, is it?" Ellar snorted. "A Prince, they said, whatever that means. With weapon-scars a year or so old, and supposedly taken in battle. A pampered pet of some alien shrine, it would seem. What use will he be to the clans?"

"Chosen of the Lady?" Mettan frowned. "A fine-sounding title, but surely that makes him no more, and no less, than the Stallion that quickens the Mare's womb? Is he the Sun Stallion of Khassan?"

"She said not. It has a High King," Myra said, stumbling over the unfamiliar Tylosian words. "He does not lead as such, but I don't know enough of her language to know all she was trying to say. If he is as she says he is, then it could be he has power. Earth-power and moonpower — as I have."

There was a stunned and unbelieving silence for a moment.

"Impossible!" Ellar snorted.

"Indeed," Rythian said, "it seems as likely as him being captured in battle."

"But it is a possibility we shouldn't neglect," Gorryn Elder put in. "What if he does have the use of Her powers?"

"He would have used them to avoid capture," Lythan Elder countered.

"If he was captured," Gorryn snapped. "Tylos trusts us no more than we trust them. Perhaps they think to dispense with our aid to their caravans?"

"Meaning?" Kardan barked.

"That they have sent one among us who will attack us from within with unnatural powers."

"Sun and Stars," Milgan sighed, "save such imaginings for the evening fires and children's ears."

"Better still," said Ellar, "don't voice them at all. There are enough hotheads out there without adding oil to the flames. They are ready to believe anything of Tylos, including that they might send something dark among us."

"Dark?" said Rythian and Myra as one, though in different tones, and the Elder flushed.

"Aye, well," he muttered, "it does seem an unnatural thing, a man using woman's powers."

"If he does," Rythian snapped irritably. "All this is sheer speculation. He is more likely to have a hidden knife than spell-making."

"And if he does have Her gifts," Myra said with the bite of anger raising her voice above the deeper tones of the men, "why should he be dark? Just because Her ways are hidden, and because She is honored in different ways in other lands, that does not make Her gifts shadowed."

But this was taking it into areas that Rythian would sooner avoid since it would not be politic to speak his mind too bluntly. "I think Ellar is right that all such speculation be left in this tent and not spread about among the people."

"That seems sensible," Mettan nodded. "Is there a dissenter? In the Eye of the Sun, so be it."

"There is another thing," Lythan Elder said. "It's all very well our Sun Stallion claiming these four people as hearthkin, and it's proper that he should under the circumstances. But what can they do? The little girl must be taken to the Hold as soon as possible, of course, but what of the others, especially if this Kherin must be watched?"

"LyDia should go with the child," Rythian agreed, "she is, after all, the only familiar face the child has now. Merse and Kherin can share my old tent and take whatever place they are best fitted for on the Trail. They'll each be given a mount. They can ride herd and tend horses at least. We'll judge what manner of men they are by their actions." That got a consensus of agreement, but Myra was still frowning.

"I will have to go with the child and LyDia," she said. "She needs someone to tend her, who can speak her language. None of the other priestesses speak it well enough to be useful. It would be an unnecessary cruelty to send these two among strangers they can hardly talk to." There was another reason why she wished to return to the Summer Hold; there was much to discuss with the Hooded One. "But be wary of Kherin."

"I have claimed him as hearthbrother, and that makes him my responsibility," Rythian said quietly. "I'll be wary. Make what arrangements you think best regarding LyDia and NaLira, and come back to the Trail Ride when you can. Take a couple of the boys with you for horse-care; Kherin and Merse can take their places."

"Perhaps Kherin should go back as well, if he is untrusty," Gorryn suggested.

"No, Uncle," Rythian responded coldly. "For that very reason he stays with the Warband. Now we need to discuss the coming meeting at the Sun Fire."

The site of the Sun Stallion's tent was chosen with care so that the Sun Fire and the spacious area around it looked towards the river. It was good that there was much room since the Tylosians came to the meeting in full force, but all their garish pomp had the air of being put together in haste. The D'Shael were now neither mounted, nor painted for war, but that didn't seem to give the Tylosians any deep confidence. Only Hasoe preserved his aloof condescension and his dignity. Rythian did nothing to threaten either.

With the Elders around him and the SwordBrethren in an arc behind them, Rythian met his guests beneath the Sun Standard. Beyond the ridge and out of sight were the horse herds, the wagons and draught-cattle; a hive of activity kept as silent as possible.

Rythian smiled a pleasant greeting and bade the Tylosians sit. After a wavering hesitation, they did so, sinking cross-legged and uncomfortable on the turf. The D'Shael knelt as was their custom, and on Rythian's signal, boys came forward with skins of ale and horn beakers for the traders and clansmen alike.

"Drink with us," Rythian said to Hasoe, making it a personal invitation. "Our ale is not as your wine, but we would share it with you to seal the treaty between us in the Eye of the Sun."

"You do me great honor, my lord," Hasoe drawled, accepting the horn beaker as if it was made of white gold.

"We are friends and allies, are we not?" Rythian drawled. Arun's younger brother filled their cups, and the trader sipped cautiously at the liquid. Then he drank more deeply. The ale was a mixture of ciders, heather ale and the almost tasteless grain alcohol that had a kick like an angry stallion, all stirred together with clear honey. It had the taste of a cooling summer draught, innocuous and pleasant. The D'Shael, knowing the power of the stuff, treated it with disguised respect. The boys kept the ale flowing, filling Tylosian beakers and pretending to fill the D'Shael.

Rythian lounged back on one elbow, long legs stretched out in front of him, a deliberate move to lessen himself and allow the trader to look down at him. "This is not as Caier would have had it," he said, a casual sweeping gesture around the assembly. "But he changed our customs."

"And you would restore them?" Hasoe asked.

Rythian chuckled "Some of them," he agreed. "Custom is one thing. The Law is another. That, also, he broke."

"And died. You are a great warrior, my lord. Invincible."

"He was old," Rythian said with the callousness of youth. "Old, fat and slow, and therefore unfit to lead us. It was time for him to die."

"I see. We in Tylos did not realise his position was so insecure. But it is well the D'Shael have a young, strong leader. Tell me, did the gifts please you?"

"Most of them will be welcomed by my people," Rythian said. "But I tell you straightly, Hasoe Trader, that NaLira was a gifting that angered us all."

"How so? If she displeases you, we will replace her with one who is more to your taste."

"You misunderstand," Rythian kept the smile on his face with an effort he hoped did not show. "She is a child and afraid, and that annoyed us. But she is blameless. As for replacing her, that won't be necessary. When she is older, she can, like other D'Shael women, choose who shares her bed. Besides, I would not insult you by returning a gift."

"You are wise beyond your years, and generous," Hasoe said smoothly. "We will not offend in that way again."

"You are not at fault. Caier told you what he wanted, did he not?"

"Yes, lord."

"I am not Caier. I don't know how much of our language you know, so you may not be aware — we have no word for slave. And that is something that will not change. No more NaLiras, Hasoe Trader. No more LyDias, Merses, Kherins, and above all, no more hawks. They are sacred to us. Now, when were you planning to send the first caravans?"

"Soon, my lord. Within the month if the passes are clear."

"They won't be," Rythian said, refilling both their beakers. "There is more snow yet to come. This winter was harder than most, and the spring will be a cold one."

"I feared that," the trader admitted. "It is unusual to see ice still coming down the river at this time. How long, do you think, until the passes are clear?"

"Six weeks, perhaps seven. I'll send word as soon as they are clear. The east is likely to be passable sooner than the west, so it would be as well to have those caravans readied first."

"I'll see to it."

"Also, over the years I've noticed the wagons and mules are more and more heavily laden. They would travel faster and safer over bad ground if you were to lessen the loads. Add more wagons if you wish; with less to pull, or carry, there will be less loss of stock and goods. And therefore more profit for Tylos."

"Ah, but Caier charged us for each head of stock," Hasoe pointed out.

"I am not Caier," Rythian repeated. "That is something I would stop, since a slow, overburdened caravan puts itself and my warriors at risk. There are other ways of assessing payment."

"Indeed, my lord. What would you suggest?"

"Payment in kind, or in gold, depending on the nature of the merchandise on each caravan," Rythian said. "The amount to be a percentage of the safely delivered goods, and that we can bargain over, Hasoe," he added, his smile all guileless charm. "But you must warn your people that there will be no breaking of the agreement, nor any attempt to circumvent it. The first time that happens the treaty between us is ended and Tylos will have no safety beyond her borders."

"My lord, you are far-sighted and of high honor." Hasoe made obeisance as best he could, swaying somewhat as he straightened. All around the Fire, D'Shael and Tylosian were in relaxed and cheerful accord. "Tell me what would please you most and I will send it to you as soon as may be."

"Please me?" Rythian pretended to give it owl-eyed consideration, refilling Hasoe's beaker as he did so. "The sword you gave to Caier the year before last was a very fine one." He dropped his voice to a whisper so that the trader had to lean closer to hear. "There are friends I would honor, men I would influence — would you send me twenty of such swords, of the same much-tempered iron?"

Hasoe blinked. "Lord, it shall be my delight to have it arranged for you," he murmured.

Rythian smiled up at him, aware of Hasoe's eyes moving over his hair and body in an almost tangible caress. "The enemies of Tylos will wash those blades in blood," he vowed. "Let us talk percentages, Hasoe."

The bargaining, and the setting out of the treaty, took some hours of leisurely discussion. Mellowed by the ale, and by the non-aggressive humour of the Sun Stallion and his Elders, Hasoe put his name and seal on the two identical sheets of vellum beside the flowing pictograph that was Rythian's name-sign. Rythian could not read more than a few words of Tylosian, but Kardan Elder could,

and there were changes made in the treaty to shape it as the Sun
Stallion wished it. Hasoe, in the cold light of the next day, might not
be so happy with some of the long-term implications. But it was
signed, sealed and witnessed by a long list of names, D'Shael and
Tylosian in equal numbers, and sworn to by the Sun and the Moon,
and the many Gods and Goddesses of Tylos.

Once that was done, the ale was poured even more generously
until it was time for the Tylosians to be shepherded back across the
river. In the cool light of dawn, the Warband joined the rest of the
D'Shael waiting out of sight behind the ridge and together the large
group moved out swiftly and efficiently.

Chapter Five

"He did <u>what</u>?" Arun asked incredulously. With a grim smile Mettan repeated the news — and Rythian's instructions. "Of all the — is he so set on being the exact opposite of Caier that he must name these outlanders his kin?"

"It is not without precedent," the Elder pointed out. "Under the circumstances, it seems to me he took the best course. As for mounts for the two men, they can have my Bakra and Ellar's Virini to start their strings. No doubt Rythian will give them their choice of the herds when we return to the Summer Hold — as he would any Shi'R'Laen warrior."

"That's generous of you," Arun muttered, face reddening. His own immediate thought had been that no Tylosian should have the use of any of his horses.

"They are to have Rythian's tent as well. He bids you see that it is set up for them tonight. Show them how it's done and make sure they understand. We can't be riding nurse-mare on them for long."

"I'll see to it." Arun didn't have to ask why he had been picked. Rythian knew he was reasonably fluent in Tylosian. Besides, unwelcome tasks are more easily given to close friends than to others.

But maybe not completely unwelcome, Arun realised as he headed for the remount herd. He was by nature a very curious man. He was now intrigued by the contradiction between the extravagant claims made about Kherin, and the man himself. Here was the chance to find answers.

There would be those who thought otherwise, of course. Arun grinned to himself, thankful that Voran was away on the other side of the camp attending to last-minute harness repairs.

The two horses were cut from the herd. Arun gave both beasts a swift grooming, avoiding Bakra's teeth with the ease of long practice, and harnessed them up. He could see the bright silks that marked out the boy Merse over by the Tribute wagons, talking with the young woman from the tribute. Arun was struck again by the beauty of the woman. Lucky the man she chose to take to bed!

Kherin stood apart, wearing his isolation and pride like an honor-robe. Someone had given him a heavy fur cloak, but it had fallen — or been shrugged off to the ground. There was a glint of gold about his wrists, and Arun frowned. Those shackles should have come off before this. He'd have to see to that immediately.

Arun swung up onto chestnut Virini and rode towards the wagons, the bay Bakra pacing at his side. The Tylosians saw him coming; Merse performed some sort of ritual greeting that involved the usual Tylosian groveling to those they considered superior. Clearly, the boy had a lot of learn.

"Kherin, who has the key to your chains?" Arun asked in his careful Tylosian as he dismounted. The stare that Arun received had a blank hauteur that raised his hackles somewhat.

"Lord," Merse murmured, "he probably does not understand. He speaks but little of my tongue."

"Don't call me that," Arun snapped. "Do you know where the key is?"

"The Lord Hasoe would have given it to the Sun Stallion, may all honor come to him," the boy said smoothly. Arun lifted an eyebrow in frank disbelief.

"I saw no such thing given," he said. "Where is it?"

"Lord, I know not."

Well, it might be the truth, but then again it might not. Arun saw his younger brother approaching at a swift trot and snagged the boy's braid before he could pass. "Whoa," he said. "Surdar, will you go and ask 'Thian if the trader gave him any keys to these chains?"

His younger brother aimed a kick at his elder's ankles. "Of course he didn't, or he'd be here unlocking them, now wouldn't he? Let me go, I'm on the Sun Stallion's business."

"So am I, brat, and this won't wait. If he hasn't the key, then tell Gallan-Smith I need his help here."

The boy glared up at him, a scowl on his fine-boned face, full of the importance of his responsibility, and his first War Trail. "Oh, as you will," he grumbled, jerking his hair out of Arun's hand. "But if 'Thian wants to know why I'm late, I'll tell him it's your fault."

"He knows you too well, scrubling."

"Spavined old gawk," Surdar grinned. He dodged the cuff at his head with a cocky swagger, and bolted off at a tangent.

Arun looked up and met the assessing gaze of the courtesan. The girl child was curled up in her lap, sound asleep, wrapped safe in the woman's arms and a great bearskin cloak. "She is safe among us, and so are you," Arun said quietly. "Did they put collar or chains on you?"

"No, warrior."

"I am Arun Therais'son, SwordBrother," he said formally, "called Winter Wolf."

The lovely face warmed to a smile. "Arun Therais'son," she repeated, "I greet you well. Neither NaLira nor I are slaves, only Merse and Kherin. As to the key, in truth I do not know where the key is if it wasn't given to your Chieftain."

"There are other ways," he said, and tore his gaze away to check over the slender youth beside him. Merse did not appear to be chained and the jeweled thing about his throat looked more ornamental than anything else. He did not seem be much older than Surdar's thirteen years, but the green eyes were frankly inviting under the long lashes. Kherin, on the other hand, was watching him as a man watches an enemy across drawn swords. *Danger.* The instinct ran through Arun's nerve-ends, tightening his muscles and sharpening vision.

"Listen to me," he said to all three of them. He spoke slowly, hoping Kherin could follow the words. "You are now D'Shael and hearthkin to our Sun Stallion, Rythian Lyre'son. Not his property, you are his kin. He names you brothers and sisters." His reward was a look of blank incomprehension on Merse's face, while on the courtesan's face there was dawning understanding. Kherin's expression did not change.

"Make sure that Kherin understands this, please. LyDia, very soon now you and the little one will be taken back to the safety of the Summer Hold by the swiftest route. Merse, you and Kherin will take your places among the warriors. For your mounts, Mettan Elder and Ellar Elder have graciously given you these two. They are called Virini and Bakra. Choose as you will."

"My lord is most generous," Merse said, taking Virini's reins warily.

Arun held out Bakra's reins to Kherin, fending off the inevitable nip from the animal with his elbow. "Watch out for his teeth," he warned. "But that's his only fault."

Kherin's dark blue eyes flicked over the stallion, but the man did not move to take the reins. To do so, Arun realised, would call attention to the golden shackles and the shame they represented. *How could a warrior live so bound?* This one wasn't taken in battle — by treachery, yes, but never in fair combat.

"You are D'Shael now," Arun said to the gaunt grim face. "A new beginning." There was no response at all. Arun sighed. It didn't need the Long Sight to know there were going to be problems ahead with this one.

Gallan cantered up on his massive raw-boned grey and swung down beside Arun. "Will this be key enough?" he asked, taking metal-cutters out of his saddle-panniers.

"Probably. Go easy with him, he's liable to be difficult."

"I've got eyes in my head," Gallan snorted. "I don't have his speech, tell him what I'm about."

"He doesn't seem to have Tylosian," Arun said wryly, "but I'll try. Merse is being as much use as a mudmoth." Slowly and with gestures, he explained what Gallan would do.

The cutters made short work of the golden cuffs, but the collar was a different matter. As soon as Gallan touched it, he twitched his hand back with a oath. "Stings like ant-bites," he growled. "By the Fires, what's working here?"

"Stings?" Arun echoed, bemused. "What does that mean?"

"Nothing clean. Some Tylosian magic forged into the metal by the feel of it. Something extra to bind him, I'd say. That's all I can tell you. I'm no Spell Weaver."

"You can't take it off, then?" Arun frowned.

Gallan's expression was grim. "There is the collar and the spell to contend with. I know nothing of spells and weavings, but I do know ores and metals. There is iron beneath this gilding; I can take out what shouldn't be there, let it ring true. That might be enough."

"Take it out? But if it is a spell — ?"

"I'm a smith! I can work metals. I can try to clean out the impurities, maybe draw the spell out — or at least weaken it. Would Rythian want it done?"

Arun gave a snort. "What do you think, Gallan?"

The smith nodded. "Best get on with then, hadn't I?" he said. He spat on his hands, rubbed them together, then knelt briefly to scoop up some loose dirt to rub into his hands. "Earth working is best done with some proper dirt on your hands," Gallan explained. "Let's see if I clean this damned thing up, maybe then I can get the cutters on it." He took a firm grip of the collar on each side of the Prince's throat.

Kherin's eyes were watchful, his stance wary.

To Arun it looked as if Gallan was trying to twist the collar free, and as the smith's great muscles bulged, Arun wouldn't have been surprised to see the metal snap. But it didn't, nor did it give in the slightest.

Gallan stood back with a grunt, and wiped the sweat of effort from his face. "The metal's clean, but the spell weaving's still there. Not so strong as it was, though," he said with some satisfaction, taking up the cutters again. He still had no success in cutting the collar past the soft gilding. Beneath the gold was iron of the same tempering as Tylosian blades; Gallan's cutters could do no more than scratch it. The smith swore under his breath and turned his attention to the lock. It was small and intricate, and no more vulnerable to the cutters than the rest of it. He swore again.

"It's no use," he growled. "I've nothing here that can get through that stuff. Back at Hold there are those fine-toothed hacksaws that Disan-Smith traded for last season. They may be able to deal with it."

Kherin made a sound of disgust. He understood the collar wasn't coming off.

"It'll be a while before we return," Arun frowned.

"Nothing we can for that," Gallan said practically. "At least the damn thing hangs loose enough to spare him sores. He'll have to be patient. Well, for what it's worth, he knows we've tried to get the foul thing off him." Shaking his head, Gallan mounted up and rode off.

This time when Arun held out the Bakra's reins Kherin took them. "There will be some food for all of you soon," he said, speaking to all but with his eyes on Kherin. "Be ready to ride out in a couple of hours time. When we leave we'll be traveling fast. Make sure you're clad well, we won't be stopping until we reach the night-camp. Do you have thicker clothing than these silks?"

"Yes, Lord," Merse said promptly, but Arun ignored him.

"I do not think Kherin does," LyDia said. "All the baggage that came with us was Merse's, mine and the child's."

"I see," Arun frowned. It would be like Hasoe Trader not to waste provisions on one he did not expect to live. He measured Kherin with his eye. "I'll see you're provisioned as soon as possible," he said quietly and scooped up the cloak, draping it around the man's shoulders. The dark eyes caught and held his gaze, and there was something in their dark blue depths that made the hairs on Arun's nape stand on end. But he was given a slight nod of acknowledgement that left him with a ridiculous feeling of success.

That feeling did not last long. The collar was still around Kherin's neck. And why had it been spelled? Arun went in search of Rythian, uneasily aware that perhaps he had been a little hasty in letting Gallan-Smith weaken the weaving.

Rythian had no such qualms. "It was the right thing to do," he said quietly. "One thing, though, don't talk about the spell weaving. I'll have a word with Gallan, ask him not to spread it about. There are enough malcontents who'll braid all manner of tales into that news. Myra will be able to do more to eliminate the spell." He hesitated, then made his decision. "But she is about to leave for the Hold — I don't want to delay her now. When she returns, I'll ask her." The Priestess' warning had been unexpected, but 'chancy' was not the same as 'dark' as she had been swift to note herself.

* * *

Voran stood up in his stirrups, staring around at the apparent chaos as men claimed their mounts from the horselines. He was heartily glad he had not been among those expected to be pleasant to the traders; there were plenty of advantages in not speaking the foreign tongue. The main disadvantage, though, was his SwordBrother did speak it, and had therefore been with those who accompanied Rythian. Voran had collected both their horses from the lines and now waited for his SwordBrother to join him.

Arun's horse tugged impatiently at the reins and Voran's threw up his head, equally eager to be off.

Surdar thrust between the two stallions with his usual casual familiarity. "'Run wants his horse over by the wagons — he's going to ride some of the way with the Tribute men."

"Why? We should be with 'Thian —"

"'Run and 'Thian thought someone should ride with them because Merse hasn't any horse-sense at all," the boy grinned. "He knows which end kicks and which end bites and that's about it. He's lucky he's got Virini. Those Tylosians make my flesh crawl."

"Whoa," Voran interrupted. "Arun's doing what?"

"Told you. Riding nurse-mare on the new ones." Surdar twitched Arun's horse's reins out of Voran's hand and sprang into the saddle. "Didn't he tell you?"

"No, he didn't!" Voran yelled after the boy's fast-disappearing back.

With a growing irritation, Voran finally spotted his Brother on foot by the wagons, talking with the dark-haired Prince Peacock. Mettan's Bakra stood hip-slack beside them, his head almost resting on the man's shoulder, ears pricked forward and apparently with not a thought of biting in his contrary skull. From Arun's gestures, he was explaining something in detail. Voran's mouth thinned as he turned his horse away.

It was well into the afternoon before Arun appeared at his side, as casually as if he hadn't spent all the time in between with the Southerner.

"Well, Merse should at least be able to stick on Virini now that he's used to him. That Prince knows horses, though — had Bakra eating out of his hand instead of chewing on it."

"Prince?" Voran said, and spat as if to rid his mouth of the taste of the word. "And what is that? A Tylosian titling and about as meaningful as frog-croaks."

"Prince is the style of a king's son," Arun said mildly, cutting his Brother's tirade off and leaving him gaping. "Or even the offspring of a noble house, by Tylosian thinking. In his own lands the man may be all they claim."

"Hah!" Voran was not impressed. "And what is a king? Do you know that, Arun Elder?"

"One who leads and rules. Like the Sun Stallion, but less since it seems he comes to the title through birth and not the will of the God."

That earned him a grunt and a very sour glare. "How is it," Voran demanded acidly, "you know so much about it? Did that little whatever-he-is tell you? Or was it LyDia?"

"Both," Arun said.

"Hah!" Another snort. "And Prince Peacock? What did he have to say for himself?"

"He says nothing. After all, what chance has he had, knowing none of our tongue and little of theirs? Both LyDia and Merse were clear enough."

"All Tylosians lie. It's a well known thing. What I want to know is why you're so interested in him."

"Because he's — different," Arun said. "Because he's not what they say —"

"Because he's a walking wonder!" Voran jeered. "A warrior taken in battle and not a mark to show for it?"

"He's marked," Arun snapped. "It's in his eyes and the set of his mouth. No man is safe from the hidden attack — we learned that during Caier's years. Don't judge him, 'Ran, and above all, don't mock him. He is D'Shael now."

"And that's another thing!" Clearly, Voran was spoiling for an argument. Arun gritted his teeth. Sometimes he found it hard to suffer his Brother's rantings, which were becoming more uncurbed. "What has the name of the D'Shael come to when it can be given to Tylosian slaves? Born and bred like cattle into bondage —"

That was too much for Arun. "So you would rather that 'Thian used them as the Bear would have?" he asked scathingly. "Listen to yourself, you sound more like your sire than my SwordSworn. As for 'Thian, I swear I'll put a knife into him myself rather than see him turn that way! We have a Sun Stallion worth the name now, and I'd have us free of Caier's poisons as well!"

"Caier would never have claimed an outlander as hearthkin!" Voran yelled, stung to fury.

"No, he'd have used them against all our laws, goaded them to suicide, or killed them out of hand! I know which course I'd prefer to see our Sun Stallion taking! And if you can't see which is wrong — and why — then you need to sit and think until you do!" Arun reined his horse away at a gallop, threading through the swift-moving convoy towards the Tribute wagons.

Voran's was not the only objection to the Sun Stallion's decision, of course, though Arun's quick ears told him the dissenters were in a minority. Caier had worn the Sun Disc for ten years. Time enough for attitudes to become set. Were the D'Shael not the very children of the Sun? And by that token, chosen above all other races? None of D'Shael blood would renounce that birthright, or wish to be any other than what they were. This natural pride had subtly altered in the Shi'R'Laen during Caier's stewardship to become an arrogance, a belief that they were superior to any other people. From thence it was a short step to the belief that all others were far less, fit only to be slave. Yet before the treaty with Tylos, the Tribe had neither the word, nor the concept of slavery.

There was a growing sense of unease in Arun's belly. He hoped that Rythian had not become Sun Stallion too late for this Tribe of the D'Shael.

There was a lot of ground to cover before nightfall, and the Tribute wagons were not permitted to slow them down. Even so it was full night before they reached the night-camp and the hot food waiting for them. It was a time to relax and celebrate their new wealth, to discuss the Tribute and the Tylosians.

Rythian was not in the mood for any such pastime. He had woven through the warriors as they traveled, questioning each man and woman on what they learned and overheard from the traders around them. The Elders went with him, saving him the necessity of another meeting to pass on the information gleaned.

Scouts had ridden in during the day, reporting on the slow thaw in the west. Word had not come from the east and that concerned him somewhat. The weather was not the only enemy along the caravan roads, not even the most deadly. Rythian had many tasks ahead before he could relax. There were maps to be studied, the position of the hostile tribes and warbands to be marked and plans to be revised. There was also the question of what to do about his new hearthkin.

Sore, aching, and more than a little disgruntled, Merse glared around the hovel of a tent. When he had been told he would be in the Sun Stallion's tent, that's where he'd expected to be; on cushions at the feet of the intriguing young barbarian who'd smiled and spoken so warmly to him during the nightmare ride. The Lord Hasoe had been right. Without the warpaint the D'Shael Lord was indeed handsome, which made it all the more infuriating to be stuck there in such cramped surroundings. He aimed a kick at the all-too-near baggage and swore. This place was not big enough for one, let alone two, and it had been made clear that Kherin was expected to share it with him.

Impossible.

Still, Kherin had proved useful as far as that damned horse was concerned. Merse had no intention of ruining his hands and breaking his fingernails tending the thing. The Prince of Khassan had obviously found his station in life among these savages. Horse-boy.

"Merse," said a familiar voice outside the tent, effectively stopping the snicker in his throat. "May I enter?"

The eunuch gave a squawk of horror and threw himself to his knees, ripping aside the tentflap as he did so. "Great Lord," he gasped, "you do me great honor," and flattened himself to the ground in proper obeisance.

"Don't do that," Rythian said. "This is not Tylos."

"But Lord, I am your humble —"

"You're not my humble anything, nor anyone else's," the Stallion said quietly. "Get up, there is much we have to talk about." Cautiously Merse rose to his knees and found Rythian kneeling back on his heels facing him, relaxed and smiling, a long braid over one shoulder. "That's better. Where is Kherin?"

"With the horses, Lord," Merse said. "He insisted on tending them both."

"So you can understand each other?"

"After a fashion. Lord —"

"Merse, don't name me thus. That title belongs to the God, not to any man. My name is Rythian."

"Yes, L-Rythian."

"Good. Since Kherin is not here, you must tell him what we have discussed, and make sure he understands. My Tylosian is adequate only. If you don't understand what I say — or mean — stop me and ask." He paused, and Merse managed to turn the incipient bow into a nod of acceptance. "Now, the laws and customs of the D'Shael are not those of Tylos, and it's best you learn that as soon as possible.

Arun has already told you that you all are part of the Shi'R'Laen tribe now, and part of my family. You are my hearthkin. You will have tasks to do — as do we all. You will have the same duties and freedom as any member of the tribe."

Finally the sense of what was being said filtered through the eunuch's mind. It could mean only one thing.

"Lord, I am not pleasing to you?" he whispered.

"Merse, you were chosen to please Caier," Rythian explained again. His tone was calm and patient, but there was an edge of irritation beneath it. "I am not Caier, and I do not find pleasure in young boys and child-maids. If I looked for pleasure with a man it would be with a warrior and a lifelong friend. Besides," and his smile transformed him, "you are D'Shael now, and therefore it is your choice with whom you would lie, no one else's. You choose."

"Oh," Merse said blankly, then panic began to set in. This was not at all what Hasoe said would happen. "B-but, Lord, I know nothing else!"

"Are you sure?" Rythian asked. "Stop and think. Others trained in pleasure and given to Caier had more skills: massage that could loosen locked muscles and restore sprained joints."

"Yes!" Merse said with a gasp of relief, more secure on familiar ground. "I can do those things, Lord. I can serve you also at meals, keep your place tidy, carry your messages —"

"Whoa," Rythian chuckled. "You've not been listening properly. You will not be serving me directly. Besides, you have your own place to care for and your own horse. Also you will be riding herd on the remounts —" a litany of horror as far as Merse was concerned. "And there will be much for you to learn. Our language for one, and weapons. Can you fight with sword and spear?"

"I know the war-dances, Lord."

"Merse, I am not 'Lord.' As for the dances, that is not important — can you use the weapons in combat?"

"I — don't know. But I shall learn if it will please you, L-Rythian," he added swiftly.

"Combat is something all D'Shael learn. There is also something that you could teach — the Tylosian speech to those that would learn it — or wish to better their skill in it."

"As you command, great prince." A safe compromise between the protocols, he thought.

"Not a command but a request," the man sighed. "You'll make sure Kherin understands all this?"

"Assuredly, my prince."

"My thanks." He rose smoothly to his feet and ducked through the entrance, then paused. "Merse, I'm not a prince, either." He smiled and was gone.

Merse relaxed with a gusty sigh of relief. Oh, yes. He'd make sure Kherin understood exactly what his situation was. He ran his fingers through his hair; it was just long enough to be bound on top of his head in the D'Shael horsetail crest, though it would fall only to his shoulders. Or he could have a respectable enough braid, if nowhere near as long as the savages wore theirs. But hair would grow and men could be manipulated; in that, at least, the D'Shael were no different to the Tylosians. He began to hunt through his baggage for his mirror.

The ride left Kherin all but exhausted, but caring for his mount was automatic. He groomed the chestnut first, after seeing the two of them fed and watered. Now he worked on the sturdy Bakra, and thought about the tall blond warrior who had given him the horse and had seen to the removal of the shackles. The man had been at pains to explain some things to him, but his Tylosian was so heavily accented, Kherin had understood little. He'd tried to Read the man, but that had been as fruitless as his earlier attempt to aid the child. All it gained him was a headache. Kherin intended to escape soon as he could. When he was free of this place he would seek the Inner Path again.

Despite the heavily accented Tylosian, Kherin understood the warning about Bakra's biting. The animal showed no such tendency now, because at the first opportunity Kherin had taken his muzzle between his two hands, shared breath with the beast and murmured the Secret Name of the Lady of Horses. It had been almost comical to see the slanted ears prick forward, and the rolling eyes calm to a moon-calf gaze. He had done the same to the chestnut — not out of any wish to give Merse an easier ride, but simply because he did not like to see a good horse mishandled.

And these were good horses. There was no doubt in Kherin's mind these beasts were the origins of the greathorses in Khassan. In fact, these horses were even larger. Seen in their natural habitat of the plains, they seemed fit for gods to ride. For a brief moment Kherin had a vision of himself leading a phalanx of of such horses down on Alzon's army with Khori on each flank slashing forward in curving arcs while the huge war-horses crushed all in their path.

Alzon. The name burned in his mind. Alzon who had betrayed both the Goddess and High King. Who had betrayed and poisoned him — who had sold him to slavery.

Fury such as he had never known before erupted in Kherin and the horse he was tending gave a squeal of anger, reacting to the surge of rage in the man. Startled, Kherin gentled him with soothing-calm. It was not easy. Slowly, he forced himself to relax and regain some measure of self-control, then he made his way back to the tent he shared with Merse. Hope began to rise in Kherin; the animal should not have reacted so strongly. Perhaps the barriers that cut him off from his powers were not as solid as they had seemed at first. Frustration and anger roiled through him and he clenched his hands into fists to stop them shaking. The D'Shael were the enemies he should be concentrating on now. Scorn and contempt did not need translating. Kherin had seen both in the faces of the warriors — men painted for battle with his own sign of the Hawk across their brows. Servants of Tylos, it seemed, bought by gifts of lives.

Or not, perhaps. He revised the thought. They had not reacted as Hasoe had expected, that much was clear. As clear as the smith's angry frustration when the steel collar defeated his tools. The collar. He touched his fingers to it, remembering the strangeness when the smith had gripped it and tried to — what? Break it with his bare hands? Whatever the intent, it had failed.

With all but a trickle of the Goddess' Gifts barred to him, he was still able to call on his wits. He was clearly not a prisoner, but without the range of his skills it was difficult to know how these people viewed him; certainly there were no shortage of hostile and suspicious looks. More importantly, he was decently clad in wool and leather now and he had eaten properly for the first time in days. Merse had looked askance at the thick meaty stew of roots and herbs and sheepflesh, preferring to pick daintily at the honeycake and curds. Kherin had eaten his fill. His next meal could be many hours away. He was more worried, though, about the chill sweat that gathered on him and the growing nausea in his gut. Kherin knew the signs. The Tylosian drugs that had been fed to him were leaching from his body, leaving him ailing and weakened in their wake. Time was not his ally.

Kherin had already chosen the horse he would take for his escape; the massive roan one of the older men rode. It looked as if it could run day and night without rest.

Tense and restless, Kherin waited until full dark. When the camp slept, he gathered together the supplies he had filched. Despite his impatience to be gone, he was moving slowly and carefully, and not just to avoid waking the eunuch. His stomach hurt and waves of heat and cold swept over him in turn. He fought it as best he could, aware it would get a lot worse before long.

In the dimness, the bundle of bedding that was Merse moved slightly, and the bright eyes regarded him. "You cannot sleep, Prince?" the eunuch whispered. "I too am wakeful. Which of us will be called to serve the Stallion's pleasure tonight, think you?"

Kherin shot him a glance of dislike, but didn't answer. He had vowed to himself that he would never speak the tongue of his Tylosian captors again.

Merse propped himself on one elbow. "Of course, whoever is passed over will most like be given to trusted comrades. Maybe you will be given to the one called Arun. I think he liked you." Kherin ignored him. Picking up his small bundle, he lifted the tent-flap cautiously, and was gone.

Merse lay back down, smiling. The Prince thought to escape. Well and good. There would be no rival now for the Sun Stallion's passion, nor any need to start using again the drug he had concealed among his belongings. Of course, without it, Kherin would sicken quickly. With luck, he would die out in the wilderness. With a small wriggle of pleasure, Merse burrowed back into his silken cocoon and sank into sleep.

"Arun?" The familiar voice was tentative, apologetic and wheedling all in one. Arun glanced round to see Voran in the night-shadows beyond the horselines, lurking like a half-grown hound unsure of its welcome. "I'm sorry. You're right about Rythian and the Tylosians and I'm —"

"A fool," Arun said affectionately. "Come here." Voran walked into the open arms with enough enthusiasm to push him back against his horse's shoulder, and locked powerful arms about his waist.

"I've been thinking," he said, voice muffled. "You're right and so is 'Thian."

"Do you mean that, or is it just to mend the argument?" he asked, stroking the springy mantle of flaming hair.

"Yes," Voran answered nonspecifically. "We don't let angry words last past sundown, you and me."

"Which, Storm Child?"

"Both," he said simply. "I love you." Which was unquestionably true.

"And I you, but I'm not going to prove it here and now," trapping the questing hands.

"Why not?" his Brother demanded, mock-indignant and pressing closer.

"Because it's cursed cold, beginning to rain, and I'd sooner make love on furs beside the fire than in freezing mud."

"I'm convinced," Voran chuckled. "Are you done here?"

"Not yet. Going to help me?"

Voran laughed and shook his head. "I'll go and keep the bedfurs warm," he drawled and pulled Arun's head down for a hungry kiss. Thus occupied, neither of them noticed the dark shadow moving cat-silent through the horselines.

Chapter Six

It was the children of the Hold who first saw the approaching rider. A group of boys climbing to the crest of the Sun Hall, ostensibly to clear the snow from the thatch, but in reality to make the longest possible snowslide into the drift below.

Shenchan, claiming the highest point as his due because his father was Sun Stallion, was poised astride the roof ridge. He squinted at the dark dot on the expanse of blue-white, then his shrill cry brought the adults running.

Two men rode out to meet the newcomer, but he did not break his horse's stride to greet them. Instead the Hold men wheeled their horses around and escorted him in at a fast canter.

They rode straight to the Elder Hall and conferred briefly with Vinar. The Elder brought out the GatherHorn, and its deep bellow summoned the Hold folk from houses, herds, and lake.

Syth dropped the rug she was shaking and herded Fyra in front of her to the door. Alais snatched up Lirren, and followed her. The open space between the Elder Hall and Sun Hall was already packed with people. Emre pushed through to join her hearthsisters, and Dreyen arrived, panting, with Shenchan as usual at his side. The boy should have been with his own kin, but Emre gathered both boys to her sides in a light embrace.

The three women glanced at each other, but no one spoke. No one needed to. They had heard the same summons often enough in the past ten years to dread it. Another Challenge. Which of their friends would be mourning a dead husband, son, brother, lover...? Nearby, Lia and Shelais stood with their arms around each other's waists, their children crowded close and silent. Lia's lips moved in soundless prayer, but Syth could read it as if it were spoken aloud. *Merciful Lady, don't let it be Voran...* Not vital, impatient, hot-headed Voran. For all that Rythian and Arun might try to curb that impetuous, flashing temper, there was a limit to what two men could do.

"There has been Challenge," Vinar Elder's voice rolled out over the crowd. "Two stood in the Eye of the Sun, and the Lord made His choice. Caier, Son of Storms, has gone into the Light, and Rythian, Bright Hunter, stands alone in the Eye of the Sun."

"Rythian?" Syth whispered. Around her was a cheering tumult, but she seemed enclosed in an invisible cocoon and the ground was tilting. "Rythian?"

"It's a mistake," Alais said, voice shaking. "He wouldn't. Would he?"

"Rythian, Sun Stallion?" Emre gasped. "Oh, Sweet Mother..."

The three women pressed close together, the reality of it dawning on them and bringing laughter and tears. Shenchan tore himself from Emre's side and bolted, head down. Dreyen noticed and would have followed, had not Shelais caught him back. "Leave him be," she counselled. "His sire is dead..."

* * *

The horse-lines were quiet as most of the animals dozed. Alert for guards, Kherin skirted the two human figures he did see, but they were too engrossed with each other to notice him. He untied the roan he had chosen earlier and led it silently away from the horselines. Taking a handful of rough mane, he hauled himself astride the wide shaggy-coated back. He was weak in his legs and fighting nausea.

Crouching low over its neck, he urged the horse out past the perimeter and onto the trackless grassland. Once he judged them out of earshot, he straightened and gave the beast its head. He was racked with chills, and yet sweating, his head pounding and swimming. But he would not stop. Eventually his way must lie southward, but for now it would be enough simply to get away, find somewhere he could lair up like a animal until this sickness passed. He was not sure what had caused it, but suspected the drugs he had been dosed with. Once the stuff was out of his system, he would be better. He would put as much distance between himself and the barbarians as he possibly could while the night lasted. Come dawn, when he and the roan were missed, they would be on his trail.

The plain was criss-crossed by rivers and smaller waterways, but they were no barrier to a long-striding gallop. The first river was wide and shallow, easily forded; the next narrow and flowing in a deep gully; it needed a leap.

Kherin felt the muscles bunch under him as the horse gathered itself and jumped. He started to slide, and tried to grab to steady himself, but there was no strength left in him. The jolt of landing finished it, and after the first bruising impact, he felt nothing at all.

"Rythian!" Kardan Elder strode towards him through the early morning light, his staff held like a warspear. "My roan's been taken!"

"What? Are any other horses missing?"

"No, not from the lines. The boys are checking the remounts now. By the Sun, Rythian, who would do such a thing?" He glared south towards the distant river.

"Do what?" Voran roared out of his nearby tent, naked, his hair unbound in a fiery cloak There was a sword in his hand and a fierce enthusiasm on his face. "There's an attack? Where? Who?"

"Drouen has been taken," the Elder snapped.

"Who by?" the Sword Brother demanded unwisely. The staff cracked across his bare hip as Kardan's temper slipped leash.

"If I knew that, you stone-brained mooncalf, would I be standing here suffering your idiocies?" he ranted. "I swear sometimes I think the Lady has struck you witless!" By this time something of a crowd had gathered, all armed and in various stages of undress, and all prepared for battle. All that was missing was an opponent.

"Where," said Ellar Elder asked, laying his hand on Kardan's shoulder, "are the two from Tylos?"

"Why would they take your damned bullock?" Voran snorted, rubbing his bruise well out of the staff's range. "They have horses of their own. Are you sure you tethered him?" Arun, fully dressed by this time, groaned aloud and ducked back into the tent.

"Whelp!" Kardan roared, advancing on the SwordBrother.

"Voran," Rythian's voice was quiet, but there was a note to it that stopped each man silent in his tracks. "You go too far. Get back in your tent and dress. Arun, come out. Find Merse and Kherin. Kardan, you are too swift to strike out. Has your grandson taken him for a dawn ride?"

"No, he was the first I asked."

"Have you sent men to circle the camp for the horse's tracks?"

"Not yet, but —"

"Rythian!" Arun called, "Kherin has gone."

Rythian loped over to the tent, ducked inside and was nearly tripped as Merse fell at his feet.

"Great Lord, I know nothing!" the boy babbled. "He was gone when I awoke! He told me nothing of his plans! Lord, I did not know!"

Impatiently Rythian reached down and hauled the young man up by his elbows. Merse's fear was palpable. His face was white, his eyes huge and terrified and leaking tears. Shudders racked through him and he hung from Rythian's hands like a broken doll.

"Why should you be held responsible?" Rythian said soothingly. "Stand up and wipe your nose. Is anything missing?"

"N-no, Lord," Merse looked around the baggage-crowded tent. "Only the cloak he was given."

"All right." He left the tent and the shaking boy. "Kardan, where was your horse tethered? Is any harness missing?"

"None. If Kherin has taken him, then he has headstall and rope alone."

Rythian shrugged. "That's more than enough," he said, "How many of us need even that?"

"He is not of the D'Shael," the Elder snapped.

"As of yesterday he is," his Sun Stallion countered. "And, Uncle, if you'd watched him yesterday, you would have seen that he is also a horseman. But that doesn't tell us why he took the horse — if he did. Merse," he raised his voice a little and the boy scurried out. He was still shivering, cocooned in several cloaks. "Where did Kherin sleep last night?"

"B-by the door, Lord — " he dropped to the ground, clutching for Rythian's ankles. "Lord, I — "

"In the God's name, get up!" Rythian barked. "And I am not your lord!"

"'Thian," Midar was at his side, breathless and grinning. "We've found the horse's tracks and a couple of bootprints before he was mounted. By the size and lack of weight, it's Kherin right enough."

"Fire take it," Rythian sighed.

"Then he couldn't have understood Arun," Kardan growled. "Burn it, if we have no tongue in common, how do we tell him the crime he's committed?"

"If, indeed, he is not of Tylos," Gorryn said.

Rythian gave an impatient snort and Kardan glared at his fellow Elder. "It's not only that flame-haired fool the Lady has struck," he snapped. "If he is a Tylosian spy sent among us, why has he left and on my horse? Or did they send him only to steal one of our best stallions?"

Rythian stepped between the two Elders. "And while we're discussing it, Uncles, he is riding further away. Arun, you and your Brother take some of the younger lads and bring Kherin back. It'll be good tracking experience for them and we'll worry about explaining our ways to Kherin when he's back with us."

"I'll go with them," Kardan said.

"No, not this time," Rythian answered. "The scout has come in from the east and the Elders need to hear his report."

In the dawn's light the grass was a filmy grey blanket over the land, heavy with a chill and unfrozen dew. It quickly soaked through their boots making walking a penance. It did nothing to improve Voran's mood. This should not be a lesson in scoutcraft for the brats, but a warband hunting down a stealer of horses. What was Rythian thinking of, to treat it so lightly? And what was his Brother thinking of, to show no more haste than if he was trailing the milk cow to the riverbank?

Voran shifted impatiently, hearing his feet squelch in his boots. One of the boys nudged him between the shoulders, shoving him onto Arun's heels. Who turned on him with a glare.

"Give the boys room," Arun snapped. "And don't overwalk the tracks."

"But —" Voran started an angry protest but his Brother had already turned away and was crouched over a horse's hoofprints, listening while one of the boys explained how he would interpret the sign.

Not that it needed much reading. To Voran's eye it was clear as a row of banners where the horse had passed — not even a child-in-arms could miss the deep-cut tracks the huge horse left. Clearly the Southerner had no idea of how to hide sign, and, moreover, had headed out in a straight line, letting the stallion have his head.

Or was that what he wanted them to think?

"This is strange," Arun said quietly.

"No, it isn't," Voran snorted. "He's just cleverer than I thought. He's sent Drouen out at a gallop while he heads off on foot in another direction."

"You've found his tracks, then?" Arun asked blandly and Voran flushed.

"Well, no — but that's what I'd do — and steal another, less conspicuous horse —"

"You'd steal another horse?"

"No! I don't steal horses — but I'm not Tylosian!"

"Neither is he."

"We don't know that!"

"You won't accept that," Arun countered. He turned to one of the boys, "Ris, lead out, stay to the left of the trail and read it from horseback."

"Wait!" Voran felt as if he was clutching at straws. "It could be a trap. So straight a run could take us into an ambush."

"Who by?" Arun demanded acidly. "The Surni? Tylos? The Mygraeans? And how did they get this close to the warband in the first place? Our scouts have been about for days. If you're so anxious, go ahead and make a sweep. Mount up and ride on, Ris."

Angrily, Voran did just that, eyes scanning the ground and the skyline alternately while the small group of riders continued at a slower pace.

Consequently he was the first to see the familiar bulk grazing along the edge of a gully. Almost at the same time, the stallion became aware of him and threw up his head, whinnying. There was no immediate sign of his erstwhile rider.

A signal from Arun sent the boys into a wide crescent, but Voran was already urging his horse into a gallop, his sword drawn and poised ready. They cleared the gully in an effortless leap. Voran's horse shied away from the sprawled body that was very nearly under his hooves. Voran was nowhere near to being unseated, but it did nothing for his temper.

"I thought you said he was a horseman?" he yelled as Arun approached the gully. "He fell off, or was thrown." It also occurred to him that Kardan's horse might well have fallen and he slid his sword back into its scabbard and dropped from his horse's back to check the other horse's legs.

In a clatter of hooves and stones, the others joined him. "The horse is sound," he reported, and got no reply. The boys were crowded round the Peacock Prince who was supported in Arun's arms as if they were enacting a scene from a battle saga.

His Brother looked up as Voran stalked towards them. Arun's face was anxious. "I don't think he's broken bones," he said, "but there's a nasty head-wound. We'll need to get him back to the camp as swiftly as possible. Drouen's all right?"

"I said so, didn't I?" Voran flared. "Throw him across the bullock's back and let's get moving, since you're so concerned."

"That's no way for an injured man to travel," Arun snapped. He stood up, lifting the man with him, and whistled for his horse. Cann came to his side and Kherin was lifted into the saddle. Arun swung up behind him, cradling the limp weight against his chest. "If I remember rightly, the gully widens and lowers further down; we'll cross there. Let's go."

With one of the boys leading the way, they rode across the plain towards the camp with Voran, silent but far from content, bringing up the rear with Drouen on a leadrein.

Ijena and a couple of the other priestesses came to take the unconscious man from Arun with Rythian and Kardan following close on their heels. The Elder went straight to his horse while Rythian waited for Ijena to finish her swift inspection of the unconscious man. Her frown was not a good sign.

"I'll let you know as soon as he wakes, Rythian," she said over her shoulder.

"Drouen is sound, at least," Kardan growled. "My thanks, Arun."

"None are needed," the SwordBrother said tautly, hunching a shoulder as Voran snarled something under his breath.

Rythian eyed them quizzically. "And?" he prompted. "By the look of you, there's more to tell."

"Nothing," Arun snapped.

"Oh," Rythian said. "Thanks, Arun."

He had little time to reflect on the SwordBrothers' problems. When he reached his tent Gallan was there with an armful of oddments left over from the Tribute.

"I've sorted out everything that's likely to be of use, Sun Stallion," the smith said cheerfully. "This is what's left. Will you look it over before we burn it?"

As Gallan said, there was nothing in the heap that could be of use to the tribe. Rythian was about to consign the lot to the fire when his eye was caught by one of the embossed leather hoods the hawks had worn. He picked it out, turning it over in his hands, wondering again at the society that enslaved a free creature. And what was more deserving of freedom than the hawk, the Dancer on the Wind?

Suddenly he was hearing an echo of Hasoe's voice. What had he named Kherin? The Hawk of Khassan? Blasphemy, yes, but... There had been a bitter pride in the man and a burning desire for freedom.

Ijena pushed aside the tent-flap. "Rythian, I've left Kherin in Merse's care. He says he knows what to do when he wakes, though I can't really see him enjoying the task of nursing the man."

"Some Tylosians have such skills," Rythian reminded her, although he also felt doubtful of Merse's ability. It might be as well if he looked in on the two of them shortly, instead of waiting for the man to regain consciousness. A head-wound could keep a man senseless for days.

Rythian's frown grew as he stared down at the unconscious man and Merse prostrated himself quickly.

"He has bruises only, Lord. And a sore head when he wakes, no more."

"He had the wit to fall soft, then," the Sun Stallion muttered, and bent to lay a hand briefly on Kherin's brow. "Why this? He had but to speak and I'd have provisioned him. He could have gone homeward, wherever it lies. He didn't need to steal a horse and leave in secret." Rythian straightened, and his gaze fell on the prostrate boy. "Oh, Fire take it, Merse, how many times must we tell you? That isn't necessary. In fact, in a D'Shael, it is insulting and distasteful."

Hurriedly, Merse picked himself up and adopted the straight-spined kneeling position the chieftain had used the previous evening. "I beg pardon, L-Rhythian," he said. "I am slow to learn. I forget."

Rythian nodded approval. "Did he speak to you before he left? Do you know what possessed him?"

Rythian meant one thing; Merse heard another and pounced on it as the answer to prayer.

"He said nothing to me. But — I do not think he was in his wits. Even in Tylos, he was — strange. Lord Hasoe has told me that in some distant lands, those who are not entirely... stable... are lodged in Her shrines, are considered sacred and under Her protection. And he is known as Her Chosen. In truth, my chieftain," he went on sternly, daring to put a hint of admonishment in his voice, "I do not think he is possessed, merely not quite — sane? — all the time."

"Oh, Lord of Fire," Rythian sighed. "Well, if you think you can cope with him, Merse, he is in your charge."

Merse bent his head, or Rythian would have seen the feral smile. "Do not fear, my chieftain. I am not entirely without resources."

Some hours later, Kherin regained consciousness. If from then on he was confused and lethargic, there were none who thought that unusual, following as it did a severe blow to the head.

For several days there were other things than the welfare of his hearthkin to occupy the Sun Stallion's mind. The command of the warband was no light matter for one who before had only captained scouting parties. Kardan's unfailing support and advice was God-sent. It was Kardan, also, who acted as eyes and ears among the warriors, bringing their comments and concerns to Rythian. Now that the initial shock of Caier's death was passing, those who had been high in his favor were feeling the chill wind of the difference. It did not go unnoticed.

"You'll need to watch your back around Marikyr," Kardan said outright as he joined Rythian in a study of the map of the trade- routes. "And a couple of the others who fawned on the Bear for what they could gain."

"They'll Challenge?" Rythian said sharply, looking up.

"I doubt it. But Caier's rule taught them less direct ways. Fire take it, boy," Kardan snapped, "don't look at me like a spooked colt. You weren't forever out scouting. You saw what went on."

"Yes. I saw 'accidents'. People who ate bad food, or water. A slipped girth. A fall. But nothing could be proved."

"Then you know what I'm saying. Be on your guard. They'll spread discontent like a plague. There were more than a few who did very nicely out of the Tributes."

"All that is changed. There'll be fair division from now on."

"Yes. But don't expect everyone to like it."

"I don't," Rythian said shortly. "But I'll not buy myself friends. Enough, Uncle. What of our scouts? Have we had word yet from them?"

"No. The thaws are late this year." He had given enough warning, Rythian would be on his guard.

"There have been late thaws before. It's news of the Surni clans and the western passes that we need most. Should we send out another scout?"

"Not yet. Wait a few more days. I'll tell you another thing that's causing concern. Kherin."

"What of him? If it's the matter of the horse-theft, that will be dealt with by Trail Council when he's recovered. A few more days only will we wait, then we'll have to send out others to scout the western passes." Rythian was silent for a moment. Then, "Why is he the cause of concern?"

"You know, of course, that Merse is spreading it about that Kherin is of the Lady and not always in his wits? He keeps telling people that Kherin is Her Chosen. Whatever that means."

"And there are enough wild imaginings to fill the gaps," Rythian agreed. "I've already had my ears and patience well-battered by fools who should know better than to look to children's hearth-tales. If he was going to strike us all impotent, man and stallion alike, or let the Moon into men's heads and drive them mad, he'd have done it before he left."

"Left on my horse."

"That's another thing. If he was returning to Tylos, why did he ride west? Tylos lies south. Or if he wanted to avoid it, then he should have gone east. Unless..."

"But the question is, why was he on my horse and not his own. Unless what?"

"I told Trail Council last year I'd learned Tylos was trying to forge links with the Surni. He might have been making for Surni lands. No." He answered his own question with a positive shake of the head. "No, he's no Tylosian spy. There's an honest hatred in him and no subservience at all, thank the Lord. Horse theft is the only crime he might be accused of, and he'll answer for it in due course."

"No 'might be' about it," Kardan growled. "He will be accused!"

"Yet it could be he doesn't know the reason himself," Rythian went on. "He was sick enough when they brought him back, and not much improved since then, no matter what Merse says."

"Merse says much to any that have enough Tylosian to listen," the Elder said. "Kherin says nothing at all. I've tried talking to him, but all I get is a blank stare. When he knows I am there, which is not always the case. That fall he took has addled his head, but he's not witless — or mad — whatever Merse pretends."

"I'll make time to talk to him myself," Rythian promised. "He has to understand we're not his enemies."

"There is another thing," Kardan said. "Some people are beginning to say his sickness is a plague sent with him that has nothing to do with his fall."

"What would that gain Tylos? Raided caravans," he answered himself. "And their border is no more a barrier to the Shi'R'Laen — or the Surni — than gossamer. No, Tylos will not move against us until she has found an army to equal our defense of the caravans. I've already told Trail Council they are beginning to sound out certain tribes along the routes. So far nothing has come of it, but that could change."

"Over the years you've spent a long time scouting the borderlands and caravan roads," Kardan said, eyeing his leader thoughtfully.

"Yes." Rythian smiled. "And I have some friends among the outlanders. There are many who hate us, but they hate Tylos more. I would have word if such things begin to come about."

"It seems to me," the Elder said, "that you've a longer sight than we'd have thought. You could have served the clans better as an Elder than a Sun Stallion, young Hunter."

Rythian shrugged. "As for the matter of Kherin, if he is well enough, Trail Council could be held tonight."

"What use? It's obvious there's something not right about the lad. He should be sent back to the Hold. Myra will know how to tend him."

"A good thought," Rythian said, "and Merse can go with him. Men on horseback will travel faster than Myra's wagon; they might even overtake her before she reaches the Hold."

"They'll need escort and guides. Send Marikyr and his cronies. It'll get them and their discontent out of the Warband."

There is a creature of the Tylosian deltas, a reptile able to adapt to almost any environment. In a land where conditions can be fair one day and foul the next; the water fresh or brack, only the cunning survive.

After only a few days away from the Warband, Merse was surprised how quickly he had grown used to traveling on horseback. He found the D'Shael clothing comfortable and practical, and easily embellished to his taste. The food, while lacking the delicacies of Tylosian cuisine, was well-seasoned and filling. The ale was rough but palatable. The handful of men riding escort were equally interesting. The only thorn in his side was the Khassani Prince, and he was controlled by judicious dosing.

Merse laced shut the tent flap and glanced across at Kherin. He was crouched on the other side of the center pole, head resting on arms wrapped around drawn-up knees. He had barely been able to stay in the saddle, hardly surprising with the amount of *au'ri* Merse had given him. Merse took the phial from his cosmetic pack and held it up to the lantern-light. The green glass glowed like a jewel, dark at the bottom where the heavy oil lay, barely a quarter full. It should have been enough for months; it had lasted only days. While Merse knew men could gain a tolerance to the stuff, the amount he was having to give Kherin would have dropped an elephant in its tracks. Perhaps this distillation was not as potent as the palace pharmacist had claimed?

Kherin's anger fueled him and had kept him in the saddle during the long ride. It allowed him to see the sleight of hand that had added drops of liquid to his food at every meal. Now, for a while, his rage and hunger for revenge had a new target; Merse, who encompassed all that was Tylos —

The attack came swift as a striking leopard and as unstoppable. One hand closed on Merse's throat, the other swept the phial from his grasp and it was crushed under their falling bodies. Unable to scream for help, Merse fought with the weapons available, long nails lacquered to metallic hardness and the serpent suppleness of a dancer. Needing both hands to defend his eyes, Kherin released his throat to trap Merse's wrists. Merse's screech of fear and fury brought the required aid.

The D'Shael did not waste time trying to get inside the tent. They merely heaved the thing from its moorings and tossed it aside like a courtesan's parasol. After that it did not take long for five tall men to subdue one who was half-stupefied by last night's *au'ri*. Merse left them to it and scrabbled among the bedfurs. The drug was unsalvageable, a sticky mess of oil and shards of glass, the reek of it making his head swim. He snatched the nearest perfume bottle and broke it over the *au'ri*. The barbarians wouldn't know what it was, of course, but they might guess it was no cosmetic and it was better to be safe than sorry. The powerful scent of jasmine swamped that of the drug.

"Merse?" Marikyr's large hands rested on his shoulders, offering comfort. "Are you hurt?"

"I don't think so," he said, raising limpid eyes to the giant towering over him. He'd broken a fingernail, he thought acidly, but they wouldn't see that as an injury. "It was so sudden — I didn't expect anything — you saved my life."

"Your throat is marked."

"It's nothing," he said bravely. The D'Shael admired bravery.

"The treacherous cur," Marikyr growled. "What was Rythian thinking of, sending him to Hold in his condition? It's as well that collar is still about his neck. We've leashed and hobbled him — the Hold will have to be warned of the danger."

"We can talk of this later," Merse purred, resting one hand lightly on the hard brown chest. "I must reward my rescuers." Yes, there were debts to pay; to the barbarians and to Kherin. Merse always paid his debts. "I have something in my packs that I was saving for the Sun Stallion, but I think it more fitting I share it with all of you."

The first mouthful of the spirit made Marikyr stretch his eyes.

"Whew! This is good! Better than the slop in the Tribute!"

"This is the pure spirit," Merse said. "Perhaps it is diluted for the Tribute." It was, as he knew well. Hasoe believed that the D'Shael would not know the difference.

"From now on, it had better not be," Loris growled, taking a swig in his turn and coughing at the bite of it. "Ae-Shae! What do they make this from? Distilled oil of snake, or ground-up scorpions?"

"If you don't like it, the more for us." Paren grabbed for the flask. "Sun and storms, but this puts fire in a man's blood!"

"All that and more," Merse purred, making his eyes long at the lean and silent Jarmin, who took the flask next, the brown throat working as he swallowed. Sargen gave a guffaw and elbowed Merse friendly-wise in the ribs.

"You're a good lad, Green-Eyes, for all you're Tylosian scum."

"I am D'Shael now, lord. The Sun Stallion has said it. I am proud to be D'Shael. In Tylos, we heard much of the greatness of the Horse People."

"Ah, but that would have been when Caier led us." Jarmin reached for the flask again. "Now, he was a Stallion!" There was a general murmur of agreement. "Didn't stint us when it came to sharing out the Tribute, either."

"Surely," said Merse, "the Lord Rythian will be equally generous."

"Mayhap," Marikyr nodded sourly. "Mayhap. But I got short shrift when I made claim to Caier's sword, didn't I? And was there any sharing after this Tribute? Not a whit. Caier would have held a feast."

Merse smiled. "And Kherin? Would he not have pleased Lord Caier?"

"That sullen bastard? More trouble than he's worth. Caier wouldn't have been as soft with him as Rythian."

"No?" Merse breathed.

"No. Broken his will in a night, then turned him out for whoever wanted the trouble of keeping him. But he'd have kept you for himself. I doubt any of us would have had as much as a smell at you." It was meant as a compliment, Merse was certain.

"I am fortunate, then, that I may... choose..." he said softly, lashes demurely lowered. "As is Kherin, though he does not appear to appreciate this. Should he not be reminded that he belongs to the Shi'R'Laen now?" He meant as property, but the men did not take it as such.

"Remind him how?" Loris demanded. "The Sun Stallion said he was in the Eye of the Sun."

"Put the tribe's mark on him," Merse whispered, eyes glittering. "He will remember then who his... benefactor... is." There was doubt in their eyes, and a measure of unease. Merse changed tack. "Besides, if he wears Lord Rythian's brand, it will surely cancel out any ill-luck he carries. The mark of the Sun Stallion must be a greater magic than any jinx."

This met with general approval. At Merse's request, Loris drew some of the Clan symbols in the dirt, pointing out what each one meant, and, after some thought, sketched Rythian's name-sign. Merse nodded. It would serve admirably.

It soon became apparent, however, that he would have to inflict it himself. They had objections he could not understand to performing such a deed. Possibly they might have been able to explain more clearly if the Tylosian spirit had not been working strongly in them; as it was, they agreed only to hold Kherin for him. Merse took his belt-knife, and laid the coveted blued steel blade in the coals. One of the men went to get Kherin.

If he had been less drunk, he might have guessed that Kherin was not going to co-operate. Semi-dazed still, Kherin realised that the man meant him no good, and kicked with both feet into the man's crotch. The large man gave a choked whine of pain, doubling over. Kherin tensed, knowing full well that he could not escape whatever was intended but determined these barbarians would pay dearly for it.

Two came to discover the reason for their comrade's prolonged absence, found their companion curled on the ground and called for the others.

Hobbled, Kherin had no chance of escape, but he did indeed make them pay for his capture. They all bore bruises, and Marikyr a painful bite, before someone had the wit to bring a fist clubbing down on the back of Kherin's head. That took the fight out of him.

"Ae-shae!" Jarmin panted, "Did you know this one was such a rock-lion, Merse?"

Marikyr was examining his bitten hand, which was streaming blood — Merse took up a strip of silk and bound the injury, lamenting the savagery of the Southerner even as his mind rejoiced at the chance for more revenge. "Such behaviour would never be tolerated in Tylos," he announced sententiously. "Does your hand feel easier, lord? In Tylos, we have ways of punishing the recalcitrant. He should be whipped, at the least."

"Well, I'd like to make him smart for this," Marikyr grunted. "Give over, boy, that'll do."

"Then take your belt to him, lord." Merse stepped back obediently, eyes feral. "Stripe him well, and then I shall mark him."

The man tenderly cradling his privates liked that idea. Two of the other stretched Kherin's limp body on the grass, pegging each limb securely. Marikyr took off his belt, winding the tongue into his palm for a better grip. Merse showed his teeth. It might not be the braided lash of Tylos, or the barbed scourge, but with Marikyr's muscle and injured anger behind it, it would serve. The slavers of Tylos disciplined their prime stock with the strap, so as to leave no disfiguring scars. The massive buckle would bite and tear, and the welts would be blackening bruises for days. The Khassani prince would sleep on his belly — if he was able to sleep at all.

The first shock of pain brought Kherin round, and his moan was out before he could stop it. But it was the only sound he made, locking his teeth on the lancing agony as each stroke ripped at his flesh and his body jerked in reflex. But the respite, when it finally came, was momentary. A hand tangled in his hair, and Merse was smiling into his eyes. "Hasoe's error, that he did not mark you as a slave before the Tribute. I shall remedy that, Prince."

It had a certain fitness, Merse considered, wrapping his hand in hide to take up the glowing knife. The arrogant Khassani prince should be branded a slave by the Tylosian pleasure-boy. Merse knelt, one knee bearing hard on the back of Kherin's right thigh to hold him immobile, and bent to his work. His victim sobbed aloud at the searing touch of the blade, then, unable to keep silent, screamed. Merse smiled, and continued to cut. The stink of burned flesh was like incense to his nostrils.

It did not take long. Merse got to his feet, appraising his handiwork. It lacked the clean clarity of a true brand, but it marked Kherin irrevocably none the less. Pleased, he smiled at the watching warriors. "He is yours now, lords, if you wish to use him for your pleasure."

It would have crowned his victory — but none of the five seemed inclined.

"I like my bedsport a little livelier than that," Marikyr said. He cocked an eyebrow at Merse, one hand stroking suggestively over the crotch of his tight breeches.

All their eyes were on him now. Merse felt his heart quicken in his breast. They had been stimulated by what had been done to Kherin — he did not think any of them would be hard to please. And if they proved otherwise — had he not been trained to the highest standards? He made a small bet with himself that he could satisfy and outlast them all — and untied the cord that held his silken trousers.

The diluted spirit that was part of the Tribute did not have the miserable after-effects of the pure kind. The morning found the five D'Shael with varying degrees of nausea and headache, fervently wishing they had either not drunk so much of the poisonous stuff, or enough of it so they did not have to remember what had happened afterwards.

The first one who first stumbled wincing into the grey daylight, found Kherin still as they had left him, spread-eagled on the sodden grass, the dew standing cold on his lacerated back, soaking the tangle of dark hair.

"Oh, Sun Lord..." The man crouched, touched chill flesh, and thought for one awful moment that the Southerner had died in the night. Further desperate investigation found a slow pulse, however, and when the stiffened limbs were freed and the man's head lifted, it was possible to get a mouthful of spirit down his throat. But he showed no sign of consciousness.

"If he dies, his blood is on our heads," Marikyr voiced their common thought. "We'll have to answer to the Hold Council, and to the Sun Stallion when he comes back."

"If the ill-luck hasn't fallen on us before then," another muttered. "As it surely will."

Merse, less affected by the drink, looked worriedly from one to another. Sooner or later, they would bethink themselves of the one who had suggested what should be done to Kherin. He did not want to be held their scapegoat. He would have a little leeway with them

— he had pleased them well last night, and knew it — if he could just suggest some way out.

"Lords," he said tentatively, "who is to know of what has happened, if we say nothing? In Tylos, we say 'The Night sees all, but is silent.' If there is no evidence..." He glanced at Kherin's blanket wrapped form.

The five D'Shael were not stupid. "Kill him, and be rid of the body before anyone sees?"

"Better yet, we take back a corpse torn up and part-eaten by a rock-lion," one of them suggested. "As if he'd gone hunting and been taken as he rode. It wouldn't be the first time."

In case they balked at killing a helpless man, Merse put in another word. "He's been untended all this night. Who is to say he will survive anyway?"

"Southerners are weak. They're not used to our climate," Marikyr added. "It might be a kindness to put him out of his misery now." He fingered his knife as he spoke, and no one made objection.

"He's certainly in a bad way." They all looked at each other. It was Marikyr who made the move, dragging the blankets loose, and pulling Kherin's head back to expose his throat for the killing stroke.

"It's for the best," he said — and in the next instant his hand was knocked aside. "What—?"

"Riders," he was told. "Over there. They've seen us. Put up — there's no time now."

"Then what tale do we give them?" Marikyr hissed. Merse, thinking quickly, tucked the blankets back. "Well?" Already the nearest rider was within earshot.

No one had an answer.

Chapter Seven

Myra's return to the Summer Hold with her two charges caused something of a sensation. That a child so young had been sent as part of the Tribute caused such fury it took the combined authority of Hold Elders and both Priestesses to prevent a warband riding out for the Tylosian border. Myra counted it fortunate that Velra was not in Hold at the time, for it was certain she would not have stood with her Sister Priestesses on the matter.

The news that Rythian had named all four Tylosians as hearthkin did something to allay the general wrath, and Syth immediately stood forward.

"Then let me take them now," she said, "the little girl looks exhausted and frightened out of her wits!"

"She is," Myra said. "She needs as much comfort and care as we can give her. Do you speak Tylosian, Syth? Do any at your hearth?"

"My husband," she answered without thinking. Then, "Ronan Alais' son, and my son Dreyen, a little."

"But you and your hearthsisters do not? Then I'm sorry, but NaLira will be best at a hearth where Tylosian is spoken with some fluency by all there, and she'll need LyDia to be with her. Syre Helia's daughter should take them in — if both she and you are in agreement."

Syth looked across at Syre's calm, wise face, and knew Myra spoke only commonsense. Kardan's birthsister would give the child — and the woman — all the quiet haven they would need to grow strong and confident in their strange new circumstances. "If Syre is willing, then so am I," she said reluctantly. "But be sure NaLira knows she has hearthkin near her age at my hearth."

"Of course," Syre agreed with a smile. "All at your hearth are, as always, welcome at mine. In fact, why don't you and Dreyen come with me now and help settle them in?"

Myra breathed a sigh of relief. That problem, at least, was out of her hands. She went with LyDia and the child as far as Syre's hearth, then quietly left. She had other matters to consider, specifically the new Sun Stallion and Chiera's plans. Although the

Hooded One was in the Grove, Myra could feel the cold fury of the Third Priestess radiating like the chill from a glacier.

Chiera's house was set among the trees of the Grove's northern edge. Myra found the door ajar for her; she entered, closing it behind her.

"Why did you permit it?" the Hooded One demanded immediately, voice harsh with fury. "How could that blaspheming — nobody — become Sun Stallion! By what trickery did he defeat Caier?"

"No tricks," Myra said calmly. "It was youth, speed, agility and a thinking mind against brute strength."

"Did you aid him?"

"No!" Myra approached the hearth and the tall, cloaked figure standing beside it. "It took us all by surprise."

"Indeed." Chiera's laugh was bitter. "I was sure I had Voran on the edge of Challenge, but he did not."

"Arun and Rythian stopped him, so I heard. Mother, Rythian has started well, I have high hopes of —"

"He agreed to the Treaty!"

"Yes, but he —"

"He should have rid us of Tylos! Instead he brings its poison into our very hearts and we must wait here for the doom to come to us. You'll not return to the Warband, Daughter. Death flies ahead of him — I have Seen the Hawk's wings spread wide over our people. In its shadow waits the scorpion. Death, Myra, and betrayal! The Dark One comes amongst us!"

Myra bowed her head in acceptance, knowing there was nothing she could say in Rythian's defence. The Third Priestess would not listen. She chose not to mention the man Kherin just yet. Time enough for that when the Hooded One was less furious.

"Syth! Alais! Emre!" Thin and high as a bird's cry, the woman's call came across the water. Alais looked up from her fishing nets. On the rocky promontory of the eastern shore stood a horse with his rider waving a red jacket above her head.

"It's Lia. What brings her out here? Something important —"

"The children!" Emre gasped.

"Or the Gather Horn," Syth said swiftly, reaching for her oar. "We wouldn't hear it this far out." There was no more talking. Alais hauled in the nets and they rowed swiftly to shore. Lia urged her horse into the shallows to meet them, the water girth-deep on her indignant mount.

"Myra told us all that your new hearth-brothers were staying with the warriors," she panted. "But both of them are here now, and the one called Kherin is like to die."

"Battle-wounds?" Syth asked over the exclamations from the other two.

"No," Lia said grimly. "The story is unbelievable. One of them — Merse, I think he is called — says Rythian had the man beaten, and the hearthmark burned into his hip —"

She got no further.

"Rythian?" Syth interrupted. "No. Never! What are we, Tylosian? This is ridiculous!"

"Myra said Kherin had been claimed by Rythian as hearthkin, like the others," Alais said. "Even if he were not, to brand him? That is not the D'Shael way!"

"Nor would Rythian order it!" Emre exclaimed. "This is a mistake, a misunderstanding."

"Well, if it is Merse's understanding that is at fault, then none of the escort have seen fit to contradict him," Lia said. "Not that they stayed more than a few moments! Turned right round and headed off at a gallop. They were Caier's men, though, and I doubt they have any love for Rythian."

"Caier Red Bear." Syth spat into the lake as if the name left a bad taste. "Lia, go ahead, we'll follow. Tell them we are coming. Sisters, pull for home."

The boat was no light skiff, but the women were strong and skilled. By cutting across the curve of the lake, they reached the landing stage only a little behind Lia on her horse. Alais moored the boat, then caught up with her sisters. Syth led the way, striding towards the open space before the Sun Hall where a crowd was gathered. She pushed through, looked at the man lying there, and rounded on the group of Elders, eyes blazing.

"Is this D'Shael law?" she demanded. "Is it Shi'R'Laen custom?"

"It was the Sun Stallion's word that ordered it," Nortan said heavily.

"I might have believed it of Caier, but never of Rythian! My husband would never countenance such brutality, and all of you know it."

"He is not your husband any more," said Vinar brusquely. "He is Sun Stallion."

"Husband he may no longer be," Alais interrupted, "but he is still our hearthbrother. Becoming Sun Stallion does not change a man. Be the metal true or flawed, it stays the same. Rythian is not and can never be another Caier, and you would do well to remember it!"

Syth knelt at Kherin's side. "I will not stay to argue further. This man is sick and in need of care, and we are taking him home. Alais, will you send Ronan for Myra?"

The three women moved about their patient with efficient skill, tending his injuries and making him as comfortable as they could, though they all became progressively more tight-lipped.

"What has Rythian been thinking, not to send him here before this?" Syth burst out. "I've seen more flesh on a winter wolf!" The hand she held in hers seemed almost fragile in comparison to her own. Yet tendon and muscle were sculpted over the fine bones of narrow palm and long fingers, and the hard pads of callus spoke of long acquaintance with sword and spear and rein.

"I'd like a few words with whoever had him beaten and branded," Alais snapped. "Marikyr was always Caier's man, but I did not think he'd sink to this!"

"Not while he was sober," Emre said quietly. "Lia said they all had the look of men still half-drunk. Except the Tylosian." There was an unaccustomed edge to her voice.

There was no opportunity for further speculation; Ronan burst in while they worked. He spilled the crock of water in his haste as he slammed the pot down, splashing the rugs and risking a crack in the earthenware. "Mother!" he shouted. "What are you doing?"

"Our hearthbrother is in need," Alais snapped, taken aback by his vehemence.

The boy was not to be quelled. The flushed, angry young face scowled down at her, fury on the pale brows. "He should be denied, spoken against!" he yelled, kicking out at the senseless body.

Her hands occupied with the senseless man, Alais could do nothing, but Syth was closer. The ten-year-old gave a squawk of pain and shock as her palm cracked across his ear.

"You won't be so sorry for him when you find out!" He stood his ground against their united displeasure. "He eats horseflesh!"

"Rubbish," Alais snorted. "Who told you that?"

"Merse, the one who came with him——"

"And since when does the Lady speak oracles though that one? We are fortunate to have one so learned at our hearth, sisters."

"It's true! I asked LyDia, and she said yes, in Tylos they eat horses as well as cattle and sheep. And that's evil, and when Rythian finds out, he'll speak against him. I'm not sitting at the same hearth as one who——"

"I am not tolerating any more of this nonsense!" Syth snapped.

"It isn't nonsense!" The boy was near to tears. "And LyDia says he belongs to the Lady." This got him the attention he wanted. "It's true. In his own lands, she says, he's the Chosen. Merse says it's as if he is husband and son to Her——"

"Blasphemy, brat?" Alais frowned. "First the horseflesh, now this. Ronan, if—-"

"But Mother — that's what people are saying!"

"People would be better served to keep the hand of discretion before the mouth of rumor, and you can tell that to any who repeat such children's tales!" The women exchanged glances, keeping their thoughts to themselves with the boy in earshot.

"But he eats horses," Ronan insisted. "It makes me sick even to think of it!"

"Hush, my colt." Alais touched his cheek in a gesture of forgiveness. "You start too swift at shadows. Has not your hearth-sire told you often not to believe blindly all you are told, but to seek answers from the source? When our hearthbrother wakes, and is strong, then ask him. And do not forget that LyDia says he comes from another land, not Tylos."

Abashed, Ronan ducked his head. "Sorry," he muttered. "Myra said she'll be here soon." He bolted out of the door. Alais sighed, but before she could speak there was a stir in the room beyond, and the Hooded One came over the threshold. She brought with her the smell of dried herbs, woodsmoke, and the undefinable scent of night, though the day was bright outside.

"The Good Goddess guard this hearth and all about it." She spoke the ritual salutation, and they rose to greet her. Syth, tall and slender, hair ash-pale in the gloom of the windowless room; Alais, taller but not so slender, her shapely breasts heavy with milk for her youngest, hair a soft honey gold; and Emre, her hair the deep rich gold of spring flowers, carrying her advanced pregnancy with innate grace.

"The hearth is honored," Syth said formally. The Hooded One gave a curt nod, and knelt beside the unconscious man with a soft grunt for her stiffened joints. Laying one gnarled hand on his chest, fingers splayed, the other on his throat, she grunted again.

"Fever, and mounting," she gave her verdict.

"Hardly a surprise, considering what was done to him, Old Mother," Alais answered.

She got slowly to her feet. "Rythian Lyre'son may choose to regret calling this one Hearthbrother. I will come again tomorrow, when I have Read again the signs of his coming."

They would no more have prevented her going than they would have doused the hearthfire. "And just what does she mean by that?" Syth wondered aloud. "I don't suppose we'll ever know. Emre, put willowbark to steep, will you? And we should think of food, too."

The sun was sinking by the time Myra came, and the man's fever was rising. Syth was sponging the restless body with cool water when the Priestess came in, speaking the blessing upon the hearth, but without the grudging attitude of her elder. Syth greeted her with a smile. She was in no awe of Rythian's mother's sister.

"The Hooded One says he is fevered?"

"Worse, now." Syth sat back on her heels. "We have tried to give him willowbark tea, but his belly will not hold it. Or anything else."

Myra knelt, rolled back her sleeves, and began a brisk examination of the patient. "It is the Lung Ill," she said finally, frowning. "It takes Southerners hard. But I have something that may help. He is vowed to the Lady, have you heard that?"

"Rumor. Gossip. Like the story that he brings bad luck. How can it be, a man in Her service?"

"Other places have other customs, daughter. But it is no empty titling. He has Her mark on his spirit." She looked down at the sick man. "He is a new thing in our knowledge. We cannot say 'this is so, because it was so before'. Even in the legends, there is nothing to compare."

"Will he die, Myra?"

The priestess smiled slightly. "That is with the Goddess. But we will fight for his life. One thing, Syth — you claim him as Hearthbrother, and so he may someday prove to be. But we do not know. Until we are certain, grant him no hearthright."

"What?" This from Alais. "Myra —"

Myra silenced her with a gesture. "No right of hearthkin," she repeated. "He has no say in the running of the hearth, no claim on any of you for anything other than food and shelter. Keep him apart from you; a bed in the barn will be sufficient. He is a stranger among us. Not D'Shael." She gazed at the women, her eyes cool blue and unblinking. "This is the word of the Middle Priestess, my daughters, and over-rides the decree of the Sun Stallion."

Myra, the person, they could have argued against, but not as the Servant of the Lady of Mares. Syth bowed her head, partly in assent, partly so that Myra would not read the rebellion in her eyes.

The priestess bent to her work, taking the herb-lotion she had brought and bathing the fevered body, murmuring charms against sickness as she did so. Yet the charms did not take hold as they should. Frowning, Myra sought the reason and found it in the collar about his throat.

Touching it carefully, she recognised a weaving — one that had been far stronger, though lessened now, it was still in place. It was an evil thing, a rusted chain eating into the living soul. "This collar — have you tried to remove it?"

"Not yet," Syth said. "I was going to wait until he was settled before I sent to Disan Smith for tools. Why? What —"

"Later, daughter." Closing her eyes, Myra set her hands on the metal, feeling the unnatural chill of it against his heated skin, and began unweaving the binding spell. Chiera, she knew, would not want this done. *He is here!* the Hooded One had said when she'd come from Syth's hearth. *The Dark One. But he's tethered and weak, thank the Lady*, and she'd disappeared into the Grove to take more omens.

To Myra's sight, both inner and outer, the only darkness about the man was the colour of his hair. The Lady's Mark was indeed on his soul, a guttering white flame wreathed about by the foul tendrils of the weaving. That was all she could See within him, but it was enough for her to know what she should do regardless of the Hooded One's will.

As a hearthwife picks loose a snarled yarn, she worked steadily at the binding spell, careful not to break the thread lest it rebound and do even more harm to the prisoned spirit. It was not melded with the metal, which made her work easier. When at last it was free, she banished it with a Word, sitting back on her heels and stroking the sweated elf-locks tangled over the sick man's brow. He calmed at her touch, and she felt the fever grow less. The rest of the battle was his to fight alone.

"The healing took a long time," Alais said. "Was he so ill, or was there more?"

"He was sick enough," Myra said grimly. "I will come back this evening," she went on, getting to her feet. "Remember what I have said."

Syth did not speak until Myra had left, and then it was with tight restraint. "A stranger among us — do we treat all who come to D'Shael lands like beasts, then? Alais, run to Disan and borrow a file from the smithy. I want that collar from his throat, to begin with. No hearthright! The least Tylosian trader is better treated, and if it is his pledging to the Goddess that folk fear, then surely we should hold him in honor!"

"I agree," Alais snapped as she turned for the door. "I've never heard the like!"

"Nor I," Emre said. "This is your hearth, Syth, yours and 'Thian's, be he Sun Stallion or not. Besides, I doubt whether the Priestess can overturn the word of the Stallion. Can she? Whatever you decide will be supported by Alais and me."

Syth gave her a hug. "My thanks! Though I expected no less. We shall obey Myra, and not offer him hearthright. But he is without kin in these lands, alone and sick. So he shall have every care that guestright dictates. And guests do not sleep in the barn!"

"You are as cunning as Rythian, sister," Emre said softly, and returned the hug.

"Alzon!" Kherin hunted through the battle-field like one of the Dark Lady's Wolves, searching for one face among the dead — one among the few who lived. "Alzon!" The heat and stench of death, the blackening pools of blood that caked the drought-parched earth, all were nothing to him. Voices called his name, but he would not hear them, no matter how well-known, no matter how dear. He cared for only one thing; sought only one person. "Alzon!"

No one betrayed the Lady. Oh, there were certain tracts among the ancient sagas — but this was no saga. The one he called cousin had dared to seek the Chosen One's death. The Chosen, who was Son and Consort. And Avenger. The Sword In Her Hand.

So, then. Let the prophecy at his birth be fulfilled. The mountains of Khassan will indeed shake, and change will come when the Chosen takes the life of the Blasphemer.

An army. He would lead an army of giants mounted on greathorses, golden warriors who burned with the Sun's own fire and Alzon, Lord of Lies and Shadows, would fall.

"Kherin."

This one voice reached through his rage and stopped him in his tracks.

"Jeztin?"

From noon and a killing-field Kherin stepped onto a beach of white sand. Before him white unhewn stone rose into a sky of dark pearl, their peaks bathed with the fire of sunrise. Behind those walls were the Courts of The Morning, all peace and beauty, where hunger and want and pain were no more.

But there was no gateway.

Jeztin stood at the foot of the walls, straight as a lance, his dark hair loose on his shoulders. He was simply clad in a white kilt belted with silver, and in his hands was a reed pipe.

"Jeztin!" Kherin tried to walk forward but his feet would not move.

"You have come unsummoned, and before the appointed time."

"Alzon has betrayed Her! Jeztin, I will raise such war that —"

"Are you certain this is Her will?"

"Yes!" Kherin raised his arms to the boundless sky. "He sought my death and has sent me to a place where I can fashion his own! Her Will in all things — what can be more clear?"

"Are you certain?" the question was repeated. "Or is this a forge to temper you...?" The last was a fading whisper of sound, then Kherin was again standing alone amidst slaughter. Doubt struck like an enemy's lance to his stomach. He staggered and fell.

Myra's remedies did at least reduce the fever, but the smith's strongest file could not make more than a scratch on the Tylosian metal of the collar. Nor would anything they coaxed down his throat stay in his belly. The Southerner was not resisting them; rather, it was as if his body refused help. As if he wanted to die.

"He's not D'Shael," Emre said worriedly, "What do we know of his customs? Perhaps, in his land, dishonor is as unthinkable as it is here..."

"Emre, you are over-tired. Go and rest."

"You're more weary than I am; you sat with him all night. I'll stay. Alais, it's been three days!"

"The Hooded One comes," Alais interrupted, brushing down her skirts and standing upright. The old woman acknowledged the courtesy gruffly and bent to peer at the patient. Alais brought a lamp nearer and had it brusquely waved away. The old fingers pushed back the tangled curls that clung to his brow, traced the dark lines of the winged spiral tattooed on his forehead.

"Mother," Alais said respectfully, "you said you would Read what Sign there might be concerning him."

"Aye." But there was no further revelation from the priestess. "Get me to drink. My throat is dry."

Emre brought a cup of herb-tea, sweetened with honey, and a dish of honeycake. The old woman sat at the hearthside and ate slowly, her sharp eyes raking the room for signs of ill-keeping.

"Myra said not to give him hearthright," Alais said.

"My Daughter gives wise advice." She put down her cup. "A pity she does not take heed of it herself. What's done is done. Get food into him. Give him strength to recover. He is weak as a newborn." She turned to go.

Emre sighed. "We are trying —" she began, but before she could antagonise the old woman, Alais cut in.

"One thing, Old Mother. This man — is he a danger to our children?"

The Hooded One faced her. "He is a danger to us all," she replied flatly. "Aye, to this hearth, to the Sun Stallion, to our clans, to all the tribes of the D'Shael. But — but he would not, I think, willingly harm your children."

She was gone, and Alais drew a breath of relief. "She may not have meant it," she said grimly, "but she has given me an idea."

He was a babe again, cradled in his mother's arms, her crooning song lulling him as he suckled at her breast.

"He'll keep that down," Alais said surely, retying the strings of her bodice.

"Will you have enough for Lirren as well?"

"For certain. It's only for a few days, until he can take mare's milk."

"I think," said Syth consideringly, straightening the bedding, "it would be well if we kept this to ourselves. The Hooded One would not be pleased. Nor Myra."

"Which is not like Myra," Alais agreed. "I think they have Seen something. They fear him. Why?"

"Probably because it's unheard of for a man to be linked to the Lady. Whatever. We'll hear in Her own time. Until then — we have a hearthbrother to tend. Whatever they say to the contrary."

He was the Hawk, wing-free in the wide sky, lord of the wind, unfettered. His body was all of air, his pinions of light. He was flying homewards, home to the Courts of the Morning, to sun on white stone and the welcome of friends and lovers...

Kherin opened his eyes to see a dark ceiling of hewn wood, lit by the flicker of a lamp and some light from beyond the threshold. He lay on fleeces, covered by a blanket. His limbs felt heavy and without strength to answer his will. Drugged again — but he had broken the phial — and this was no tent.

A shadow blocked the light, and a woman was bending over him, exclaiming something in the D'Shael tongue. Others came. Kherin lay and endured their ministrations.

He had been the Hawk. But the Hawk does not fly shackled by the chains of flesh. She had not called him home to Her. He was back in the world, and it was as new to him as to a week-old puppy, eyes just open. He could not resist the pull of it, and the nightmare retreated a little. Something had changed. Kherin wasn't sure what it was and could not concentrate long enough to pin it down...

Women — the three of them — who tended him were gentle but firm, as they might be with a child. He was encouraged to sit up, to move from his bed as soon as they judged him strong enough, to sit at the hearth, or to go out and take the air. He swiftly came to realise that his status was not at all as Merse had told him. He was not a slave. He was attached to the household of the man Rythian, who was now Sun Stallion. His food and care were the responsibility of that hearth. The women there were either wives or sisters of the absent man, he was not sure which. The one called Syth was chief among them, but wore her authority lightly. There were a number of children, to whom he was first a curiosity and then for the most part accepted.

Syth asked him once who had ordered the beating and branding. She had faced him, kneeling back on her heels, spine as straight as a spearshaft and her eyes like shards of crystal. Kherin did not need the Inner Sight he could no longer use. Her honor and strength were like war-banners. 'My enemy,' he'd answered. Then he realised, with a fierce leaping joy, that he had Read her. Whatever had bound and blinded his Inner Sight was gone.

Somehow Kherin kept hidden his joy at the return of his power. He focused on healing and growing strong again. Within days he was learning their tongue — slowly, because it was a complicated matter, but with delight. He could hear the music in it; their speech was like song. In the quiet hours of the nights he healed the injuries done to him and explored the resonances left in the collar. Without the drugs that confused and destroyed his control, he could See it clear enough. Prenin's work, without a doubt, yet the metal was not tainted. An image formed in his memory; the giant hands grasping the collar — a true-smith, untrained in mage-work. Another image; a woman's hands, strong and gentle, unravelling a stained thread not of her spinning...

The collar was still there, but now it was only metal. A reminder he did not need that there were enemies to be dealt with. The one named Marikyr and his companions had returned to the Warband, but Merse had not. The Tylosian would pay the price as soon as Kherin had a chance to track him down.

Alzon, though, was the true goal of his life. The very thought of his cousin's name was enough to send fury surging through his blood. As soon as he was fit, he would ride out on the hunt that would end in his quarry's downfall and death.

Yet there were shadows in his mind. Was he wrong? Insidious doubt surfaced every so often. Was the hunger for revenge from within himself, or was it truly sent by the Goddess? Was his anger blinding him to Her will? And if that was the case, then why was he here?

Kherin picked up the rudiments of the D'Shael language quickly and Syth, pleased by his progress, decided he should join Merse, LyDia and NaLira in the more formal schooling in that tongue. Kherin accepted her wish with alacrity. Not only would it be his first excursion further than the porch, but it would bring him within reach of Merse.

That particular goal remained temporarily unattained. Kherin caught a glimpse of the eunuch as he approached the Elder Hall. Merse promptly turned tail and disappeared among the longhouses and did not show up for the lesson.

The schooling was a well-meant error on Syth's part, but an error none the less. The lessons were conducted by Nortan Elder. She had never seen him teach and didn't know his methods. Nortan had been chosen solely because of his knowledge of Tylosian, which was comprehensive. For three years, he had been one of the Trail Council intermediaries between the traders and the tribe, until arthritis made riding impossible.

Whatever his usefulness in bargain and barter, however, Nortan had scant patience and no love for his task. He tended to reward errors or inattention with a sharp rap from his staff. He did not know, nor would he probably have cared, that Kherin had determined to neither speak nor listen to the language of his bondage save by his own choice. The man's presence at the lesson, sitting mute and blank-eyed, began to irritate the Elder.

"Fire take it, Southerner," he burst out at last, after a totally unfruitful afternoon, "even the child could understand a simple phrase in an hour!" NaLira took offence to that and unseen, poked her tongue out at the Elder. "Are you a wittol, or mule-stubborn?" Nortan spoke as usual in Tylosian, so Kherin paid him no heed. But as the staff swung up, Kherin moved. Fast and without hesitation, he snatched the staff from the Elder's grasp, and with one clean and economical movement, broke the hard carven wood between his hands.

"You have no authority over me, Old Man," Kherin said in careful and stilted D'Shael, and dropped the two halves at Nortan's feet before walking out.

Kherin did not return to the hearth. This was the first chance he had to go about the Hold; it was time he hunted down the enemy closest to hand.

It was common knowledge among the children of the hearth that their other new hearth brother had no love of manual work. It was a matter for scorn and much giggling that Merse would sooner laze in the shelter of the willows by the lakeside. Out of sight there unless anyone went looking, he was free to do as he pleased.

Kherin's guess had been right. Ducking under the trailing branches, he saw Merse sitting cross-legged with his mirror propped in front of him, both hands occupied in restyling his hair. The half-finished braids gave Kherin a good handhold as he lunged, cat-silent. He hauled Merse to his feet, pushed him back against the tree and held him there. Merse's squawk of fright was stifled by Kherin's hand over his mouth.

"Hear me," Kherin said softly in Tylosian. "The spells that bound me and kept me from my own powers have been broken." The eunuch's fear became obvious terror. "It's time you paid your debts. You owe much, do you not? A beating and a branding, at the least reckoning. What recompense for those, Merse? What recompense will you offer the Goddess? In marking me you put insult upon insult on Her, and of a certainty you will pay!" It was as if he had all that was Tylos in his grasp; the urge to rend and destroy was a madness that hammered on the walls of his self-control. Kherin spared one hand to grip the slender throat, felt the racing beat of blood under his fingers. It would be so easy to stop that pulse. He would not even have to tighten his hold, just slide his will into the weaker mind and —

No.

The Word came from within and without, unmistakably the voice of his Goddess. Years of schooling had instilled an unthinking obedience to Her will and he drew back a little, loosened the hand across Merse's mouth.

"Please!" Merse wept. "Please — great Prince, I only did as I was ordered —"

"You are a liar," Kherin said. "You would not know Truth if She sounded Her Horn in your ears!" His fingers tightened and the eunuch's howl of panic was choked off.

No.

Behind Kherin's eyes was the shape of a vast tapestry. No recognisable forms, just colors and patterns in a rich sweep of beauty beyond words. One thread, of dark and light, wove its way through a small part, twining briefly about ribbons of moon-silver and sun-gold. The message was clear; Merse had a part in the Goddess' intentions, and it was not his time to die. It was a bitter truth and Kherin was slow to accept it.

"So," he hissed, "I doubt that Tylos sent you here as a gift, whatever others think. Am I right?" He knew he was, could Read him as easily as a written scroll.

Green eyes wide in panic, Merse gave a muffled grunt and nodded as far as he could.

"I'll give you fair warning, then. These people are not the fools Tylos takes them for. They may play your game as it pleases them, but be very sure they are not blinded by your trickery. I do not know how they deal with traitors but I would guess your death will not be quick, nor easy."

The green eyes went even wider, and Kherin smiled. It was not a pleasant smile. He may be forbidden to take Merse's life, but She had not banned him from putting abject terror into his erstwhile quarry. "As for myself, if my Goddess willed it, I could strike you dead in a heartbeat — or better yet, put an end to that beauty you prize so highly." Merse looked as if he were about to faint, or be sick. "What shall it be? A mass of festering sores? A twist in your backbone so that you cannot stand straight? Tylos already took your manhood, but I can take your pride."

Merse gave a moan of anguish, knees buckling. Kherin's grip held him upright. "You ordered me flogged, Tylosian. Slave that you were, did you ever feel the lash?" His Sight showed him the answer: never. Merse had led the pampered, idle life of one who had been bred to be beautiful and graceful — simply a living ornament and source of pleasure. They rarely felt the harsh blows of a lash.

"If you were a warrior, I'd give you a weapon and make a duel of it. But you're not, so I'll pay my debt in another coin." Kherin took his hand from Merse's mouth and reached for a thin branch, snapped it from the parent tree. He spun Merse around, and with one hand on the nape of his neck, held him flattened against the trunk. With his other hand Kherin jerked down Merse's leather breeches. The eunuch guessed his intent and howled in earnest, screaming for rescue. He screamed again as the first stroke lashed across his buttocks. Two more fell, raising livid welts.

"Those are for the beating and the brand," Kherin told him over the screeching. "These are for the afront to the Great Goddess." Three more stripes and the makeshift whip snapped. Kherin threw it away and let go of Merse, watching him dispassionately as he crumpled to the ground.

"I am the blade in my Lady's hand. As She commands, so I do." Kherin stepped back from the writhing, sobbing Merse. He could feel the pain and abject terror in the eunuch's mind. "Remember it is only by Her Will that you live. For now."

Angry and dissatisfied, Kherin left the willow grove and went back to the hearth. His muscles ached with weariness, as if he had fought all day on foot. It was gall to him to leave such an enemy living, but She had Spoken — so it must be. For now. Besides, it was clear to Kherin that he had not yet fully recovered from his sickness. He would have to stay a while longer to regain the lost strength.

Wait.

Her Word again. So be it.

The news of his confrontation with Nortan ran before him. Emre greeted him at the door, her lovely face distressed. "You should not have broken his Staff, Kherin," she said.

"I am no dog for him to beat," Kherin told her, sorry that he had been responsible for anything that upset her. Of the three women, it was Emre he found most attractive. Even great with child, she was as graceful as a bending willow, and plainly loved by all at the hearth. It was she who stopped the children's squabbles and interceded when one was at odds with another. His Sight gave him the truth of her gentle spirit, bountiful and loving and infinitely generous, the Peace-Weaver of the Hearth.

"Of course not, and he was wrong. But to break his staff — it is a symbol of his rank. Sit down and I will explain."

The staff was to Kherin simply a weapon. Now he learned that an Elder's Staff was a potent symbol of his responsibility and power, the most precious of possessions. Each one was individually crafted for its owner, presented by the Sun Stallion, and prized throughout his lifetime. At the Elder's death, the staff lay on his pyre. To put violent hands on it was in a way worse than attacking the Elder's person, for it violated the authority of the Council.

Kherin had a staunch champion in Syth, who had not waited to speak to him, but had gone immediately to argue the case with the other Elders. Alais, however, was at the hearth with her nursing child, and she gave Kherin a grin. "It was time that man met his match. How such a pompous, self-important old fool ever rose to be an Elder, I do not know!"

"Tch!" Emre scolded her sister for the benefit of any listening child. "Show some respect!"

"To those who earn it, aye. So, my sister —" she said to the grim-faced Syth as she entered. "What says the Hold Council?"

"They are split," Syth took off her wrap and held out her hands to the hearth, "and so the casting vote will be Rythian's, when he returns." She looked across at Kherin. "Hearthbrother, I could wish you had not done this thing."

He bent his head in apology to her.

"And?" Alais demanded. "There is more, I can see that by your face."

Syth gave a sigh. "Oh, they say that if he is strong enough to break an Elder's staff, then he is strong enough to do a man's work about the Hold. Kherin, what skills have you?"

He blinked. "Lady, I am a warrior."

"We know," Alais chuckled. "But what else? Do you know woodworking? Leather-craft? Smithcraft?" His blank expression made her shake her head. "Well, there is always the herding. You have knowledge of beasts, Kherin?"

"I know horses," he said, with truth.

"Well, there's a start. We could use help in the stable. Later, maybe with the herd."

"Ronan will not like it," Emre warned.

"Ronan, sweet sister, will do as his Mam tells him," Alais said firmly. "Here, do you take this great lump of a babe, Syth, and I will show our hearthbrother his new domain."

If it was meant as some kind of punishment, it was hardly onerous, Kherin reflected, pausing for a moment in his grooming of the in-foal Tribute mare from last year. The stable block was big enough for more than the five horses, one pony, and the house-cow who were lodged there. Oh, and the cat, he amended, as she wound her furry body between his ankles, purring. Cats, in Khassan, were known to be often chosen messengers of the Goddess.

Amber, the horse he was grooming, shivered and stamped, showing the white of her eye at the sound of raised shrill voices outside. Kherin frowned, soothing her with hand and voice. She was lightly-made and the foal large. Kherin guessed she would have a hard foaling.

He went to investigate the sounds. Outside a small herd of boys were gathered, dusty and blond and all but naked. Two of the boys were embroiled in a rough fight, rolling in the dirt. The other boys were screeching like jays, shouting names of one or other of the combatants.

None of them saw Kherin until he was among them, reaching down to take each of the fighters by the scruff and haul them apart. Several women were already hurrying toward the scene. Kherin gave the two boys a shake and let them go. They stood hunched like bantam-cocks, glaring at each other. The women scolded and the boys scattered. Kherin went back to the horse's side.

He was still there when a freckled face peered in from the doorway, followed by a small brown body. It was one of the young fighters, standing hesitantly on the threshold, both hands clutching a large honeycake. This time Kherin recognised him. Clean of dust, but with a bruise darkening on one cheekbone, Dreyen Syth'son stood watching him intently.

"Mam says I am to give you this," Dreyen said. "It was to be mine, but I am to learn not to fight close to the horses. I am sorry about frightening the mare. Mam said I was no better than a Tylosian and — I am sorry, I forgot."

"You need not apologise," Kherin said. The honeycake the boy held out was fresh, warm from the oven. He broke it in half, held one portion out to him. "Or not for that."

"Mam said I was not to bother you. With questions, that is."

"Surely," Kherin said, with a half-smile, "the son of the Sun Stallion may ask what he will."

The boy's chest swelled visibly. "He'll be the best there has ever been. But Shenchan — he's Caier's youngest son — he says his father ruled for ten years and was the bravest man in the clans until my father killed him with bad magic. So I fought him because Da doesn't do bad magic. This is good honeycake, isn't it? My Mam makes the best."

Kherin held out another portion. This little colt of the Sun Stallion's seed had a clear-eyed directness that he liked. "Shenchan is your enemy?"

"No." The boy cocked his head, considering. "No, he's my friend, really, most of the time. He only fights people because his father is dead. He thinks he has to. Is your father dead? Is that why you broke Old Nosy's staff?"

"My father..." Kherin paused, blinking at an unexpected surge of grief. "I am a Child of the Goddess, Dreyen."

"Like my cousins, the twins? My aunt Myra is a priestess," he added importantly. Before Kherin could respond, Alais' voice called.

"Dreyen! Brat, where are you?"

Sighing, the boy got up. "I have to go. But I am glad we talked. May I talk with you again?"

"I shall be pleased," Kherin said carefully. "May Her Hand shelter you."

"And you." Dreyen gave a quick urchin grin and dived for the door.

Dreyen's interest had plainly been simmering for some time, for once permission was granted, he began to regard Kherin as his own personal oracle and repository of knowledge and inexhaustible exotic stories. He extended his access to Kherin to include his circle of companions, the belligerent red-head Shenchan among them.

The young ones would bring questions, along with small offerings of dried fruit or honeycake. Kherin gave them the same kind of grave concentration he gave embassies who came to the Sanctuary. The concentration was necessary, or he would never have understood them their swiftly spoken idiomatic D'Shael, but his understanding of the language progressed by the day.

Soon Kherin understood most of what was said to him, and much of what went on around him. His world was still circumscribed by the Hold, more particularly by the boundaries of the Hearth, but he knew that his time to leave was not yet.

Wait, She had said.

When She called on him, Kherin knew he would take with him more than the one horse — that an army of warriors would follow him. Why else was he treated as kin in this house?

Chapter Eight

It was D'Shael custom to break fast at sun-up and eat again at sundown, but the women of the hearth, most particularly Emre, were insistent that Kherin eat at midday as well, as the children did. The wandering young ones rarely came to the hearth to be fed at noon, preferring to take their noon-piece with them on their daily adventures. Kherin soon discovered that he was not allowed such laxity. If he did not appear, one or the other of the hearthsisters would hunt him down.

It was Emre, this time, who called him in. He came obediently, rinsing his hands at the threshold. Emre smiled at him, talking as she filled his dish. Kherin accepted the bowl she filled for him. When he sat to eat, he murmured his customary thanks to the Goddess for Her bounty.

Emre's smile abruptly changed to a grimace and her hands went to her belly in a gesture he could not mistake. She cried out, a soft breathless call for her hearthsisters.

Kherin dropped his bowl and crouched beside her, his hands on her shoulders to support her. The other two were suddenly there and they all were talking at once.

Syth took charge. She helped the gravid woman to the bedchamber and settled her on the wide bedplace. She held Emre's hands and talked to her. For all Syth's confident attitude, Kherin sensed an underlying concern. Silent, he bent to retrieve the pieces of the broken bowl. He traced the ancient luck-signs in the grey ash of the hearthstone, invoking the Great Mother as he did so.

"Breathe deep," Syth commanded. "Come, Emre, you know what to do."

"It is early — by nearly a moon —"

"So perhaps you miscounted. Or he is merely impatient to be born. Breathe deep. Are the pains worse?"

"I don't think so. No. I'm sorry, it startled me, coming so suddenly."

Syth laughed. "All Rythian's children have wills of their own. So, rest a while. You have work enough ahead of you!" As she spoke, her hands moved gently over Emre's swollen belly, examining the lie of the infant. "Rest."

Her confident smile faded as she left the chamber. She crossed to where Alais sat, sorting the linens for the birthing. "The babe lies across the womb," she said quietly. "I can feel head and heels here and here," pressing her hands on her own flat stomach. "Go for Myra. The baby will have to be turned." Alais didn't question, she just dropped the cloths and ran for the door. Feeling other eyes on her, Syth turned to meet the intense, dark blue gaze of her hearthbrother, and hid her anxiety under a bright smile. "You have not eaten, Kherin."

It was the beginning of a long afternoon and a longer night. Kherin saw to the beasts and came back to the hearth. No one told him to go elsewhere, so he stayed. There was considerable coming and going; the Hooded One was there for some time, as was the Middle Priestess, Myra. When she left, she took the children with her. Kherin knew then that things were not going as they should for Emre.

Kherin caught the deep-set eyes of the Old One on him in displeasure more than once. Perhaps the D'Shael held the presence of a man ill-omened during what was, of all things, a woman's greatest mystery. But no one had forbidden him, so he waited as the voice in his soul dictated.

The night dragged on, but no one slept. Kherin became aware of a change in the atmosphere. They did not speak to him, indeed hardly knew he was there at all, but tone and expression told him enough. When the first screams ripped into the murmur of voices and he heard their fright, he knew that Emre was losing the fight to bring forth her child.

Syth did not waste breath by telling Alais to go rest. Such a watch is best kept by two. It was better for Emre to have both of her sisters with her, whether she was aware of them or not. Once again the Hooded One had turned the child in the womb, but even as they lifted Emre into the birthing crouch, the next contraction undid the effort.

"There is no more to be done," the old woman said, as Alais cradled the barely conscious Emre. "It is with the Lady now. I think the cord is too short to let the child come down as it should."

"No...!" Alais moaned. "She cannot die..."

"It is with the Lady," the priestess repeated. "It may be that this hearth is in need of a reminder of Her Hand."

Alais drew breath for an angry retort, but before she could speak, Syth said politely, "Perhaps there are others for you to tend this night, Mother. We would not keep you."

A thin smile curved the seamed mouth. "You do not, daughter. I go where She bids me, none else. I'll return in a while. It may be we can save one of these."

"What will you do?" Alais asked in a small voice.

"Cut out the babe," she said grimly, and was gone into the night.

Kherin heard the harsh pronouncement and went to the threshold of the inner room as soon as Chiera had left the house. Syth and Alais were holding Emre in their arms, stroking her hair and crooning to her, but Kherin saw only Emre. She was panting like hard-run doe, sweat sheening her face and throat; her hair was dark with the sweat, strands sticking to her skin. The veins showed blue under her fair skin as she strained. Her eyes were wide but unseeing. She did not react when he slipped to her side and knelt there, touching her brow in salute before laying both hands flat on the glistening mound of her naked belly. His eyes blanked as he turned his Sight inward to discover what he needed to know. He never heard her hoarse crowing scream as the next contraction racked her, only felt the impatient children within the womb. Two, the lower turned to lie across the birth passage, blocking it.

A voice spoke his name, questioning, but there was no time now for speech. What must be done must be swiftly done, while the woman still had strength to help. Kherin went out to the hearth. There was water seething in an earthenware crock. He poured some into a basin and immersed both hands to the wrist and beyond, letting the cleansing powers of fire and air and water work their magic. He prayed to Her who watches over the creation of all things, She who bore sun and moon together and knows the travail of bearing. *Great Goddess, Mother of the World, be merciful...*

She has been kind to me. She shall not die.

There was a crock of oil at the foot of the bed. He spread it lavishly over both hands. "Be ready," he said to the staring women.

Emre scarcely had strength left to groan, but the muscles were locked in spasm. He waited until it eased. "Be strong, Beloved," he whispered in Khassani. "You must be brave a little longer, only a little..." And again he turned his vision inward as he slipped a hand into the dilated opening of her body. He sought and found the doubled legs and tiny feet of the obstructing child and eased it into position. "Now!" Alais and Syth together lifted, and he suddenly had both hands full of slippery and bloody baby, kitten mouth opening in a wail of displeasure. He barely had time to lay the boy to one side before the second followed her brother. The sisters laid Emre down, but she was hardly aware. "There is new life in the world, little mother," Kherin said in Khassani.

The after-birth followed fast, and after that, more blood — far too much. Kherin laid his hands on Emre's lower belly, pressing down and speaking the Words of Power as he had been taught. The flood slowed to a trickle, no more than there should be.

He sat back on his heels, drew a deep breath. Syth was cleaning the twins, Alais tending their mother. Kherin bent his head in fervent thanksgiving. *Goddess, I give thee thanks and praise. Three lives Thou hast granted, and I rejoice; where there was sorrow and lamentation, all is turned to exultation. Honor to Thee, Lady!*

Since there was nothing further he could do, he left Syth and Alais to their work and went back to the hearth. He washed his hands, while inside his rejoicing went on. He felt as a dry and arid land must feel, after a cleansing rain. For the first time in many days his anger was distant from him.

"Kherin." He turned.

Alais was standing in the doorway, tears on her cheeks.

"Is it well with Emre?" he asked, suddenly afraid.

"Very well," she said, and caught her breath on a sob. "But it would not have been, but for you." And without warning, she took his hands in hers and kissed them.

"Lady..." Startled, Kherin tried to draw back. "This is not fitting."

"Is it not, when you saved my sister's life, and that of her babies?"

"Thank the Mother," he said quickly, "that the skill was mine to use."

"Be sure we shall. I go now to call Myra to examine the babes."

It seemed a good time to be elsewhere. Besides, the sky was ripening into dawn and there was work to be done. When Alais returned with Myra, Kherin was no longer at the hearth.

"They are fine children, and strong, and perfect," Myra said, laying them back in their nest of fleece beside their drowsing mother. "Thanks to the Mother of All."

"We thank Her indeed," Alais said softly, and led the priestess back to the hearth, where Syth had herb-tea waiting. "My sister would be dead now, like a butchered heifer, and most like the children with her if the Hooded One had had her way."

Myra's lips tightened. "The Third Priestess would not do such harm."

"She has no love for us at this hearth," Syth put in calmly. "And for sure if we had heeded her word — and yours, Myra — Emre would have been beyond help. It was the Lady's Grace that brought Kherin here and made him hearthbrother."

"Kherin?" Myra repeated. "He was at the birth?"

And Syth told her the way of it, with interjections from Alais, until the Middle Priestess had heard all.

"This is beyond me," she said at last, shaking her head. "That a man — and an outlander — should have such knowledge..."

"You said when he came that the Goddess had marked him."

"That much was clear. But what that meant..." She fell silent again. "I must think on this."

Spring finally came to the D'Shael lands. The transition was swift; it was as if the Hold went to sleep still gripped in the dregs of winter, and woke the next morning to a changed world of greening warmth and flowering sweetness.

For Kherin, spring held a special kind of enchantment. It was a time of gladness, of new life in all things. He felt a kind of peace filling him. Though far from his homeland, he sensed the Maiden's presence, and knew Her blessing lay on this country and this people.

With the new warmth, the women of the D'Shael put off their heavy garments of wool and quilting, blossoming out in light bright fabrics, silks and cottons from Tylos and their own fine-woven wools and linens. D'Shael women liked bright colors; their fabric was dyed and embroidered in a profusion of colors.

The younger unwed girls in particular caught the eye, with their skirts kirtled up for riding or wading. Their unbound blond hair tousled on bared, browning shoulders. They gave laughing sidelong looks and found reasons to linger when Kherin went to the well or the river. He had to pretend not to understand the nature of the words they called out to him.

But they were beautiful, these D'Shael — even by Khassani standards. They had the carriage of queens and courage of lionesses. He saw the Goddess' hand in their shaping, as if She said: *These too are my children, and behold, they are fair.*

He would never dispute that.

At Syth's suggestion, Kherin carried Emre from her bed to sit among cushions in the strengthening sun. Her twins were placed in a shallow wicker cradle beside her. The babies' fresh skin bloomed rose-gold with the sun's kiss, their soft hair bleaching even more silvery. The boy they called Emryan, and the girl Kerah.

Dreyen was openly jealous of the attention lavished on the new babies, and importuned Kherin to bring Amber and the other stabled beasts down to the meadows at the lakeside, where the new grass grew lush. The animals grazed there from dawn to sunset, sleekening daily, while Dreyen and Kherin taught each other to fish.

The days grew into weeks, their passing scarcely noticed. Kherin's nights were of unbroken sleep without nightmares and dark visions, and he did not often ask in his thoughts *When do I go from here?* Merse avoided him; LyDia flirted her eyes at him with gentle malice and spoke only D'Shael in his hearing; NaLira chattered like a jay and played with the other children of the hearth as if she had known no other place but the Summer Hold. And then there was the Grove. The Goddess' Power hung about it, but he did not go there. No man did, he was told, unless summoned. But he knew himself watched from the trees, and by no friendly eye.

But all things come to an end. So it was that Ronan sought Kherin and Dreyen out by the river.

"Our hearthsire is coming back to the Hold," the older boy said, reining in his pony. His attitude towards Kherin was still stiff and unsure, although he knew now that horse-eating was as far from Kherin's taste as it was from his. "The scouts rode in at noon. They are perhaps two days ahead of him. Mam sent me to tell you."

Dreyen gave a whoop of delight, dropping his fishing line and capering like a monkey. "The clans will gather, and he'll be acclaimed Sun Stallion before all the people!" Ecstatic, he did a cartwheel as Ronan rode away. "He'll hold his first full Council and give judgements and —-" He broke off, gazing into Kherin's impassive eyes. "You mustn't be afraid," he said earnestly. "He won't hurt you, Kherin."

Kherin busied himself pulling the lines from the lake, coiling them and stringing the catch for carrying. "I broke Nortan's staff," he reminded the boy gently.

"Yes, but — you didn't know. You were outlander, you couldn't be expected to understand. Anyway, I'll speak for you. I won't let anything happen to you, I promise."

Kherin straightened from his task, moved by the child's simple sincerity. "Thank you, Dreyen."

The boy hugged Kherin's neck for a moment, then vaulted astride his pony, kicking his heels into the shaggy sides to urge it into a canter. Kherin watched him go.

Even if the child was favored by his father, it was doubtful if his pleas would be heard in Council. The women at the hearth would speak, but he was unsure how much weight their words would carry. Whatever came to pass, one thing was sure. His time of waiting was almost over. Somehow he would gain Rythian's allegiance. With the Sun Stallion came the army that would wreak the Goddess' wrath on Alzon.

Kherin gathered up tackle and catch, mounted Bakra and rode back towards the Hold.

The excitement infected everyone, it seemed. The three women were in a frenzy of making ready. The older children were left much to their own devices, which led Dreyen to take advantage of the chaos. The boy crept to Kherin's side long after he should have been asleep.

"Tell me a story, Kherin?"

Kherin, who had been lost in thoughts of his own, blinked down at the flushed face. "You should be in your bed, young one."

"I was. But I felt sick. And then I was — just a little." As a means to awaken sympathy, it was not entirely unsuccessful. Kherin touched a hand to the smooth brow under the tousled blond. There was no sign of fever. He diagnosed over-indulgence in honeycake. The sky-blue eyes pleaded wordlessly. Kherin, whose thoughts had not exactly been comfortable ones, was glad of the small diversion. He shifted so that Dreyen could clamber onto the fleece-draped settle.

"So, a story. A new one? Or one you know?"

"A new one."

Kherin kept his voice pitched low, relating a tale from his own childhood concerning a magical cat — who looked amazingly like the house-cat dozing by the fire — that had the power of speech, and a youngest son. Kherin never finished it. Dreyen's weight grew slack against him, and the pale head drooped, for all his valiant attempts to stay awake.

"...and the cat spoke again to the monster, saying, 'I have no doubt your power is great, O terrible one—' He broke off, and Dreyen made no protest, curled fast asleep at his side.

Syth looked up from her seat on the woman's side and smiled as Kherin lifted her son in his arms. "The rest of the tale will wait, I think," he murmured, ducking into the boys' room and gently laying his burden beside the others, covering him with the blanket. "May Her hand guide your dreaming, brother," he whispered, and left the child to sleep.

"Kherin," Syth said quietly. He had been about to go and see the beasts settled for the night, but he halted obediently.

"Lady?" He gave the title the inflexion due her rank as mistress of the household and senior wife of a chieftain.

"Before you go out to see to the horses, I have a word to say to you." She rose to her feet and came to stand before him, a woman of his own height and a little more. "You have heard that Rythian will be here shortly."

"Ronan told me so."

"That is well. Nortan Elder will bring your — action — before the Sun

Stallion."

"I understand, Lady."

"I wish I could be sure that you do." She hesitated. "Kherin, the women's side do not choose to interfere often in the councils of men. But you have brought life to this hearth, and that will never be forgotten. This I promise. May She, whom we both worship, bear witness."

Kherin bent his head in acknowledgement.

"You are of this hearth, Kherin," she went on, choosing her words carefully, "and not only by the Sun Stallion's word. Indeed, Rythian is no longer Guardian of this hearth, so it would be for us to choose — Alais and Emre and I — and your place is here, never doubt it."

He sensed her confusion."Lady, I am grateful."

She reached out abruptly as if she would say more, but checked herself, and smiled, letting her hand drop. "Goddess guard you, hearthbrother." It was scarcely more than a whisper.

Kherin murmured the response. "And you, and all at this hearth, as well." Then he was gone, moving silent as a shadow into the stable to tend the horses.

Syth remained in the room, standing quite still, her arms across her breast. She was weary, but not yet could she go to her sisters. There was pain in her, one that had been sown when the riders came to tell of a new Sun Stallion. Over the weeks it had grown and strengthened. With his coming, the pain would grow even stronger.

Rythian. She drew her breath sharply. Lover and beloved no more. *Goddess, I could bear his absence with patience; I could even bear his death, for that I could mourn. But this...*

She sat again at the hearth, using the fire's light to aid her hands as she took up her spindle. The carved wood - of Rythian's making - twisted and spun in counterpoint to the chant forming within her. She had heard her own mother make similar lament, but she had never dreamed she would know the same anguish.

He has gone from me, my Bright Hunter,
with no touch, no word of farewell.
I am a woman without husband,
vows set aside, nullified,
whose man is dead
and not dead.

So had other women lamented, generation on generation.

He is gone from me, my life-friend,

the warm companion of my nights,
bringing pleasure like wine
in a cup of sunlight.
The beloved friend of my days,
builder of hearth and home,
sire of my children — dead
and not dead.
How can I mourn him?

Her inner eye showed him as she remembered him.

Spear-tall and golden, behold him.
He stands in the Eye of the Sun.
All his youth and proud strength,
all his manhood and potency and beauty,
taken and returned for a while —
but not to me —
until Hawkwings brush his brow
and the Stallion stumbles and falls.

All men die. But she had hoped for many years together, seeing their children grow.

I rejoice that the glory is his,
rejoice that he has found favor,
rejoice that the high honor
is his, and mine, and his sons'... And yet, and yet—-
No more the step on the threshold.
No more the hand in my hair.
No more the smile across the hearth.
No more the weary, wounded head on my breast.
No more the wide shoulder to take my tears.

If he were dead, I could mourn him.

Sun Stallion, I should rejoice.
Sun Stallion, thou hast my heart.
Sun Stallion, wilt thou remember me?

She bit her lip against the keening wail of loss, tears dripping unnoticed onto the bundled fleece in her lap. *Wilt thou remember me? My Rythian, my heart's joy — Sun Stallion. Mother of Mares, how can this be?*

And then — *with the morrow he will come. My man no longer. Has he changed? Caier was but a loud savage before he became Sun Stallion. What will Rythian have become?*

Her thoughts raced with the rumors and tales that were being told. Tales of cruelty corroborated by Kherin's arrival. He had come helpless, sick, and abused to her hearth. Merse said Rythian had ordered it. *No! I did not believe, nor do I now!*

I am a woman without a man at hearth. Then she stopped herself. *Lady, forgive me.* She did not mean to slight Kherin. Nor had she really, but in her grief she forgotten the quiet, self-effacing man who had taken up residence with them.

She thought of him now — not tall but lean and strong. Hair like night's own cloak, and eyes that spoke mysteries. He had shown favor to no woman of the D'Shael, though she had seen his gaze linger on Emre.

Yet I have rarely seen you smile, Kherin. Or laugh, and then only for the children. They love you. I could love you, for you are man of this hearth now. But how should I speak so to you?

Even if it were not so — *oh, Rythian, my dearling, I am empty without you!*

The spindle dropped and rolled, unreeling a trail of new-spun wool, but Syth, arms wrapped around herself, did not heed. She rocked a little, crying silently. *Yet I will bear another son for you, if the Lady wills it so. A Sun Stallion's colt... Great Mother, grant me that.*

Syth straightened out of her slump, palming the wetness from her cheeks. *I will not be less than my mother in courage. I will not soil your honor with my grief, beloved.*

She took up the spindle again, rewound the thread, and found comfort in the ordering of it. She would not go to her hearthsisters for solace, although she knew they understood her confused feelings, and shared them. Their gentle love and caresses were not what she needed — she knew the balance of her life was gone. Rythian's strength matching hers, each complimenting the other, making the perfect whole.

Now there was a space in her life that could never be filled. It was a man's strength she needed, a man's shoulder to lean on for a little while.

But the only man she desired was hers no longer.

Chapter Nine

*A*mber was not in her stall. Kherin fingered the frayed headrope, frowning. He knew well that a mare in foal will sometimes seek seclusion when her time approaches. It seemed that Amber had taken it into her head to do just that.

He had to find her. Knowing how she was treasured by the hearth, he could guess how it would grieve them to lose her.

He could only hope she had not gone far. Quietly, he saddled Bakra, took hard journeybread and honeycake from the store, and went out into the night.

She was not in the lakeside meadow, as he had thought she might be. He followed the trails she would know, around the rim of the water. With the risen moon lighting the land, he cut her path at last — leading westward, away from the bustle of the Hold.

He turned his horse's head in that direction, and they set off with the moon ahead of them slowly fading as dawn approached from behind. Soon the sun was on his back, sending their shadow long and black before them over the dew-diamonded grass. It was a wonder to him how many kinds and colors of grass there were — some as straight as spear-shafts, thick or thin-bladed, some silvery and fine, or veined with purple and blue. There were flowers in profusion, too, with the spring warmth. Flame-flowers, golden and violet and white, sprang in clumps from green sheaths to make bright splashes of color. There were tiny white star-flowers, and the clustering gold of the sacred asphodel. Unmistakably, the Maiden was decking Her spring robe for the Great Rite.

Unlike the barrens of his old hunting, this rich land held spoor well, and by noon he was climbing into higher, broken ground.

He halted at a spring that bubbled into a moss-lined basin to break his fast and water the horse. When a small she-finch fluttered inquisitively near, he coaxed her to take crumbs from his fingers, imitating her chirrup.

There was a gift not given to many, said the teachers at the Sanctuary, one never to be misused. This touch of mind to mind with their kindred of the beast-kind was not a trick for mountebanks, but a thing as solemn and joyous as the meeting of human souls. More important, in a way. These little ones were easily swayed by superior strength, for good or ill.

Cautiously, he put forth his will to reassure the small creature, encompassing her feathered body like cupped and sheltering hands. She stilled, her fear gone, and closed her eyes as he stroked her breast.

It gave him an idea that might shorten his search. Letting the finch go, he searched the skies for a larger bird, and found his namesake riding an up-draught from the scarp. It scarcely twitched a feather but glided smooth and easy on the warm wind. The hawk did not know that another was seeing through its eyes, but Kherin saw the group of moving shapes made small by distance, and recognized a wild horse-herd. It could well be that Amber had found refuge with them, and they were not far away.

He left Bakra beside the spring to graze and climbed the rocky hillside to a ridge that he had seen from above. From here he could look down on a broad sweep of valley and the horse-herd that ran there. The high sun gilded them all, catching light in the flow of mane and tail and the gloss of satiny hide. Kherin did not move from his vantage point. The vision held his gaze, filling his eyes and heart alike. In all Her creation, he found few things more lovely than the horse-kind, and he knew why the D'Shael regarded themselves as close kindred to these other Children of the Plains. All horses were sacred to the D'Shael, but a wild herd more than most, for here also a Sun Stallion held sway.

Kherin had no trouble identifying that one, a great grey animal, tall in the crest, vigilant as his mares grazed. Many of them had foals at foot. The herd prospered.

He began to walk down into the valley, taking his time and making no attempt to conceal himself. The stallion scented him first. Its head came up, swinging to keep him in sight. But when he continued his slow advance, the animal came towards him.

The stallion circled the herd at a canter, head snaking low, violence in the dark eyes. Kherin did not check until the stallion came between him and the herd, rearing with a shrill scream of warning fury, forehooves lashing.

But the intruder neither ran nor responded, merely stood there, hands still and empty, unafraid. Unthreatening.

Kherin reached for the food he carried, took out a piece of honeycake, and held it on extended open palm, reaching out with his mind again. He saw the ears prick, and nostrils flare at the unfamiliar, tantalising smell. He made no move as the stallion strolled forward, stretching the arched neck. Lips like living velvet delicately quested over his palm, taking the sweetmeat as an emperor may accept tribute. He allowed Kherin to stroke one hand down his nose as he lipped hopefully at the empty palm. The alert ears pricked as he whispered the Secret Sacred Name of the Mother of Mares.

The stallion tossed his head again, and Kherin half-turned, giving the soft trilling whistle he used when he fed, groomed, and watered the horses of the hearth. Somewhere in the grazing herd, an answering whicker. He whistled again, sending out a silent summoning as well, and Amber came trotting inquisitively towards him.

The stallion sniffed at her, but made no move to drive her back to the other mares. Kherin looped his belt around her neck, caressing the satiny hide.

He led Amber away and up the slope, talking to her softly as they picked their way over the rocky scree, and feeding her on crumbs of honeycake. He could sense that she was very near to her time now, and doubted that he could get her back to the Hold beforehand.

* * *

Not all of the Warband returned to the Hold. Some were escorting Tylosian caravans, while others patroled the lands bordering the trade-routes, but the celebration of the Hold-folk was not lessened for that. They came out to meet the Warband, a laughing joy of festival for the new Sun Stallion in sound and bright colours. The Gather Horn blared over all, announcing, summoning, and greeting all in one.

The warriors who rode in the vanguard dropped back to let Rythian go ahead alone. Rythian's eyes touched on each face. He knew them all; their clan, their names, and their line. They were his people. He had always been aware of that sense of kinship, of belonging, within his family and his clan; also within the larger complex of the tribe and the great amalgamation of tribes that were the D'Shael nation. Now that awareness was intensified to a degree that for a moment it seemed to refract his vision as light through a crystal. He saw a living tapestry, each thread of the pattern set with purpose and meaning.

"Da!" Shrill as a bird-call the familiar voice rose above the deeper chant of the crowd. Rythian's eyes focused on his hearth-family. Loved faces every one, and abruptly his heart ached to be with them.

Dreyen made a bid to break free and reach him. Ronan pounced on the child and picked him up, ignoring the howl of protest. The older boy was laughing, tears tracking dusty cheeks. Rythian smiled at him through his own mixed emotions. *Sun Lord, don't let my Hearth be changed towards me.* He met Syth's gaze, read the mingled joy and pride and sorrow in her brilliant eyes, and saw the love there too. Emre and Alais, nearly as well-beloved; and the children; these last too young to know anything but that their sire was come home. Only Ronan, hearth-son, but not blood-son, understood the destiny of a Sun Stallion.

Abruptly the Hooded One stood before him, with her skull-capped staff planted in his way. Zaan threw up his head and half-reared, but Rythian calmed him with a touch. This too was Ritual.

"Sun Stallion," she said, eyes pale as ice slivers, "your time may be a day of shining, or a season's warmth, but both have their ending. It is all one to Her."

Kardan had coached him on the correct response. "I stand in the Eye of the Sun," Rythian told her, "until He sends the Hawk to call me home. A day, a season, or the brief flare of noon, it is all one to Him. And to me." This last was a lie, and he knew she knew it.

Her lips thinned in a mocking smile. "The brighter the sun, the blacker the shadow," she said, which was not Ritual, and stepped aside. Beyond her was the Middle Priestess, hair loose over a cloak of green and gold, seated on a red mare. No longer Myra, his mother's sister, she was that aspect of the Goddess most loved and revered, the fertility of land and beast and people. The red mare was in season and Rythian's stallion called to her, nostrils and mouth flaring.

The Priestess turned her mount on its haunches and rode her away from the Hold towards the distant Grove. The mare was fast, but Zaan would have caught her had not Rythian held him back. To catch her too soon was not part of the Ritual.

On the edge of the trees, beside the grey pillar of the standing stone, Myra reined the mare in and slipped from its back, letting the horse go free. Rythian swung down and loosed his stallion after the mare and followed the Priestess into the Mother's Grove.

Some part of the Mystery he already knew. As Sun Stallion he must lie with the Priestess to ensure the continued fruitfulness of the Land. And he had no fear of Myra, whom he had known from childhood. But his mistrust of the Goddess was something else. This place, like the Sacred Lands to the east and the caverns beneath the Winter Hold, was full of Her power.

"This is the well-spring of the Mother of All," Myra's voice said softly. "It is your right and your privilege to be here. At this time, in this place, we are priest and priestess. All else is forgotten..."

The chestnut stallion was grazing peacefully near to the stone when Rythian left the Grove. He spent a few minutes with the horse, trying to sort sense from a tangle of confused thoughts. He gave it up eventually and rode back to the Sun Hall.

The business of preparing for celebration made the Hold hum like a beehive. The Sun Hall, at least, was quiet, and Rythian was tempted to stay there for a while, but there was too much to be done before nightfall. Apart from Council business, he wanted to go to his hearth — what had been his hearth — and spend time with his family, but that too must wait on custom and tradition. Truly, in some things, the weight of the pectoral was heavy indeed.

The Council was waiting for him in the Elder Hall, with a good proportion of the tribe packed in as well. Rythian went to the dais, lifted a hand, and the noise lessened enough for him to be heard.

"Before the assembly begins," he said, "there is a matter that must be settled. I have brought Caier's weapons. Now I call upon his children. Palen Kaji'son, I have the sword of your acknowledged sire. Do you make claim to it?"

The boy was urged to the front of the crowd. He flushed scarlet, a tall twelve-year-old with the wide shoulders and musculature of a smith, which was the skill to which he was apprenticed.

"No, Sun Stallion," he said. "I don't want it."

"So be it. In the Eye of the Sun, the sword has been refused. Shenchan Mabe'son, do you claim the sword of your acknowledged sire?"

As pale as his half-brother was red, the child came forward.

"Yes," he said defiantly, and Rythian smiled at him.

"In the Eye of the Sun, then, it is yours, young warrior. It is a fine blade — be worthy of it." He laid the blade across the boy's outstretched hands. "Give it to your mother to keep for you, as is custom."

Shenchan carried the sword back to his place with a monumental dignity, but before Rythian could speak again, a familiar voice rose from the body of the hall, clear and strong and imperious.

"There is another matter, Sun Stallion," Syth announced. "A wrong has been done to my hearth. I ask your justice."

Kherin walked into a Hold alive with activity and strange faces, leading Amber and her foal. The Sun Stallion had arrived, and with him, the Warband. A fierce hope rose in Kherin. If the Goddess was kind, the man called Marikyr, who had lashed him, would be within his reach. As soon as he was done with the mare, he intended to start looking for him.

No one spoke to him, or detained him as he took the horses to their stable, stripped down to his doeskin kilt, and set about their welfare.

He was halfway through the grooming when Alais found him.

"There you are!" she scolded, breathless. "We've been all over, looking, as soon as we discovered you and Amber both gone."

"It is a healthy colt-foal," Kherin began, but she cut him short.

"Time for that later. We have to be in the Elder Hall. Come now, quickly, and maybe we'll be in time."

Kherin did not question her; he merely followed her to the largest building of the Hold. He had never been inside, though he had admired the carving that made the outside of it splendid. As he entered, he noticed the inside was dominated by a hearth in the center, and by a carving on the far wall behind the dais, a great golden Sun Symbol — three times man-height and sheathed in glittering gold. It was here that the Sun Stallion stood with his council around him. Alais pushed a way through the crowd to where Syth stood in the front.

"Four outlanders you claimed as hearthkin," Syth was saying, "making them D'Shael and Shi'R'Laen by ancient law. How is it, then, that my hearthbrother came to the Hold sick and close to death, with no excuse given for the way he had been used save that you ordered it? How was it that the hearthbrother of the Sun Stallion was lashed and branded by Shi'R'Laen hands?" Her voice rang with her anger. "Are we a free people, children of the Sun and Moon, or still in thrall to the Red Bear?"

Kherin studied Rythian, remembering the face from his drug-shrouded days, but he remembered little else about the man. Used now to the height of the D'Shael, men and women alike, the Sun Stallion's lack of physical stature took Kherin by surprise. Yet somehow Rythian was not dwarfed by the Elders standing around him. Kherin sought to Read him and it was strangely difficult, like gazing through a heat-haze. He could sense Truth in this man, a desire for what was right, and above all at this moment, bewilderment. But that was all.

Syth whirled, pulling Kherin forward. "Our hearthbrother was flogged, Rythian, and a mark put on him that stains the honor of my hearth," she repeated. "See for yourself."

And before Kherin knew what Syth intended, she reached out and tugged loose the fastening of the kilt, so that he stood naked in front of the assembly. He saw the blue gaze harden into midwinter ice as the brand on his hip came into view.

Rythian felt a killing fury wash through him, quickly followed by a wave of shame. His name-mark, used in such a way! He lifted his eyes from the mute accusation of the brand, swept his gaze over the people; they were waiting, judging him. "Who did this?" he demanded.

"It was done at your command, or so Merse says," Syth replied. "Whose hands did branding and beating I don't know. Kherin has not told us."

"Merse was wrong," Rythian said, holding his voice level with an effort that made his jaw ache. Marikyr, Loris and the others had volunteered for the border patrols instead of returning to the Hold. He'd wondered at that, but accepted it at the time. Now he understood their reason. Merse's part in this was not so clear.

"Kherin," Rythian said in Tylosian, looking directly into Kherin's steady and unreadable eyes. "I did not order this done." There was no response for a moment, then a mere inclination of the head, but it was enough to tell him his word was accepted. "It is not the D'Shael way, and I offer the apology of my people and myself. You are owed recompense for what has been done, and I'll see that all is as honor demands."

"No need," Kherin said in clear D'Shael. "I have taken what is due from one. I'll take from the other when I have tracked him down."

"Who?" Rythian demanded. "Give me names if you know them."

"That is a matter for the Lady and I," Kherin replied with a lift of his chin that told Rythian more than words.

"Of course, but if two of the five who rode here with you are more guilty than the others, I will have their names. Merse, stand forward." The eunuch was, after all, the only other one who was within Kherin's reach. A stir and a murmuring grew as the people looked around for the eunuch. "Merse?" Rythian called again. Still there was no response and Rythian frowned. "So. What part did Merse play in this, Kherin?"

"It is finished. Let it be." It was not a request and their gazes clashed like crossed blades.

"So be it," Rythian said; an agreement, not a concession. "Hear me, Shi'R'Laen," he went on, pitching his voice to carry, "and remember: if any are so enamored of Tylosian ways and customs that they cannot let them go, then so be it. But they cannot remain D'Shael. If any choose Tylosian ways, then they shall go to Tylos and trespass never again on the soil of a free people. We shall have no more bending of our Laws to suit the whim of individuals. If new laws must be made, then they will be, by the Sun Stallion and Elders and Priestesses, and with the consent of the people. If any would challenge this, speak now!" The silence was so intense the crowd might have been holding its collective breath. "In the Eye of the Sun!" Rythian shouted.

"So be it!" bellowed Kardan, and the assembled Elders' staffs pounded down.

Rythian looked at Syth. There was disappointment clear in her face, and her lips moved. He did not need to hear the words. *It is not enough...*

Rythian knew it wasn't, but for the moment he had nothing further to offer. He stepped down from the dais. People parted before him as he strode for the doors, hands reaching out to touch, eyes smiling. He returned the smiles, but was aware also of Syth and Alais, with the light of battle still glittering in their eyes.

Rythian did not leave the Hall unescorted. Arun and Voran were beside him, as he had known they would be.

"Lionesses," Arun said admiringly, "With one cub between them. I wouldn't care to cross them."

"Nor I," Voran grimaced. "What witchery has that Peacock put on your hearth, 'Thian?"

"None save that of a good-looking male," Arun snorted. "You may have made a mistake, letting that black-maned stallion run with your mares, man."

Pain and loss tightened under his ribs, but Rythian did not show it. "I have no mares, and all mares," he said evenly. "No hearth and all hearths. Syth and Alais and Emre have the ordering of their own place, as they always have."

The Sun Hall was silent and still. Rythian stood by the cold hearth and fought down a darkly bitter surge of jealousy. Arun's *...letting that black-maned stallion run with your mares...* rang over and again in his head. All he could see was Syth and Alais flanking the Southerner, robed only in dignity, yet proud as a stag. Hearthbrother, they had called him. And what else, he wondered savagely; what else, to prompt so swift and fierce a defense? He knew he had neither right nor cause to question who they chose, be he Sun Stallion or just Rythian Lyre'son, but that did not lessen the pain. It was a reminder of all he had given up when he Challenged.

Well, neither law nor custom could break the bloodlink with the lives he had sired. He had children at that hearth, and it was his right to satisfy himself of their welfare. Also, there was Emre — no longer pregnant. Was her child living or dead, male or female? As the child's acknowledged sire, his was the right to hear it named; as Sun Stallion, no hearth was closed to him. He would go there, and soon. He took off the pectoral and hung it in its place, and stood staring at it for a moment, blindly.

"Sun Stallion." Nortan Elder stood on the threshold, with the Hold Council behind him. Rythian raised an eyebrow, but gestured them in. "There is a matter that must be brought to you," the Elder announced. "I was given neither the time, nor the opportunity, in the Elder Hall." There was outright accusation in the tone.

"Speak it then, Uncle." Rythian schooled his voice to politeness.

"The Southerner, Kherin, broke my staff," Nortan said, spreading empty hands. "It was an act of defiance and insult. I require a fitting punishment for him from both Sun Stallion and hearthbrother. And reparation."

"Say you so?" Chill and soft, Rythian's voice did not raise the echoes as it had in the Elder Hall, but it carried more menace. "And as Sun Stallion and hearthbrother, what would you have me do? Brand his other hip? Or perhaps cut off his right hand? Instruct me, revered Uncles. I await your guidance." He made a mock obeisance in the Tylosian fashion, and Nortan spluttered objection.

"Of course not! That would be unthinkable! But—"

"There are no 'buts'. Reparation will be made. A staff will be fashioned and carved to replace the one broken. Yet as to punishment — I tell you, my Uncles, that had he broken every one of your staffs ten times over, it still would not equal the shame done to him — and not one of you spoke against that, nor saw the guilty punished."

Nortan looked as if he would argue further, but thought better of it.. "Well, if there is to be reparation..."

"I have said it. In the Eye of the Sun."

"So be it," Nortan echoed automatically, and sealed the matter whether he wished it or not.

The doors closed behind the departing Elders, and none too soon. Fury and frustration battered at Rythian's self-control. He wanted to strike out — at anyone, anything — but could not. He wanted to see the guilty brought to justice, to remake all the ways that Caier had unmade, to bring the Shi'R'Laen back into the Eye of the Sun by the scruffs of their collective necks —

"Da?" It was a reverent whisper. An eye peered hopefully through the crack where the great door had not latched, and a small voice said, "Da?" again.

The dark mood was banished like a summer shower. Rythian grinned, pulled the door open, and seized his son in a bear-hug. "Dreyen! Should you be here? Does your mother know?"

"Mam's busy," said his son, nearly throttling him with an answering embrace. "And I wanted to see the Sun Hall — I can come in now you're Sun Stallion? I waited and waited for you to come to the hearth, but you didn't come, so—"

"So you came to find me, brat! Well, as to the Sun Hall — you can come in when I am here, yes, but you have to ask, understand? As to my coming to the hearth — I had business to attend to first."

"It's because you're Sun Stallion. Mam said. But you'll come now? Won't you?"

Rythian set his son down. "Yes, I will come now. So, tell me, what has been happening?"

Dreyen's view of events was of necessity one-sided. "Amber's had her foal," he said as they walked away from the Sun Hall. "It's a colt, and Kherin says he'll be like Zaan when he's grown. Ronan says he thinks Kherin has the Summoning like you and I do. And Emre had twin babies."

"They are well?"

"Kherin helped," Dreyen said. "They cry a lot."

Which told him nothing. But the porch of the longhouse was ahead, and Fyra was playing there. As she saw him, she launched herself at him with a shriek and he had to catch her in mid-leap. Laughing, Dreyen and Fyra together dragged him up the steps. But there he paused. Tradition demanded that he wait to be invited.

"'Thian!" Alais ran out into his arms, laughter and tears together on her face. "Don't stand there shuffling your feet — come in!"

Syth was on her feet, her spinning spilling from her lap. Rythian hesitated, but she did not — her arms locked tight around his neck in a stranglehold much like her son's. She was weeping his name, and he knew that whatever else might have changed, he was still first in her heart.

"Oh, 'Thian, I swear I could beat you senseless!" she whispered when she had breath to speak, wiping her eyes. "I am so proud of you."

"I wondered," he said, still holding her, "when you railed at me in the Elder Hall."

"Ah, and that is a matter we have yet to talk about! But come, sit — are you hungry? Thirsty?"

"Both," he said. "But first — Emre?"

"Twins," Alais said concisely. "A boy and a girl, growing strong. We would have lost them, and Emre too, had it not been for Kherin."

"The Old One would have cut —" Syth begin indignantly.

"What?"

Between them, Alais and Syth told the story. As they reached the end of it, Emre came in, skirts held high to let her run, and Rythian stood up and snatched her off her feet. She laughed, and returned his kiss.

"You're well?" he demanded.

"Perfectly. Your children, too. Come and see."

But Alais had already brought the wicker cradle out to the hearthside. Rythian looked at his new son and daughter. "Their names?"

"Emryan and Kerah," said Emre as Rythian took a pinch of ash from the hearthstone and touched each brow.

"Emryan and Kerah," he repeated, speaking their names at the hearth formally, acknowledging them. Then he kissed both babies, and Emre again for good measure. "And it would seem I am in debt for all your lives. Where is our hearthbrother?"

"With Amber and her foal," Syth said. "And that is a tale for telling, also. Oh, Rythian, did I hurt you with my words in Elder Hall? I spoke to the Elders and the clans rather than to you."

"You spoke for the wrong done to our hearthbrother," Alais said strongly. "And the words had to be said. It was Merse's doing, the branding. Kherin made him suffer for that as soon as he was well. But it was Marikyr who beat him almost to death. Not that Kherin said so, but Merse let slip enough for folk to put it together."

"I will remember," Rythian told her. "And I was at fault — I wanted Marikyr and his cronies out of the Warband. I should not have given Kherin into their keeping. There will be recompense, regardless of what he says... But what of the other people of the Tribute? The child?"

"She and LyDia are with Syre at Kardan's hearth. Myra thought it would be best for her to be with those who speak Tylosian, and indeed, she was right. NaLira's settling well, and she's a joy. Merse flits from bed to bed so fast I can't tell you who he's with."

"And we care less," Alais finished Syth's speech for her. "What recompense will you order, Rythian?"

"Oh, not now, Alais," Syth begged.

"No, she is right," Rythian agreed. "It's for Kherin to deal with Marikyr and his friends. But for my guilt in this... I think I will ask Kherin to accept Llynivar as his mount." The silence told him their shock. "Well? As hearthsisters, will it be fitting recompense?"

Emre was the first to recover her speech. "That — is more than generous," she said, "but we had thought Amber —?"

Rythian looked at her in surprise. "The time for brood-mares is later," he said, "for now he must build up his warstring."

The three women glanced at each other in consternation. "You ride to battle so soon?" Syth said. "Thian, you've only just come home..."

"And in a couple of days we shall be riding out again for the Surni borderlands. If he wishes, Kherin will go with us. How much of our speech does he understand? He was fluent enough in Elder Hall, but there is much I need to explain to him and I cannot risk any confusion."

"He understands very well," Syth said tightly, "but say no word of Tylosian to him. Enough of that for now. You have been gone from us for a long time, and soon we shall lose you again to the wartrails. Can we not talk of other things for a while?" He met her eyes and felt her pain — and shared it. He sat down at the hearth and took his new daughter into his lap.

It had been made clear to Rythian that the three women did not wish him to leave the Summer Hold so soon. It was also equally clear they did not wish Kherin to go either, and for similar reasons. Restless and ill-at-ease, Rythian did not go back to the Sun Hall after he left his erstwhile home, but took another path, joining Arun on the bench that leaned somewhat drunkenly against the rear wall of the SwordBrothers' barn.

"I have decided," Rythian said after a while into the companionable silence, "that I'll ask Kherin if he wishes to ride with us."

"What?" Arun nearly dropped the leather reins he was braiding. "Are your wits astray, man? Voran may not always talk sense, but he's right when he says that one is a danger!"

"What danger there may be is in Voran's head. What threat has he been to the Hold? None, or I would not have sent him here!"

"Thian," said Arun reasonably, "You sent a sick man to the Hold."

"He looks to be well enough now. Besides, if he is a danger, then the best place for him is under my eye, is it not? Anyway, the choice is his, and I haven't asked him yet."

"Then I can hope he'll refuse!" Arun put down the leather and seized Rythian by the shoulders. "Listen, I know you owe him a debt, in more ways than one. But to have him ride with us? Have you thought this through?"

"Of course."

"When your eyes are limpid as a child's and you put that look of innocence on like a mask, I wouldn't believe you if you said grass was green. Have you thought it through? Truly?"

"Truly." And there was a note of finality in his voice that Arun knew better than to challenge.

"This danger you insist on — you have Seen it?" Rythian asked.

"No, not exactly," Arun admitted. "Oh, I have no hatred for him; on the contrary, I like the man. But he is dangerous."

"Well, so," said Rythian, "am I. So are you, and every one of us."

Arun tried another track. "We'll have trouble with Voran, you know that. He's taken against Kherin, and there's nothing anyone can say or do that will change his mind."

"Well, that fool is in your care. This one," tapping his own chest, "is in the Lord's keeping."

"Since when did you give any credence to the old tales?" Arun snorted.

"Since it suits me," Rythian grinned and left him to his work.

The narrow back-path led past the long-house and curved towards the lakeshore behind the dwellings of the Elders. And it was here that the Third Priestess stepped into his path, planting herself and her staff in his way.

"I would speak with you," she said curtly. Obediently, he halted, looking down at the covered head. In her youth she would have been spear-tall, close to his own height, maybe more, but age had shrunken her.

"Speak, then, Old Mother," he said, matching her curtness. The hackles on his neck bristled, as they always did in her presence.

"The man Kherin. He should not be permitted to remain at your sisters' hearth."

This was unexpected. "Why should he not? Has he done harm to any there?"

The heel of the Hooded One's staff cracked down on the hard-trodden ground. "Why should he not?" the old woman mimicked cruelly. "I swear, Lyre'son, the first word you uttered was a 'why'! Because, fool, he is dangerous!"

"I've heard that word already," Rythian cut in, irritated. "Dangerous how?"

"Because he is marked by the Goddess," she hissed, and the bright eyes gleamed up at him under the hood. "I will take him to the Sacred Caverns under the Winter Hold. There we shall see what —"

"No," Rythian said abruptly, his gorge rising. No man knew for sure what rituals were conducted in the Sacred Caverns, but there were rumours enough. In ancient times, there had been youths who had 'chosen' to go to their deaths there, to feed the Earth Mother. Or so the tales ran.

"You deny me?" Chiera drew breath, startled.

"In this, yes. He will not remain at the hearth, however. He will ride with me, as befits a warrior and my hearthbrother."

The bent back straightened as she lifted her head to look into his face, eyes blazing. "You dare defy the Third Priestess?"

Anger flared up in him "You dare to defy the Sun Stallion? As you speak for one aspect of the Lady, Chiera, so do I speak for the God. And I say Kherin rides with the Warband." And so saying, he stepped around her and went on his way.

The decision being made, he supposed the next thing was to find out whether Kherin was willing to comply. Rythian made his way to the stableblock, and in through the rear door. Kherin, as he had hoped, was with Amber, her foal leaning against his hip while he scratched the wool between its ears.

Kherin's thoughts were not on his surroundings. The Goddess, he had found, was in no hurry for punishment to be meted out to the second transgressor; Marikyr was many leagues away and retribution would be postponed. The mare whickered a soft greeting, Kherin glanced around and saw Rythian.

"They're doing well," the blond man remarked casually, sitting down on a haybale.

Kherin said nothing, trying to Read through that strange heat-shimmer around Rythian's inner self. His silence did not sit comfortably with the visitor. Kherin could feel his unease, but only as a kind of echo.

"The Warband rides south and west shortly," Rythian said abruptly. "We're scouting the fords and the passes, and reminding those who need it that the Shi'R'Laen guarantee the safe passage of the trade caravans. There will be fighting. Will you ride with us, hearthbrother?" In the dim light of the stable, the man's eyes were dark sapphire, and unreadable.

"Is this your wish, Sun Stallion?" Kherin asked quietly.

"Yes. A wish only, you understand? The choice is yours."

Goddess? Kherin asked silently, but got no reply. The choice was indeed his. To ride with the Warband would gain him the allegiance and friendship of this Chieftain and his warriors, the Goddess willing. Would thus bring the downfall of Alzon that much closer. It might also bring him closer to Marikyr. Kherin nodded. "Yes. I will come."

"There is also the matter of recompense." Rythian picked up a straw and began to twist it between his fingers.

"For Nortan's staff?"

"No. That has been dealt with. From me, for the — dishonor done to you."

"That was not of your doing," Kherin pointed out.

"I was at fault," Rythian said quietly. "I thought I was doing what was best for you, sending you back to the Hold. But I shouldn't have sent you with those five. They were Caier's men, and if I did not trust them to hold true to me, I should not have trusted a sick man to their care."

"True," Kherin said coolly.

"Therefore you agree I also owe recompense by D'Shael law. If it is offered, will you accept it?"

"Why did you Challenge Caier?" Kherin asked abruptly, seeking to catch him off-balance and adding a subtle compulsion to the question.

"Because he was corrupting us, changing us." Rythian answered without hesitation, then frowned, eyes suddenly blade-keen. *The man had felt the compulsion?* "Could it be because the God called you," Kherin suggested to distract him.

"No." Rythian gave an irritable shrug. "It was my choice, my decision. Fire take it, don't you start as well. I've had enough of that from Kardan and the rest."

It was spoken as a grumble, as if Kherin was a friend of long-standing and not a virtual stranger.

"The recompense?" Rythian returned to the matter at hand.

"From the Sun Stallion?" Kherin asked.

"Of course."

"What of the hearthbrother?" Kherin queried and saw a reddening of the shadowed face.

"Doubly so from him," Rythian said, shifting uncomfortably on his haybale. "I'm sorry. It should not have happened. I cannot unmake it — I would if I could. What more can I say?"

For a moment the shimmer-shield sank and Kherin could Read Rythian's grim determination to shoulder responsibility regardless of cost, his innate compassion and pride, and his tiredness and loneliness, before they were hidden behind a wall of yellow flame. This was a man of his own age, but without the years of experience in leading and commanding, struggling to do what he thought was best for his people. Making mistakes and learning from them. Kherin weighed what he had Seen and knew that if this man had come to him in Khassan and asked to be of his Khori, he would have had no hesitation in accepting him. And training him for high rank. More importantly, with Rythian he felt a sense of kinship, of shared goals.

"Between hearthbrothers," Kherin said quietly, "there is no need. But —" abruptly remembering the hearth that still buzzed like an angry hive, "will this other recompense you offer satisfy Syth and Alais?"

"For now."

For the moment they understood each other perfectly, and with the understanding came recognition of a fast-growing friendship. "Then I will accept. Hearthbrother," Kherin replied, receiving a smile from Rythian that was all Dreyen.

The smile became a grin of relief. "Then that's settled. There is a horse, trained for battle. His name is Llynivar. I'll bring him to the front of the Elder Hall in the morning. The gift has to be seen and witnessed." Rythian glanced towards the door that led into the hearth and gave an almost imperceptible sigh. "As for the rest, tell our sisters you'll be riding with us, they'll make sure you're equipped. And you'll need a couple of remounts. Ronan or Dreyen can show you the herd to choose from. Take your pick."

Kherin nodded. "I will be at Elder Hall," he said. "Will you not join the hearth for the evening —" he began hopefully.

"No. I have to be in Sun Hall." Rythian turned away with obvious reluctance, then paused briefly at the outer door. He did not look back. "The debt I owe you for Emre's life," he said quietly, "and that of our children, I can never repay," and he was gone into the night as silently as a cat.

"No need," Kherin said to the empty space. "No debt. They are as dear to me as they are to you. Hearthbrother."

Kherin's hearth accepted the news of his leaving without surprise.

"Rythian said he would ask you," Alais said, "and we guessed you would want to go."

"We have already begun to gather what you'll need," Syth went on.

"We will miss you," Emre said quietly.

By contrast, Ronan Alais'son was openly pleased, and come the dawn he disappeared with his hounds to bring Rythian's horse-herd closer to the Hold. He was one of the few to miss the impromptu ceremony in front of the Elder Hall.

Llynivar was waiting; saddled, bridled and groomed to a satin gleam. Kherin had guessed the stallion would be a good one, but even so he was taken by surprise. Not so tall, maybe, as most of the D'Shael mounts, the horse was amongst the best he had seen.

"There are weapons also," Rythian said quietly as he handed over the reins, "though it is only a pair of spears. I do not have a sword

yet to give you. Disan-Smith has unfinished blades at the forge. Go
see him and he will find one for your height and reach, and fit the
hand-grip for you."

Kherin nodded. "I will," he said. "This is a splendid horse."

"Yes," Rythian agreed with some complacency. "He is young, just
six, but battle-trained and -tried. He'll not falter and he'll not refuse.
If there are other things you wish to teach him, you'll find him quick
to learn. Is the recompense accepted?"

"It is. Let there be no more talk of recompense, hearthbrother."

The transforming smile came briefly to Rythian's face and he
nodded his acknowledgement. "Go to Ronan now. He has brought in
my horses for your choice. They're out beyond the willows by the
lakeside. Later, on the trail, perhaps we'll have a chance to talk, get
to know each other better?"

Kherin returned the smile. "Brothers should not be strangers," he
agreed.

Rythian's herd had both the tamed and the untrained in their
number, and in anticipation of Kherin's choice, Ronan had separated
them out. Kherin walked past the small group of gentled beasts
towards the larger milling gathering of their wilder kindred. He
stood for a moment just drinking in the sight of them, the free power
and grace. He began to walk towards the grazing animals and
Ronan snatched at his arm.

"You just point out the ones that you want to see. Hammer and I
will cut them out."

"There is no need," Kherin said gently. "We of Khassan are not
without horse-lore. They will not harm me."

And they would not, for it seemed to Kherin that the Goddess
moved with him. He walked among the horses, touching a flank, a
forelock, a mane, talking to them softly, laughing as a velvet nose
nuzzled at his bare breast. Any of these would be fit to carry an
emperor, and yet it was not until the roan shouldered inquisitively
at his side that he made his choice, feeling with that inner sense the
contact of spirit to spirit. "You were foaled to carry me on your back,"
he murmured in Khassani, "I name you Rooinar, and we shall go
into battle together, you and I."

The roan bent his fine head, as if in agreement, and Kherin took
a handful of mane and swung up on to his back to ride him out of
the herd. The young horse, never before mounted, checked and
shuddered, head thrown up. Then he answered to hand and heel and
will as if he had known Kherin from the moment of his foaling.

From Ronan's scowl and set jaw it was clear he was not entirely surprised. Kherin did not need Sight to read the boy's resentment that an outlander had the D'Shael gift with horses. Ronan would have been more ready to see Kherin trampled or kicked.

Like the grey Llynivar, Rooinar had probably been bred for Rythian's own use; light-made for a D'Shael stallion. Kherin knew the roan had just the temperament to make a peerless war-steed, with the added endurance that was necessary for a long trail.

Kherin spent the rest of the day with the horse, grooming and talking to him, letting him get used to being handled and allowing him to become accustomed to Kherin's scent and voice. By the time Kherin went in to the hearth, the household were asleep — but a pile of goods were folded ready for packing. The women of the hearth had been busy.

Moving quietly, he lifted the items one by one. There was a thick cloak of new wool, the oil still in it so that it would shed water like a turtle's shell. It was large enough to cover him head to heel and serve as blanket in the chill of night. There were four shirts, two of quilted Tribute silk and two of combed wool; breeches of supple leather cut to fit his lean hips and long legs. The boots were of tough hide, made for riding. They felt stiff and strange after months of going barefoot or in soft shoes.

All he lacked was a sword.

There was a movement from the shadowy doorway, then Alais stepped into the light. "I thought it must be you," she said, smiling.

"I am sorry. I did not mean to wake you."

She made a gesture of dismissal. "The twins were restless — I was nursing them so that Emre could sleep. Have you eaten? No, I thought not. Syth left this ready for you." The covered dish held a tender baked fowl, cooked with honey and herbs and fresh greens.

Kherin hadn't realised how hungry he was until he started to eat. Alais sat and watched him.

"Is everything in order?" she said at last, indicating the heaped clothing. "We didn't pack it, because we thought you'd better see what you had."

"I am better provided for than I could ask," he told her, tipping the picked bones into the fire. "You have been most generous, sister."

"It would ill-become us to see one of our hearth go to war ill-prepared," she demurred. "And Emre was insistent that you do not go shirtless. The silks are of her shaping. Syth finished the cloak on the loom just today." She hesitated, as if she would say more, then reached down behind a bench and took up a long, wrapped bundle. "It is for us to arm you, hearthbrother, since you have no birth-family here. This belonged to my father." She shook away the bindings. It was a sword fashioned of bronze, the leaf-shaped blade polished so that it gleamed no less than gold. "In life or in death, carry this blade in triumph," she said and held it out.

Kherin accepted the weight of it, struck speechless for a moment. "This is a gift beyond any other," he said finally. "But Ronan —?"

"Has my man's sword. He was Syth's brother and he died fighting the Surni. Lirren is too young yet for blades of any kind." she added, forestalling his next question. "Not all fight as do the D'Shael, and since I do not know how you make war in your own lands, there is this, too. It was my husband's." A bow, a double-curved horseman's weapon, made of horn and strips of supple woods bonded together, a thing of elegance and power. "He made it himself. There are arrows, as well." There were four hands of them in a foxhide quiver, fletched with barred goosefeathers.

"It is the work of a master-craftsman," Kherin said quietly. "I have never seen better." Nor had he, not even those of the Tsithkin who rode with the Khori.

"Then take it and use it," she said. "With my love." There were tears standing in her eyes, he saw. Laying the sword aside, knowing what was needed, he went to her and took her in his arms. She drew a shaken breath, and then another. "Kherin, we will miss you... Goddess guard and protect you, hearthbrother."

"And you, and all at this hearth," he murmured, and gently kissed her brow. Then, pulling free, she turned and ran to the bedchamber, her hand to her mouth to stifle a sob.

The flames flared high as Chiera added a handful of dried herbs. The scent of them filled the chamber and the priestess breathed in their essense, eyes closed.

"Voran," she said, as if he stood before her. She took up a strip of bloodstained cloth bound about by some long fine strands of bright copper-red hair. "Listen to me. This man Kherin is a danger. To the tribe and to the Sun Stallion. Do not trust him. Do not let him work his magic on you as he has the others.

"Listen to me. Arun is snared. Rythian is snared.

"Listen to me. The time may come when you will have to kill him. For Arun's sake. For Rythian's sake.

"Listen to me." She breathed on the small bundle and held it to her breast as if it was an infant. "Obey me..."

Chapter Ten

$\mathcal{A}$nother sign. Kherin let out the breath he had been holding and looked down at the sword in one hand, the bow in the other. The bow was Her weapon, echoing the youngest and the oldest Moons in its shape and beauty, and Kherin was a skilled archer. According to Dreyen, to the D'Shael the bow was a hunting weapon, not to be used in warfare. The Khori, the Chosen's Honor Guard, had other ways. Kherin packed his gear, then with reverent care put sword, bow and quiver with it.

Now it begins. Kherin put his last lingering doubts aside. Everything was following a pattern; he had horses, weapons, and the friendship of the chieftain. Now he would ride to war where he could prove himself in the eyes of those who mistrusted him. After that, surely it would not be long before he was leading a war-band, then an army, with the Sun Stallion at his side. Once he entered Khassan at the head of such an army, the Khori would rush to his banner and bring with them most of Khassan's army. Alzon was doomed and damned.

There was another consideration, one he had been avoiding thinking about: the High King Teiron, whom Alzon claimed was Kherin's father. Kherin had to admit, if he was honest with himself, that he had sometimes wondered if Teiron was indeed his sire. It was a thought he did not dare to dwell on. But if it was true, it added another dimension to Alzon's sin. For brother to raise hand against brother was evil enough, without the foulness of striking at the Goddess' Chosen.

It came to Kherin then that if Alzon had sunk to such evil, then perhaps he could encompass another. Heir that he was to the throne of Khassan, perhaps he grew weary of waiting. Perhaps Alzon had — or would — take the Throne before the due time. Perhaps Teiron was already dead... Wasn't slaying the Chosen just a short step from slaying the High King?

That night, sleep did not come easy to Kherin.

The D'Shael rode to war in no fashion Kherin had ever seen. Used to the drilled discipline of the Khori, he found the loose shifting formation unsettling, particularly as he did not know his place in it. The men and women of the Warband rode where they would, with friends or kindred, except the SwordBrothers and the Elders of the Trail Council. They rode together with the Sun Stallion.

Kherin knew very few of the Warband; other than Rythian, Arun's was the only other vaguely familiar face. The desert tribes of Khassan rode in clan-groups; he would do the same, which meant riding as close to his hearthbrother as protocol allowed. Kherin edged through the pack until he was riding behind Kardan.

When Kherin had first joined the Warband, Kardan had greeted him with a smile and a nod of welcome. This Elder, at least, seemed to have neither hostility nor overt suspicions towards him, which could not be said for the rest of the Elders. Even so, Kherin was surprised when Kardan checked his horse and settled in beside him. He was also grateful; he wanted answers to certain questions.

As the Elder settled his horse in alongside Kherin, he momentarily felt dwarfed by the size of man and his horse. He remembered somewhat guiltily that he had stolen the massive roan that paced sedately at his side.

Kardan showed no resentment of the theft. His only reference to it was a nod of the head in Llynivar's direction, and a casual, "You'll not need to borrow a better mount this time."

Kherin smiled, patting the arch of the milk-white neck. "No, Uncle. I think not."

"Not as mute as a mole any more, either. That's good."

"I had good teachers," Kherin said, straight-faced.

"Nortan is not among them, eh?" Kardan grinned. It was no secret that the two Elders had no liking for each other.

"That one couldn't teach a fish to swim," Kherin said wryly.

Kardan gave a snort of laughter. "True enough," he agreed.

"Uncle," Kherin asked, since Kardan seemed more than ready to talk, "Rythian has told me we are to patrol the Surni border; can you tell me more of these people? Also I'd have thought the Warband would have been greater in number?"

"Some of the warriors have gone south and east to make the caravan routes safe. As for the Surni, the Sun Stallion suspects the border tribes to be making alliances against the D'Shael — particularly against the Shi'R'Laen tribe."

"Isn't that all the more reason to be riding in force?"

Kardan shook his head. "There will be no pitched battles," the Elder told him. "That is not our way, although we can if we need to. We prefer to make swift punitive raids, strike hard and fast."

"The D'Shael fight like the wild desert tribes of southern Khassan," Kherin commented.

He did not add that defeating those wild tribes had been his and his Khori's main task. For himself, Kherin needed to know more of the D'Shael's enemies. Kardan needed only a little prompting to tell him all there was to know about the Surni and the other tribes.

By the time they made camp at dusk, Kherin had a comprehensive view of the border peoples, and a deepening respect and liking for the Elder. A swift Reading had shown him the enduring strength and majesty of the man, and an integrity as uncompromising as a honed steel blade. "You're welcome to eat at my fire tonight," Kardan had said. "Mettan and a few others will be joining us."

Among those few was Gallan-Smith, a massive red-haired man. This was another familiar face, Kherin realised; this was the smith who had weakened the binding spell on the collar he wore. Gallan was, he discovered, the eldest son of Caier, but was also a staunch supporter of the new Sun Stallion. Gallan had little good to say of those who complained about the change in leadership. Kherin listened more than he spoke, and learned more of his new tribe and of his hearthbrother.

A growing physical uneasiness took his mind away from the conversations around the fire. The rich stew he'd eaten sat heavy in his belly. Soon the unease became severe discomfort, and it drove him from the fireside and into the bushes beyond the horselines.

The worst of the sickness soon passed once he had emptied himself, but a weakness invaded every limb. It did not wane after a few minutes. Rather it increased, until it was all he could do not to collapse onto the grass. He could feel the weakness eating into the barriers of his mind. This was nothing natural. This was spell-cast. Kherin propped his back against a tree and gathered what strength he could. Then he turned his mind outward, seeking the source of the evil trying to overwhelm him.

It was harder than he expected, freeing his spirit from the confines of the flesh for the Sending. The winds of a wild magic buffeted at him until he thought he would be torn apart, but he found the thread, and held to it, letting it draw him, unresisting, back to its source.

His vision opened out. To his startlement, he was at a D'Shael hearth. Facing him was the Third Priestess of the Tribe, a figure he had seen around the Hold, always at a distance except for the one time they met during Emre's labor. He sensed her brooding emnity then, but he had not expected her to move against him like this. Chiera's hood was thrown back and her long white hair hung loose over her shoulders. She held a small bundle in one hand; pale fabric stained with blood — his blood from when he was brought injured to the Hold. With her other hand she tossed something into the flames, muttering an incantation. Then her ice-crystal eyes fixed on him and widened. He read her hatred in them. Her free hand began to move in a pattern he recognised, but since he was not — yet — a ghost, it had no power to banish him. He had not expected to be attacked on this level. He cursed himself for a fool. This was the mind that had Watched him from the Grove. He should have gauged her powers then, while he was at the Hold, not waited to learn what they were when she already loosed them on him. He had been lax in many ways in that respect. No more.

"Why are you come here?" she demanded.

"What harm have I done you, Chiera?"

His use of her name angered her. "Harm? You ask that, witch-spawn? You should be dead! I made sure—"

"Not sure enough, Old Woman."

"That can be remedied." She made a hissing sound like a cornered cat and began a weaving with hands and voice. Kherin felt the beginnings of the binding, as if invisible cords were tightening. Even weakened as he was, he understood the extent of her power.

"Unwise, Old Woman, to seek to slay Her Chosen." He broke the weave as if it were cobweb.

"You dare call on Her!"

Kherin could not feel an equal hatred for Chiera, though her rage and fear battered at him.

"What do you fear of me, Chiera? Tell me!"

She straightened, and with both hands flung a scattering of dry stuff into the flames. "I have the Long Sight," she said. "I see an end — an end to all we hold dear! The D'Shael — clan, tribe and people. I see death and dishonor to the Sun Stallion, brought about by you!" The flames leapt, and Kherin Saw her vision. Change, yes, and an end to many things, but the most vivid part of the Vision for Kherin was Rythian, with his long bright mane mired and tangled in the dust. The Sun Stallion fallen like an axed tree.

Kherin knew it was a true Seeing. A Gift from the Goddess, using one of his enemies to show him the way ahead.

"We are all — you, he and I — together in Her Hand," Kherin said with ringing conviction. *"Goddess, in all ways and in all things, be Thy will done!"* The bloody fabric in Chiera's hand suddenly caught fire and was consumed. Chiera dropped it with a startled cry. Smoke roiled up from the fire, obscuring his vision.

Faintly, as from a vast distance he thought he heard a scream — then all faded to nothing.

Then he knew himself in Her presence, enfolded in Her embrace as he had not been for so long. *"Beloved, Son, Chosen of Mine, you do well. This is as I decree. You are here to work My will in the world and among these people."*

"What of Khassan?" he dared to ask.

"Khassan is no longer your home, Beloved." He felt a stab of wrenching loss, but sorrow was transmuted by Her gift. Yet there was another need in him.

"The High King?" he pleaded, *"Goddess, of your mercy —"*

"He lives and rules," came the answer. *"Khassan is as it has always been. Do not grieve for either."*

"And Alzon, his crime against Your will?"

The reply was remorseless: *"Who are you to know all My will? Accept this; Khassan is closed to thee, Beloved."*

He bowed his head in acceptance. Obedience had never cost so much.

All his life Kherin had been trained to unquestioning acceptance of his Goddess's will. Now the phrase *Khassan is closed to thee* echoed in his head with a terrible finality. So be it. There must be another Chosen in his place and he could not, therefore, cross the border. Since Khassan and Alzon were barred to him, that left him free to strike at Tylos — the people who enslaved him.

A distant scream woke Kherin, the hunting cry of a rock lion. He opened his eyes on deep night, broken only by the sweeping arch of stars showing through the branches over his head. He was cold; dew coated his hair and shoulders, but there were no symptoms of what had driven him from the fire. Carefully Kherin got to his feet, stretching the stiffness out of his muscles. Despite the pain of exile, he felt purged and clean, as he felt after a stay in the Sanctuary. He also knew he could not afford to be so unwary again. The signs had been there, all around him; there were those of the D'Shael who could mind-call their horses, who had the Fore-Knowing, the smiths with the deep earth-fire in their souls; of course their priests and priestesses would have greater skills. Kherin frowned. Did they have priests? He had seen none, nor heard of any. The Elders served no priestly function he could see, but that didn't mean there were no magic-weavers among the Warband. Kherin sat in stillness and built an armour about himself, protection against almost any assault.

By the time he was done, the eastern horizon showed a pale seam of light. Above, the herald of morning glowed like an unset gem. Kherin lifted his hands in salute, then made his way back to Kardan's fire.

Rythian expected an increase in border-raids. He wasn't wrong. Two of the forward scouts rode back on lathered horses; the news they brought wasn't good.

"Two hundred and sixty-three Surni warriors," the first scout said as he reined in his mount.

"And their remounts?" Rythian asked, ignoring the rumble of disquiet and anger from his Trail-Council.

"In a blind valley," the other scout reported, quickly sketching a map in the dust. "At least three hundred head of horse, pack beasts as well as war steeds. The mouth of the valley is blocked by rolls of bloodthorn. Their main camp is here —" drawing a crude hand shape, and pointing to the palm of it. "The remounts are in the thumb, with the others in the fingers, and the wrist is blocked with a palisade of stakes filled with bloodthorn. There's water, but little grazing. Two days, three at most."

"By now they will know our numbers," Gorryn Elder pointed out. "Forty and nine, Rythian."

"What do you suggest, Uncle?" Rythian asked calmly.

"Ride wide of them," Gorryn snapped. "Anything else is folly."

"And leave them to attack us from the rear, as well as leap down like wolves on the caravans? I think not. Kardan?"

"They outnumber us by five to one," Kardan said slowly.

"Yes. And while they are united, no caravan can dare the pass."

"We could summon the clans?" Mettan suggested.

"How long would that take?" Rythian asked, not expecting an answer, nor did he get one. "Listen well. This alliance threatens more than the Tylosian caravans. If the Surni succeed against us now, then other tribes will follow their example. They must be defeated so conclusively that they lose heart as well as lives."

Gorryn snorted. "And just how do you propose to do that?"

"There will be a way." Rythian said. He reached into his pack on impulse, taking out the Sun Disc, and their eyes were drawn to the sunlight glinting on the ancient gold as he hung it about his neck. "Tonight we camp at Split Rock," he stated, reining Zaan away from the Elders.

For a while Rythian rode in silence, Arun and Voran flanking him, Kherin a few paces to the rear. The weight of the gold on Rythian's breast felt strange. The enemy would not have to come close to know a Sun Stallion rode with the Warband. Such a potential prize could bring them out too soon and too fast for caution, which would be to D'Shael advantage.

The valley floor was a tangle of broken ground, where rocky outcrops and scrubby copses offered cover for friend and enemy alike. The D'Shael rode hand on lance.

"You're mad," Arun said beside him.

"Maybe," Rythian acknowledged. "I need to think." He let the reins lie loose on Zaan's neck and turned his thoughts inwards. Somewhere in the tangled threads of information lay the knowledge he needed.

The Surni were akin to the D'Shael, both being nomadic horse warriors. They even shared bloodlines as clanless D'Shael sometimes found shelter among the Surni. So, what was the best way to defeat a horse-warrior? The answer was obvious — unhorse him. Any horse warrior was weaker when fighting on foot. It would be a blow to the heart indeed to take their horses out from under them.

Suddenly there was a picture before his eyes. Rythian choked on the rush of nausea it brought him. The solution was there, horribly clear. It went against every instinct of custom and upbringing. But it would work. Try as he might, Rythian could see no other way. Nothing else would have the same crippling impact, bringing not only a chance of victory but the possibility that his own losses would be light. Rythian knew that as clearly as if it had already happened, but he didn't know if he could make the Trail Council see the wisdom of his plan. Or if he could convince his warriors.

Rythian called the Elders around him when they paused to water the horses. "Split Ridge is ahead of us, Uncles. We will set up camp between the ridge and the river. We will not be circumspect about it — the Ridgemen and Surni must know where and who we are. They will not be able to resist the challenge as well as the chance to take a Sun Stallion's head. I will send a small party, maybe six, to their valley, to wait until the battle is joined. Then they will fire the brush to stampede the remounts through the camp and onto the plain."

"This is madness," Gorryn burst out. "They'll ride over us like a grassfire!"

"No, Uncle. Our camp will have the scarp behind us and be walled by cut brush and thorn. Within that perimeter there will be spears hidden, shafts bedded in the ground, blades pointing outward. The enemy will not see them until they've ridden onto them. Unhorsed, they will be unable to stand against us, however we are outnumbered."

Silence greeted his plans, speaking louder than words.

"Why not launch an attack on their camp?" Kardan said coolly. "Why this — trickery?"

Rythian was in no mood to meet dissension with diplomacy. "Because this way we will break their hearts and their courage!" He bit the words out. "Because this way we have a chance to win, my Uncles, and be sure they will not trouble us again this year. And because I have but recently put on the Sun Disc, and I have no wish to lose it. Those are my reasons. In the Eye of the Sun!"

Kardan put hand to staff, grim and frowning. "So be it," he said. "But I tell you, Lyre'son, the warriors will not like this."

"They do not have to like it; they only have to stand and fight!"

Kardan was right. Word of Rythian's plan spread like ripples in a pool and he met with more than one objection. He heard them out, but he did not change his plans. The six he chose for the firing of the brush accepted their part most readily of all and left the Warband well before the campsite was reached. They left behind their spears, though.

To any watcher — and Rythian did not doubt there were watchers — the camp was set up in usual D'Shael fashion. But after dark every warrior gave one or more spear to Rythian, who with a small group of warriors, set them among the thin scrub. The glint of the bronze blades was hidden by smeared dirt. A charging rider, intent on the enemy, would not see them. By midnight all was in readiness.

The sun was high in the sky. Kherin watered his horses and talked to them softly in Khassani as he teased the wind knots from their manes. His horses were restless, like all the beasts. It did not surprise him. Kherin could feel it in himself. He had listened along with the rest of the warriors to Rythian's plan — and had watched with his Inner Sight. That strange heat-shimmer had flared strongly about Rythian and Kherin knew it now for what it was. The God's touch was on him, and the horses recognised it as well. Horses would die this day as well as men. Kherin hoped Rythian would take their deaths upon himself, as the Chosen must. It was no surprise now that there was a fast-growing kinship between them. The touch of their respective deities made them brothers indeed.

With a wry smile Kherin remembered their conversation in the barn and Rythian's denial of his God's call. He wished there had been more time for them to talk. Goddess willing, there would be in days to come. *Grant us victory, Lady of Battles,* Kherin prayed. *We are in Thy Hand.*

The word finally came to mount up. Kherin settled on Llynivar, and found his place in the line. The sun's face was clouded over by dark thunderclouds. The air shuddered with the gathering tension, thick as syrup. From overhead came an ominous booming rumble. A storm was about to break — one that did not seem right.

Schooled in the skills of weather-working, Kherin wondered briefly if some mage of the enemy was at work. But this didn't feel like skill; rather it was like some monstrous anger, shifting as it built and built. Kherin could detect no control here, or not enough to hold the storm's power in check.

Like a wild horse whipped to frenzy, the storm struck with a scream of wind. Scything lightning bolts slashed down behind the enemy line, sending the horses mad with fear, driving them forward. The voice of the storm found echoes in the harsh warcries of the warriors, the drumming thunder of many hooves. The D'Shael did not spur forward to meet that charge; they braced for the impact and the battle was joined.

Rythian's plan worked. The headlong charge broke like a cresting wave on the deadly angled spears, men and horses screaming as the impetus drove them onto the cruel barrier. The front ranks crumpled; those following were too close to turn aside, stumbling and falling over the thrashing bodies of the injured. Then the D'Shael threw their remaining spears and charged.

Part of Kherin fought as he had been trained to do. Another part of him sought the core of the storm. He found it unstable, and he bent his will to tame it as he would tame a wild horse.

Fighting two battles at once took all his strength — and all his attention. He had no ability, or energy, left to sort the details of either battle. He didn't even know what battle he was winning or losing until the raging storm became sheeting rain that finally drizzled into thin mist that dissipated on the wind.

He became slowly aware of his surroundings. He had swords in both his hands, red-wet from points to hilts. The grips were sticky with blood that gloved his hands from elbows to fingertips. One was the blade Alais had given him; he could not remember who he had killed to gain the new weapon. The screaming chaos of the two battles swamped all detail.

Both battles were over, and there was calm. There were no more enemies to fight. Those of the enemy who could do so had fled the field, leaving their dead and dying behind. It was late afternoon, and the setting sun painted the retreating clouds slaughter-yard-red.

Kherin had been fortunate; the Lady's hand had shielded him. He had only cuts and bruises, but he was trembling almost as badly as Llynivar. He dismounted, leaning against the grey horse's shoulder, stroking the foam-dripping muzzle. The horse's injuries were as slight as his own, for which Kherin was fervently grateful.

The currents of the fighting had swept them away from the camp. With one arm across his mount's withers, Kherin made his way back to the tents, Llynivar's head drooping beside his own. Kherin picked up a lamed warrior on the way, put him up on the grey and took him to where the healer-priestess worked.

Kherin took care of his horse's small hurts and left him by grazing and water, then unobtrusively began tending the wounded. Rythian, he found, had already come and gone — not to have his own wounds dealt with, but to spend time with the injured.

There were some twenty men and women in the care of Dari, the healer-priestess, four in serious need. Dari, a tall handsome woman who reminded him a little of Alais, gave Kherin a hostile stare as he crouched over the first man he came to.

Combating the storm had drained Kherin, so he could do little more than ease the pain and offer additional strength to the man. The man was conscious and aware; he gave a gasp of surprise and sigh of grateful relief. Kherin moved on, continuing to offer what little he could. Once he had done what he could for the injured, he did not linger. There was more work for him elsewhere. On the battlefield.

What awaited him on the killing ground was worse than the fighting. The Sun Stallion's battle tactic, inspired and successful though it was, had left an agonising detritus. Those of the enemy whose wounds were not life-threatening had been dragged away and left at the edge of the field. The dying had been sent swiftly on their way with the cold mercy of a sharp blade. But it was the uncomprehending pain of the dying horses that cut like a barbed spear in Kherin's gut. He drew the knife from his belt and went in among the wreckage of the animals to put an end to their pain.

He was not the only one at the work. Rythian had taken the duty upon himself, as was the right of leadership. But it was only as Kherin straightened from killing the last horse, the hot stink of blood in his nostrils, that he saw Rythian's face clearly. There was less emotion there than on a carving in stone. Kherin looked beyond the mask and Saw the total weariness that follows unskilled wreaking. Abruptly he knew the unchannelled storm had been Rythian's doing.

Anger rose in him. The first law of the weather-worker is not to meddle except at dire need — and to keep control throughout.

Rythian had done neither; he had let his summoned storm rage unchecked to do what havoc it could. Rythian was a fool, under the God's Hand or not. Kherin opened his mouth to speak, but before he could Voran thrust past him, bloodstreaked but with no serious wound, looking for Rythian.

"I thought the battle would have put an end to you, Tylosian." It was spat over the redhead's shoulder. "But that will wait on another day."

"Guard your tongue," snapped his SwordBrother, "unless you want Kardan's staff across your brainless skull. Kherin, will you take Zaan to the horselines while we see to our Stallion?"

Schooling his own face to a mask, Kherin gave a nod and took the reins. As he led the horse towards the river, he heard Rythian's voice refusing aid, denying injury, and Arun's deeper tones arguing. He walked upstream until he found a clear place and let the horse drink before beginning to wash the blood from its pale hide. Aside from minor cuts, the horse was uninjured. He rubbed the stallion down with handfuls of grass and turned him loose to graze with Llynivar.

Kherin rinsed the bloodstains from his shirt and breeches, spreading them to dry on a bush, before wading waist-deep into the cold water to cleanse himself. When he looked up he saw Rythian alone on the edge of the shallow, kneeling in fouled mud to drink from cupped hands. He plainly did not know Kherin was there. Rythian's head drooped and his shoulders slumped from exhaustion. Kherin decided it was a good time to Read the man more deeply and discover the extent of his powers of weaving and casting.

Before Kherin could do more than test the strength of Rythian's shields, his outward sight took note of a wound. Rythian's left shoulder blade had been all but laid open, a long slash from the outer curve of the shoulder almost to the spine, clotted black now. He frowned. That injury needed urgent tending and he was surprised Arun had not seen to it that Rythian was in Dari's care. Unless the SwordBrother was not aware of the wound. It would have been hidden by the blood-matted blanket of Rythian's hair and if the man did not admit to it nor let anyone examine him for injury — he remembered the half-heard argument and shook his head.

Kherin spoke Rythian's name, and when that got no response, he waded over and touched him. The sharp intake of breath was that of a man waking from an unquiet dream. Kherin spoke his name again, putting a hand towards the injured shoulder. The ragged edges of the wound were dry and crusted and clotted with hair from the loose mane. "This must be cleaned."

"Leave it," Rythian said dully. "It doesn't matter."

Kherin did not waste time in arguing, merely took up a handful of absorbent moss and set about soaking the mess of blood and dirt and hair away. Either the D'Shael were schooled to show no pain, or the wound had not yet made itself properly felt, for he was able to swab the slash clean without the man so much as wincing. A little fresh blood came, but not much. While outwardly cleaning the wound, Kherin tried to probe the cut with his mind, but the wildfire sheen within that guarded Rythian would not let him past the surface. There was little Kherin could do in any case, exhausted as he was. Just cleanse it a little ...

But contact brought additional knowledge. Kherin leaned against those shimmering shields with impunity. Their heat was that of a banked fire, built by instinct. It was clear that Rythian had no knowledge of his power. It was amazing. If Rythian thought of it at all, he probably regarded the storm as a fortunate accident of nature. The danger of his ignorance could be catastrophic. Rythian needed to learn how to control, and wisely use, the power in him. But that must be for later. With a jolt of shock and rising elation, Kherin realised that he would be the one to give that Knowledge. A piece of the the Goddess' Pattern had fallen into place, revealing more of Her Will. Yet the Crone's vision of desolation and death had been a true one and he would do well to remember it.

"You fought well today," Rythian said abruptly, rousing himself.

Kherin doubted if Rythian had actually noticed him, but he accepted the accolade. "I am a warrior," he said simply.

The wide-set blue eyes, hazed with the aftermath of the battle, lifted to his face. "I know." That was all. Yet it felt as good to him as the acclaim of the Khassani war-princes. "There is blood in your hair," Kherin said gently. "Come into the river and wash it." It would clean the stains from the rest of Rythian's body as well.

Rythian docilely obeyed. Kherin carefully freed the worst of the clotted tangles from the pale mass of long hair. The water had darkened it little so it lay in heavy sodden ribbons over Rythian's shoulders and back. Rythian flinched a little when his hair snagged in his raw wound. Kherin carefully gathered it into a loose tail and tied it at the nape of Rythian's neck with a leather thong. Kherin was aware that the water was reviving Rythian to thought and feeling, could sense the growing mental as well as physical anguish that found voice at last in a sob of caught breath.

"The horses..."

The Khassani, although they honored horses, did not reverence them as the D'Shael did. Still, Kherin could understand Rythian's grief.

"It was necessary," Kherin said firmly. "If you had not done as you did, the enemy would have swept over you like a wave, and it would have been Shi'R'Laen beasts and men left for the carrion-eaters." He did not intend to say more, but the words were there to be spoken. "Their Mother called them home, and they went to Her. Rythian, as the river washes away the blood, so shall time wash away this grief. There is no stain on your honor in this action."

Bleak as midwinter, Rythian looked at him. "Is there not?" he whispered, and turning, waded back to the riverbank.

Kherin followed, gathering up shirt, boots and breeches. He called the two horses from their grazing. "Rythian, let Dari tend you now — or Arun —" but Rythian did not look back.

By dusk, with wounds treated and bellies full of meat and ale, the warriors turned to tales of valour around the Sun Fire. Kherin, sitting in a shadowed corner outside the pegged back entrance of the Sun Stallion's tent, listened to the proud boasts with half his attention, the other half focused on the Trail Council going on within the tent.

Kherin bent his head over the burnishing of his new-gained sword, checking it critically for flaws. The blade caught the flame-light as he turned it, glowing like gold. It was more slender than his D'Shael blade and a couple of handspans shorter. A good weapon, for all it was bronze and not steel, though it was not as fine as the blade Alais had given him.

"Well?" Kardan's voice, sharp above him, indicated the Council was over.

Kherin looked up. "Uncle," he responded politely.

"What was your view of this fight?" Kardan asked, but before Kherin could answer, a voice interrupted from the crowd around the Fire.

"From a distance, most like," Voran said snidely, ducking an exasperated swipe from his SwordBrother.

Kherin did not look at him. "I have swords," he said simply. "Let who will try to take them from me."

Kardan gave a bark of laughter. "Ha! The South breeds raptors, sure enough! Arun will need to keep a tight rein on his SwordBrother, I think." His face became abruptly serious. "Enough of this. More important, the Sun Stallion needs care."

"Care!" Voran whooped. "He's invincible!"

"And wounded," Kardan snapped.

"And like wounded wolf, too." Arun cut in, pushing through the celebrating crowd to join them. "He'll let no one near him. Dari managed to get a bandage on him, but no more than that. She's tried over and again, so have I, but he'll have none of it."

"I know," Kardan sighed. "This battle has cost him dear, particularly since he probably felt each horse's death — and knew he was the cause of it. He says he wishes to be alone awhile. We'll try again later when he has had a chance to come to some sort of terms with this. Will you eat at my fire tonight, Kherin?"

"I thank you, Uncle. I will."

Of all the Elders, Kardan was the one Kherin felt most at ease with. He might almost have been one of the priests of the Sanctuary, although he had none of their arcane skills. Kardan had as much wisdom and insight into the hearts of men as any priest, which was not the case with all the bearers of the Staff.

Kherin served Kardan with meat and bread as formally as if he were a senior priest, and Kardan accepted his service as gravely. As they ate, they talked about Khassan, about the Chosen's Khori, the desert — an alien concept, that — and the tribes that lived there. There was in Kardan Elder a hunger for new knowledge, and it was getting on for midnight before Kherin left for his own tent.

The camp slept, save for the guards. The moon was high in the sky, washing everything in silver, when Kherin followed a sudden impulse and slipped silently into Rythian's tent. He was not surprised to find it empty and the bedding undisturbed. But he had seen the depth of the man's wound and knew that if left much longer, it could turn green. Rythian did not have the luxury of isolation, no matter how much he wanted — needed — the solitude he could not find in a crowded campsite. It was his right, as Chosen and Chieftain, to be alone with his God, and Kherin would have followed the same path himself in such a time of need. But with such a wound needing tending, now was not the time. Besides, Kherin could feel there were Shadows gathering, and Rythian was their quarry.

Kherin went to his own tent, took up the bow and arrows Alais had given him, and left the camp. The sentries did not see him as he left the perimeter and struck southerly into rising ground, finding the goat-tracks that led up towards the ridge's sheer crest.

Rythian had not covered his trail, but even if he had, Kherin would have had no trouble following him. There was clearer sign than prints for eyes that could See; a blood-spoor of the spirit, the dark hearts-blood of a man hurt to the edge of endurance.

Kherin knew he had been right to come when he reached a ledge that overhung the plain. Rythian crouched there, doubled forward so that the unbound hair touched the ground.

The moon was almost at the full. The Moon of Knowledge the Khassani called it, and Her light was pitiless. Someone had managed to get a bandage on Rythian; it showed starkly white, the fresh blood-stains like ink in the night.

Something moved in the black shadows, a furtive stalking. The light caught the liquid glint of eyes that gleamed greenly. There are creatures that are drawn to any spent battlefield, the scavengers of the wild. Those would be gorging on the plain below. This was other, and Rythian was its chosen meat. Kherin fitted arrow to string, drew and loosed. There was a squall of pain, a scrabble of claws on loose rock, and the rock-lion was gone.

Rythian had not moved; Kherin came closer. "Rythian," he said quietly, kneeling beside him. After a few moments, the man stirred, sitting back on his heels. There were tracks of tears in the dust on his face.

"Kherin? Why are you here?"

"You weren't in your tent," he said.

"And I should be. I know. There is no answer for me here."

Rythian got stiffly to his feet, turned back to the narrow trail. Kherin did not try to stop him. *You are wrong,* he wanted to say. *There is an answer for you, if you would but open your heart to Her.*

Kherin could See Rythian's pain and despair, clear as a thorny cloak. He wanted to lift the weight of it from him, to make him realise that he carried it unnecessarily, but he didn't know the words. Not yet. Perhaps if the Goddess willed it, later there would be a way.

Rythian paused for a word with a guard on the way to his tent, so Kherin was there before him. He had Dari's potion ready in a cup. Rythian made a wry face. "If I must."

"Dari and Kardan ordered it."

"Yes, they would. Can you loosen this binding first?"

It was stiff with blood and knotted tight. It would need to be cut off and the wound redressed. Kherin drew the lamp closer and took up Rythian's belt-knife. The man braced himself, head tilted to the right, long hair swept aside to bare his shoulder. The arch of throat curved smoothly into hard brown muscle and strong cords of tendon, and beneath, the vulnerable beat of the blood pulse. Kherin eased the knife-point under the wad of fabric, slitting it. Where it pulled away, fresh blood welled. Kherin blotted it away, tried again to explore the wound with his mind, but could not. It seemed clean; that was all he could See. Kherin reached for ointment and fresh bandages, bound the injury as securely as he could.

"Thanks," Rythian said. He made a visible effort to respond normally. "That feels better."

"Good. But that wound troubles me. What does Dari say?"

"That it's clean and will heal. If I am sensible." Rythian pulled a rueful self-mocking expression. "I have not been sensible, have I?" Then he hesitated. "Could you perhaps comb out this tangle for me?" With the injured shoulder, he was effectively one-handed. Kherin took up the comb.

"I have no skill in this," he warned.

"It's no different to a horse's mane," Rythian said dismissively.

But it was. There was none of the coarseness of horsehair. It was a weight of heavy pale silk that drifted and clung as Kherin combed the dust and snarls out of it. He braided it as he had seen the other warriors do into a wrist-thick rope that reached more than halfway down the man's back. Kherin was tying it off neatly with the leather thong when the companionable silence was broken by a bellow of outrage, and Voran was lunging through the tent door.

Rythian's uninjured arm held the intruder back as he came to his feet. "By the Fires, Voran, what now?"

"Man, are you mad? You let that moon-mage touch your hair — weaving the Lord alone knows what evil charms and ill-wishing into it —!"

"Enough!" Rythian snapped. "Evil charms and ill-wishing? You should go back to the Hold and play with the children. You let the old women frighten you with their tales!"

"He's Southern witch-spawn!" Voran howled. "Who knows what mischief he could do?"

"He has had ample opportunity," Rythian said tightly. "I am still here and healthy. If you think he has put ill-luck into my hair," and he picked up the belt-knife, "then cut it off."

"What?" It was a yelp of horror.

"I do not need a nurse-mare," Rythian said, temper barely held in check. "Still less do I need your hysteria, Voran. You will make your apology. Now. In the Eye of the Sun."

"Apologize?"

Kherin could have told him that Voran could no more make any apology than he could fly. Equally, Rythian was angered beyond reason.

"For the dishonor done to my hearth." It was bitten out. The fire-basket spat out sullen sparks, flames rising from the charcoal.

"The dishonor isn't from me," Voran snarled, "but from him! Can't you see how he has snared you? No, of course you can't. Then I challenge him!"

Astounded, Rythian stared at him. "Voran — "

"It's the only way to rid you and your hearth of his spells," Voran said flatly. "Challenge, witch-spawn! Do you accept it?"

"No!" Rythian shouted. "I forbid it!"

"You can't. Once challenge is given, not even the Sun Stallion can halt it," Voran said with immense satisfaction. "You are as dear to me as a birthbrother. I will not stand aside and watch you destroyed by this serpent." He stared at Kherin over Rythian's shoulder. "Will you accept? Or be known by all the clans as a coward."

Kherin was suddenly weary of Voran's antagonism. "Challenge is accepted," he said. "Are weapons used — or is it hand-to-hand?"

"Both," Voran said quickly, before Rythian could speak. "This is not a Stallion Challenge, but a dispute between a warrior and — between warriors," he amended.

"So be it," Rythian said quietly, anger held simmering by iron control. "I would prefer not, but if it must be, then tomorrow at mid-morning."

Chapter Eleven

The site most suited for the combat was the wide circle where the great Fire had burned the previous evening. The debris had been raked away, leaving a level blackened surface.

Voran took up his stance, his best spears in his hands, his sword sheathed on his belt. He crooned a war-song under his breath, blood high and racing. He would give the Southerner a quick, clean death for Rythian's sake. With the man dead, the spell would be broken, and they would know he had been right.

But Voran was uncomfortably aware of Rythian standing among the crowd with his arms folded and a frown on his face. But more painful than that was Arun's absence. His SwordBrother had not agreed with his actions; in fact Voran could not remember when he had last seen the usually cool-headed Arun so furious. Maybe his Brother was right? The doubt was nipped in the bud before it had chance to grow.

Kherin came to the killing ground carrying two swords but no spears, which caused a buzz of comment among the watchers. He walked light and seemingly unafraid, with the bulk of Kardan half a pace behind. Kherin was stripped to his doeskin breeches, his black hair tied back from his brow with a length of scarlet silk. Kherin was lean and hard-muscled and as brown as a hazelnut.

Suddenly Arun pushed through the crowd, holding out his own pair of fine spears to Kherin. "You have no spears," he said. "Use these." Fury ran in Voran at Arun's treachery. Was every soul in the camp glamored by the creature?

Kherin shook his head. "No," he said. "I have no need. I thank you for the offer."

Kardan said something in Tylosian, arguing, but Kherin repeated his refusal.

More fool he, Voran thought, though it caught in his craw. It would be less a challenge than a butchery, with little honor in it. Nonetheless, he could not withdraw now. He would not, even if he could.

Kardan stepped between the two combatants, staff planted firmly on the ground.

"Challenge has been made and accepted," he announced. "In the Eye of the Sun, let the combat begin."

Voran had the sun behind him as he planned, the dazzle of it in his opponent's eyes. He saw Kherin poised like a cat, dark eyes keen, measuring. Voran balanced himself, gauging the distance, and feinted his aim so that Kherin's dodge took him into the path of the spear instead of away from it. The warriors gave a kind of concerted gasp, but Kherin raised one arm, deflecting the deadly thing with the flat of his blade as it dropped from its glittering apogee.

Ae-shae - he was as fast and nimble as a goat! Voran felt a moment of uneasiness.

Kherin stood waiting, hands down at his sides as if the weight of the two swords was too much for him. His face was serene, his body relaxed.

Anger burned in Voran's blood and he lunged forward, spear thrusting fast as an adder's strike. But not fast enough. Somehow Kherin caught the haft between crossed blades and twisted. The move was totally unexpected; the leverage was enough to bend back Voran's wrist and wrench the spear from his weakened grasp. Voran threw himself after it but Kherin snatched it up and tossed it to the edge of the circle. Swearing, Voran whipped out his sword and crouched, aware that he was being made to look a complete novice. All the advantages should have been with him; his height, weight, reach and strength all were greater than his opponent's. But so far they had counted for nothing. Voran's hatred of the man grew to new heights and he came forward in a fast, slashing attack.

Three blades clashed, slid together, and Voran's sword hooked under the curved hilt of Kherin's shorter blade. Even before Voran could give it the twist that would disarm, Kherin let go of both his swords. Voran suddenly found his extended arm held in a vice-like grip and he was inexplicably flying through the air. He landed hard on his back in the black grit, a cloud of ash settling around him, swordhilt a dozen feet away from his clutching fingers.

Voran lurched to his feet and shook his hair back from his eyes. The slight figure of his opponent was poised, unruffled. Kherin stepped sideways as neatly as a cat as Voran circled him. No strategy now — Voran wanted only revenge. But fast as he was, Kherin was faster. He avoided every lunge, sending in punishing kicks to Voran's exposed flanks, reminding him of Rythian's fight with Caier. For an instant Voran faltered. It was enough. He was thrown to the ground in a tangle of limbs, the taste of ash and defeat in his mouth.

There was a heavy thudding, a pounding like a pulse. Voran wondered if it was his own heartbeat — or the spear-butt salute of D'Shael warriors for his adversary.

Tricks! Tricks and witchery! Voran's blood was raging, his anger blinding, and he lunged from a crouch, fast as a rock-lion, hitting Kherin hard. He bore him back and down, but even as his hands clawed for the throat, Kherin's knees drove up and straightened, the explosive power lifting Voran and sending him up and over in a somersault. He fell hard, the breath driven from his lungs This time, although he tried, Voran could not get immediately to his feet. Coughing and wheezing, he fought for breath. Kherin stood over him, straddling him, looking down at him, and there was a sword in his hand.

Challenge, even if not so stated, is to the death. There is no defeat for D'Shael, only the cleansing of honor in the Sun Fires of death. In the eternity between heartbeat and heartbeat, a thousand confused thoughts swarmed in Voran's mind — regrets, primarily, for Arun's grief. For Rythian's, also. For Arun would have to challenge Kherin, and Kherin was Rythian's hearthkin.

"No," Kherin said. "I kill only my enemies."

And Voran's own sword was thrust quivering into the hard earth a handsbreadth from his head. Not the D'Shael way, but there was a buzz of approval from the assembled Warband. It continued even after Arun had given Kherin a nod of acknowledgement and thanks, then dragged Voran to his feet and hauled him to the river to wash off the dust and ashes of defeat. Later it was noticed that Voran came back not only clean, but with more bruises than Kherin had given him.

Kherin also went to the river to wash himself off. He returned to find the Sun Stallion mounted and holding out Llynivar's reins.

"My thanks for his life," Rythian said quietly. He was starkly pale, but there was a wryly humorous quirk to his mouth. "I hope you won't have cause to regret it before he finally sees sense. There is no real malice in him."

"I know," Kherin said, taking the reins and swinging into the saddle. But there had been something inside that fiery head that should not be. Kherin had Read him as the man lay defeated and found an insidious dark thread running through the essential pattern of him. Voran was an uncomplicated mixture of fierce loyalty and devotion. His was a basically cheerful nature. It seemed likely that his unreasoning hatred for Kherin was tied in with the dark weaving.

So Kherin drew free the dark thread, letting it loose to rebound on the weaver. He had a good idea of where it went.

The pace Rythian set was a fast one, towards the distant Tylosian border and the first of the caravans. Behind them, at the battlefield, rose the smoke of Surni funeral pyres as the survivors gave their dead their dues.

As before, Kherin rode beside Kardan. The Elder told Kherin that although the warriors were surprised at Kherin's mercy, they generally approved of it. Voran was well liked, and they were too few to lose any warriors. Kherin was pleased as well. Although there had been no calculation to the gesture, it brought him that much closer to his ultimate goal of leading an attack into Tylos. So too had his work with the wounded. Men do not forget the healing hand.

At noon the Warband paused briefly to change mounts. Scouts, who had been ranging forward, came back reporting the evening's campsite was secure with no sign of enemies' tracks. Rythian heard the scouts' reports but spoke little to them. That was not his way, and Kherin gave the Sun Stallion a hard look. Rythian sat straight-backed in his saddle, his bandages marked with dust and sweat, but his color was high under the travel-dirt.

"Dari should —" Kherin began.

"Say nothing yet," Kardan interrupted quietly. "After all, a little fever's to be expected. In any case, there's nothing that can be done until we reach the night camp."

When they finally reached the place it was clear that Rythian had more than a little fever. He was barely conscious, slumping in his saddle. Kardan plucked him from it as if he was a child and laid him on the grass. Kherin knelt beside him, pouring water from his flask onto a cloth and wiping the dust from Rythian's face. Arun joined them and handed over another flask while Voran hung back, then turned and walked away.

Kherin gave Arun a quick smile of thanks while the injured man drank thirstily. Over Arun's shoulder Kherin could see Voran organising the setting up of the Sun Stallion's tent.

"This should not be," Dari snapped, pushing between them to lay her hand on Rythian's forehead. "It comes too swift and hard. The wound was clean, I'm sure of it."

"I'm all right," Rythian said, trying to shove them aside. "Let me up."

He was ignored.

"It was clean," Kherin said, "but —"

"But what?" Kardan demanded.

Kherin did not answer immediately. He closed his eyes and tried yet again to reach into Rythian, to find the source of the fever. The shields flared strongly, keeping him out, but through their heat-haze shimmer he could See an edged shadow. "There's a piece of metal in him. Deep. In his back, by the shoulderblade and working beneath it. It will have to be cut out before it kills him."

For a moment there was a stunned silence, then: "You cannot know that!" Dari hissed and thrust him away. "Didn't you dress his wound, before Voran challenged you? What have you done to him?"

"He's done nothing to me!" Rythian got an elbow beneath him and half-sat up.

"Why would Kherin do anything to him?" Kardan barked, easing him back down. "The man has healing in his hands as Myra has."

"Then why hasn't he healed Rythian?" Dari demanded.

"I've tried! I have not —"

Kardan gave a snort of impatience. "If Kherin says there's a shard in his back, there's a chance there might well be a shard in his back. You think it might be an infection, no matter the source. So do something about it, both of you!"

Despite Rythian's cursing protest, Kardan lifted him over onto his belly, held him there with one massive hand while Kherin and Arun hovered anxiously. As white now as he had been flushed, Rythian lay still; his eyes were closed but he was far from unconscious.

With a glare for Kherin, Dari cut away the bandages, gently baring the wound. It was raw-looking, but not inflamed. In fact, it looked to be healing well.

"No infection," she said grimly. "Which leaves only poison — or worse."

"It is there," Kherin insisted. "By Her Sacred Name, I swear it! Cut and you will see, Dari."

"I will not," she snorted. "Another wound for a man already fevered and weakened by bloodloss — and the Lady knows what else? It is healing clean and sound. I will not put him to further risk, especially on your word!"

"Why do you hate me?" Kherin asked quietly. "What have I done to you?"

"Nothing. Yet. But the Hooded One has Seen." Dari stood up. "I will bring him a potion for the fever."

"Kardan," Kherin turned to his one ally. "It must be cut from him!"

"No one but Dari has that skill," the Elder said.

"What is to be done, then?"

"Done?" It was a croak from the man between them. Rythian struggled up onto his good elbow again. "Nothing! I'm all right! All I need is a little rest!"

"Your tent and bed are ready, 'Thian," Voran interrupted.

"The Sun bless you for that, boy," Kardan said. "Hear that? You'll rest while Trail Council and Priestess talk," Kardan said. "Kherin, can you do nothing for him? If you have aided the others, then surely you can help him?"

"I will do all that I can, I swear it, but the metal must be taken out."

"Fire take it, stop talking over me!" Rythian demanded weakly.

"Hush," Kardan said. "We'll see how you are in the morning."

"There's nothing wrong with me!" Rythian flared. "It's just a cut! What of the others? The ones who are truly injured? Arun, tell me!"

"Doing well enough. All four of them are," Arun said. "Better than you, that's for certain. Dari, Uncle, maybe Rythian should go back to Hold and Myra for healing." Unfortunately, his commonsense statement triggered a fever-fueled explosion of temper that few would have credited from Rythian Lyre'son. But it was short-lived and his attempt to stand up sent him into unconsciousness.

Arun carefully scooped him up, meeting Kherin's eyes as he straightened. "Shall we share the night-watch?" he asked quietly.

Kherin nodded. "That would be best, I think."

"You get him settled, then, while Voran and I see to the horses. We'll bring our meals and yours when we are done." Arun carried Rythian's limp body into the tent.

But only Arun returned, carrying a small cauldron of steaming stew and three bowls. Voran had elected to eat his meal outside the tent and keep out unwanted visitors. One bowl was filled and set aside for Rythian, Arun poured stew into the other two bowls and held one out to Kherin. "So, tell me," he said with a singularly sweet and innocent smile, "this fighting with the two swords, is that the way of it in your land?"

"Yes," Kherin replied gravely. It was clear that Arun's intent was to get as much information as possible from him in friendly conversation. Kherin had no quarrel with that — could understand and sympathise, but he did not intend to let him know too much. It was not easy; Kherin liked the man and the contrasts within him, appreciated the cool logic and ice-cold relentlessness that was above and around the deep fire that was his love for Voran, and the quieter warmth that was for Rythian. Winter Wolf was a true naming. At the same time Kherin acknowledged that this was not the time to tell of what he had found in Voran's mind. Likely Arun would neither believe nor truly understand.

However, in one matter they were in perfect accord: Rythian must return to the Summer Hold.

Hours later, Kardan entered the Sun Stallion's tent, coming from the Council meeting. He sank to his knees beside the fire basket and let out his breath in a gusty sigh.

"Fetch me ale," Kardan told Kherin. "I'm dry as ash." Kardan's eyes were focused on the bed, and the restless figure that turned and muttered. Kherin brought the ale. Kardan swallowed a few welcome mouthfuls. "I saw Voran outside. He told me that Rythian is worsening," the Elder went on gloomily.

"As you see," Kherin said quietly. "Each bout of fever lasts longer and leaves him weaker."

"He should not go on with the Warband," Arun said.

"We all know that!" the Elder snorted. "Except him. Luckily it seems that the border tribes aren't inclined to be troublesome —"

"Luckily?" Kherin interrupted grimly. "Luck has nothing to do with it. He won us that at the slaughter-place, and maybe that's part of his trouble. Arun has told me none among the Brethren or the other warriors blame him for the horses. What of the Council?"

"None there, either. The victory of so few over so many has had a way of rearranging men's views of such things. Doubly so since we lost no lives. No one blames him — he only blames himself."

Which was unanswerably true.

"I have done all I can and it is not enough," Kherin said quietly. "Ordinarily I should be able to banish the fever, drive out the poison and heal. But not this time." He stared into the glowing charcoal, frowning. "His shields are very strong — I can't break past the barriers to help his body heal itself. Perhaps Myra can reach through where I cannot. Therefore he must go to her and soon, before he's too weak to ride. What has the Council decided?"

"The Council is divided three and three. The Priestess says he should go."

"So be it," Kherin said with finality, drawing on his authority as the Sun Stallion's hearthbrother. "He goes to Hold. I'll ready him for the journey. We leave at first light."

"But not alone. You'll need one or two at the least to ride with you."

"Arun, by choice," Kherin said with a glimmer of a smile at the SwordBrother, "even if it means Voran and dealing with his temper every step of the way."

"We have already discussed it," Arun agreed.

Kardan drained his ale. "Make your packs ready for the dawn," he said. "There'll be no dissenters in Council."

"What are you doing?" Rythian asked suddenly.

Kherin glanced round, knotting the last thong tight on his bedroll. "I am preparing to ride."

Rythian struggled to sit up, frowning. "You're going somewhere?"

"We are going to the Summer Hold," Kherin said, sitting back on his heels. "We ride very soon, now. At sunrise, with Arun and Voran."

The sea-blue eyes, dark in the fitful lamplight, burned with anger and fever. "By whose word? I gave no —"

"Your wound has turned sick. You cannot lead the warriors until you are fit. You should rest. It will not be an easy journey."

"It will not be a journey at all. Arun!"

The SwordBrother came into the tent, but only to pick up the fastened packs.

"Send for Kardan and Mettan. And the Council. I will not be packed off like some unwanted child!"

Arun slung the packs over his shoulder and knelt beside Rythian. "Fevered again," he said over his shoulder to Kherin.

"I'm not raving, Fire take you!"

"No, 'Thian, but you're not in your wits either. It's no good you railing at me or Kherin. You need better care than we can give. If it were one of us, you'd do the same. In fact, you'd have acted sooner. Kherin, is there any of the sleeping draught left? Drink this, 'Thian, and sleep." By speed and sleight of hand he got Rythian to swallow some of the mixture. He glanced wryly at Kherin. "I've had practice enough with Voran," he said softly. "Everything is ready bar your horses. We thought you'd want to see to them yourself."

"My thanks, I would." Kherin slipped silently from the tent, and Arun intercepted the cup as Rythian pushed it away.

"Finish it," he commanded. "'Thian, see sense, will you? I don't need another fool to look out for. Voran's subdued for now, but it's all I can handle persuading him not to stick a knife between Kherin's ribs. If you start giving me grief as well —"

"Arun, I'm Sun Stallion," Rythian protested. "I can't leave the Warband!"

"You have no choice," Arun told him, not without sympathy. He took the cloth from the bowl beside the bed and laid it across Rythian's brow. "'Thian, this is not a time to argue. Kherin rides with you and will stay with you at the Hold. 'Ran and I will go with you and return; the Warband will be less by two warriors, no more."

"One of which is Sun Stallion."

"Who is wounded and in need of healing," Arun said unanswerably. "As for Kherin, you know for yourself that he's best under your eye. I don't want him with the Warband, 'Thian, not even in Kardan's care. He is dividing us. Some think him a gift of the Goddess because he took away their pain and eased their wounds, others still talk of moon-mage and sorcery."

"He fought as well as any against the Surni."

"Oh, he is a warrior, right enough, and he understands honor. But Voran has another view of him, and if there is another challenge Kherin might not be inclined to let him live. You know what would come of that."

Rythian's brow creased, and he closed his eyes. "When are we going to be able to beat sense into that brainless red skull?" he muttered.

"Maybe in another fifteen years. 'Thian, I ask you, keep Kherin with you at the Summer Hold while you heal. I can't ride herd on Voran all the time. Hopefully if Kherin is out of his sight for a while, he'll cool down and find some acceptance. Kherin should stay with you. For my Brother's sake?" Arun held his breath. It had seemed a good argument when he had first thought of it, and it had the benefit of being mostly true.

Rythian's blue eyes, disconcertingly brilliant and glittering, fastened on Arun's face like spearpoints. "Kherin will not harm Voran." It was said with utter conviction.

"You'll take him home? Keep them both safe?"

Rythian blinked, the brightness of his eyes that of fever, nothing else. "Yes," he said, and then, "Kherin's always safe. In Her Hand." Rythian fell back asleep almost immediately. Arun sang a silent praisesong.

Rythian was fenced about by fire. He did not fear the flames, but the barrier angered him. In one direction lay the Tylosian caravans, in another the Summer Hold. In a third was the soaring height of the GodStone, its crest alight in the rising sun. There was a choice to be made. He wanted to ride on to the caravans, but commonsense told him Arun and Kherin were right. If he returned to Hold he would heal and be ready to ride the wartrail again. But the GodStone pulled at him — he needed to go there, had to go there. The urge was as stubborn as a rock. Rythian dug in his heels and refused. Duty to his people dictated a return to Hold. No other path would be taken.

A monstrous rage swept over him, coming not from within, but from somewhere beyond his Sight. It seared with the intensity of a forge-fire, pushing him towards the distant Stone. But he would not be driven, though the flesh was scorched from his bones and his being crumbled to ash. He would not be driven. His choice, his decision. His world dissolved in fire and agony.

The trip back to Summer Hold was as bad as Kherin feared. The fever that burned in Rythian grew worse daily. Yet each morning he somehow managed to pull himself into the saddle and stay there against all probability. Arun was an invaluable help, with his calm competence and reassuring manner. Voran took the horses and the trail-scouting as his tasks and avoided Kherin as much as possible.

It took three days — each a small eternity — before the small party came in sight of Summer Hold. Voran reined his horse in beside Arun. "They'll have seen us. We'll hear the Gather Horn soon."

Arun nodded and glanced across at Rythian slumped over Zaan's neck, staying in the saddle by instinct and sheer stubbornness. Arun took a firmer grip on the lead rein and urged the horses on.

The Gather Horn sounded as they passed the mark-stone. Its strident bray even penetrated Rythian's sickness-induced stupor. He straightened in the saddle. "Where — ?" he began huskily.

"You're home," Kherin said. "Be easy."

The news of their arrival preceded them to the Meeting Ground in front of the Sun Hall.

"Let's get him inside," Arun said.

Syth broke from the crowd. "No. Rythian comes to his own hearth," she began, until Nortan Elder blocked her path.

"The Sun Stallion is nursed in the Sun Hall, woman," he said sternly. Rythian registered her presence and objections, tried to pull free.

"Peace, 'Thian," Arun said gently, not letting go. "Kherin, the inner room."

Arun, carrying Rythian and with Kherin beside him, went into the dimness of the unlit hall, while Voran saw to the horses. The inner room, at the rear of the main hall, was less imposing and better suited as a living quarters. Arun eased Rythian onto the heaped furs of the wide bedplace. They stripped Rythian of boots and breeches, and were sponging him off when the Middle Priestess arrived. Kherin drew back a little to give her space, but she gestured him forward to help turn Rythian for her examination.

"Who has had the care of his wound?" she asked as she carefully removed the bandages.

"Dari, primarily," Arun said. "And myself and Kherin — when Rythian would let us. As soon as he turned sick, we brought him here."

Myra examined the wound gently. "It looks well enough; still there is something..."

"A shard of metal," Kherin said quietly. "It has worked its way beneath the shoulder blade. There is infection around it."

Arun nodded. "Dari says the wound is healing clean, but fever like this doesn't come from a clean wound."

"I'll need but a short time to gather what I need. Bring him to the hearth where the light is better." She hurried away.

Rythian could not walk unaided, although he tried. He was half-carried into the main hall and laid on a raised pallet beside the hearth.

Myra returned, her features calm and composed, wreathed in a herb-scented steam that rose from the cauldron she carried. Her presence steadied Rythian. Then his eyes caught a movement behind her and he focused on the Hooded One. There was an expression of grim satisfaction on the old, strangely twisted face. Rythian could read her thought as clearly as if she had spoken aloud. *Thus are all proud men brought low, to come as errant children to the Mother's knee...*

But it was not only the Third Priestess who looked out from under the hood, but Chiera, the woman, who hated him as well. Night-shadows lay about her like a cloak, the dark sterility of her an affront to his maleness. From somewhere Rythian found the strength to push Myra aside. "Out!" Rythian commanded the Third Priestess, pushing himself up on his good arm. "You have no place here. Get out."

"'Thian, hush." Myra reached to him. "Be still. Of course the Third Priestess must be here for you."

Rage flared fierce as pain. "Chiera, get out, and take your darkness with you! I want no enemy close to me!"

"In none of Her guises is the Lady your enemy," Myra told him. But his eyes were still on the contemptuous face of the Hooded One. He could see himself mirrored there — all brute male strength humbled and awaiting Her mercy.

"Out!" he demanded the Third Priestess again. "Get your malice out of the Sun Hall, Chiera Gatre'sdaughter! Keep your gall in your own belly!" And he used his will to drive her back towards the doors, her face slack with shock. "I will not have your darkness in here! Get out of the Sun, Shadow-Woman!"

"Be still." Another face filled his vision with compassionate night-blue eyes. Rythian did not see the dark shape creep out of the Hall, one leg dragging in a limp.

"Be still, brother." Kherin's hands were on Rythian's shoulders, holding him. "There are no enemies here." The soothing accuracy of Kherin's statement settled Rythian. He let his eyes close, his body slacken, trusting in his hearthbrother's strength. Careful hands turned him to lie on his stomach.

"We must be swift," Myra said. "I will need to cut deep to find the infection, but I think he is too weak to struggle over-much. Even so, you and Arun must hold him still." She washed the wound with an infusion of herbs and took up the knife.

Kherin felt Rythian shudder as the blade touched his skin. He tightened his hold with both hand and mind. Although Rythian's mental shield was like a glowing furnace, Kherin was able to channel most of the pain away from Rythian.

The priestess reopened the new-healed gash, wiping away the blood that welled out. She probed deep into the exposed muscle.

Kherin caught her eye. "Deeper," he said quietly. "Beneath and against the bone." He felt when the knife point touched the area, and caught his breath at the sharp stab of pain as the splinter moved.

Myra made a small sound of triumph as pus abruptly welled up, thick and curdled. Something shifted again under the pressure of the knife. She reached for a pair of fine tongs, inserted them and after a breath-held moment, slowly drew out a finger-length sliver of jagged metal.

"Mother of Mares," Arun whispered sickly. "He had that in him? Why isn't he dead?"

"The Lady is merciful," Myra murmured, eyeing Kherin sharply as he drew a ragged breath. "Lift him a little towards the light, my sons, and let the poison flow out."

Rythian's eyes were part open, but blank and unseeing; he was a dead-weight in Kherin's arms. Blood, streaked with the thick pus of the infection, pulsed from the wound as Myra kneaded the flesh around it. The scent of the healer's herbs did little to mask the stench of putrid infection. Arun was no stranger to wounds; still, he was the color of whey by the time Myra pronounced the wound clean.

Kherin's attention was fully on Rythian, so he did not see the glowing blade Myra took from the coals. He only became aware of it was when the unexpected agony of the cautery seared into his own nerves; he gasped with the shock of it.

"Steady," Arun said, his hand on top of Kherin's. "I'll take him."

Myra bound pads thick with salve on top of the wound, bandaging the whole with strips of soft linen. When she was finished, Arun carried Rythian back to the inner room.

Kherin did not follow. His knees were none too sure. He sat down abruptly beside the hearth, using hard-won discipline to regain his composure. A hand touched his shoulder, and he looked up into Myra's serene, wise eyes.

"My Son, is it well with you?"

"Yes, Mother." He answered her in the same manner, priest to priestess. "I thank you."

"Drink," she said, and gave him the cup. Honey-sweet, fiery and strong, the spirit ran warm into his veins. "That was well done, Kherin." She gave his name a slight lilting that also made it an endearment. "You were right about the broken blade in Rythian's wound; we must speak together more on that later, and on the way you took away his pain. For now, your hearth requires you."

"I should stay with Rythian."

"I will stay with him. Go to your hearth," she repeated. "Tell them that Rythian will be well. They will need that word. And you," she said, smiling at Arun who had come up behind them, "go to your Brother. He needs to know this as well."

Syth met Kherin at the door, her eyes wide with fear — and hope. "He will be well," Kherin said quickly.

"Thanks be to the Goddess," Syth breathed. "Alais, Emre — you heard? Come inside, hearthbrother, and eat."

There was a dear familiarity about the place and the people that struck Kherin's heart. The novelty of the feeling of homecoming in this place so intrigued him that at first he did not realise that Syth had seated him in what had been Rythian's place. When he did, and would have moved, Alais laid a hand on his arm.

"Is this not a good enough place for you, hearthbrother? Or is the food not to your liking?"

"This..." Suddenly his knowledge of D'Shael was barely adequate. "This is..."

Syth shook her head. "Rythian is Sun Stallion now. His hearth is the Sun Hall. He is hearthbrother here, yes, but this hearth is no longer his responsibility. You are most senior of the men at this hearth, Kherin, therefore this is your place."

Kherin sat in confusion, his food cooling before him. It was irrefutable logic, save that he was D'Shael only by adoption. It would appear that made no difference. "Is this the wish of all here?" he asked, needing to be sure.

"It is," Syth smiled; Alais nodded, and Emre gave him a dimpling glance beneath her lashes. Kherin looked at the children.

Ronan would not meet his eyes, but said gruffly: "It is."

Dreyen, with a wide sunny grin, announced: "You are my hearthsire as well as hearthbrother now. That means twice as many stories!"

Kherin could not remember knowing a family. He was a child of the Goddess, to whom all people were as brothers and sisters. To find a close family at this point in his life was a warming, painful, good feeling. He was not entirely sure what his new status entailed, but no doubt the women would enlighten him as it became necessary.

As the evening continued, it seemed his changed status little altered the evening routine. He was still required to tell Dreyen and Fyra their favorite stories; Ronan wanted details of the campaign and battle; the women needed reassurance about Rythian.

The evening grew late, and the children were abed, and he started to go to the place that had been his.

Emre caught his eye.

The Man of the Hearth had other duties to be fulfilled.

The room the hearthsisters shared when Rythian was absent was the largest room beside the hearthroom. He had been here only once before, during the birthing of Emre's twins. It was different now, warm and sweet with woman-scent, lit by lamplight. Emre was waiting for him, the great fur spread covering her to the waist, her unbound hair over her breasts.

"We do not know the customs of your country, hearthbrother, but it is the way of the D'Shael for a woman to choose what man she takes to her." She held the covers back for him.

He came into the bed, shivering a little at the sweet nearness of her. It had been a long time since he had been with a woman. Her warmth and scent made his head swim. "It is the custom of my country also, lady," his voice hoarse with the desire rising in him. "I am honored by your choice."

She gave a little gurgle of laughter. "I would have spoken before, but you went away. Oh, Kherin, no more talking. Love me?"

After the first urgency was spent, they both drowsed a while, until the need returned to his loins and she took him to her again. She was honey and wine and fire, taking fierce joy in his strength and potency, meeting his passion with a wildness that equalled his own. He knew her at last for Who She was, the Bride Incarnate, and he did Her worship.

Then she was Emre again, holding his head at her breast, crooning to him. Kherin slept deeply at last.

At dawn, Kherin was back in the Sun Hall. Rythian had come through the night well, and Myra expressed herself satisfied. She packed her things into her basket and checked her patient once more. He was already drowsing. Kherin straightened the furs around Rhythian and looked over at Myra.

"Come, my son," she responded to the question in his eyes. "It is time, and past time, that we talked."

Kherin followed her out to the hearth, where she paused, sighed, and sat down. "It must be here, I suppose, since someone must remain within call. Let us be plain, Kherin. We both serve the Goddess."

"In all ways and in all things," Kherin agreed softly.

"For a man to be Summoned to Her — that is a thing unknown in these lands. Not even in legend. Is it usual for men to serve Her your homeland? And you; Her Chosen, I am told. What is this title? What does it mean?"

Kherin told her as much as he could of the role of the Chosen, the Sanctuary, and the lesser Mysteries. She listened in silence, only questioning the matters she found unclear.

"And the healing arts?" she said, when he was finished.

"I am not skilled as the Healers in the Sanctuary, but I have some knowledge — such as would serve a warrior."

"It was not warrior-skill that saved Emre," Myra pointed out.

"The Goddess guided me." He could not hold back a small smile. "It was not the first time I have brought young things to birth. Though it was the first time I have helped a woman."

Myra caught her breath on a chuckle. "I see." Then she was serious again. "When you came here, we were not sure you would live. Could not your skills have helped you? Or can you not aid yourself?"

"When I was taken by Tylos, I was drugged. Otherwise I can heal myself, by Her will."

Myra was silent for a moment. Then: "My Mother, the Old One, believes you dangerous."

"Does she not think all men so?"

"Perhaps, but she has the True Seeing. As, I think, do you."

This was deeper water. Kherin said carefully, "A little. Yes."

"How? In the fire, or the smoke? Water or crystal?"

How could he describe it? "When it comes — when She speaks to me... It is like a dream. And a Voice. Mother, forgive me, but this is not mine to speak of."

Myra began to object, but then caught herself back. "We too have our Mysteries, Kherin."

Kherin now felt the tentative touch of her mind, light and probing, as a swordsman tests the guard of another. Kherin smiled and met her probe, turning it easily aside. Myra's eyes widened in surprise.

"The Old One did not tell you," Kherin said aloud. "She cannot Read me. Without my consent, no one can."

"So it seems. Did you know that she is ailing?"

"She is lame now, I saw that much. Is it the joint-ill?"

"No. It came upon her suddenly, the night after the Warband left. I heard her call out, and when I went to her, she was lying awry, half her body paralyzed. She could neither speak nor move for several days."

"That night, she Sent a curse on me," he said slowly. "I warned her of the Goddess' wrath. It seems She was indeed angered."

Myra gazed at him. "You returned curse for curse?"

"That is not how I was taught. But a curse unset rebounds on the sender. That I did. No more."

"Have you any healing knowledge that might ease her, then?"

He shook his head. "It is in Her Hand. We saw such cases in the Sanctuary."

She sighed. "I feared it would be so. What of Rythian? There is something that I cannot explain. I felt it when he first became Sun Stallion, a change in him other than that which comes to a man when he stands for his people before the God. Now when I touch him, try to Look into him, there is this — something. I cannot See past it. Kherin, you are a Seer. As priestess to priest, I ask you — what is happening?"

Invoked thus, he had no choice. He opened himself to any word the Goddess might wish to Speak, but all that came into his mind was a tale he had heard in childhood. "Once it was that the Goddess heard the prayer of a young mother for her child, which was sickly and like to die, and She foresaw a great future for the infant. In the guise of a wetnurse, She came and tended the child. Each night, when the mother slept, She would lay the babe in the heart of the fire — and each night, a little more of his mortality was burned away..."

Myra stopped him with a gesture, eyes wide. "Enough. What will become of Rythian? This is not the hand of the Lady on him!"

"I don't know." Kherin did not prevaricate. "All I can say is there is nothing of Darkness there."

"The Old One has told me her Seeing," Myra whispered. "The Sun Stallion fallen, trampled in the dust..."

"I have Seen it, too. But not by my hand, nor by my will. I swear by Her whom we both serve. But the events leading to — and from — that Seeing are still hidden. It may be other than it seems."

"May She grant it so."

Chapter Twelve

There was a constant stream of visitors to the Sun Hall the next day. Hold Council arrived, held a consultation, and went away without seeing the Sun Stallion. LyDia brought a cooling sherbet for him, and left it with Kherin. Dreyen and Shenchan came and had to be evicted. The Old One came to the door of the Sun Hall, but did not enter. She stopped at the threshold with a sharp gasp of pain and anger mixed, turned and hobbled away.

Kherin was grateful for that. Crippled she might be, but she was still a formidable enemy.

By late morning Rythian was restless and muttering. Kherin was glad to hear Arun's step outside.

"I've brought fresh water," the Sword Brother said, setting down the pitcher. He noticed the sherbet; the smell of it made his eyes widen. "One of Myra's brews?"

"No. LyDia. I think she did the best she could without the right kinds of fruit." Kherin poured a cup and held it out.

Arun tasted it, coughed, and wiped his eyes. "Ae-Shae! It's not fit for an invalid, but I'll not let it go to waste."

Kherin gave him a half-smile. "I thought it had fermented a little. Do you leave to return to the Warband now?"

"Yes. We're come to say our farewells. Kherin, I thank you for the care you've given 'Thian. Next to Voran there is no one I love more." Arun hesitated, his grey-eyed gaze as direct as a spear-thrust. "Part of me wants to trust you as he does, part of me cannot," he said.

Kherin nodded. "I understand," he said. "Time will show you the truth of it. I would ask one thing of you both," he went on as Voran came in with Myra on his heels. "Put no trust at all in Tylos."

"None is given." Unexpectedly Arun gave him a swift hug while Voran gave him a slap on the shoulder. "Listen, you'd best know this. Rythian is a very bad convalescent."

"Emre has already told me."

"Did she tell you she was once driven to box his ears?"

"No, but Syth did. Take care of yourselves. Rythian will have need of you both."

"Maybe," said Voran, meeting his eyes with a straight stare, "Just maybe — I was wrong about you."

Then they were gone and Kherin noticed the grimness on Myra's face for the first time. "What is it?"

"The Hooded One came to me complaining you have Warded the Sun Hall against her."

"What? I have done no such thing!"

"I know. But someone has, and it isn't either of us. Go look at the threshold. Use your Inner Sight."

Kherin got no further than the door of the room. He could See the flames that stretched from doorpost to doorpost in a shimmering curtain. He had not Seen nor sensed it in his comings and goings, so it was set there against one person only.

"Rythian did this," he whispered.

"Who else? I can't lift it. It is like the barriers around him..."

"The Hand of The God is strong on him."

"It is like to scorch him to death before it's done!," Myra snapped. "Kherin, I have never encountered anything like this, nor heard of it in legend! What are we to do?"

"What we are doing. Give him what strength and healing we can, despite his shields. Otherwise I am as lost in this as you are."

It was late that night before Kherin could leave to go to his hearth. Rythian was increasingly restless and Kherin was loath to leave him. Myra had commanded him, using her Goddess-given authority, so he had obeyed. This time Alais was waiting for him in the furs. He was not surprised.

Still he didn't expect to find Syth waiting for him in the big bed on the next night. Unlike the others, she was dressed in a long night-robe, and her hair fell over her shoulders like liquid gold, but there was nothing of invitation about her. She was here, he guessed, because she felt it was his right. She was not to know that he could no more lie with an unwilling woman than fly.

He made no move to take off his boots or breeches, but instead sat on the edge of the bed and reached for her hand. "Syth," he said quietly, "hearth sister, there is no need for this."

"You are the man of this hearth," she said. "We chose you, my sisters and I."

"And I am honored by your choice."

"You do not desire me, perhaps."

He was touched by the odd mixture of pride and hope in her voice. "Any man would desire you, my sister. And I am a man."

She looked at him under her lashes, and a smile dimpled her mouth for a moment. "Yes. Emre and 'Lais told me."

"So, then. But there is that in you that does not want me, that is still wed to Rythian whatever law and custom say to the contrary. Syth, you are my sister, and I am your brother. That is a great thing, and unless you require it of me, I ask for nothing more."

Her hand tightened on his then, her head bowed. "Tell me again he will recover."

He could have given merely the reassurance that she had asked for, but he knew that she needed more. "It is not in his fate to die in bed, my sister."

"What Sun Stallion ever has?" she said bitterly. "Oh, Goddess, was not my mother's grief enough?"

The Sight gave Kherin understanding and a small foreknowledge. "Your father was Sun Stallion, but your mother never bore him another child to lessen the pain. May that which will one day wax within your womb bring you joy."

She caught her breath, staring at him. "Is that Long Sight?"

He nodded. "Within a year." Syth let out a long sigh and he held her close, brother to sister. She slept that night in his arms like a tired child. He could guess her anxiety had kept her from her rest until now.

Myra met him on the porch of the Sun Hall at dawn. She was displeased, he saw that in the set of her mouth.

"Rythian spent a good night with no fever to speak of," she answered his unspoken question. "In fact, he's feeling frisky as a colt. I am to summon the Hold Council for him, so we are not needed this morning, my son. Go hunting. Zaan and Llynivar will relish the exercise, and so will you."

Hold Council heard their Sun Stallion tell of the battle without interruption. They did not like what they were told. Rythian heard their mutters as they left. Well, it had been years since most of them had ridden to war. They forgot what it was like.

Rythian turned restlessly and turned again. The soft furs itched his skin. The dressing over the wound chafed, and when he inadvertently shifted that shoulder, a twinge of sharp pain reminded him why it was strapped tight. But he could not lie still. It was too warm, and the scents of the herbs used in Myra's potions and unguents were too thick and cloying.

Awkwardly, wincing, he sat up, fumbling the covers away with his free hand. It was unwise, he knew that, but if he could breathe clean air, feel the wind fresh on his face, it would do him more good than a wagon-load of potions.

His legs did not want to hold him. With barely the strength of an hour-old foal, he used whatever came to hand to support himself as he edged to the door, and through it into the hearth-lit dimness of the Sun Hall. Its very spaciousness made it seem more airy, but he wanted to feel sun on his skin, needed it with an intensity that was more than hunger.

The doors might as well have been on the other side of the plains; his legs would not carry him that far. Well, if nothing else, he could sit at the hearth and have a change of scenery — at least until his nurse-mares came back. The meeting with Hold Council had tired him more than he'd thought, but at least he was free of the fever-dreams that had haunted him. Dreams of being hunted, herded, driven towards a hidden goal; he had fought every step of the way —

The outer door swung open and a figure stood silhouetted against the noonday brilliance. Rythian knew him at once; that stag-proud bearing could belong to no one but his hearthbrother.

"Good," he said. "Kherin, help me up."

Kherin came to his side and got him on his feet again. "You should be in your bed," he stated mildly, starting to steer him back towards the inner room.

"Not that way," Rythian snapped. "I want out of this place."

Kherin halted. "That is not permitted yet."

"Permitted? Who denies me? I am Sun Stallion, and I say I will go out!" Fever, weakness, and anger at that weakness all combined to fuel Rythian's sudden temper. Not for the first time, Kherin stood firm.

"When Myra says you are fit you can go out. Not until then." He had no trouble supporting Rythian. It was an added irritant to one who expected his body to answer the demands he made upon it. He was unused to being handled and manipulated like a fractious child.

"I need to breathe, damn it! I am stifled in here!"

"If the inner room is too confining, I can bring your bed out to the hearth," Kherin's stubbornness matched his own. "But without the Priestess' word, you cannot go outside."

"Out onto the porch. No further." He should not have to plead, but when he tried using his will to force Kherin to agree, he came up against a rock wall.

"Ah, but it is I who would have to answer if you grew chilled. The wind is keen today."

"The wind..." He could smell it on Kherin, the scents of fresh air and grass and the good clean smell of horse. "You've been hunting."

"Zaan needed the exercise. How about if I open the doors and you sit here in the sun?"

Rhythian knew it was the best he could get just now, and nodded his agreement.

Kherin propped the doors open and helped Rythian settled into a patch of warmth where the sun lay strongest. After fetching an armful of rugs and cushions to prop Rythian comfortably, Kherin sat down beside him, cross-legged.

The sun's heat sank into Rythian and he let out a long sigh of relief. He could see the dust of the street, the rich green of grass, and the blue sky with small racing clouds. He sniffed the cool air like an animal testing scent. It made him want to throw off the furs, to leave the Hold, to race with the wind. Suddenly he hated the lithe, fit strength of the Southerner, envied his freedom to move, run, ride — go where he would, whenever he would.

"How long," Rythian burst out, "am I to be caged in here?"

Rythian Lyre'son, what do you know of cages?

The words in Rythian's head were as clear as if Kherin had spoken them, but the man's lips hadn't moved. Kherin wasn't even looking at Rythian; his eyes were focused at some distant place only he could see. A vision came to Rythian's mind of silk-draped slave-wagons, with elegant filigree-work disguising the cage's secure bars. Rythian knew it was Hasoe's slave-wagons, although he had never seen them. Hands gripped white-knuckled at the unyielding metal — the same hands that now lay loose and open on Kherin's knees.

The clarity of the Seeing startled Rythian. Never had he so clearly shared a vision before. With others, there had been shadowy glimpses, but nothing like this. And with the vision came feelings of frustration, a feeling of still being a captive, the harsh longing of a prisoned hawk for freedom.

"Nothing holds you here." It came out more roughly than Rythian intended. "You're free to go where you will."

Kherin was as still as a statue in copper and bronze. "If that were so — even if that were so..." Kherin turned his head and the dark blue eyes looked into Rythian's. "When you are healed, Rythian, you will ride out, go where you will — all this wide country is home to you. But I can never go home."

The stark statement brought with it a fleeting vision of sunlight blindingly bright on white stone; towering buildings, soaring and elegant and astonishing; a land harsh, unforgiving, but beautiful. The vision was gone before Rythian could properly register it, leaving behind a sense of aching emptiness and loss. He found himself staring dazedly at the expressionless face of his hearthbrother, and all he could say was: "Why not?"

"You say your God does not speak to you."

"No, of course not. Nor to any that I know of, save in ancient tales."

"The Goddess has told me that Khassan is closed to me." Kherin's eyes flinched closed, briefly, in a reflex of pain.

Was that why Kherin had only once tried to leave? Rythian wondered; *was it because he had nowhere else to go?*

"I waited on Her word," Kherin said softly. "And so I was answered."

There was no bitterness in his voice, only a fatalistic acceptance of the fact and the pain.

"You are my hearthbrother," Rythian said awkwardly, his own temporary sufferings seeming trivial. "You have a home here now."

"I know — and it is truly a home." Still an unspoken 'but...' hung between them.

That night Rythian's fever returned, burning more fiercely. Myra came, but could not ease it; neither could Kherin help. The wall of fire around Rythian was burning high; they could not reach through it. It seemed to Kherin that Rythian was battling an unseen foe; what few words they could understand were of refusal, denial. As if Rythian fought for his very soul, for life itself, maybe. Fear such as Kherin had never known caught him by the throat.

"Rythian!" He snatched the man's shoulders, half-lifting him, shaking him. "Damn you, man! Let me in! Let me help you!"

With shocking suddenness, all barriers were gone and Kherin fell into the fever-dream.

They were on a plain, level and golden with ripe grass. Ahead was the GodStone, blazing in the sunlight; behind them was the Grove of the Lady, deep with cool shade. There was a collar around Rythian's neck and from it a golden chain stretched into the distance, seeming to drag the Sun Stallion towards the GodStone. Another chain, of fine silver links, tethered him to the Grove. Racked between the two, Rythian fought for the freedom to pick up something that lay coiled in the grass - a braided rope of grass, grain, the manes of horses, and the long blond hair of his people. A rope that would link him to Hold and Clans.

"He has made his choice!" Kherin shouted. "It is enough — let him be!" He drew a sword he didn't know he was wearing and swung it in a double arc. True Tsithkin steel cut through the chains as if they were silk. Rythian fell to his knees, clutching the Hold-rope. His other hand reached out to Kherin, who dropped his sword to take Rhythian's hand in both of his. "Your choice..." he said softly. In the dream and in reality, Kherin carefully gathered the exhausted man into a gentle embrace, bending his full will on the wound.

Nothing barred him. Kherin wove muscle, flesh and sinew together, making them whole and strong, while Rythian lay in a dreamless, healing sleep.

Drained of energy, Kherin shook himself back to awareness, lifted his head and met Myra's astounded gaze. "He will be well," he whispered, laying the sleeping man down on the furs.

"You have Healed him? Lady be thanked! Kherin, the Gathering of power I felt was — incredible. You must rest. Go to your hearth; I will be here."

Wearily Kherin trudged along the dusty street, seeing little until a flutter of leaf-green silk caught his eye, and a drift of exotic perfume came on the breeze. He had frequently seen LyDia about the Hold, settling into her new life and happy. As was NaLira, who ran and played with as much enthusiasm as any of the D'Shael children, at home among them as if she had known no other way. Since his encounter with Merse, Kherin had seen little of the man, save at a distance. Which was no surprise.

Now LyDia approached him with a smile. "I greet you, Prince." Her D'Shael was fluent, if heavily accented. She alone persisted in using his title. From her, he accepted it.

"How fare my hearthbrothers?" she asked.

"Lady, we are both well. And you?"

He hardly needed to ask — she had found a new beauty with the Shi'R'Laen, and the pale exquisite courtesan of Tylos was glossed with sun and happiness.

"I am content," she said simply. "Syre has made me most welcome. We are sisters in truth." LyDia hesitated a moment before continuing. "Prince, I would speak to the Sun Stallion."

"He is sleeping, Lady. Perhaps tomorrow?"

"Then I will speak to you, as hearthbrother." She glanced around, but the morning was young and few were abroad from their hearths. "When word came to the Isle, asking for one to go with the Tribute, and pledging gold in return, our Elders took the omens. When the Goddess made Her Will plain, I was chosen to serve Her in this matter, though we did not know what form this service might take. Hasoe had another idea. I was to be his tool among the D'Shael, his eyes and ears. And not I alone."

"Merse." Kherin did not have to guess.

"Just so. But we are no longer Tylosian. We are D'Shael. Shall we betray our new family for those who saw us only as tools, not caring if we lived or died?"

From the corner of his eye, Kherin saw a figure at the edge of the street. He would have had to be blind not to have seen the changes in Merse. Even the hearthsisters, while not forgiving him, had acknowledged the change in him. Gone was the painted pleasure-boy. In his place was, to all appearances, a young D'Shael. No warrior, certainly, but at the least one who was not afraid to stand in the Eye of the Sun.

"Is this Merse's word, Lady? Or yours alone?"

"We have spoken together on it, Prince. His heart is as mine in this. But because of what has been between you, he has asked me to speak for him. He has changed, Lord Kherin."

Kherin had cause to know Merse's skill in guising. He reached out with his mind to Read the eunuch. Wariness and fear of him were the first things to be found in Merse, but beneath that was an earnest wish to never again be a slave. Kherin frowned. Perhaps Merse's change was more than skin-deep. Time would tell. He beckoned the eunuch closer; Merse approached with a straight spine and his head held high.

"Explain to me how you have changed — and know that I can Read lies in a man's soul," he commanded. "Then tell me what you would wish Rythian to hear."

Merse's chin jutted. "I will not lie," he said in D'Shael. "I know you do not trust me, and have good cause. That was before I — came to understand —" He met Kherin's judgmental gaze without flinching. "I have learned the language of the D'Shael," he went on, " and their customs and way of life. It has changed me." he said. "I don't know how to explain it." For the first time Merse looked down. There was an honest confusion in him, and every word he spoke was the truth.

"After you whipped me, Rythian came back with the Warband and sought me out. I thought he would beat me also, but he didn't. He said you had settled the matter as was your right, and in the Eye of the Sun, it was finished. He told me that his quarrel with me was the using of his name in a lie, and he asked me why I had done it." Merse paused, lifted his head and met Kherin's gaze again. "I told him the truth: that I hated you because Hasoe thought more of you than of me; because you were everything that I was not. He told me I was past the age to act like a spoiled brat, but since I had already been thrashed as a child he would not do the same. He said that I had stained his honor and that in recompense I, more than any other, must live in honor from that time on. That I must hold his honor above my own, and if I did not, then I would be spoken against and would be no longer his hearthbrother — or even Shi'R'Laen. I would be driven from the plains. He spoke to me as a warrior to another warrior, Kherin. As a free man to a free man. I truly understand the extent of the wrongs I did to you and to him. I will live my life in honor; I will repay him in this way. I will not go back to the slave I was. In the Eye of the Sun I am Shi'R'Laen."

Every word, every shade of thought, was the truth. The image of the Sun Stallion was treasured in the eunuch's mind, a glowing figure close to godhood, all but worshipped. Kherin nodded. "Tell me, then, what Rythian should know."

"Hasoe plots against the D'Shael," Merse said. "He has spies and contacts among the Surni and the traders who cross all lands. He seeks an alliance with the Surni; once he has that, he will also control their allies, the tribes of the hills. Then he will move against us. He fears the D'Shael. That is all that I know. Things might have changed in the months since the Tribute was given. But I believe that sooner, or later, one will come to hear what LyDia and I have learned."

"Merse speaks truth, Prince," LyDia said. "Let the Sun Stallion think on what he wishes us to say."

"I will tell Rythian what you have said," Kherin said gravely. "For this warning, Hearthkin, he will surely thank you both."

"He might do more," LyDia said, with a flirt of her lashes. "Myra tells me that Midsummer Festival is tomorrow."

"That is so," Kherin said, not sure of how it was celebrated by the D'Shael. After thanking them again, he walked away, thinking about LyDia's remark. He decided to go back to the Sun Hall to talk to Myra.

"What is Rythian's role at the Midsummer Festival, Mother?"

Myra, blending herbs beside the hearth, gave a snort. "It should be the stallion's role with the mares. But even though you have healed him, I fancy he'll be weak as a new foal for a while. No matter, the Goddess will choose a substitute. Her Rite will take place as it should."

"But without Rythian? Will it not fret him?"

"He won't know what he missed," she said shortly. "This is a women's mystery, and not to be spoken of. What happens after, here in Hold, that's another thing. But he'll not be fit for that, either."

During the ten years of Caier's reign, only two of the Maidens chosen at each Midsummer had conceived by the Sun Stallion. The last Midsummer Maiden gave birth too early to a monster that was stillborn, and she herself had died soon after. Myra had known then that Caier's rule was coming to an end, although she did not know how.

On the eve of the Midsummer, the women gathered in the Sacred Grove for the Goddess to choose one from among the unwed who had not borne a child to be the Year Maiden. Myra had the lots ready in the covered bowl, the single moonstone among the dark river pebbles. One by one, all those eligible drew a stone, both Hold women and Huntresses.

When all had taken the lots and the bowl was empty, Myra lifted her hands in invocation. "Goddess, Great Mother, we Your Daughters await Your choosing." It was the sign for each woman to look at what her closed fist held. There were audible sighs from some — of relief or regret? — and a sudden cry from the group of Huntresses. One of them was staring at the softly-glowing moonstone on her palm.

Kherin, thinking about Midsummer in Khassan, was falling into a doze on his fleece-strewn bed when he heard a voice speaking his name. Or rather, not speaking, for he was alone; the voice was in his head.

It is moonrise. It is time. Come to the Grove. It was no request, but a command.

The moon was at the full, a glowing pearl of light that shed a silvery sheen over the dew-thick grass. The Grove was a dark cluster of trees not far from the lake. Just outside the Grove, Kherin paused for a moment, looking into the trees, into the light-and-shadow, silver and black, that lay within.

This was a place of the Goddess, and forbidden to men, save only the Sun Stallion. Even he entered only when ritual demanded. Kherin, in common with the rest of the D'Shael men, had never been any further than the outer trees. Now, obedient to the summons, he stepped into the darkness.

Unmarked and unseen, the ancient paths drew him inwards. There was no sound of bird or beast, only a sighing murmur, like wind in the highest branches, or surf breaking on a sea-shore. Kherin moved towards it, the sheltering growth brushing his body with cool wet leaves, caressing him, until he was in the heart of the Grove. The glade was filled with women.

Kherin could not tell how many women there were, nor did he immediately recognise any of the shadowed faces but Myra's, though he knew his hearthsisters would be among them. The women were silent, all eyes on him as he crossed the springy turf.

"What is this, Myra?" A voice was raised in anger. "A man comes here who is not the Sun Stallion?"

"No man may defile the Grove," said another. "That is the Law."

Myra took Kherin's hand. "He is here at the Goddess' will." she smiled, and kissed him. On her brow she wore the Full Moon, and a sleeveless white robe fell sheer to her feet.

"Is he so?" This was a strange voice, harsher than any Kherin knew. A woman stood forward, clad in leather and fur, with a knife thrust in her belt. A Huntress. "If he is indeed an entire man, he has no place here. Is he some lover of yours, Myra, and you so besotted that you allow him even the Mysteries? Or are we to return to the Old Ways in truth, and give his blood to the Goddess?"

Kherin read a feral hatred in her eyes. This one would joy in the killing.

"You have been long from the Hold, Velra," Myra said without rebuking. "You do not know of Kherin."

"We know. My sisters and I, we know. The outlander. No D'Shael."

"D'Shael before the Law," came the strong calm voice of Syre, Kardan's sister. "Claimed by the Sun Stallion as hearthkin, and acknowledged by the Council."

"Man's Law — for men!" Velra turned on her like an angry cat. "Ours are the Laws of the Goddess!"

Myra held up a hand. "Do not presume to instruct, Velra Etha'sdaughter! Though you serve the Lady in Her Maiden aspect, it is through me and through my Mother that She speaks." There was a movement behind her, and Kherin made out the hooded figure of the Third Priestess. If any was to speak against him, surely it would be her?

But Chiera remained silent. Kherin looked at Myra. "Lady, may I speak?" She gave assent and he turned to face the Huntress. "Sister, you say truly. My blood is for the Goddess. She made it Hers at my sacring and it is Hers to take again, whenever She chooses. It is also true that I was not born D'Shael. I am of Khassan, Kherin Tyril'son, and she who gave me life was Priestess to the Goddess, the Maiden of her year."

Fists planted on hips, Velra looked him over. "None of which gives you the right to enter the Sacred Grove, outlander."

That won a murmur of agreement from the other Huntresses, but Myra shook her head. "He has the right. In his own country, he is the Chosen One of the Goddess, to speak with Her Voice and do Her bidding as Her mortal Consort. To become for his life-span the Ageless, the Twice-Beloved."

Even this statement, news to most of the women, did not convince Velra. "This is a thing of his country, not of ours."

"The Goddess we serve is the same," Myra said, imperturbable. "And it is She who summoned him here." She spoke with all the authority of the Mistress of the Rite, and not even Velra could argue further. "My Son," she said, turning to him again, "the Maiden awaits."

They parted and she was there, a veil covering her from crown to ankle. He knelt and kissed the bare dew-dappled feet in reverence.

He did not know the form their mystery should take, but the Goddess would guide him. Gently, a priest performing a rite, he stood and lifted the veil. She was none of the women he knew, or had seen before, but there was a familiar look about her, all the same.

She was as tall as he, her hair a cloak of silver bound at the brow by the horned crescent of the Maiden, her naked body as dazzling as the moon.

And she was afraid.

He could read it in her, feel it through her skin as he took her hands. They were cold, and bore calluses from the use of weapons. A Huntress, then. Was that why Velra had spoken out? Because one of her own, perhaps a favoured one, had been chosen?

It was the will of the Goddess.

"Be thou blessed," he said softly, formally. And, formally, touched her lips with his.

For the first moment, it was like kissing a stone. Then the spark and the tinder took flame, and she was fire under the ice. The Goddess in her responded to the God incarnate and there was no more hesitation. It was only when she cried out once, sharply, that he knew that she had been virgin indeed, but neither of them heeded it. The Goddess had them in Her Hand, and if the moon had fallen from the sky, they would not have known or cared.

Kherin woke to find himself alone in the Grove. The moon was westering and the small soft wind of pre-dawn was rustling the tree tops. Someone had covered him with a doeskin cloak against the dewfall. It fell away as he slowly sat up, feeling the weight of mortality again after the divine flight.

Something stirred in the shadows. He was on his feet in a moment, balanced for action, before he realised that nothing could harm him here in Her sacred place. The something emerged, halt and lame, the moonlight glinting on the knife in her hand.

Kherin knelt.

"You do not fear that I will cut your throat, outlander?" Chiera asked harshly. "Perhaps I am going to offer your blood to the Mother, as Velra wished."

"If the Mother requires my blood, it is Hers to take," Kherin said steadily. "I am in Her Hand."

She gave a snort. "Bow your head, then, in thanksgiving to Her. I shall take a lock of your hair, as the ritual demands." He felt the tug as the knife sheared through. "You do not fear that I shall use this to bind you?"

"I think you have found the unwisdom of trying to harm Her Chosen," Kherin said. He got to his feet. "One thing, Mother." He gave her the courtesy title. "The Year Maiden, is it permitted that I know her name?"

Under the shadow of her hood, her eyes glinted at him. "Her name? Why not? She is Rynna, daughter of Lyre."

"Lyre's daughter?" Kherin questioned back. "Rythian's sister?"

"His birthsister."

The next morning Rythian was lounging on the porch of the Sun Hall, basking in the warmth of the sun. The bandaging was gone, and save for a loss of weight, he looked fit and well, as if he had never been wounded. Kherin gave due thanks silently to the Goddess, and a cheerful greeting to his hearthbrother.

"Myra tells me you healed me," Rythian said. "For that I thank you, even if I remember nothing of it."

"No thanks are needed," Kherin smiled. "Come back to the hearth with me, let our hearthsisters see for themselves that you're sound. They'll not believe it otherwise. Can you eat another breakfast?"

"Foolish question."

Side by side, they strolled down the street. Kherin was filled with a contentment he'd never before known. Long ago, in scant periods between campaigns, he had known a shadow of this feeling with Jeztin and Tarvik. But to them, he was always the Prince, the Chosen. Their friend, their leader and comrade, but always set a little apart. With Rythian he was Kherin, companion and hearthbrother, and there was no distance between them. It seemed to Kherin a priceless thing.

There were, of course, many D'Shael who did not trust him. Even now Kherin could feel an occasional hostile stare. But the memory of Voran's parting words warmed him. If that one was coming to see things differently, there was hope that all would. Admittedly some of Voran's hostility was probably augmented by that dark thread of arcane control, but now that taint was gone, the man could reason for himself. For a moment Rythian wondered if he should have said something about that to Voran or Arun. Or maybe now to Rythian, but Kherin decided against it. The hostility between Sun Stallion and the Hooded One was hot enough without adding fuel to the flames. Least said, soonest mended, Kherin decided — especially with Chiera crippled. Then the joyous welcome from their hearthkin was all around them and he put the Hooded One, and her plotting, from his thoughts.

After the second breakfast, Rythian did not stay long at the hearth. The walls irked him, he said, so Kherin and Rythian walked down to the lake. In Kherin's opinion, the water was too cold for swimming; Rythian believed otherwise. He stretched his healed muscles swimming while Kherin was content to watch. The long scar on Rythian's back was fresh-pink, but it would fade soon enough to match the other pale marks on the tanned skin. Certainly it did not trouble the man; he swam with the easy competence of an otter.

Soon they would be able to rejoin the Warband. The thought reminded Kherin that he had not yet passed on LyDia's information, so he called Rythian from the lake. Once the Sun Stallion was on shore, Kherin told him what LyDia had said.

"Do traders come from outside?" Kherin asked Rythian when he finished.

"Once or twice a year. Usually it's Kasha Den and his family. They come through Mygraea to us and then go down to Tylos. There could be Tylosian spies among them," he agreed thoughtfully. "We'll have to decide what we want any spy to know of us, I think."

"Devious," Kherin smiled. "Another thing to consider — perhaps you should lift the barrier you placed against the Hooded One."

"Barrier?" Rythian stared at him blankly. "What barrier?"

"The one you set at the doors of the Sun Hall while you were fevered."

"I don't know —"

"Come on, I'll show you."

And with their arms across each other's shoulders, they walked together up the dusty path from the lake, Rythian protesting his ignorance of any arcane wall.

In the space of a single heartbeat, though, the arcane wall was forgotten as a man stepped out of the shadows beside the Elder Hall to stand in front of them.

"I am Cathan, called Iron Hand, of the Dh'Ryor Clan. I would lead the Shi'R'Laen, by the God's will."

It took Kherin a moment to recognize the formal challenge. He had never witnessed a Challenge; this was the first of Rythian's rule. Shock sent a numbing chill through Kherin, for he knew this moment had been planned. The faction behind the Challenge believed Rythian still weak and unfit, not knowing the extent of his healing. Even so, Rythian's shoulder was untried.

Kherin was afraid that the man who was his friend and hearthbrother could be going to his death.

Before Kherin could move or speak, Rythian strode the little distance to where the Standard was planted in front of the Sun Hall. He set his palm against the wood, turned to face his opponent. "In the Eye of the Sun," Kherin heard the calm voice raised in formal response, " I am the God's choice."

"He has turned from you to me."

"Stand forward, then, and prove your claim. Let the Sun Lord show to all who stands in his favor."

People were shouting, running — the deep bellow of the Gather Horn sounded once, twice, again. Kherin felt as if he moved through a milling vortex, with the Challenge ground at its center. He saw Nortan Elder hurry to Rythian's side, but he could not hear what was said. Rythian stripped off his kilt and unbound his wet hair.

Someone brought the Sun Disc pectoral to hang on the Standard pole. Rythian touched it, and walked the few paces to the cleared area fronting the Sun Hall. It was ringed now two and three deep by watching D'Shael. Kherin saw his hearthkin in a close knot opposite him. Syth stood spear-straight, her hands on Dreyen's shoulders. Kherin could have gone to them, should have gone, for he was the man of their hearth. But he could not move. His eyes were fixed on the two men about to fight to the death, and his heart was gripped by a fear he did not want anyone else to see.

Is it now? Is this the reality we both Saw, Chiera and I? The Sun Stallion sprawled naked in the dust, hair tumbled like the bright banner of a defeated army? Must I stay to witness this?

Kherin had no choice. Like the rest of the Shi'R'Laen, he must stand and see it happen in the Eye of the Sun and do nothing.

An Elder extended his Staff between the two, his deep voice calling for silence. "In the Eye of the Sun," he announced, and the Staff was withdrawn and the combat began.

The dust churned like smoke about their feet, their long hair swirling like the manes of their horses. Rythian was as fast as the great cat that was his name-beast and as deadly, but Cathan had seen him fight and watched his tricks. He was no easy target. Cathan also had some speed, if not so great, but he was campaign fit, taller, stronger and uninjured. He also knew the weak point on Rythian — and that was where he concentrated his attack.

Rythian's new-healed shoulder could not withstand the assault, and he was suddenly down in the dust. But as Cathan hurled himself on top of him, Rythian's feet came up and caught his opponent in the belly. The man's own impetus carried him over in a perfect arc to land hard-winded in the dirt. Rythian snapped back to his feet and pounced before Cathan could stand again. Kherin saw fatalism dawn on the man's face as Rythian arched Cathan back against his bent knee, forcing the spine to the point of fracture, muscles straining and taut with effort. The watching crowd was as still as a carved frieze, and then, in the breathing silence, came the sharp, shocking crack of breaking bone.

For an instant it was as if Kherin felt it in his own tense body; a painless loosening of every sinew so that he had to support himself briefly against one of the housepoles. His vision swam as if he were sunstruck. The deep ululation of victory rang in his head, the accolade of the tribe for their Sun Stallion. He didn't wait for the Elders' acclamation or the ritual declaration. He was driven by an urge he did not understand to step back into the shadows and make his way to the Sun Hall.

It was dark inside and cool. Yet, Kherin was shaking and his heart was pounding as a war-drum in his breast. What do I have to fear? he asked himself, through the churning confusion that was in him. And why am I here? What am I waiting for?

That which was Written for you before you were born. The Voice within him was the Voice of the Goddess, clear and unmistakable. *It was for this you came here, Chosen of Mine. Through you, he will come to Me.*

As in the Sanctuary when She spoke to him, Kherin was calmed by Her Presence, and his acceptance of Her word was rewarded by a depthless serenity.

In all ways, in all things, Goddess, I do Your Will...

Her peace lapped around him, holding him within it as the shell holds the pearl, and he did not know how long the ecstatic timelessness lasted.

Only that at last there was movement in the dimness, and light slanted from the door that gave onto the Hall, gilding sweat-and blood-glossed skin, firing the streaming tangle of pale hair to living gold.

"Kherin." No questioning tone, though for the moment, until his eyes adjusted, Rythian would be almost blind. But maybe his God had spoken to him, also.

What will be, will be.

Kherin smiled, and a quicksilver quiver of anticipation ran through him.

"I am here," he said.

The night was velvety black; the furs warm and enfolding. Rythian's hair was like spun silk falling through Kherin's hand. It smelled of sun and dust, and more potent than the most exotic of perfume.

A sigh of content.

"I didn't know..."

A murmur of wonder. Kherin felt Rythian's caressing touch, and pushed his head into it as a cat might. He wanted to purr his contentment. "Neither did I."

The newness of it all held a kind of innocence, a tenderness that neither of them would have guessed at. It was unexpected, but cherished the more for it. The edge of passion blunted, they were at completely at peace with each other, all stretch and strain eased. Kherin had never felt this way with a woman, even Emre — even at the peak of delight, they had not been as closely linked as this moment, when he and Rythian lay comfortably entwined.

"You are the wellspring ..." Rythian whispered. "I didn't know what I lacked, before..." Then, as if the thought had just struck him, "This is not something forbidden among your people?"

"No. Among warriors, it is a thing of honor. As with your SwordBrethren. But until now, there was never anyone —"

"No warrior you loved?"

"There was one whom I was close to," Kherin answered softly, "but it was not like this." The bond he had felt with Jeztin was not of this nature. And as much as he had loved Jeztin, his friend and companion and brother-in-blood, Rythian was more. "He died before I came here."

"I'm sorry."

"It was his time." The old wound was healed; Kherin could think of Jeztin without pain. "And he is with the Mother now."

Rythian's hand stroked Kherin's cheek, offering comfort. Kherin turned his head, and kissed the hard palm. He knew without having to be told that Rythian had been a virgin in this as well, even though Rythian had taken much of the initiative in their lovemaking. Well, that was, no doubt, the God in him, whether Rythian acknowledged it or not. But the Gods had had their due; what came next would be for Rythian and himself.

It was so different. So much to explore, to learn; new sensations, and those already known but made different, intriguing. Male muscle instead of soft woman-flesh, strength matching strength. Kherin gave into his passionate nature, offering all he was to his lover, as he would to the Goddess in worship, nothing held back. He was the Hawk again, a hawk whose every feather was a flame, who carried the sun at his center, burning and yet not consumed.

Kherin

He opened his eyes on a moonlit plain, the pure white walls of the Courts of the Morning reflecting back the glory of it.

Beloved, My Chosen One, come to Me now.
"Great Goddess, Thy will above all — but —"
Walk the path I have set for thee, Beloved. The Son of the Sun will follow after. So it is written; thy lives are forever joined. Come to Me.
Slowly, Kherin began to walk across the plain towards the towering walls. There was an empty space at his side that made his heart ache.
Soon, She told him, *he will follow thee and all will be as it should.*
So Kherin gave himself in trust to the dream.
When he awoke he was not in the warmth of Rythian's bed. Instead he stood naked and shivering in long grass. Confused and disorientated, still half asleep, he stared around him. Pre-dawn greyness hung over the land and the Summer Hold could not be seen. Horses moved nearby and a familiar shape loomed out of the mist. Syth's mare Chyren, let loose to graze with the herds. She came to him, curious and hopeful of a tidbit. Kherin slid his hands under her mane to warm them, and tried to clear his head.
It was not the first time his Goddess had called him in his sleep and he had woken to find himself elsewhere. Always before it had been from his bed in the Sanctuary and he had opened his eyes on Her Shrine. Kherin opened his heart to Her, asking Her will, and heard an echo of Her Summons.
Where? he asked. The answer wasn't clear — to the Grove, maybe. Kherin swung up onto the mare's back, then realised he had no idea where Hold nor Grove lay. All direction was lost in the mist. The mare would not be so confused.
Chyren, he touched her mind with his own. *Let us go home.*

* * *

"'Thian," a voice murmured, with an edge of urgency to it that cut through Rythian's sleep. "Rythian, wake up! There is news."
"Arun?"
The room was dim, lit only by the embers in the firebasket. The mane of pale hair above him was ashy in the pre-dawn. His mind cobwebby with sleep, Rythian struggled up onto one elbow and found himself alone in the tangle of sleeping furs. Which wasn't as it should be. "News?" Rythian repeated. "What are you doing here? You should be with the Warband — it is Voran?"
"He is well. Some of us returned with the Trail Council. Rythian, the Tylosians have crossed the river by the GodStone in force and they're building a fortress."

"How many?" Rythian said sharply. He had been expecting something like this.

"All told, three hundred and some fifty. Of that, two hundred are warriors. By now, who knows? They are being watched."

"Damn them." Rythian reached for his clothes. "Arun, have you seen Kherin?"

"No. He'll be at his hearth. There is more. Half a day's ride away we came on Kasha Den and his pack-beasts. He told us that a warband of five hundred has crossed into our lands to the north. They are moving this way, burning Mygraean border towns."

"More Tylosians seeking to outflank us?"

"Allies of theirs, more like. A breed of men never seen before, according to Kasha Den. Their horses are small and light, and they ride like the Sons of the Wind. Warriors, too, he says, although nothing in Mygraea would have tested them much. The Council is gathering, 'Thian. Let me help you."

Wherever Kherin was, he would have to wait until after the Council. "I am sound," Rythian replied, pushing away Arun's helping hand. "Thanks to Kherin."

Kasha Den was waiting in the Sun Hall. A short, stout figure, he told Rythian and the Elders what he had seen of the invading warriors. He was no stranger to the D'Shael, but he was nervous and sweating. He kept twisting his broad-brimmed hat in his hands, over-awed by the place, by Council and Sun Stallion alike.

"Is he lying?" Mettan wondered aloud

"No," Rythian said. "He speaks truth as he sees it. This threat is real enough. Our thanks, Kasha Den. Go now. The SwordBrethren will see that you and yours have our hospitality." He waited until the doors closed behind the man, then beckoned to Mettan. "Send Arun to me, Uncle. Kardan Elder, who else rides with Kasha Den?"

"His sister, two sons, three cousins and his sister's new husband. All but the last have been here before often enough."

"I want them watched, but with care so they don't suspect it. The danger could be closer than it appears. Arun," he went on as the SwordBrother joined the Council, "LyDia has warned me through Kherin that Tylos will send spies among us. They may be with Kasha Den's folk. Go to LyDia and tell her that if anyone contacts her, she is to tell them I am a insecure, weak fool who rules with lies and poisons, and the tribe is afraid to speak against me. That she is in my bed and in my confidence, as is Merse."

"I will," he grinned. "Poisons, is it? That'll be your trail-cooking, no doubt," he added over his shoulder.

"What will that gain us?" Mettan frowned.

"Complaisancy, perhaps. And time while we deal with these

invading warriors."

"What of our own warriors?" Gorryn demanded. "Shouldn't we call them back from the borders and caravans?"

"Not yet. That would alert the Tylosians. For now leave them where they are. The fortress isn't going anywhere, after all. These warriors could be on us any day. As soon as Kasha Den leaves, our people and the herds must go to Winter Hold."

"We must recall our trail-warriors!" Nortan insisted. "We have not much more than two hundred fighters here!"

"Winter Hold can be held by a dozen," Kardan snapped.

"Peace," Rythian held up his hand. "Send out scouts, but no more than six. I want these invaders found and watched. When we know their direction, we can better judge what must be done. Is there more to be said? No? In the Eye of the Sun," he announced, terminating the gathering. He turned to Kardan as the others left. "Uncle —"

"It is a testing," the Elder said quietly. "Find stillness. All will be well."

But there was another anxiety in him, which should not be there when his people were in danger. But where was Kherin? Rythian could feel, somehow, that he was not with his hearth, nor anywhere in the Hold.

The nagging fear was realised as he left the Sun Hall and Ronan came running. "Chyren's not with the herd," he announced breathlessly. "Gethan says he thinks he saw Kherin take her before full light, but the mist was thick and —"

Rythian caught the boy, holding him firmly. "Where did Kherin go?"

"Gethan said north-east — and Emre is crying. She's Seen something and won't say what. At least," he added fairly, "she wouldn't tell me."

"Damn it!" Over the boy's head Rythian saw the black-cloaked figure of Chiera bearing down on him. Myra was at her side, pale and angry. Behind them came a phalanx of Hold-folk, all grim-faced.

"Sun Stallion," the Hooded One called, voice harsh as a Tylosian war-trumpet. "We are betrayed!"

"That is to be proved, Mother," Myra countered.

"Proved it will be." The old woman came to a halt in front of him, eyes of sharded ice probing. "Enemies are at our northern flank," she announced. "Do you deny it?"

"Of course not."

"Kherin Southlander has ridden out before dawn, heading northeast. Do you deny that?"

"Gethan believes it," he said. "What of it?" He knew what her next words would be.

"He rides to meet them with word of our numbers."

"No." Rythian held fast to his temper. "Kherin is true to us."

"Then where is he, Sun Stallion?"

Rythian couldn't answer that, and Chiera smiled her triumph.

"If he rides to meet them," Kardan said coldly, "which I doubt, the scouts will know and send back word to us."

"You think him a warrior like any other?" Chiera laughed. "I think not. Moon-mage, he is, sworn to the Darkness." Growls went up from the crowd, of dissent as well as agreement. "Do you deny he has the gathering of power?"

"No," Rythian said. "He healed me — and others as well."

Chiera snorted. "A child's trick. One that any can do if they have the gift and the will. What else can he do? Cast spells and ill-wishing — I am his enemy and he knows it; look at me, Rythian Lyre'son, and see how he strikes at his foes."

"It's a wise man that knows his enemies, Chiera," Rythian said softly. "Do not provoke me, or you may find I strike harder and more swiftly."

"Can you?" She eyed him up and down, as if he was a beast for the slaughter. "Perhaps. All the better if you can. But save your skills for him. You'll need them when you fetch him back."

Startled, Rythian stared at her. "I will not go after him," he said. "It grieves me that he has left, but he is free to ride where and when he will, as is any of us. As you so rightly said, there is an enemy coming from the north. I will be riding with the Warband, as befits the Sun Stallion."

"What says the Council to that?" Chiera demanded. "I invoke their word! Does the Sun Stallion stay with the people, or does he ride to bring back the moon-mage who has betrayed us?"

"Have you lost your wits, woman?" Mettan exploded. "If half of what you say is true, how do you expect Rythian to contend with a spell-weaver?"

"He is Sun Stallion!" Chiera snapped with the speed of a striking adder. "And the Hand of the God is on him. Who else can defend us against the Darkness?"

"No one knows more of Darkness that you, Shadow-woman," Rythian said. "What is the will of the Council in this? Would you have me charge off like some poor fool in a fireside tale — or take my rightful place with the SwordBrethren defending my people?"

The twelve Elders chose by walking to stand by the person they supported. Five stood by Rythian, seven walked the few paces to stand beside the Third Priestess.

"So be it," he said quietly. "But what do you gain by this?" and saw her flinch away.

But her unspoken reply did not falter. *Your death. It has been Seen — and not by me alone. Maybe his also. Best it happens soon, so neither of you can bring more harm to the Shi'R'Laen.*

"You are wrong," he told her. "Are you so blinded by your hate that you dare the wrath of Lord and Lady alike?"

"Since when," she snorted, "did you give a dog's turd for either? Sing another song, Lyre'son. That one falters. Council has made clear its will. I wish you good hunting."

"I will not forget this, Shadow-woman," Rythian promised, stalking away. He called Zaan from the herd.

Voran and Arun joined him as he was saddling the stallion. They carried saddle-packs with them; their faces were strained and angry.

"This is truly insane," Arun growled. "Your place is with us!"

"I know it."

"We can ride with you," Voran suggested.

Rythian shook his head.

"No," he said. "It's bad enough the Warband is losing one. Three is out of the question. Guard my hearth for me. All of them, LyDia and Merse as well."

"We will," Arun promised. "Rythian, is it true that Kherin healed you? And that you took Challenge and won yesterday?"

"Yes. Cathan thought I'd be weak. Easy prey. Thanks to Kherin, I was neither. There is no evil in him, I swear it," he went on abruptly. "He is my hearthbrother and — " He broke off with a shrug and finished strapping the two packs behind the saddle.

"So," Arun said, eyes shrewd on his face. "And more than brother?"

"More than brother," Rythian agreed and mounted the horse. "Hopefully we'll be back by tomorrow's noon."

At a fast canter, Rythian headed northeast across the plain towards the distant mountains. He was a good half-day behind Kherin, but the trail was clear enough. It ran spear-straight towards the high pass that led to the Wetlands beyond, a land clogged with marshes watered from mountain streams.

Kherin could not know where he was going. Rythian was certain of that much. If the man meant to take ship for his homeland at some port not allied to Tylos, he should have headed east, then due south. North-eastward lay only the Wetlands and the mountain plateau that held the Sacred Land — and by now, perhaps, the alien warriors, coming south. Which might have been a reason if Kherin had known of them — if he had wanted to meet with them. But he didn't know. He'd ridden out before the news. Why had he left?

Chapter Thirteen

By late afternoon Rythian was in the foothills. Rocky slopes slowed his passage and Kherin's trail grew harder to follow. It seemed likely that Kherin, not knowing the land, would choose the easiest path. Which was not the quickest. Rythian cut across broken ground and the scrambles of scree, reached the first ridge of the pass and crested it. The footing was treacherous, but better than what lay ahead in the Wetlands.

The sun was westering when Rythian finally won clear of the pass. He drew rein briefly to look northwards, towards the dense veil of cloud that hid the plateau of the Sacred Lands rising out of the Wetlands.

Lady, he thought briefly but fervently, *Lady, if You love him, hold him in Your hand.*

Below, seen intermittently through skeins of heavy mist, was a tangle of tall spear-bladed grasses, scrawny willow trees, expanses of tough heather, and patches of bright turf bordering murky moss-and-leaf-clogged pools. Tufts of bog-grasses blew white plumes of warning to the unwary. How could a man from a desert land know of the hidden dangers lying in wait? The seemingly-solid mat of floating grasses would draw him as the best path.

The mists lifted, giving Rythian his first clear view. It was enough. He urged Zaan down the slope.

The first quagmire had been Kherin's downfall. The terrified mare was belly-deep and slowly sinking. Plastered with mud, Kherin was at her head, keeping her calm with the touch of his hands and his mind. The matted heather that promised sound footing was only a spear's length away. As Zaan's hooves met the uncertain ground, Rythian flung himself off and began wading into the liquid mud.

"She's caught," Kherin told him breathlessly. "Her nearside hind. Give me your knife." Without waiting for a reply, he snatched it from Rythian's belt and ducked under the surface of the thick wet morass. Suddenly the mare gave a great heave, and Kherin broke the surface, white teeth showing triumphant in a mud-mask.

"Tough roots," he commented briefly. "Come up," he encouraged the mare. "Good girl." Floundering and half-swimming, Kherin and Rythian guided her to firmer footing.

They were all three coated in filth, and the mare was badly lame. Zaan nickered from a short distance away. He had found good water and a clear pebble-bedded stretch of stream. It was what they needed. The mare snorted and showed the white of her eyes when they got there, but they got her in and sluiced her and themselves down, getting rid of the worst of the muck.

It wasn't the time for questions, but Rythian couldn't wait — time was running out.

"Kherin, why did you leave?" he asked bluntly.

Kherin looked up from checking the mare's forelegs, black curls matted against his scalp, mud still streaked on face and throat. Trickles of blood from small unfelt injuries showed scarlet.

"I was called by the Goddess," Kherin shook his head, as if trying to clear it even now. "I dreamed, and when I woke I was not in bed but out on the plains and mist-locked. I thought the mare would bring me home — "

"Dreams!" Rythian's relief at finding Kherin safe and unharmed gave way to anger. "Dreams! Man, we're being invaded!"

"I didn't know," Kherin replied simply. "But even if I had, it wouldn't matter. When She calls, I obey Her." He began to wade clear of the stream, a little unsteadily, his hand on the mare's neck. It was then that Rythian saw the four leaf-shapes clinging to Kherin's naked thigh, patching the tanned skin from hip to knee. There were more around his ribs.

Rythian swore softly, snatching a long willow branch from an overhanging tree. He flicked the end at the leaf-shapes, ignoring Kherin's bewilderment. Carapaces split and filmy citrous wings spread, carrying the insects back to their swamp.

"Mud-moths," Rythian said. "Sit down before you fall down."

He was obeyed, but possibly because Kherin didn't have much choice in the matter. The venom of mud-moths was very powerful; it could paralyse with frightening speed. The moths did not of themselves kill, but they laid their eggs in the bites they made, creating great ulcerating sores. If not treated, the sores turned to gangrene and death soon followed. Rythian turned away from Kherin to begin hunting for the low-lying, rosetted leaves of the sandwort that would poultice the wounds. He knew they wouldn't be returning to the tribe within a day.

The Sacred Land they were in was the Lady's domain, as surely as the Grove and the caverns beneath the Winter Hold. An eerie place of hot springs and geysers, it also offered a more effective remedy for the venom of the mudmoths than the sandwort in the hot, malodorous mud that oozed in certain places.

Rythian found a game trail leading from the marshes up the plateau's flanks. For two large horses, one of them lame, it was difficult ground to cover. Rythian was on foot, leading Zaan with Kherin slumped unconscious over the stallion. The mare, on a long tether, had little trouble keeping up the pace. They followed the path into a small, densely-wooded valley, and from there to the verges of the great bowl-shaped plateau. Here there were strangely-shaped formations, pools of water that steamed, and rocks that were hot to the touch.

It was full night by the time Rythian made camp under a sheltered overhang, close to a stream of cold water. Not far away a small hot spring put a sulphurous taint into the air. Rythian folded his cloak beneath Kherin and placed a blanket over him. Kherin's breathing was harsh and difficult, and his skin hot to the touch. The venom had taken a strong hold, and since it paralysed the mind much as the body, Kherin couldn't heal himself.

Rythian gathered enough dry wood for a small fire, more for light than anything else. He fetched water from the spring and returned to his patient. He peeled off the leaf mash poultices, bathed the affected areas and tied on fresh poultices. Come the morning he would make some broth, but for now there was nothing more he could do for Kherin. Rythian ate sparingly from the limited supplies in his saddle-packs, then settled in to keep vigil through the short summer night.

Tomorrow, if his memory was true, he would find the spring he sought.

LyDia watched Rythian ride from the Hold. She was no stranger to politics, and the treachery implicit in them; she knew the Sun Stallion's enemies had won this bout. It brought an uneasy feeling to her stomach.

"What passes?" said a quiet voice behind her, speaking in Tylosian.

LyDia turned with casual grace to look at the woman stranger who smiled at her.

"I am Sulie Den," the woman introduced herself.

LyDia recognized the name; sister to the trader, Kasha Den. And possibly an ally or a tool of a Tylosian spy.

"Our Sun Stallion rides to battle the moon mage," LyDia shrugged in answer. "Or not. It's probably a trick to see who is still against him."

"Like the old witch?" Sulie Den pulled an expressive face. "I remember her from other visits."

"Could she be forgotten?"

Sulie Den chuckled and shook her head. "It has been long since I was on the Flower Isle," she said. "The roses grow there like nowhere else in Tylos — I remember the way their perfume filled the temples ..."

"Ah," LyDia smiled sweetly. This was the phrase Hasoe had told her would identify the contact for sending information back to him. "To me it seems another life away." They drifted away from the crowd until there were none near to overhear.

"We will be leaving soon now," Sulie Den said, "since the Horse People go to their mountain Hold. We have never been permitted to go there. What word to I take to the Lord Hasoe?"

"That all goes well. Rythian is as Hasoe thought, young and cunning." She glanced around, saw Merse and caught his eye. He sauntered over and joined them with an air of languid boredom. "We have him snared between us, Merse and I."

"Safe and sure," the eunuch snickered. "How do we steer him in the matter of this fortress?"

"That is not of Hasoe's planning. Year-President Behmath ordered it as soon as you left for the border. He fears Hasoe's influence and motives, it is said."

"Wise of him," LyDia tittered, "but too late, I fancy."

"Indeed. The Lord Hasoe has long had his measure. Behmath plans to put two legions in garrison there and strike when the D'Shael come to protest it."

"They'll do more than protest," LyDia said. "The Warband will ride."

"So?" Sulie Den shrugged. "Even if the D'Shael break the Treaty and pull their warriors from the caravans and borders to augment those they send from here, they will still be some five hundred at the most against two thousand of the finest soldiers there are."

"So how will Hasoe turn this to his advantage?" Merse asked.

"He has the War Lord Thetar in his hand. The Legions will not slaughter the D'Shael, merely force them to surrender. If the Sun Stallion commands it, they will obey."

"Surrender?" he frowned. "The D'Shael? They never have, nor will."

"Then change the word if not the deed. Alliance, not surrender. After all, there is much they had never done, until the Red Bear ruled them. This Rythian seems little different, save only in bulk. Make sure he sees Hasoe as a true friend and ally. After all, riding at Hasoe's side, he will become the leader of a great vassal state with none to challenge him, second only to Hasoe himself."

"And when Hasoe becomes President of Tylos, he dispenses with the yearly election," LyDia chuckled. "Which he will be able to do with the dreaded D'Shael as his personal honour-guard... Oh, how I miss Tylos!"

"And I," Merse sighed. "You cannot know how much. It will be as Lord Hasoe commands. This other band of invading warriors," he went on. "Is that also of our Lord's planning?"

"No." Sulie Den shook her head. "No one knows who they are, or where they come from. It will be good if they can delay and weaken the D'Shael; it will give Hasoe more time to undermine Behmath. As long as Rythian is not killed. Whoever replaces him may not be so easily managed."

"Yes, he will," Merse smirked. "We can see to that. We have already decided that Arun Winter Wolf will be the best choice. Should it be necessary, soft words and poisons will make sure he becomes Stallion."

"Indeed," LyDia purred. "He is another young fool, easily led — if not quite so cunning..."

"But he does not need to be, with us at his side," Merse added.

"And his SwordBrother?"

The two looked at each other and laughed quietly. "Voran is ours," LyDia said.

Summer Hold was a hive of activity, preparing for the move out. It was well past sunset by the time LyDia and Merse were able to report to Arun. At the last twist to the tale, he stared at them with his jaw dropping, while Voran's smothered chuckles became hoots of laughter. There was little else to laugh at.

"Damn Chiera," Arun growled. "Rythian should be here, not chasing across the plain on that black crow's whim."

"True, but what else has she planned?" Merse said. "I do not believe she says one word without due thought behind it. There is more to this."

LyDia nodded. "So do I believe," she said quietly.

Neither Arun nor Voran argued the point.

That night Arun's sleep was haunted by a dream of death. Of Rythian's death. At almost every hearth, one or more of the Shi'R'Laen shared a similar dream of death and disaster.

Before dawn the Hold was roused by the Gather Horn. The D'Shael came from their beds with weapons and torches in their hands, but there was no foe. Only the Third Priestess standing between Elder Hall and Sun Hall. Her hood was thrown back and her unbound hair rippled to her knees in a sheet of gilded silver.

"The Sun Stallion is gone into the Darkness and is lost to us," she cried. "I have Seen it! The omens have confirmed it! Rythian Lyre'son, our Bright Hunter, has been taken from us by the treachery of the moon mage! Council of Elders, there is no one to stand before the God for our people!"

Silence greeted her words until Kardan and Mettan pushed through the stunned crowd to stand before her, staffs planted firmly in the dust.

"We have no proof of that," Kardan said.

"Ask the clans," she countered. "They will tell you of the same omen; a dream of the Sun Stallion lying dead in defeat, and the Shadows wrapping him around to hide him from our Sight. Nor is it the first time this vision has been sent to some. Emre Nianre'sdaughter and Arun Therais'son have also seen it." There were other names as well, but none more telling than those.

"His death will be proved with his body, then," Mettan said. "Until that time, we will continue with his plan — "

"Who," Chiera interrupted him harshly, "will stand before the God for our people?"

The silence stretched again.

"There is no one," Chiera answered herself. "The omens tell me the God has turned his back on the Shi'R'Laen tribe. It is time to return to an older trail. Too many new ways have been forced upon us, first by Caier, then by Rythian. So the Lord has walked away." An uneasy murmuring ran through the assembly. "The Lady, however, will never walk away from Her children, no matter how wayward they are. In the times before legend, a new Sun Stallion was chosen each year. To this day the Maiden and the First Priestess are so chosen. In distant times, three Elders and Three Priestesses ruled the clans in Her Name. It must be so again if we are to defeat the evil that threatens us."

Shouts of protest went up, but so did some of agreement.

"What says the Middle Priestess?" Kardan bellowed. Myra came forward to stand beside Chiera.

"I have been taking the omens as well," she said. "By one reading it is as my Mother has said. By another," she went on, raising her voice to be heard above the sudden uproar, "the Sun Stallion faces trial by ordeal and the outcome is not certain. The God..." she hesitated and the silence grew again, "is forging a weapon in the furnace of His Fires. Its likeness and purpose is hidden."

"My Daughter," said the Hooded One, "does not yet have my skill in reading omens. The Lord of the Sun has turned from us; his Stallion is lost in Shadows and Mists. There is only the Lady left to us, my children."

Kardan summoned Arun and Voran to him. "Go after Rythian," he said. "With or without Kherin, with or without his life, bring him back!"

The Sacred Land was filled with thick mists, the first long rays of the sun painting them rose and gold. Rythian led the horses, with Kherin on Zaan, down the shallow slope to the site he remembered from his own childhood encounter with mudmoths. It was unchanged. Steam still wreathed above the pools of mud and water, and the rocks were warm underfoot. There was the overhang for shelter, and beyond a tumble of boulders was a tiny spring of cool, untainted water.

Kherin was conscious, but he lay like a dead thing. Only his eyes were alive, and Rythian didn't know if he understood what was happening. Rythian talked to him anyway as he worked, plastering the bites with the hot stinking mud, and coaxing sips of water and herb tea down him until Kherin slept. Rythian poulticed the mare's lame leg in the same way and she seemed to find comfort from it.

As the sun rose, and the mist lifted, Rythian found a warm clear pool close by to wash the last of the marsh from himself and his clothing. He spread his wet clothes on the flat rocks at its edge, then sat beside Kherin.

The heat of noon baked into his bones, easing weariness, which freed his mind to worry about the gathering problems. The invading warriors would be getting closer to the Summer Hold. The tribe should be on its way to the Winter Hold. He and Kherin should be well on their way to join them, but if venom, ulcers and treatment took their usual path, it would be days before Kherin would be able to move. But He was the Chosen of the Lady — how strong did he need to be to heal himself?

Using a handful of spongy moss soaked in water, Rythian carefully wiped Kherin's face. The man's eyes squinted open, focused on him, and knew him. Incredibly, a croak followed, that might be interpreted as a greeting.

"Yes," Rythian said. "Very probably." He was grinning like an idiot, but couldn't stop it. Carefully, he lifted Kherin so he could drink from the water-flask. "Do you know how worried I've been?"

"Did you say we are being invaded? Mudmoths, are they? We don't have them in my country," Kherin managed hoarsely, as if by way of apology.

"You can thank your Goddess for that, then."

"We have serpents. And scorpions. And there is a certain lizard..." Kherin's voice faded, but the smile remained. He struggled up onto one elbow. "What is this place?"

"The Valley of the White Mare, in the Sacred Land. Your Lady Goddess guards you well. By rights you should still be venom-bound and unconscious."

"I wish I was," he whispered. "This hurts like no war-wound I have ever taken! Why are mud-moths invading?"

"No, you misunderstand. There is a Warband of some five hundred warriors heading south across our lands. They may or may not attack the Holds. The clans are on their way to Winter Hold."

"Rythian," Kherin said coolly, fixing him with a stare that had nothing of weakness in it, "Why are you here then, Sun Stallion? Your place is with your people, not me."

"True," he said. "But the Third Priestess declared that you are a moon mage riding to betray us to the strangers, and that I must bring you back for judgement. There were enough of the Council agreeing with her to give me no choice. Kherin, can you heal yourself?"

"I — don't think so, not just yet. I don't have enough strength yet. You should go. I will follow as soon as I can, my word on it."

"I won't leave you," Rythian said quietly. "You can neither hunt, nor ride, nor defend yourself. If it's strength you need, use mine. There are enemies about and the clans have need of both of us."

Kherin nodded. "I'll try. I've not drawn on another before, although I know the way of it." He clasped Rythian's hand loosely, leaned back against his supporting arm. "Open your shield-wall, 'Thian."

"Shield-wall?"

It is here, a voice smiled in Rythian's mind and he could See behind his eyes a barrier of golden fire.

No walls of any kind between us, now or ever, Rythian replied and willed the flames to part. Then Kherin was there within his mind, a flame of living silver. Somehow he could See himself in Kherin's mind; a flame of gold. The two became one. It was a soaring ecstasy like nothing Rythian had ever experienced, a deeper union than any he had known before. He could not tell if it lasted moments or hours, but when the two flames parted, still there was an echo of Kherin within him.

Strength flowed back into Kherin like wine into a cup. By mid-afternoon he was on his feet and able, with a little support, to make his way to the clear pool. He sank into the water with a sigh of pleasure and bathed away the caked mud that plastered the bites.

"This is disgusting stuff," he said, deeply aware of their new closeness and relishing it. He had found the one person who was truly the brother of his soul, and the joyous wonder was a praise-song in its own right.

"It worked, though, didn't it? I used it on the mare, too. She didn't complain."

"Then she has no sense of smell."

It was good to feel the water silken on his skin, and it was a while before Kherin waded from the warm pool. He sat down thankfully to let the sun dry him. Rythian, hands pillowing his head, was staring up into the blue above, frowning a little. Kherin felt the shadow in his thoughts and reached over to tug at a blond hank. It got his attention.

"Where have you flown to, my beloved?" he asked softly.

"I am Sun Stallion, Kherin," Rythian said awkwardly.

"I know." Kherin folded arms on knees, studying the beloved face feature by feature, as if he had not seen it before.

"If I were anyone else — if I were not Sun Stallion — then we could be more than what we are. I could almost wish — "

"We are what we are," Kherin said, slightly puzzled.

"Yes, but we could be more. We are lovers. But that is the least of what I would choose." Rythian sat up. "I have told you already, you are the very wellspring of my life, completing me where I did not know I lacked."

"So are you to me," Kherin smiled.

"If I were free, if I were Rythian only, then I would ask you to be SwordSworn with me."

"There would be no need to ask," Kherin told him gently. "It is my wish also."

"I know. That is why... Oh, Sun and Stars, why could we not have met a year ago?"

"Because it was not in the Pattern."

"And it is in the Pattern that I must deny you your right?"

"I do not understand this," Kherin said. "I have your love, so..."

"If we could be SwordSworn," Rythian went on doggedly, "then nothing would part us. We would take the vow together." His eyes were very blue and intent. He began to recite the ancient words, as if he only now realized what they meant. "I will walk at thy side in the light of the Sun, lie at thy side in the light of the Moon. In the forge of battle, we will stand together, and we will not be sundered. In life and in death, there will be nothing I will not share with thee, nowhere I will not go with thee..."

Kherin heard him out. "In life and in death there will be nothing I will not share with thee, nowhere I will not go with thee," he repeated softly. "You know my heart as I know yours; the SwordVow is an affirmation of what already is between us, is it not?" and smiled at the bewilderment in his lover's face. Then slowly a grin began there.

"You're right!" Rythian said wonderingly. "Just because it's never been before doesn't mean it can't be." He pulled Kherin to stand beside him. With only the Goddess for witness, the words were spoken.

Arun dropped from his horse's saddle and crouched in the grass. "Here Zaan sprang into a gallop," he reported. "'Thian must have sighted something."

"Yes," Voran said. He was standing in his stirrups, eyes shaded under his hand. "This valley is not so wide. We must sweep it for any sign — 'Run, look yonder."

Arun followed the pointing finger and saw the vivid green carpet that spread to fill the narrow, steep-sided valley ahead of them. The hoofprints headed straight for it — Zaan had been at full stretch, the day-old tracks clear-cut in the turf. They heeled their own horses to a faster pace, their keen eyes at last finding other horse prints under Zaan's. On the very edge of the swamp was a churned-up tangle of sign, mostly indistinguishable. Arun dismounted, feeling the treacherous ground quaking under their weight. There was a growing knot of icy sickness in his gut as he read the story. "Kherin's horse stumbled and went into that filth. 'Thian jumped from Zaan and went forward —"

"Zaan wandered here and started to graze," Voran said from the higher ground. He quartered the turf on foot, searching for a man's footprints with desperate eyes.

Arun edged forward until the mud began to draw at his legs. He salvaged a long branch and probed ahead of him. Foul smelling gasses belched up, but he could feel no obstruction, no bodymass — and then no bottom at all. The mud was moving under his feet, loosening. He lurched back a few paces, sought another way forward, aware on the edge of his vision that Voran was searching along the edge of the swamp. Something else moved, a light leafy flutter and something brown was clinging to his makeshift staff. He swore and dropped it, ducking as a handful of mudmoths drifted past his face.

"Arun — come out!" Voran yelled, "They're thick as autumn out there!" The moths were taking to the air in greater numbers.

Arun knew he had no choice. Voran, on his horse, was already plunging towards him. Arun was jerked from his feet as Voran snatched his belt and heaved him out of danger.

While daylight lasted they searched — Arun with increasing anguish, unwilling to believe the evidence. Voran was more fatalistic, if no less appalled.

At nightfall, with no sign even of man or horse, they crouched over a small fire in grieving silence. "He's gone," Voran whispered into the darkness. "It's no use, Brother. He's gone. They both are."

Arun nodded. "We'll keep hunting," he said. "A little while longer."

Voran did not argue with him.

Sleep did not come easy to Arun. When eventually his eyes closed he was again trapped in nightmare images. This time Rythian was choking and drowning in the fetid mud, his flailing arms forever just out of Arun's straining reach. He could see with unnatural clarity the ridge of muscle in his own outstretched right arm, the sweat and mud that streaked his skin, the glitter of gold that banded the bright coppery braid of hair on his wrist, the line of bone and tendon as he reached further out for Rythian.

Still he could not reach him. No one could. And then someone was moving past him, walking on the mist-wreathed muck as if it was rock. The warrior reached down to take Rythian's hand in a strong clasp, pulled him free and raised him to his feet, clean and unstained.

For a moment the two men looked down at Arun, one grave, one smiling. They stood close together, shoulder to shoulder. On their wrists were slim bands of braided hair. Rythian's had a braid of Kherin's raven black hair while Kherin's wrist was bound with twisted silver-blond strands from Rythian's hair.

The two turned without speaking and walked away until the mist swallowed them.

Arun cried out in his pain. He awoke, held close in Voran's arms. "Hush," his Brother was saying. "It's only a dream. Just a dream, beloved." But it wasn't. Clear and sharp, the images stayed with him. Haltingly he told his vision, feeling Voran's arms tighten around him. "They can't be SwordSworn," Voran objected. "'Thian's Sun Stallion. Maybe it's what they would have been, but they couldn't ...."

"No," Arun sighed. "If Caier was still Sun Stallion, Kherin would be dead. All I know is, wherever they are, in this world or out of it, they're together. And they are SwordSworn."

"No Sun Stallion ever took a SwordBrother, not in life," Voran said softly.

"But in death?" Arun shivered and Voran pulled his cloak around his SwordBrother's shoulders. There was a long pause. Then: "Tomorrow," Arun said, "we'll search east along the edge of the Sacred Lands, then return west. I'd like us to find Zaan, if nothing else."

"Yes," Voran agreed through the grief that choked in his throat.

Later Rythian separated a long strand of blond hair, cut it and plaited it to a thin ribbon, tying it around Kherin's sword-wrist. "When we are back in Hold," he said, "Disan Smith will fashion gold to bind it in the proper style."

"This is gold enough for me." Kherin took the knife and cut a lock of his own hair, but it was harder to fashion it properly. It kept springing obstinately into curl. They got it done at last, and bound around Rythian's wrist. "So, SwordBrother, tell me again of this invasion?"

Rythian told him all that he knew and what had had been surmised of the Warband, drawing a map in the dirt to show Kherin the lie of the land and the probable route the strangers would take.

"Winter Hold is here, the Wetlands and Sacred Land here, and Summer Hold is in the centre of the plains between the two — "

"So I was traveling directly away from home?" Kherin interrupted. "Goddess!"

"You were. If we travel west along the lee of these hills, it will take us clear of the Wetlands. Then we go back to Summer Hold from here and follow the tribe to Winter Hold. The outlanders' path, according to Kasha Den, will take them due south, possibly missing Summer Hold. But if they come on the trail our people will have left, they might decide to follow it to Winter Hold. If they take an eastern curve, they'll skirt the mountains and be on their way to the Tylosian border, missing us entirely," he finished. "If you can heal your horse's lameness, we'll make better time. Three days at the most, before we are at Winter Hold."

They were heading out of the Sacred Land in less than an hour, but could not travel fast. The country was uneven and broken, with steep escarpments and skirts of scree, riven by streams and deep gullies. By dusk they had reached a wider valley that offered margins of meadow along the river, a good site to camp.

They ate the last of Rythian's pack-rations for their evening meal. Shortly after dawn the next day, Rythian left Kherin sleeping, hoping to catch some fish or small game for their breakfast. Stripped to breech and barefoot, Rythian waded upstream, past the grazing horses. He moved from one small meadow to another as the river twisted around outcrops and trees.

Ahead of him suddenly, metal chinked on stone, sending birds into the sky. Rythian froze, becoming one with the tree shadows. Again the sound came, followed by the familiar ripple of sound of a horse blowing through its nostrils.

Silently Rythian drifted out of the shadow of the tree, cursing his stupidity. All he had for weapons were his hunting knife and a sling. His sword was with Kherin. Rythian climbed among towering boulders, flattened himself on a warm rock and eased forward. He overlooked a wide barren gully, cut across by the narrow river that flowed towards Kherin. There were twenty armed men on wiry ponies moving purposefully beside it. They were poised and watchful, speaking in quiet voices. Small, swarthy men, like none Rythian had seen before. Weapons, though, are a language any can understand, and it did not need Long Sight to know that this was the vanguard of the outlanders. They had not taken the obvious path across the plains, but were following the foothills. They were pointing downstream. Were they going to follow the fresh water? If they did, they'd come on the camp soon enough. Kherin, of course, would hear them coming and find himself a hiding-place. Chyren and Zaan were not so easily hidden. They could not afford to lose those horses.

He had to turn them back the way they came.

Rythian made a mental suggestion to the lead pony that it did not want to go that way. There was a rock-lion. He backed up the image, cupping his hands to his mouth and imitating the lion's hiccoughing roar. The pony stopped, head flung up, but did not bolt.

The other horses had heard the sound. Rythian widened his suggestion and image to include them. They all became restless and uneasy. He used the resulting distraction to slide back and cross the river out of the warriors' sight. When he next peered from cover he was behind them. They were scanning the rocky heights, bows drawn.

The best way to send them where he wanted was to give them something to follow.

The sling sent a river pebble skimming silent through the air to strike squarely on the metal that covered a warrior's back. The distance was too great for it to have any real impact, but that was not its purpose. Another stone flew, stinging a pony's rump. The warriors turned in their tracks and began a swift darting advance. At the same time Rythian heard a sound behind him. He ducked further back into cover, but too late. A shout went up and an arrow hissed past his head.

So be it. He was not going to wait holed up in the rocks like a toothless bear. He drew his knife, pausing long enough for the group of riders to enter the gully. Then he was among them, using the rock-lion image to panic the ponies and the knife to strike at man and beast alike.

Trained for war though the ponies were, the conflict of image and reality gave him advantage. So too did the crowding press of close-quarter work to his benefit. He gained an unfamiliar sword, lost that and took another — the one thought in his head was *Lady, keep Kherin safe —*

Then he had no blade at all and they were many.

A flock of birds rose into the sky ahead of them, their alarm-calls sharp and staccato. Arun and Voran reined in. "We didn't put them up," Voran said quietly.

"No. They wouldn't rise like that for a riderless horse, either," Arun replied. "We'd best check this out."

They left their horses tethered out of sight in a stand of trees and went on foot to the higher ground. Then edged along until they found a vantage point that overlooked the plain. As they had suspected, they found the intruders. From above came the plaintive whistle of a lake-dipper; one at least of the Shi'R'Laen scouts had also found both them and the intruding Warband.

Arun's face was grim as he lay watching in the shadow of a split tree trunk. The outlanders below were resting their horses, supply wagons were circled, but they didn't seem to be pitching camp.

Silent as a hunting wolf, Voran joined Arun. "Outriders are coming out of the hills," he reported. "Where are they going? Fire take them, we should have called back the warriors with the caravans to defend the Winter Hold."

"And break our oath with Tylos?" Arun said quietly.

"I know," Voran sighed. "At least we can bring back a warning, if not 'Thian. We're only two or three hundred less than they. It'll be a good fight, when it comes."

Below the SwordBrothers a troop of riders left the foothills and approached the main Warband. They moved in an ordered fashion, but for one loose horse running free alongside. A D'Shael horse, chestnut of coat, blond of mane and tail. Then came the stallion's bugling battle challenge.

"Zaan!" Voran gasped. "Mother of Mares! How did he — ?"

"And why does he stay — wait, there's the mare Kherin rode out on — in the forefront, between the two greys!"

There was a figure riding the mare, wrapped in a bright cloak. Arun felt his heart lurch. It was Kherin. He was a little slumped over, but he was being greeted with salutations like a conqueror. When his group reached the main party, he was half-lifted from the mare's back and escorted through the Warband in triumph.

Tents now began to quickly spring up in neat rows, but Arun was scarcely aware of this efficiency. He noted that in the new group, there were more than a few ponies who carried bodies slung over their backs. One pony bore a distinctive burden thrown across its withers, a naked man whose pale blood-streaked hair hung down to trail in the dirt.

Voran's breath was sobbing in his throat. Arun felt his Brother flinch as enemy hands tipped the body from the pony's back to sprawl at their feet. This was what he had Seen, this was his Vision made real, and the pain all but stopped his breath.

The God was cruel, forcing His Children to mourn a friend's death twice.

Arun vowed that he would make these people pay a price in the coming battle for every drop of Rythian's blood that had spilled.

It was not to be so simple.

"Sun-Lord!" Voran gasped. "They're tying him. 'Run, he isn't dead!"

"Yes," Arun said, voice distant and steady. "He is. If not now — he soon will be."

"And Kherin?" There was an aching disbelief in Voran's shaking whisper. "The Sun knows I've never liked the man, but I — he — SwordSworn, you said — "

"I was wrong." Ice was in Arun's chest, spreading through him to numb the pain. "Count their dead and re-reckon their number. By the looks of it they'll make camp here for a while. This news will have to be taken to Hold."

Voran nodded. The flame in him burned steady and strong. He could wait. Time would give him his due revenge.

He lay cradled like a moth in silk, cocooned in comfort and half-asleep despite the dull pain at the back of his head. Kherin investigated it, his groping fingers finding a bandage with a swelling beneath it, sticky with unguents. The surroundings, when he opened his eyes, were not familiar. He lay on piled fleeces, not bracken. The covering over him was quilted silk, not Rythian's cloak. Nor was the face hovering over him Rythian's, but dark-featured, intense, concerned, a face out of a lost dream... Kherin wondered if he spoke the name, would the face disappear?

"Tarvik," he said, surprised at how rough his voice sounded. The man bent closer, touched fingertips to his brow, and showed white teeth in a grin.

"Blessed be the Lady, my Prince. You are yourself once more." A soft crooning purr that had been part of his dream deepened and intensified. A rough tongue licked his shoulder and throat; a hard, wet nose pushed at him; a large paw pushed at the covers.

"T'Shayra...!" Kherin's fingers found the old accustomed pleasure-place under her jaw. The great cat laid her head on his breast, eyes slitted, claws working in ecstasy, her purr a rumbling thunder.

"Since she was placed in my charge, we have not been apart, my Prince. She rejoices, as we do, that you are come to us again."

Fragmented memory was drawing together to form a picture; the sounds of distant fighting had wakened him from a true-dreaming of bright, unsettling images. Then had come the certainty that Rythian was in danger, and it had driven all thought of the night-vision from his mind; he had ridden on a half-crazed Zaan to find his Brother in the midst of a pitched battle. Even as Kherin had thrown himself into the fray, Rythian had gone down, overwhelmed by numbers. Kherin had fought his way to him, had stood over him, sword — Rythian's sword snatched up in camp — held ready as the warriors charged again. Then darkness.

Memory showed him what he had not recognised at the time: Khassani faces and Tsithkin faces, Khori and Tsithkin war-harness, Khori battle-cries.

"Rythian. Where is he?" Kherin knew he was not dead; he'd know that by the agony in his soul. The content of his dream came back to him with a jolt, and with it a sense of great urgency. He eased the weight of the cat's head off his chest and started to sit up. Tarvik put both hands on his shoulders.

"Rest quiet, my Prince. All is well."

Kherin fixed him with a stare. "Tarvik. Very little will be well if I do not have answers. Where is he ? The man you were fighting?"

Tarvik sat back on his heels. "You have been as dead for many hours. I feared that I had struck you too hard. Forgive me, my Prince."

Kherin pushed himself back up on his elbows. A moment of concentration, of gathering, and the pain and swelling both were gone. "You are forgiven for that at least." His throat felt strange; when he lifted a hand to it, he found the Tylosian collar was gone. Of course — it would have been gall and wormwood to the Khori, and their Tsithkin smiths would have made short work of the metal that had baffled the Shi'R'Laen. "Is he here? I must go to him."

Consternation crossed the dark face. "It would be unwise for you to rise yet, my Prince. Your head — "

"— is healed. And it would be unwise of you to prevent me, my Hound." Tarvik had only Kherin's well-being in mind; he knew that. "So we shall go together."

That was when the expression in Tarvik's eyes really registered. Kherin sat up and reached to the man's shoulder. He could Read the consternation and growing horror, but not their cause unless he would cut deep into the man's mind and lay it bare. That was not for such a one as Tarvik. He was no enemy.

"Tell me," he demanded. "What has happened?" A sudden fear gripped Kherin — fear that he had unwittingly killed one of his own Khori in the fight, and Tarvik was searching for the words to tell him. What the man did say was more chilling.

"My Prince," Tarvik said carefully, "this man is D'Shael. We found you collared like a slave, branded, yet you came to his defence like a leopard enraged and knew us not. It was as if the man had spelled you. In the land beyond the border, called Mygraea, they told us of these D'Shael, that they are half-demon and wholly mad. It seems to me that they were not so far from the truth. This man, if man he be, lies wounded and close to death."

"Then do not keep me from him!" Kherin came to his feet in a swift movement. "Where is he! Now, Tarvik!"

"Yonder, my Prince, close by the tree to which we had bound him." Kherin was already out of the tent, running with Tarvik sprinting at his heels.

Rythian lay sprawled as Kherin had seen him in the Vision, save that here there was much more blood. Kherin turned the limp body and saw the weak rise of the blood and mud-streaked chest and gave a sob of relief. Charred ropes were about his wrists, but Kherin barely glanced at them. All his attention was given to the four great wounds in Rythian's chest and belly, where spears had thrust deep.

"Who did this?" he hissed. "I swear by the Goddess' own Blood that — "

"Himself," Tarvik cut in quickly, before the curse could be pronounced. "He was bound, great Prince, but when he came to himself he called upon his God — and the ropes burned through, freeing him. He charged upon the spears that were levelled to hold him back. This I swear by thine own name, Chosen of the Goddess."

Stunned and shaking, Kherin laid his hands on the bloody chest and sought to hold back the escaping life.

He knew that the D'Shael warrior-code did not admit surrender, and to be held prisoner was the deepest shame. But knowing it, and accepting the ultimate implications, was another thing entirely.

Kherin's head swam, and for a moment he could not find the stillness within that he needed to Heal. T'Shayra pushed at him, and briefly he rested his face in her fur. When Rythian knew that he had not been defeated and bound by enemies, he would understand. But first he had to stay alive.

Chapter Fourteen

There was much to be said to Tarvik, much to learn from him. But that would have to wait. There were two lives in the balance; Rythian's and his own. Healing his Brother's wounds, terrible as they were, would be the easy part; the harder part would be calling Rythian back from his journey.

First things first. Kherin stilled his mind, took control of his turbulent emotions and banished them. Then, when the pure silver of his inner self was a steady pillar of light, he reached into Rythian's injured body and began the weaving that would heal the flesh.

Time was of no importance in this other sphere. He was aware of the increasing distance between himself and Rythian, of a bond stretched thin. Stretched, but unbroken.

"SwordBrother," Kherin said softly to the distant, death-seeking mind. "Beloved, my soul's mate, halt your journey a space." Then a Sight swamped his eyes and mind. His breath caught in his throat, spasm knotting in his chest like pain.

He Saw their joined hands on a swordhilt — his own, thin, brown and long-fingered, and Rythian's, broad of palm and long of fingers, the little fair hairs glinting on his summer-tan skin. Then the image changed and shifted as if seen through running water. Suddenly Rythian was not Rythian but another, nor was he Kherin any longer; they were different and yet the same, linked together always as their hands were linked, sworn and bound each to each down an infinity of times and places past and to come.

How could I not have known?

But that was folly. It was not given to all to know of the Great Dance, the endless chain of existence. There were many who forgot what their souls once knew, as he himself had forgotten his ancient bond with Rythian.

He had not called the Power, but suddenly it was there in full; the winged glory that he had not practised for so long. Then more still flooded in, a surging golden force that augmented in ways undreamed of. Even as Kherin struggled to bring the wild magic under his control, he knew it was Rythian there with him, returned of his own will. Which was as it should be.

Kherin knelt in the blood that had pooled in the dust, his hands splayed over Rythian's chest. The man's heart was beating strongly in step with his own. The gaping wounds were closing, forming thin pale scars against the light brown of his skin.

"He lives," Tarvik said reverently. "All praise to Her Name."

"He lives," Kherin agreed softly. "Now he will need to regain the strength he lost with his blood. Help me lift him."

"Huh," Tarvik snorted. "This young giant of thine, my Prince, has more leg than a giraffe-colt."

"This young giant, Tarvik, is not counted tall among his people. Of less than the common height, in fact." They got Rythian's arms about their shoulders and heaved the limp body into the tent. Carefully Kherin stretched him out on the bed he himself had not long left.

Exhaustion weighed Kherin down, but he would not rest until he had washed the blood and dust from Rythian and covered him with silk. Only then did he let Tarvik help him rinse the sweat from his own body, dressing himself in the garb of a Prince again, silver-sewn blue and white. The forgotten touch of Khassani silk on his skin was like a lover's caress. Kherin was about to tie his hair back with a Khori headband when Tarvik forestalled him. With reverence, he unwrapped a circlet of beaten silver, shaped over the brow into the winged double spiral that matched the faded mark on Kherin's forehead.

The Prince took it into his hands. "I know better than to ask how this came to you."

"I never believed you dead, my Prince. This was yours, and should be yours again. No other could wear it."

It was the final touch. Kherin stood at last truly a Prince of Khassan again. Tarvik knelt at his feet and pressed his lord's hand to his brow, tears standing in his eyes. Kherin raised him to his feet and embraced him wordlessly for a moment, his own eyes wet. Then stepped back and sank cross-legged to the floor. "Sit, my Hound. Tell me how fares Khassan? The High King?"

"Both grieved for you, my Prince, even when another Chosen was announced by the High Priestess. As for the great Lord Teiron, he was — distraught. The Prince Alzon has been a great solace to him."

Kherin's hands clenched into fists but he made no comment. The Goddess had made Her own Will clear on the matter of Khassan and Alzon. The great cat leaned against him, her deep rumbling purr soothing.

"The Prince has steadied down," Tarvik was saying, "like a good horse to its harness. He will do well, I think."

"I am glad to hear it," he said neutrally. "Now tell me how it is you are here."

"My Prince, I was about to ask you that same thing?"

"Hasoe of Tylos took me prisoner with drugs and sold me to slavery," Kherin said. "There will be a reckoning. Later. For now, tell me about your journey."

Tarvik shrugged. "As I said, Lord, I would not believe the story put about of your death. Not that I doubt Prince Alzon, you understand." The last was said with a slight inflection that left no doubt as to his true meaning. "Still, it is known that Alzon has little skill in tracking and could have misread the signs. So I searched, asked discreet questions. I found nothing." Tarvik paused for a moment. "It was then I had a vision of the Goddess. The Lady appeared to me in Her guise of the Silver One. She spoke to my heart, saying that you are not dead, and that I should gather certain things and travel across the sea to find you. She said She would be my guide. I did as She commanded. I left Khassan with those of the Khori and Tsithkin who would follow me. A goodly number," he added modestly, "though they came for thee, rather than following Tarvik the Hound."

"All praise to Her Name," Kherin laughed. "She brought you at a good time. Tylos encroaches on this land and with the Khori to ride with the Shi'R'Laen, they will be swept away like driftwood on the tide!" Then cold reality took the delight from him. "If the Khori will still follow me," he added slowly, "and if the Shi'R'Laen will follow Rythian..."

"For these mad barbarians, I cannot speak," Tarvik snorted. "For Khori and Tsithkin I can. My Prince, we will follow thee to the nethermost Pit and beyond. Do not doubt it."

"With Rythian at my side? How many did he kill before he was brought down?"

"Well, that could be another matter, my Prince. He killed five and of the rest, many have wounds from him. He is a great warrior and clearly God-touched. There are those who say he has bewitched thee — " and broke off at Kherin's snort of amusement.

"So say certain of his people of me. Go on."

"But most say there is none more powerful than the Goddess and you are Her Chosen. She would not permit such a thing. Therefore you have bewitched him and he is thine."

"No witchery or spells, Tarvik. He is my soul's companion. Moreover, as I am to the Goddess, so is he to the God — although he denies it," Kherin added ruefully, smoothing the silken cover over the sleeping man's shoulders. "There are things I would have you know, Tarvik, and understand; for this is a land and a people the like of which we have never before seen. Rythian is Sun Stallion — the Chieftain of his tribe. The tribe isn't large; their Warband is perhaps five hundreds of men and women both." Tarvik's jaw slackened at the mention of women warriors. "But I have never known their like in battle, and I would not face them as enemy. I tell you this because we are sworn spear-kin, you and I, and I cannot fight against you. Yet neither can I fight these D'Shael, even if he and I were not SwordSworn, for I am D'Shael also, by their law and the will of his hearth. They took me into their family and made me one of them." It was hard to explain the concept of adoption to one who had no word for it. "I have a hearth-place with them, I am guardian and protector." He thought fondly of Syth, Alais and Emre, who had no need of guarding or protecting and would deal summarily with any foolish enough to be so presumptuous. But such was not the Tsithkin way.

"Is it so?" Tarvik said thoughtfully. "Then this hearth, and the people, are for the protection of my spear, also. Do not fear for them, my Prince. What of this — Sun Stallion? He sought to take his own life on our spears. Why?"

"A D'Shael warrior will not live with defeat."

"He was one against twenty. Besides, the Goddess calls men when She chooses," Tarvik said with a shrug.

"It is a matter of honor, my Hound," Kherin said quietly.

"And his honor must be regained?"

"Or he will be outcast. Spoken against. His family, even his spear-kin, will turn from him. That is why he must Challenge and be Sun Stallion again."

"There is another in his stead?"

"Yes. The Goddess called me and I went. He followed. Last night She sent me a dreaming and I Saw another wearing the Sun Disc, hailed as Sun Stallion. I Saw our hearth weeping and bereft. I Saw his enemy smiling. There had been foretellings of his defeat before I left, Tarvik. One at least was a true Seeing. Out there before the tree, I saw the reality of that Seeing." He stopped and took a deep breath. "Another has been set in his place; Rythian must fight him alone." Kherin was quiet a long time before he spoke again. "And I must be there. I will have to watch it, Tarvik. I know he will win, for he must. But — "

Tarvik heard and responded to the pain in Kherin's voice, and touched his shoulder. "Her Will be done, Kyri."

"All ways and in all things," Kherin responded. "But — " Kherin felt, as much as heard, the change in the sleeping man's breathing and let out his own breath in a sigh of relief. "He wakes. Tarvik, will you leave us for a while? Later we will talk to the doubters, to all the captains."

The man obeyed with a silent bow, but Kherin was not aware; all his attention was given to Rythian. "Brother of my soul," he whispered, "open your eyes. We have much to do, you and I. It is not time yet to fly to the Sun."

"Kherin." A breath, but it carried his name. Kherin. An echo in his mind and a gentle touch of velvet fire.

"The outlander Warband are not enemies," Kherin told him, "but my people, sent from Khassan by the Lady's Will. We have work to do, given us by the Goddess and the God."

Rythian's eyes opened, bleak and bitter. "I can help but little — I am no longer Sun Stallion."

"Yes, you are. That will never change while you live."

"I cannot in honor live. I have been defeated. Captured. I am unfit."

"No, the Gods test us," Kherin said urgently, remembering suddenly what Jeztin had said to him in a distant dream. "We are being tempered in Their forge, fashioned by Their Wills."

Rythian swore and came to his feet in a surge of fury. "You mean all this is Their doing, to make us tools fit for Their use?"

"Yes."

His response was not entirely unexpected, but even so, the vehemence took Kherin by surprise. "Then damn Them to Their own Hells! I'll have no part in it."

"We do not have that choice."

"I fought Caier for the sake of my people," Rythian blazed, "not at the whim of a God. For my people's sake, I did all that I could and I paid the price willingly. Now I am shamed; I cannot do any more for them — or for you — save die in some semblance of honor!"

"You and I, we are Chosen. It is not for us to decide the time and place of our deaths. My Brother, there is still Tylos. The Lady and the Lord have laid a doom on that land and we are Their — "

"Then let Them strike at Tylos."

"They will. Through us. For this they sent my Khori — "

"I will not be used so. I serve my people, not a God more fickle and wilful than a spoilt child."

"You'll go from me, then?" Kherin asked quietly.

The angry face softened into a smile of infinite sadness. "You know I will not. Did I not say it in the SwordVow? Will you walk with me, though I am shamed and not dead?"

"Your honor will be restored," Kherin said, putting all his conviction into the words. "In Her Name, I swear it. But I have to obey Her Will. Rythian, do not go from me."

"I will go where you go," he said simply, "since Holds and Clans are closed to me."

"And if I go to Winter Hold?"

"There also."

"There is another Stallion. I have Seen him — dreamed of him — and Chiera smiled. You must Challenge."

Rythian shook his head. "No," he said. "I no longer have that right. Kherin, you do not understand. I have no clan or tribe, neither kin, nor hearth, nothing and no one, save you."

"When you Challenge and win, you will have all back again."

Rythian seemed to draw away into himself. "You have not heard me," he said. "Don't talk to me of the plans of Gods and Goddesses. If you wish me to Challenge — then I will, my life offered in the Eye of the Sun."

Kherin knew he had to be content with that for now; it was a step forward. "So be it, then. Here are your clothes from our camp, and your sword. 'Thian, you have met my Khori in battle; soon you shall meet them in peace." But there was an unease in his heart. Five dead. No matter that it was one man against twenty. Rythian's blood was forfeit by Khori code and Tsithkin laws. Kherin could not deny the law, but he had to find a way around the letter of it.

Tarvik hesitated before entering the tent that had been his, unsure what he would find. But the council of captains was ready, and there were matters the Prince must know. He ducked under the flap. The barbarian was kneeling half-turned away and the Prince was combing the tangles from the long blond mane, saying something in a strange soft tongue, smiling. The barbarian responded absently. From the measuring looks he was exchanging with T'Shayra, sitting watching the proceedings with slit-eyed interest, both were uncertain of each other's motives. Tarvik gave a discreet cough.

"My Prince, your pardon."

"Tarvik." Kherin's eyes lifted to his in question. "The council?"

"They await you, Lord."

"Thank you, my Hound. What are they saying?"

Tarvik kept his gaze on the gently moving hands that worked patiently on the few remaining knots in the mantle of hair that fell almost to the man's waist. "Lord — they are unsure." That was true enough. "And they are concerned for you."

"I thank them for their concern," Kherin said mildly. The comb ran smoothly now, and he was gathering the sleek mass up between his hands. "Of what are they unsure?"

Tarvik reminded himself that never had the Prince condemned any man for merely speaking truth. "Of the barbarian, Lord. Among warriors and captains, more are now saying he has bewitched you."

"So. What else?"

"They will speak their hearts, my Prince."

"They would not be Khori or Tsithkin else." With the ease of practice, Kherin knotted the hair up on the crown to fall shining like a stallion's proud tail. "But you, my Hound — what is in your heart?" He used the old intimate speech of the Khori. Tarvik could not prevaricate.

"He is in truth your heart-friend and blood-friend?"

"In truth, and before the Goddess." Kherin's eyes, darkly blue as midnight, fixed on him gravely.

"Yet he was your enemy and he held you captive."

"My enemy — never. And my captivity was none of his doing. The collar was still about my neck because the D'Shael do not have the tools to cut Tylosian steel."

"He killed five, Lord, Khori and Tsithkin. The blood-price — "

" — will be offered for payment, Tarvik. I swear it."

There was nothing more to say. Perhaps, Tarvik thought miserably, he truly is bewitched and the barbarian was indeed a demon in quasi-human form. What else could cast a spell over the Chosen? Behind his back, Tarvik made the warding sign. "I have heard you," he murmured. But still the blue eyes held him. Kherin urged the barbarian to stand beside him. He topped the Prince by two handsbreadth — more! — a giant out of legend.

"Tarvik," said Kherin quietly. "I have need of you in council. You are my captain and my dear friend, sworn to me. Will you serve me so indeed?"

Tarvik did not try to avoid his eyes, the love in his heart swelling in his breast. "Lord, I am your Hound. Now as always I serve you." Yet even as he spoke, he guessed what would be required of him and every sense cried out against it.

"Rythian is my Brother, chosen of the Chosen."

"Yes, my Prince." *Only do not ask it, Lord!*

"Will you then salute him fittingly, my Hound?"

It was not a command. If it had been, Tarvik would have had no choice. Truly, the Prince was wise! Tarvik stared up at the alien face of the D'Shael, tried to read what lay behind that expressionless mask and failed. "Lord..."

"I would know that we have one friend in the council."

I would die for thee! Tarvik said in his heart. *But do not ask this!*
There was a long moment's pause, then, "I am in all things your
friend," Tarvik whispered, capitulating. He dropped to one knee and
touched his right hand to the booted foot of the blond man.

Kherin pulled him up into an embrace. "That was not easy for
you. I thank you from my heart."

Tarvik bent his head. It would have been easy for the Chosen, in
the full awesome possession of the Power, to have pressured his will.
Kherin, Tarvik knew, would never do that. His Khori were here in
this foreign land by free choice, seeking the Chosen One they had
sworn to. The Tsithkin not so oath-bound were there because Kherin
was the voice and mortal power of their Goddess. Neither Khori nor
Tsithkin would accept another Chosen while he lived.

Tarvik had never understood the ways of his Prince's mind,
although there had been times when he had thought he had come
close. Now, since that moment of astonishment and joy when he
heard the familiar clear voice ringing across the rocky defile and
saw his Prince spring like a leopard into the fight, he failed to
understand or predict anything.

Normally Tarvik's place was by Kherin's side as Captain of the
Khori, but at the council his place was elsewhere.

The five captains and their lieutenants were already seated cross-
legged on the carpets when Tarvik entered the tent. He took his
place in the fore of the crescent, directly facing the two enclosed by
its horns; the Prince with the winged spiral on his brow, slender and
straight in Khassani silk; and the inhuman height of the barbarian,
his mane of barley-fair hair falling bright over a black fur cloak.
T'Shayra lay like a sculpted lion, head up, paws folded, behind
them.

"We are met," Tarvik said, "at the asking of the Prince Kherin."

Kherin took the long knife from his sash, laid it point first before
him; the Khori sign of a warrior among warriors desiring justice.
There was a muted buzz from the captains at that, which fell silent
when Kherin began speaking in the familiar argot of the Khori.

"I am Kherin, Prince of Khassan, born of the Royal House, known
as the Hawk of the South. I am Chosen of the Mother, Beloved of the
Lady, the Winged One. I am your father, your brother, your voice
before Her. Here in the council I am all these things, yet I choose to
speak as Kherin the Hawk, for in distant Khassan we have fought
together and shed blood together. That is our bonding. Therefore, as
is our custom, let any who wishes, speak: and after that, hear me."

That was well said, Tarvik thought. But many of the dark eyes still watched the silent figure of the blond man, wary, mistrusting. Tarvik knew what they would say; and they did, each speaker making the age-old claim of blood for blood, a damning tally demanding the barbarian's life. Kherin listened, impassive, unspeaking.

When Tarvik's turn to speak came around, he deferred, unable to meet the Prince's gaze. He would not add his voice to those asking the blood-price, yet he could not deny them the right to ask it. He too had lost comrades.

Kherin waited until all were silent before reaching down and taking the knife into his hand. "I have heard you," he said levelly, "Now I say this. By law you claim the blood-right. By law this cannot be denied you. Nor do I deny it. But by law, if another offers his blood in place of the offender, it is accepted before the Goddess. Rythian of the Shi'R'Laen is my heart-friend and blood-friend. If you wish his blood, you must take mine instead."

This time there was no buzz of comment, but an uproar of disbelief and anger. Kherin stared them down.

"The blood-price is offered," he said steadily. "Take it, or forfeit it."

"Lord." One of the Khassani captains spoke up. "Lord, we cannot. You know it. To spill the blood of the Chosen would bring a curse on the man who even thought of it!"

"I will lift that curse," Kherin said. "But who will lift the curse I will lay on the man who raises a hand against the chosen of the Chosen, blessed by the Lady?"

Again, uproar. Tarvik saw that several of the captains were almost weeping with frustration. The D'Shael, plainly understanding nothing of what was happening, sat as immobile as the statue of a God. *My Lord bargains for thy life*, Tarvik thought. *As he would for Jeztin, if Jeztin lived. Or for me. But thou art more to him than we ever were. If this is not sorcery, then what art thou?*

The blue eyes turned towards him suddenly, as unreadable as sky — steady, unblinking and terrifyingly knowing. Tarvik drew breath harshly, right hand clenching in the warding sign, though what good that might do with a creature powerful enough to bespell Kherin, Tarvik did not know. He would have as soon outstared a basilisk, but pride would not let him look away.

Kherin was speaking again, his voice an edged blade to cut through the rising bedlam. "We are sworn each to each, life beyond life. As it is, so it was and will be again. This the Lady has shown me."

Beside Tarvik, a rustle as a captain got to his feet. "Lord, none of us here will shed your blood. We rejoice that you are come among us again, free and alive. You say this man is your blood-friend, and so it must be since truth is ever on your tongue. Yet he has killed our brothers and Khori law cries vengeance. He is ours. For blood spilt, blood must pay."

The captains buzzed assent, and Tarvik let slip his gaze from the barbarian to Kherin again, seeing the unshaken serenity in the fine-boned face, emotion only betrayed by a fractional tightening of the mouth.

"So be it," he said softly. And before any of them could move or speak the knife flashed and scarlet leapt upwards across the bare brown wrist, spurting strong to splatter on the white silk. Tarvik, like the rest, moaned with shock at the unprecedented omen. No man could shed the blood of the Chosen with impunity, and they had done this impiety as surely as if theirs had been the hand on the knife. At the same time the giant's hand clamped above the wound to lessen the flow, his features no longer impassive but shocked and angry. "As his honor is mine, so his blood is mine. It is shed, therefore, and at your will. The law is fulfilled. As for the dead— no curse stains them, for they did only their duty, and they died like true men. Their names shall be remembered with honor, and the Mother has received them into Her hand." His own hand ran with blood from his slashed wrist, but it seemed Kherin had forgotten about it. "Remember also that one warrior stood against twenty, downed five and wounded many before he was overcome by sheer weight of numbers. If he had been of the Khori, Khassani or Tsithkin, his name would be sung throughout the land!"

Tarvik shook his head despairingly. "By your leave, Lord," he murmured and untied his browband. He twisted it around the arm above the wound, watched the pulsing flow ease to an ooze. Finally the D'Shael released his hold and spoke swiftly and with true anger. Tarvik did not need a translation to tell him that the Prince Kherin, Chosen of the Lady, was being given a candid opinion of his stupidity and in no uncertain terms. Tarvik found that oddly reassuring. A captain passed him a kerchief and he bound it over the slash, the whiteness staining crimson.

Kherin smiled at Tarvik, but his words were for the council. "What now, brothers?"

The captain who had spoken before, his color sallow with shock at the Prince's action, cleared his throat. "Blood has been offered for blood. The law is fulfilled, Prince. You have said it."

"I thank you, Alar," Kherin said. "Yet may each man speak his mind."

There was none to dissent. But one of the Khori, a man who had served Kherin from the beginning, found courage enough to say what was on many minds. "Lord, the life you have bought is sacred now to you. But you went from among us without sign, and your people talked of sorcery. Now you are returned, and with you is such a one as we have never seen. No man has hair so light, nor stands so tall."

"Shall you speak to the Great Goddess, then, Nemor, and tell Her so? Rythian is a man of the Mother's shaping, as you are."

"We hear you, Lord. But it is in our minds that he has bewitched you." There was a growl of assent.

"So. The Lady guards Her Chosen so meanly then, that I am easily bewitched?"

"We did not say easily, Prince."

"That I may be bewitched at all, Nemor, is a sad comment on Her care of me, is it not? Rest easy. There is no witchery in this."

Nemor's stance did not change. Stubborn, he held to his charge. "Lord, he has branded you. We all saw it, the demon mark put upon your flesh."

Kherin's hand lifted again. "Listen now, all of you, and I shall tell you how it came to be. Yes, I carry the D'Shael brand, yet it was not a D'Shael hand that laid the iron to me. Tylos stole me from my homeland, by treachery and betrayal. Tylos sent me north, a slave, a Tribute to the D'Shael horse-clans who guard the caravan-trails. The hand of Tylos put this mark upon me and Rythian, seeing it, was angered, for the D'Shael brand only cattle. He freed me, gave me a warrior's status and a place at his side, for he is Sun Stallion, leader of his clan before the God."

The Tsithkin were engrossed. The subtle variations in Kherin's voice, tone and inflection, held them as surely as a storyteller in the marketplace. "He has cared for me, unknowing of who or what I am, and the Goddess blesses him for it. Having given him honor, She promises greater glory yet. I know, for I have Seen it." He paused, gauging their reactions. "How should I doubt it, when She has sent you, my brothers, my Khori, to join with the D'Shael people against the enemy, the Accursed Ones, the defilers of Her Chosen? It is from Tylos you shall claim the blood-price, brothers, Tylos who shall pay for this sacrilege tenfold!"

Even Tarvik was caught up in the raw flood of emotion Kherin evoked. The Tsithkin were baying still for blood, but not that of the barbarians, who had been transmogrified from enemies into friends. The clear ringing voice of their Chosen, their Beloved, whipped them to a peak of fury before he stilled them once more. "It was in ignorance, I know, that you took this man for enemy. Yet still he is owed some recompense." And he twisted, gracefully, to kneel and touch Rythian's foot. "Forgive these my people, Brother, as you love me."

It was unheard of. It was unthinkable. The Chosen owes fealty to no man, not even the High King, for as Consort of the Goddess he is above mortal authority. Like the others, Tarvik stared, struck dumb. Kherin said something in the swift cadences of D'Shael, and they saw Rythian's hand touch the dark curls briefly. Kherin took it, kissed the palm, and pulled the man to his feet. "Behold, I present to you Rythian, Chosen of the Sun, Chosen of the Lady's Chosen. I call upon you to do him honor."

Tarvik knew then why Kherin had required his homage earlier. Once done, it was less difficult the second time, and he was thus the first to kneel before Rythian's feet and utter the words of fealty, and after him, each of the captains.

Afterwards, Kherin went from the tent to heal those Rythian had wounded, and the Khori became more settled with the barbarian's presence. At dawn of the next day, the Khori would ride to the Winter Hold.

There was no sign of the Shi'R'Laen as they crossed the plain, though the prickling down his spine told Kherin they were out there.

"We are watched," Rythian said.

"I know. Will they attack?"

"Perhaps. If it were me leading them, I'd —" He broke off with a shrug. "—be waiting with a feint attack, and retreat to draw us into an ambush among the boulders and gullies, since you are so greatly outnumbered.

"And if the Elders are guiding the false Stallion?"

"Wait, most like, behind the gates of the Hold."

"My thinking, also. So we had best show them we do not come to make war."

They left the main body of the Khori on the edge of the plain, and they approached the Winter Hold from the west. Only twenty honor guard rode with them, Kherin, Rythian and Tarvik well in front of the rest. All rode with swords sheathed and spears carried blade-down, signifying that they came in peace.

Kherin's first sight of Winter Hold was across the wide canyon it commanded. A terraced and walled fortress, Winter Hold seemed to Kherin hewn of the very rock itself — and impregnable. The sun glowed on the red and ochre of the rocks, picking out the trail that wound up from the valley floor.

There was no sign of life. The Winter Hold turned blank eyes towards them, but all knew they were being watched.

"We go to the foot of the canyon," Kherin commanded. "And we approach no nearer. Now they must come to us."

There was not long to wait.

"A rider comes from the fortress," Tarvik reported, shading his eyes. "By my father's blood! Was that beast born of mares?"

Neck arched, Kardan's massive horse paced between the line of mounted Outlanders. On his back the Elder sat spear-straight, his Staff poised erect in the stirrup-boot. His loosened hair formed a white mantle about his wide shoulders. His upper body was bare, brown-tanned skin over still-firm muscle dappled with warrior-scars. The rugged, handsome face was cold and grim as rocks in winter. He was formidable and awe-inspiring, and it needed no word from Kherin to silence the turbulent Khori.

"So they send an envoy to treat with us, my Prince?" Tarvik murmured.

"No. Be silent, make no hostile move. I would have the Shi'R'Laen as friends and allies, not death-foes."

"Death-foes?" It was an alien word to Tarvik, and he frowned.

"This people neither give nor accept quarter, in warfare or in vengeance."

"Never, Prince?" his captain inquired again, his eyes offering a question to the silent man at Kherin's side.

"It is for my sake he lives, not his own. I have already told you; he is their chieftain, the Sun Lord's Chosen, and they must be reminded of that. As must he."

"Is it this old giant he must fight?"

"No, my Hound. Be still."

With cool anger and scorn in his eyes, Kardan studied the Outlanders, Kherin, and Rythian in turn. He dismissed them all, and when he spoke it was to Kherin, using the Tylosian tongue. "Well, boy?" As if he had been caught in some illicit and shameful escapade.

Tarvik shifted, but made no sound.

"Well, Uncle?" Kherin returned in D'Shael. "Do you not greet your Sun Stallion?"

"I did, this dawning. I see no Sun Stallion here, only a Warband of outlanders."

"Outlanders, yes, and a Warband. But not enemies of the Shi'R'Laen," Kherin said clearly. "When I was a Prince in Khassan, these warriors were of my Khori. Remember, we spoke of them on the wartrail we shared, Uncle? Now they have found me again and would ride with me as before, against my enemies and yours."

"That is a matter for the Council and the Sun Stallion," the Elder said shortly.

"The Sun Stallion is here, the rest of the Hold Council yonder. Shall we discuss it then, Uncle?"

"Boy," Kardan growled, "you may or may not be ignorant of our customs, but there is one here who is not." He had reverted to his native tongue. "Rythian, if the sword at your side is blunt, I will fetch you mine. Or give you my knife. There is no cause to shame the Sun with your life."

Under his earlier scrutiny, Rythian had not met his gaze nor seemed aware of his presence. It had been easy for Kardan to dismiss him and feel a sorrow for what Rythian had been. Now those blue eyes focused on him, shards of sky-stone, hard and razor-keen: yet with something else behind their unwavering stare — bleak despair and a kind of grieving pride that struck an empathic chord in Kardan's heart.

"There has been a time of late," Rythian said, voice cold and distant and all but expressionless, "when I sought death. But I have been told it was not to the Lord's liking. Since that road is closed to me, I will stand in the Eye of the Sun and offer Challenge. I will be Sun Stallion, or I will be dead."

"You would Challenge Marin?" He had succeeded in startling Kardan, and the question came out in a threatening bellow.

"How did Marin become Stallion?" Rythian asked coldly.

"There was no contest, no Challenge. No one stood forward in the Eye of the Sun save him. It took Elders and Priestesses only a day to agree he should be elected — elected! — until the God's choice be made clear."

"It will be made clear now," Rythian said. "Go sound the Gather Horn and tell them all. The Khori will not approach any nearer to the Hold. Kherin and I will enter alone."

Kardan's hands jarred on the reins. "'Thian, you cannot!" The words broke through custom and protocol. "Voran and Arun witnessed you taken living by enemies! For whatever reason, you were defeated, shamed. And you Sun Stallion! How can you be worthy of such high honor again?"

Rythian smiled, and Kardan felt ice in his spine. "Then, Uncle, I shall be dead. Go now. I will come at noon."

It was not long to midday. Less than an hour. Rythian felt torn, part of him wanting the comfort and pleasure of Kherin's companionship for whatever time might be left him; another part dwelling in isolation, remote and empty.

If Marin was destined to be Sun Stallion, then he should become so in a true Challenge, Stallion to Stallion. If he, Rythian, should win, then his honor and Kherin's would be vindicated. Wouldn't it? Rythian needed some time alone to settle his mind before the coming fight.

"My beloved," Kherin's voice drifted up to Rythian. "It is nearly time."

Rythian did not speak, but came down from the sunlit rock that had been his perch and called Zaan from the horselines. Tarvik approached, carrying harness.

"I have a whetstone, if you wish a finer edge to your blades," he said, voice gruff, off-hand.

"Sun Stallions," Kherin murmured, "do not fight with weapons, my Hound." He reached up to unbind the blond hair. Rythian stood still to let him do it, then stripped himself of boots and breeches. When he swung up onto Zaan's back, the great horse reared, savage challenge bugling from his lungs to rouse the echoes of the mountain to life. Almost to a man the Khori moved back a pace, jaws slack.

"But — Prince!" Tarvik was outraged. "He cannot go naked to such a duel!"

"It is the way of the D'Shael," Kherin said, his voice filled with pride and love. "So do they contest the leadership. He is the Stallion of the Sun, and stands this day in His Eye."

The Winter Hold was an ancient fortress of an age gone by, hewn by a people long since departed. Kherin had heard enough about it to know that it had never fallen to an enemy. It could house the whole of the clan, with ample room for their livestock and chattels beside. It was a fit place to wait out the hard grasp of winter, or to block an invasion, perched as it was overlooking the only good pass through the mountains. Kherin's warrior eye saw all these things, even as he registered the stone-faced rank of SwordBrothers waiting to either escort them in — or challenge their approach. Their swords negligently balanced across their horses' withers, their loosened manes of hair, all were clear warning. To them, he was the enemy, the interloper. As was, to a degree, the man half a length ahead of him on Zaan.

Kherin saw Arun's gaze flick over them and away, pain in his eyes. Voran's face was streaked with angry tears.

They think shame to him for living with dishonor. The thought burned like a brand.

The SwordBrethren parted but not to let them through. The great gates stood open, but the Elders barred their way, the Sun Standard in their midst. Beyond them, Kherin could see his hearthkin standing a little back from the other groups. The women's eyes were dry; their heads carried proud. If they saw Rythian fall, they would not weep. To them, he was better dead. Would they weep for Kherin?

Marin, the elected Sun Stallion, stood forward from the Elders. He was taller and heavier than Rythian; he was also older, a seasoned warrior. Otherwise naked for the battle, sunlight glinted on the great pectoral on his breast. For a moment, Kherin felt pity for the man. So brief a day of glory...

Rythian's voice rang out in Challenge. Marin answered, and it was like the screaming of stallions before the combat, bright manes tossing, hooves sharp in the dust, teeth bared.

Kherin shivered. Mother of Mares, we are in Thy hand. Marin was taking off the Sun Disc; Rythian, already naked save for the SwordBrother bracelet, was a breathing statue. Kherin found a scowling boy at his heel, taking the horses' reins from him. "The Goddess sent you, Ronan hearthson," he said softly, and the scowl deepened.

"No one else would come. Dreyen wanted to, but they won't let him. So I came to ask you — to see if what everyone says is true. Mother and Syth won't tell me, but I knew you would."

"And what is everyone saying? That Rythian is no longer fit to be Sun Stallion, unworthy to stand in the Eye of the Sun? We shall see the falseness of that, I promise you, before this day is passed."

"But if he was dishonored — "

"Ronan, son of my hearth," Kherin put both hands on the boy's shoulders. "No man has put dishonor on Rythian. I will tell you the tale of all that has passed, I swear to you, and soon. We are SwordSworn, he and I: you see this," he held up his braceleted wrist. "You know what it means. If Rythian were dishonored, would his Brother let him live shamed?"

"No..." Hope was being born in the blue eyes.

"So. Remember that men and women lie and are afraid, but the Lord and Lady see all truths. Listen now, for I have a duty for you, hearthson. When the combat is over, take twenty head of meat-cattle from our herd and drive them over the ridge to the warband, my Khori. They are my spear-brothers. They understand Tylosian, so tell them their Prince greets them, and they are free to feast and to hunt the northern and western slopes for their needs, but only that and no more. Tell them if I do not come to them within three days, then they are to depart this land without further troubling, and all is as the Goddess wills. To their leader, Tarvik, you say this — at the Moon of Fallows, remember us."

Ronan's lips moved silently as he repeated the message to himself. He nodded. "Yes, Kherin. I can do all that."

"Go back to the hearthkin now, and take care of them for me until I come again."

For himself, he had to witness the combat. Rythian was fighting for both their lives. But where SwordBrothers could fight shoulder to shoulder, he must stand by while Rythian fought. And Rythian must win. The consequences otherwise were unthinkable.

Kherin stood apart from the thronging D'Shael. He was aware of them and their excitement; aware of the Elders; aware of Arun and Voran, nearest to him yet not quite close enough to touch. Kherin had never felt so alone. He could not watch. If he did, he might not be able to stop himself gathering power and using it. Rythian would not accept such a victory. Yet he could not, in honor, leave the field.

Well, there was another way. Kherin opened his mind and let his Inner Self go free, winging like the hawk that was his namesake, beating up into the thin mountain air. Sunlight cradled him like a cupped, sheltering hand. Kherin rode its strength, uplifted and supported. This was as it should be, and for a timeless space he let it carry him. Then he sensed a change; growing, swelling, like water behind a dam. A force, a power that could not be denied.

Nor did Kherin try to deny it. He opened himself up to it, and felt it rush into and channel through him. The winged Self stooped on that great surge of light as the falcon stoops on the wind, an arrow, a blazing spear, pinions of fire brushing the brow of the Stallion — Marin died in that instant, snuffed out of life by Rythian's hands. The Hawk screamed triumph as the very air itself seemed to catch fire, coalescing into the figure of one man standing naked over his fallen adversary. Rythian — Sun Stallion now in all truth.

The same swooping descent brought Kherin back to his body. He watched Rythian stalk through the breath-held quiet to the Standard, take the Sun Disc from it and place it around his neck. The paean saluted him then, raised first by the SwordBrothers, then the Elders; and the very echoes were shattered into shards by the clamoring voices of the people.

Chapter 15

Rythian walked through the gates of the Hold like a conqueror. Bruised and bleeding from half a dozen places, alone but for his SwordBrother pacing at his side, he climbed the twisting path to the Sun Hall. Only there did he halt. Even in the dimness within, Kherin's Inner Sight saw him still blazing with sunlight. By rights Rythian should have been exhausted, but he was half-fierce, half-defiant, and fresh as if risen from sleep. Kherin watched him warily. Sooner or later, events would catch up with him. But not, it seemed, just yet.

"There's a bathing room in the Sun Hall," Rythian said. "I won't go to our hearth all over dust and sweat. Come help me, Brother."

"The Elders will be calling a Council," Kherin reminded him, following him through to where a pool had been sunken into the rock. The water was warmed by the sun streaming down a light-well into the cistern. Kherin stripped and sank into it. The water was blood-heat, silken on the skin.

"The Council can wait on the pleasure of the Sun Stallion," Rythian said and ducked under completely, coming up with a feral grin on his face. "By the God, they danced attendance often enough on Caier's whims. Now let them wait on mine."

Kherin chuckled. "I'm sure that will delight them." He leaned back against the pool rim, looking around him. "This Hold is not what I expected. It is old. Did your people build it?"

"No. Legend says we took it in battle. Domen Stonehand struck down the gates with one blow of his fist. Have you not heard that tale? It's one of Dreyen's favourites."

"Yes. But I did not expect this. And are there indeed caverns beneath?"

"There are. I explored some when I was a child, though I have little love for them. Ask Myra, she knows far better than anyone except Chiera." Rythian hauled himself up and out of the pool, twisting his hair to wring some of the water out of it. "Tell me a thing," he said thoughtfully. "These Khori of yours — where were they bound, before they came upon us in the Sacred Land?"

"They searched for me," he answered, following Rythian out.

"And now?" his Brother said softly.

"Now their swords are at your service," Kherin said simply. "You have seen the way they fight."

"They are warriors indeed. This fashion of the two swords, the greater and the lesser — "

"It is the Tsithkin way. I have fought so for most of my life." He ran his hands over Rythian's injuries, healing the small wounds without effort. "I will show you my swords. They were among the things Tarvik was instructed to bring away..." His eyes grew dreamy. "D'Shael swords are good, for all they are bronze. But mine — I can bend the blade into a curve like that of a drawn bow and it will spring back, supple as a willow wand. It has an edge like the winter wind. The Tsithkin smiths are the best in the world. You think Tylosian steel is fine, but — "

"You have the secret of that metal?" Rythian cut in, his fingers biting into Kherin's shoulders. "And you did not tell me?"

His SwordBrother blinked at him. "You didn't ask," he said reasonably. "I do not, but they have the way of it."

Rythian gave a great whoop of delight and pulled him into an embrace. "Lord, Lord, for this gift, our thanks! We can have swords to equal those of Tylos?"

"Equal? Better! Have I not said, the Tsithkin smiths are the best? Even in Khassan, we do not have as fine."

"The question is," Rythian said intently, excitement reined back, "whether they will be willing to teach the skill."

"I make no promises. It is their mystery, and jealously guarded. Such knowledge cannot be bought. And there are tales of what they did to those who tried to steal it from them."

"All things in the Eye of the Sun!" Rythian said. "They will at least be willing to discuss it? Good. I'll have Disan and Gallan, all our best men in smithcraft to meet with your Tsithkin." He stood up and stretched. "And now the hearth. Though in truth I'd rather face lions. Lionesses."

Kherin laughed. "I'll not let them scold you."

"How?" Rythian snorted. "You have only two hands to cover three mouths. And Alais bites."

"I know. Dress yourself, and let's dare their anger!"

Rythian refused to have his hair bound up or braided, however, and Kherin did not press him. They walked together down the rock-cut streets, but there was no hope of them coming unheralded to the hearth. Word ran before them, and by the time they reached the paved yard in front of the house, the three women were there waiting for them.

No one scolded. Syth did not speak at all, but wrapped her arms around their necks and held them. Emre cried and laughed at the same time. Alais kissed Kherin, then Rythian, then Kherin again. The two men were borne inside on a tide of welcome. There were questions asked and answered, and more embraces, and more tears. It would have been exhausting but for the love there. Arun and Voran came with Lia and Shelais, and everything had to be explained again. Then Kardan brought Syre and LyDia, saying that Council would wait for the morning. By the end of the evening Kherin was wondering if the place could hold any more people.

The celebratory gathering spilled outside, soon encompassing the neighboring houses and much of the street. Into this came Myra, smiling, wearing the robes of the Middle Priestess and giving Rythian the formal greeting as Sun Stallion. "I doubt you have need of any word of mine that you are blessed by the God and Goddess alike," she said, looking at them with fondness. "But it is your right to know this, both of you — the Maiden has quickened."

"Rynna? My sister?" Rhythian asked startled. His question was accompanied by a stifled sound from Kherin.

"Who else?" Myra asked rhetorically. "You do not need to be told, I think, that this is a good omen."

"And Rynna?" Kherin asked.

"Is well. Though not, alas, any more reconciled to her role. She is a Huntress born, that one."

"She is the Goddess' choice," Kherin said.

"True, but like her brother, she is not easily backed and bridled, even by the High Ones. Oh, don't fear, she'll settle to it. As will he."

For want of something to do during this time of celebration, Tarvik cleaned and polished harness; his own, Kherin's, and that of the man Rythian.

All the Tsithkin had gathered to watch the combat from the hilltop. After, while their minds still buzzed with what they had seen, the boy had ridden up with a small herd of good cattle, telling them in the Prince's name to feast and hunt, until he came again. The lad also brought another message that had chilled Tarvik's heart.

Rythian had been victorious, but there had been no word, no sign, since then. Tarvik wondered when he would know. Although Rythian had walked from the killing-ground, who was to say what injuries he had received from the taller, heavier man that would need the Chosen's healing touch. Like desert-leopard against lion, it had been, though some of the Khori swore they had seen stallions in truth fighting with hooves and teeth in the blaze of noon.

He wondered also where T'Shayra was; she had gone off about her hunting. Although he guessed she would be back when her belly was full, he was no longer certain of anything. T'Shayra was no tame hearth-cat. Kherin knew that, but Tarvik did not want to have to face him with the news that T'Shayra had gone back to the wild. She would be back. It was not the first time she had hunted alone. He was starting at shadows.

The rising sun touched the face of the valley with rosy light, contrasting against the shadows of the canyon. Kherin watched it from the open doorway, at ease and deeply content. Goddess grant that now these people would accept the Lord's clear choice and there would be no more Challenges against Rythian for many years.

Behind Kherin, an inner door opened and Rythian came out to stand yawning beside him, laying an arm across his shoulders. In the other hand he carried the Sun Disc, as casually as if the shaped gold was an old belt. Yet it had not gone beyond his reach since he had regained it.

"A fair morning, Brother."

Kherin smiled, leaning into the embrace. There had been no question of them leaving to return to the Sun Hall as custom demanded, and it was as well the bed was wide enough for five. Not that there had been much in the way of sleep for any of them. His smile widened and his contentment deepened.

"Indeed," Kherin agreed. "And a fair day to come."

"Hot," Rythian replied, scanning the sky with a frown. "And I'm not at my best penned within walls. This place is bad enough in winter. In summer I think it will have me foaming at the mouth within days. It's as well we're not staying."

Kherin felt no oppression from the weight of rock about them, but it did not surprise him that Rythian should. "Have you eaten?" Kherin asked.

"Later, maybe. There will be Council first. Right now I'd sooner face half a dozen lions than the Hold Elders."

"You," said Kherin, making the one word a caress and gentle teasing, "are such a coward."

"Don't doubt it," Rythian chuckled. "They'll be sending for us soon, and I'd prefer to be ready for them." He shook his hair back and put on the Sun Disc, settling the cool weight of it on his chest.

"Shall I braid your hair?"

"No. This Sun Stallion could well be at war with his Elders."

"Do you still doubt?" Kherin smiled.

Rythian laughed, all his confidence and new-found joy in living ringing into the morning. "I do not, though I won't be driven like a plough-ox by anyone, mortal or God. Come then, Brother. Are you ready for the fray?"

Kherin took up his Khori headband and tied it about his brow. "I am ready."

The Elder Hall of the Winter Hold was not hewn entirely from the rock as the Sun Hall was, but built partly of dressed stone and roofed in thatch. The doors stood open; the sun baked down unchecked, and the air was still and stifling. Kherin, standing beside the ancient carved stone chair, was used to conditions like this. The Council were not. He watched them sweat. Tendrils of blond hair clung damply to Rythian's brow, too, and moisture beaded his upper lip. But that could have been for reasons other than the heat. This meeting was as difficult as Rythian had thought it would be.

Nortan was holding the floor, having claimed first right. His new staff was beating an angry underscore on the stone flags. "How is it," he demanded, "that the Sun Stallion who pledged to restore our ancient laws and customs has himself broken them?" It was a question in many minds. "The battle with the Surni gave us victory," he went on, "though the manner of it left an evil taste, and it cannot be seen as a thing of honor."

There was a growl of dissension from Kardan, who had ridden with the Warband.

"That is past," he rumbled. "The matter of defeat and capture is more important."

"I am Sun Stallion, Uncle, by right of Challenge twice over." Rythian was barely holding his temper in check. Kherin saw the knuckles of the hand on the arm of the chair whiten.

"Sun Stallion you were," Nortan agreed, "and Sun Stallion you are, no one denies that. But in between — what were you then, Lyre'son? It was seen in visions by the Hooded One, and in dreams by many others — your own hearthsister among them — our Sun Stallion, naked, weaponless, defeated, beaten down into the dust. Those who came searching for you, they saw the reality. Yet you live. The Sun Stallion is the pride and honor of the tribe. Where was our pride and our honor then? Where is it now?" A buzz rose into the hot stillness. Kherin saw Rythian stir, sensed his self-control.

"The Shi'R'Laen's pride and honor were not questioned when Caier dragged both in the mire," he said tightly. "For myself, I gave Marin the opportunity to be Sun Stallion in truth, by rite of Challenge.

If I was unworthy in the Eye of the Sun, how is it I am here and he is not? Since it seems the choice of the Sun Lord that I lead the tribe, then for the good of the Sh'R'Laen I stand ready to be His Sacrifice. I stand in the Eye of the Sun. But what we should be debating is what to do about the Tylosians. They are building a fortress by the GodStone. We need to defend our lands against them — that is what we should be discussing here."

There were nods of agreement, but Nortan was not appeased.

"So you say, Lyre'son. But I say this: you are blind and bewitched!" He had to raise his voice to a shout to be heard above the roar that went up from the other Elders. "You came back to us defeated and shamed, with your conquerors victorious about you! And they are led by one sent to us by Tylos, who you have named as SwordBrother! You have brought our enemies among us, into our very hearts!"

Kherin could not let that pass. "I am no enemy to the D'Shael," he said steadily, his voice cutting clean as a blade through the continuing arguments. "Nor are my people." He stepped forward a pace to confront Nortan. "I have a word to say on this, since there are those who still hold me in mistrust. Have I the Council's leave to speak?"

Kardan's assent cut in on anything Nortan might have said. "Speak your piece, SwordBrother."

"I thank you, Uncle. Hear me, then. I was brought here by Tylos, it is true, but I was captive, taken by treachery, kept spellbound and drugged. In my country, it is dishonor, as it is here, to be defeated. Truly I thought myself forsaken by all I held dear.

"But it was not so. The Gods themselves decide who they will honor. Even as a swordblade is tempered and tested, so it is with those whom the Gods choose.

"Yes, Rythian was cast down. But the God has raised him up again to the high duty of Sun Stallion — "

"More likely it is witchcraft!" Nortan howled, staff raised as if to strike. "You bespelled Rythian into naming you SwordBrother, you bespelled Marin so that he would die at Rythian's hand! Now you would glamour us, witch-spawn — "

Rythian surged to his feet. The fury in him would not be checked any longer. Although he held no weapon, it seemed for one blinding instant that there was a spear in his hand. Without thought Rythian hurled it, an arc of red-gold leaping from his outstretched hand to explode Nortan's staff in his grasp.

"Be silent!" Rythian commanded. The banked Hearth surged into full flame, flaring almost to the louvers in the rafters and licking at the thatch.

As suddenly as it had come, the blaze died, leaving the Hall in dimness and stunned silence. But only for a moment. Then everyone began to shout at once.

Rythian did not heed them. He sprang down from the dais and through the Elders, not seeing them shrink from him, and left the Hall.

Chaos ruled behind him. Kherin hesitated only a moment before going to Nortan's side. The man was being helped to stand. His eyes bulged in a stark face, but he was unharmed save for singed hair and clothing. But the shock held him speechless. "You will be well enough, Uncle," Kherin smiled, turning from him to the others.

It was Kardan who recovered first. "SunFire, by God..." he rumbled. Then bellowed it. "SunFire!"

"Do any of you doubt the God's choice now?" Kherin demanded, and left them to their speculations.

Instinct told him he would find Rythian in the Sun Hall. He was staring at the great golden emblem covering the end wall as if it could speak, answer all his questions. Kherin made no sound, but Rythian spun on his heel, thrusting out a hand as if to ward him off, and the sullenly-glowing coals in the hearth sparked into flame.

"Shall I fear my SwordBrother?" Kherin asked calmly. The rage in the man was held in check, but the energy of it seemed to crackle in the air about him. Seen with his Inner Eye, Rythian was a coruscating blaze of power and anger, all that he was now come to full glory. Sun Stallion. Exaltation grew in Kherin. "They will not doubt you again, my soul's Brother. Nor will any."

"Sun Fire..." Rythian whispered, some of the anger fading into awe. "A thing out of stories. No one has ever seen SunFire." Rythian fell silent again, still struggling to understand and accept what had happened — what he had done. "Was Nortan harmed?"

"Singed a little. Mostly shocked." Kherin found the wine flask, and poured a generous measure. "Here. Drink."

Rythian took the cup, but did not taste it. "Singed!" He spat.

"His staff, though," Kherin went on, taking a quick glance at the new flames growing in the hearth, "is so much ash."

"By The God, he does not deserve to bear that staff!" Rythian snapped. "I wish I had the unmaking of him. I'd put you in his place!"

"Indeed?" Kherin's mouth quirked in a smile. "Truly the Goddess honors me. SwordBrother to the Sun Stallion; Elder of the D'Shael Council; Prince of Khassan and Her Chosen. Shall I be Year-President of Tylos also?"

Rythian glared at him for a moment, too angry at first to see the gentle mockery. Then he smiled. "I deserve that," he said. "Did I imagine it? Did I call Fire? SunFire..." He shook his head. "How can it be! It's a legend, tales for the evening hearth!"

"Legends frequently hold truth in their hearts," Kherin smiled. "The gifts we have are there at our birthing, and grow to their flowering at their proper time. Who more fitting than you, of all men, to have SunFire, my Stallion of the Sun?"

"But is this magic—? It can't be — I am not a mage! It was illusion only, wasn't it?" There was undisguised pleading in his voice. Long ago Kherin had known something of this bewilderment himself, when the Goddess had marked him for Her Chosen. Now, drawing on that memory, he could comprehend and guide this contentious and questioning Chosen of the God.

"Ask Nortan, then, if the cinder that was his staff is illusion," Kherin said softly. "Be at ease, beloved, you are no stranger to 'magic', if that's what you'd call it."

"What? How can you say — "

"You have the Summoning. Speaking to men, to Zaan, to any beast, mind to mind."

"That isn't witchery!"

"That word again? No, my Brother, it is a gift. Like woodcraft. Something at which you are skilled."

"And my father before me." Rythian was still confused.

"I know. Remember the storm that lashed the Surni at the slaughter-place — that was a manifestation of your pain and anger. Now the SunFire. Do not fear it; do not mistrust it. It is a weapon, yes, but it is also a gentle boon to you and your people; think of a hearthfire on a winter's night. Also, have you not told me the scourge of the summer plains is the lightning strike that starts a grass fire that can destroy all in its path? Such things have a purpose, but those who can create fire can also end it."

"I can?" And then the question Kherin had been waiting for. "How?"

"I will teach you." Thus, finally, were the strands gathered up for the Gods' Weaving. All would follow now in due course. "And it'll be best if the first lessoning is now, because news of SunFire will be all over Hold. Dreyen, for one, will want to see it proved, and I'll not have him lose his eyebrows." As Kherin spoke, the Gather Horn blared outside, a wordless paean awakening echoes that shuddered through the rock-cut maze of the Hold.

"Rythian..." Syth whispered, hearing that summoning. "Mother of Mares, no! Not another Challenge!"

"Who would dare?" Alais said fiercely, wrapping her in a swift embrace.

Emre ran into the chamber, her face flushed with heat and emotion. "Something happened in Elder Hall," she gasped, "and Chiera says that Kardan has run mad! He is calling 'SunFire!'"

"What?"

"Kardan is saying Rythian..." and her voice faltered, "has Sun Fire..."

"No," Syth gasped. "That's not possible!"

"It's a trick," Alais said with certainty, "to silence Nortan and his cronies."

"They are building a fire on the Challenge Ground beyond the gates," Emre said in a small voice. "Everyone who can carry is to bring wood for it, even the outlanders."

"It'll be a trick," Alais insisted. "Some sleight of hand. Perhaps Kherin knows a way..."

"He would not be part of such a thing," Emre snapped.

"Neither of our menfolk would," Syth cut in. Something inside her breast was beginning to hurt, the way it had when news of Rythian's first Challenge had been brought to the Summer Hold. Bleakly she followed her sisters to the woodstack and took a length of oak, the marks of Rythian's axe still on it. She stared at the piece of wood, rough and solid in her hands.

"Syth?" Emre questioned.

Syth straightened her back and squared her shoulders. "I'm all right."

Sun Fire was the final vindication. In legend, only the greatest of the Sun Stallions had been able to call it. The sisters walked through the gates and the crowd parted for them. Syth's pain grew.

They placed their wood on the mound and moved back to the edge of the throng. Rythian stood not far away, but he did not see them. He was facing into the sun, head high, gaze unblinking. Something had changed about him; she could not see clearly what it was. He looked no different. He wore only a brief kilt like most of the men, but the pectoral on his chest took the sun's rays and gleamed as if it was already afire. His hair was loose, lifting on the light wind that came up the valley. He was a man apart, more so than he had been when first he was Sun Stallion. A movement at Rythian's side caught her attention. Yes, Rythian was apart, but not alone. She gave silent thanks that Kherin was with him.

The Elders raised their staffs and the clans fell silent. Rythian did not move, nor speak, and Syth did not know whether to pray for him to succeed or to fail. Then she saw his chest rise as he drew a deep breath, and his head dropped back a little as if pulled by the weight of his hair.

She was so intent on watching him that she did not see how the Fire came, only that the carefully stacked wood erupted in one towering conflagration of heat and light that drove everyone back. All but Rythian. Now he was indeed standing alone. Syth knew she had finally lost him. The words of the lament came back to her, achingly bittersweet.

Spear-tall and Golden, behold him. He stands in the Eye of the Sun...

He was truly gone from her now. Syth laid her hands on her flat belly and remembered both the love-making of the night and Kherin's prophesy an age of the world ago. "Please, Lady..."

"SunFire," whispered Chiera, leaning on her staff at the edge of the crowd. Her gaze was locked onto Rythian, both the outer sight and Inner. He was so glorious, so brilliant, he hurt her mind. "My son... You should have been my son..."

"Mother?" Myra's voice drifted to her.

"I saw the Fire in him, but did not know the power of it, nor the meaning. Now they will follow him like sheep! All the dreams I sent that night — I should have shown more — he will destroy us yet."

"You sent? It was no true vision, then? How could you so defile —" For a heartbeat Myra longed for Fire of her own.

"All of it I had already Seen," Chiera spat, "and more to come!"

"Old Mother," the Middle Priestess said coldly, "in the Lady's Name, you'd best go down to the Caverns. The Sun will burn too bright for you from hence forth."

Sun Fire. Merse neither knew nor cared what that meant. All that he could guess was that Kherin must have fired the timber. What was clearer to the eunuch's eyes was the love between the two men, and that scorched him more than mere flames. Kherin had stolen what would have been his.

Sun Fire. Tarvik whispered it under his breath. He had not doubted his Prince's word, but somehow he had not been able to fully comprehend what being the Chosen of the Sun would mean. The Tsithkin do not have villages and cities as did the Khassani, so they were closer to the reality of the desert, of the heat of the noon sun. They, too, had legends of SunFire, and they were not comfortable tales to hear. The God of the Noon Day was a harsh Lord and Tarvik did not think that was changed in this gentler land of lakes and rivers, mountains and rolling grassy plains. He looked around at the Khori mingling with the Horse-People; dwarfed for the most part, they had been received with curiosity, suspicion, some hostile words in Tylosian, but mostly with guarded acceptance. Word of the God's Touch on Rythian had seen to that. It seemed the Khori were, for the most part, looked upon as tools in the Sun Lord's Hand rather than potential or present enemies. He did not know whether to be insulted or relieved. The Khori, on their part, were as wary of their hosts as the D'Shael were of them, but Kherin's word made sure that there would be no clashes. That and the uncomfortably close interest the Gods were showing in the two Princes. The Goddess had always watched over Her Children, but the Great Lord of the Sun was a different matter.

The Council gathered again in the Elder Hall. This time there was no contention.

"In the matter of Tylos' intrusion," Kardan began. "This fortress they are building inside our border — Kherin, will the Khori ride with us as allies?"

"Yes. Willingly," he answered. "They know it was Tylos that took me by treachery. They have a price to claim from them for that."

"If we recall the warriors already with the caravans, we will be a thousand strong," an Elder said.

"First," Kardan stood forward, "hear what Merse and LyDia learned from the Tylosian spy who came with Kasha Den. Soon — before we can be there — two legions will be stationed within the fortress. Two thousand men. Hasoc seeks your surrender. He wants you to swear allegiance to him. He plots not only against us, but the Year-President as well."

"Two thousand, three thousand, it makes no difference," Rythian said quietly. "Our army cannot be reckoned with numbers alone. We will drive this infection from our lands. Cauterise it. With Fire. Send messengers with the swiftest horses to the caravans. At sunrise tomorrow we will ride for the GodStone. There will be no need to push the horses."

Two thousands of Tylosian legionaries, agleam with armour and weapons, were lined up in three phalanxes, banners bright, in front of their stronghold. The fortress had a stone base, quarried from the GodStone itself, with timber palisades, gate and watch towers. By Tylosian standards, it was a formidable structure.

D'Shael and Khori alike were unimpressed.

The Khori had ridden mingled with the D'Shael, hidden by the taller warriors on their great horses. Before they came within clear sight from the watch-towers, they peeled away, dismounting in a gully and led their ponies to the east of the fort. The D'Shael rode on.

As far as the legions were concerned, no more than some two hundreds opposed them. With iron discipline, the Tylosians waited. The D'Shael, a shifting, seething band with no obvious semblance of order, stayed just out of bowshot. None of the D'Shael were armoured, or carried shields. Their hair lay like banners across their shoulders; on their foreheads were black stylised hawk wings.

High above them, a bird flew in wide spirals. Kherin, sitting on his horse, his eyes blank, was with that bird. "No pitfalls, no hidden traps," he murmured. "Tarvik and the others are in position."

"Then, my Brother, we go to war."

Rythian paused for a moment, gathering his Power, feeling the freely-given support and strength of Kherin at his side.

Above the GodStone the clear sky darkened with eerie suddenness as cloud boiled up, slate-black and shot with lightnings.

A bolt arced down, a brilliant lance, striking one of the gatehouses and shattering it into fiery splinters. Thunder bellowed like the wrath of an angry god, drowning the screams of injured men. A second strike went straight into the heart of the central phalanx, with it came rain in a hissing sheet.

It was chaos. Against tangible foes, these were seasoned fighters. But never had they faced anything like this, when the elements warred against them. The ranks began to waver —

Rythian laughed softly, kneeing Zaan forward. The D'Shael ranged with him so that he came at the Tylosians in a solid wall of horseflesh. The pikes levelled against them were useless, bursting into flame like so much kindling, despite the sheeting rain. Arrows fell short as bowstrings were soaked. And the Khori came howling from the east to hit that flank, while D'Shael who had been with the caravans took the west, crumpling the outer phalanxes inward to crush and hamper the centre. Men were throwing down their weapons, running for the haven of the fort. As the ranks wavered, the warriors of the Winter Hold crashed through, wheeling and surging back to drive the panicking legions before them.

It was not a rout, but a slaughter. Those who made good their retreat slammed the great gates on their attackers, and for a moment there was stillness as Shi'R'Laen and Khori circled the stronghold.

Khori captains, SwordBrethren and Elders flanked Rythian and Kherin as they sat on their restless horses in front of the gate-towers.

"Now," Kherin said. "It is no more than kindling the Fire at Winter Hold."

But it was, for as yet Rythian lacked fine control over his Power.

Kherin Saw the golden flame at Rythian's core, wrapped it around with his own Moon-Power, steadying and guiding. There were no gestures, no chanted incantations to warn the watchers, only a sense of Gathering. Then lightning struck once more. Gates and towers erupted into searing fire, running like a monstrous quicksilver to engulf palisades and watch-towers, its roar swallowing the screams of men. It boiled up in a pillar of flame that seemed to lick the sky and even the stone footings cracked in the intense heat.

Kherin's grip tightened on Rythian's wrist. "Enough," he said. "They sue for surrender."

Those Tylosians that could, were crawling from the embers of their fort.

"D'Shael do not take prisoners," Rythian stated. "Kardan, Mettan, tell them to gather their wounded and get beyond the river. They have an hour."

Of the two thousand, barely two hundred made the river-crossing.

Kherin turned his horse's head away from the wreckage. "There is yet another thing we must do here," he said quietly to Rythian, "but at moon-rise."

Alone but for Rythian, Kherin left the mingled encampment of the Warbands and walked back to where the fortress had stood, the destruction showing as a blacker scar in the shadows cast by the GodStone. The moon was high enough for Kherin to do what he wanted, and in the silver light he knelt, laying his hands on the ashy ground. As he healed men, so he would heal the land of this cautery, make it whole again.

He did not know how it would be done, only that She would work through him. He stilled himself, opened his mind — the Knowledge was there, and the Power. Like a gentler lightning it surged through him into the earth beneath his hands, and he felt ripples flowing outwards, spreading. Life was flowing through him, into the seared earth, renewing fertility. As Rythian watched, new grass pushed forth, cloaking what had been sere ground with living velvet — and when at last Kherin lifted his head, the plain stretched unblemished to the river. Rythian helped him to his feet, and they stood there unspeaking for a moment. The sounds from the distant camp were of celebration, rejoicing in victory, and more. Over and above the laughter and song rose a new chant, the voice of the Shi'R'Laen Warband.

"SunFire!" they shouted. "SunFire!"

Rarest gift of their God, no matter that He always exacts a price. "SunFire!" A new beginning, new trails to ride, new battles, new boundaries to be set and held. "SunFire! SunFire! SunFire!"